Coco[illegible]or the [illegible]aint

Debra Spark

**in memory of my sister Cynthia (1965-1992)
and for all of us who miss her**

This is a work of fiction. Names, characters, places and incidents are imaginary or are used fictitiously. Any resemblance to events or persons, living or dead, is entirely coincidental.

AVON BOOKS
A division of
The Hearst Corporation
1350 Avenue of the Americas
New York, New York 10019

Inside cover author photo courtesy of Michele McDonald
Published by arrangement with Faber and Faber, Inc.
Library of Congress Catalog Card Number: 94-3329
ISBN: 0-380-72630-0

First Avon Books Trade Printing: January 1996

Printed in the U.S.A.

OPM 10 9 8 7 6 5 4 3 2 1

Acknowledgments

Portions of this book appeared, in slightly altered form, in *Agni*, *The Boston Globe Sunday Magazine*, *Epoch*, *Prairie Schooner* and *The Madison Review*.

For support while I was working on this book, I am grateful to The Bunting Institute at Radcliffe College, the National Endowment for the Arts, the Wisconsin Institute, the Wisconsin Arts Board, the Writers' Room of Boston, Ucross Foundation and Corporation of Yaddo. Many, many thanks to Jesse Spark, Luis Felipe Arroyo and Victoria Besosa for their generous assistance and to Kim Witherspoon, Jessica Treadway, Elizabeth Searle and Joan Wickersham for their invaluable editorial advice. Finally, thanks to Don Lee for, among other things, leading me to my wonderful editor, Fiona McCrae.

"You do not come to Euphemia only to buy and sell, but also because at night, by the fires all around the market, seated on sacks or barrels or stretched out on piles of carpets, at each word that one man says—such as 'wolf,' 'sister,' 'hidden treasure,' 'battle,' 'scabies,' 'lovers'—the others tell, each one, his tale of wolves, sisters, treasures, scabies, lovers, battles. And you know that in the long journey ahead of you, when to keep awake against the camel's swaying or the junk's rocking, you start summoning up your memories one by one, your wolf will have become another wolf, your sister a different sister, your battle other battles, on your return from Euphemia, the city where memory is traded at every solstice and at every equinox."

—Italo Calvino, *Invisible Cities*

"The coconut is also a saint."

—Migene González-Wippler, *The Santería Experience*

Prologue: The Blue Street

(1968)

Of the four pale people, the man and the three small girls walking down the blue street in the center of the pastel city, there is only one person who does not look dazed, only one person who is really on the street, saying, *Yes, here we have blue bricks. Here, houses painted like candy*. It is not the adult in the group. He sees, but he sees the past. And of the girls, one sees the future, and one simply sees herself, piously resolving not to finger the mosquito bites clustered at her wrist. It is Tata—who has no desire to be grown up or perfect—who is content to be here, herself, a five-year-old child on an adventure.

"It's hot out," she says, once, loudly in English, but no one responds, not her father and not her sisters, Beatriz and Melone. Miffed, Tata glares at her family. She is used to a starring role in the adventure that is her life, but it's too warm to insist that everyone pay attention to her. She shrugs once and reluctantly allows herself to become, with her sisters, part of a different story, her father's story. There is no mother's story, no immediately apparent one, as these children have been half-orphaned since birth. Of the three girls, two are aware that they are traveling with a man who has lost his wife.

Years later, when they account for their presence on the island—to themselves and to strangers—each of them, for her own reasons, will forget boat travel, disremember the initial hotels, the long week in the filthy rooming house. They will recall only the walk down this road, the absolute security they feel in having a destination. And they will all think of themselves not as they are now . . . noting first the stores, then the gaped mouths of various windows and the fried turnovers and lemonades being dispensed from curbside stands . . . but as they must appear to the man at the end of the street. They have all noticed him, all chosen not to mention him. Yet they are moving steadily toward him as if he is, when considered as destination not person, inevitable. He is crouched the way only crazy people crouch, down low but peering up and rocking from the pads to the heels of his feet. No intention to rest—that much is clear—by standing up or sitting down. From the low vantage point of this man, the family, pale and stiff, as they are, and set, as they are, against the blue of the sky, seem to be figures on a slowly advancing frieze. So the man—his name is Angelo—says, as if in response to their approach, "You must remember this. A kiss is still a kiss." It appears he means absolutely nothing by this. He talks in burps, the funny, Jew's harp sound of someone who has had his voice box ripped from his throat.

The crouched man isn't the only one observing the advancing family. There are eyes everywhere . . . behind the plaza statue, in dark doorways, coffee shops, balconies, garbage piles . . . the whole obvious array of hiding places as the three girls and their father make their way through the street. The stares are natural . . . and not just because the girls—Tata, Melone, and Beatriz—match each other in all the crucial areas: height and weight, color of eye and hair, turn of the foot, set of the hip. It's their paleness. Though the father has Spanish blood, they are all but *gringos*, and they will learn soon enough to be ashamed of the privilege implied, even here, on this most democratic of islands.

The father—he goes by Sandrofo—is tall and slim. Handsome, save for the way his entire face slopes back into his forehead, making his head look a bit like something the eyes had to climb in order to rest in their favorite place, the sockets. Once there, one of the eyes, the left one, turns slightly inward; the other stares resolutely forward. The uneven gaze makes the father appear indecisive, as if the problem here is one of character: this is a man unable to commit to anything as defining as crossed eyes.

In one hand, he holds a piece of cardboard, which he brushes against the stubble of his cheek, as if amused to find that it makes such a distinct sound. So he is an adult after all, and this despite the way he moves, like a boy trying to restrain himself from running mountains, swimming channels, exhausting himself for the pure joy of exhausting himself. The free hand dangles at his side. Occasionally, he uses it to pat the curly brown hair of one of his daughters' heads.

When he is within shouting distance of the crouching man, Sandrofo says, "*Perdoneme.*" The man is not a likely person to ask for directions, but Sandrofo is hot and tired, and since it is *siesta*, there is really no one else on the street. He calls again, "*Perdoneme.*"

There is no response; the man is, for the moment, absorbed. Indeed, as the family draws close, he no longer seems to see them, though his eyes are, more or less, on them. A folded newspaper lies at his toes, and he is wearing gray pants, brown shoes, a green and blue sweater worn thin with age. The whole arrangement is topped by a blue and red checked sport coat. The outfit is wrong in every way it could be. Other men on the street are dressed in short-sleeved cotton shirts. The girls wear clothes the color of after-dinner mints. They shuffle their sandaled feet. Ordinarily, the father would say, "Don't stare," to the girls, because there is something about the boxiness of the fit of the man's sweater—it looks as if the man might have a cage around his torso—coupled with the clear scrawniness of the legs that suggest there is a substantial deformity here. But whether from exhaustion or confusion or a simple failure to concentrate, the four arrive at the man's feet and stop to watch him. They gaze at his puckery, red face as he removes a piece of paper from his right interior pocket, studies it and then folds it into his left jacket pocket, full as it is with an assortment of papers. They watch as he reshuffles a piece of paper from his pants pocket into his other interior coat pocket, also thick with folded material. He removes a stub of a pencil and a knife, puts the knife back, stores the pencil away, takes out a longer pencil, reaches in to retrieve the stub, only to toss it away. Then he takes out his knife and cuts the wood away from the lead of the long pencil. Disgusted, he throws the wood on the street. Tata pulls at her father's hand, and he motions her to be silent till the man picks up his paper and starts to read, the lead of his pencil poised, it seems, to make editorial comments.

"What are you doing?" asks Melone, and the scene, like so much dirt under a sponge, dissolves. The man rises from his impossible crouch to look at the assembled group.

"*Perdoneme*," Sandrofo says one last time and in his most perfect Spanish. He has been, he imagines, on this island before, although that is not technically true. Still, he pretends that this is where he met his wife, where he wooed her with dinners and flowers and walks by the lagoon. Everything his imagination was then capable of to win a heart without losing himself, his own stern sense of the importance of love, the silliness of expressions of love. "Could you direct me to a bakery by the name of Madeleine?"

"I speak English," the man responds. A form of an insult, an explanation necessitated by a flaw in Sandrofo's skin, not in his language. "I speak English, and it's closed."

Tata tugs on her father's hand. She knows something is wrong here, and she wants an explanation. Beatriz and Melone lean slightly forward, comical hunting dogs, sniffing out absurdity or wondering, at the very least, why the funny man's funny voice seems to be coming from the air to the side of him rather than from his body proper. For his part, Sandrofo seems not the least bit surprised by the man's voice. He has always known that real life is to the side of life, and he is happy, at last, to have some physical fact articulating this ineffable truth.

"Are you a puppet?" Tata asks. After all, puppets' voices always come from somewhere other than their mouths.

Melone reaches over and, apparently because she thinks the question is rude, slaps Tata gently on the wrist.

"I know it's closed," Sandrofo says quickly. "But I would like to go there anyway."

The man steps closer, and Sandrofo resists the urge to pull himself, and his children, back. The man seems to be at the border of all substantial disgraces of the soul. Or this is the way Sandrofo interprets filth, drug addiction, madness. But the man doesn't clearly, *absolutely* suffer from any one of these weaknesses. The clothes might simply be old, the face red with sunburn, the body wracked with unavoidable diseases—some of which may or may not have affected the brain.

"You don't understand. It's closed. For good."

"Not for good," Sandrofo says. "It belongs to me . . . and these three little bakers," he says, glancing down. "We plan to open it."

The man stares at him, the sort of intractable stare that makes Sandrofo feel he has no choice but to dance around whatever judgment is implied in the look. Another day, Sandrofo would have tried to match him, iris for iris, for implacability, though on Sandrofo it would only be a feigned implacability—really a combination of shyness, anger and pride. Today . . . force of the easy weather, he supposes, it makes one agreeable . . . Sandrofo does something he rarely does. He explains himself.

"It belonged to my wife's father. Madeleine was the name of his mother, his French mother, my wife's grandmother."

The man winces slightly.

"And the cookies," Sandrofo continues. "The place was named for her and a special kind of cookie that looks like a shell."

"OK, OK, OK," the man says, flapping his hands, still gripped about the lead and paper. "I've heard it all before." He continues to flap his hands, as if Sandrofo's words are so many pigeons he is trying to shoo away. Then his hands stop suddenly. He asks cheerfully, an odd but welcome shift in the tone of his chirpy voice, "*La Panadería y Repostería?*"

"Yes," Sandrofo says.

"I would be most honored to give you the guidance you require and offer my services."

Sandrofo raises an eyebrow, none too eagerly.

"As butterer and flourer of pans, beater of eggs, sweeper of floors . . . these are just some of my many talents."

"We'll see," Sandrofo allows.

"Pourer of coffee. Softener of butter," Angelo continues as if he hasn't heard the response.

"No," Sandrofo says firmly. "I will not be hiring anyone. This is a family operation." As a fugitive from his own life, even something like this—the status of an employer—will, he feels, draw too much attention to him.

The girls, silent all this while, begin some quiet protests. "If I were home right now," Melone tells her father, "if I were home, I think now's about the time Grandma would give me lunch."

"It'll just be a little longer," Sandrofo says.

"She makes egg salad for me," Melone explains. "But Tata and Beatriz like tuna fish."

"Just a little longer, then you can have whatever you normally have for lunch."

"It's normal," says Melone seriously, "to be eating egg salad or tuna fish."

"OK, a bit longer," Sandrofo says.

"That's right. You're almost there," the man says. "And you can call me Angelo, because I'm like an angel with a little something extra. An 'angel' with an *o*. And you're . . ."

"Sandrofo, and my three girls."

"Tata," Tata says.

"And I'm Melone," Melone says, "and this is Beatriz, but she doesn't talk." Then, as if getting down to business, "If you're wondering why we all look alike, it's because we're triplets."

"I see. Triplets," Angelo says and nods at Melone before looking up at Sandrofo to ask, "How do you tell them apart?"

Sandrofo blinks stupidly, as if this is the first time he has ever heard the question, and says, "They're my children."

"Well, then," Angelo says, paying no attention to the answer. "Right this way." He turns stiffly around to make his way down the street.

Sandrofo imagines Angelo as some self-appointed guard to the interior and is reminded of all those Gate to Heaven jokes and stories, where entrance depends on puns and bits of moral knowledge, elusive, even to the best of petitioners, for reasons of pure semantics.

"There," Angelo turns and points. Such ceremony for such short distances. He has walked fifty feet, past four boarded-up storefronts. "*Arturo y Mara*," Sandrofo reads the childish blue paint scrawled on the boards, then looks up to see a chipped, thin blue sign, covered with yellow letters: *"La Madeleine,"* and under it, in smaller letters, *"La Panadería y Repositería."*

This is it. How odd now that he is finally here to feel more tired than curious. A fault in his character, he supposes, this sudden weariness that sneaks up on him; just when he imagines other people would be genuinely fascinated, he has to fake fascination. He shifts the weight of his feet, almost impatiently, while Angelo tears a hole in the rotting piece of plywood. Inside it is not what Sandrofo has imagined, but then this is not quite true. Part of what he has imagined is that when he finally arrives, it will not look like what he has imagined. Through the hole in the board, he can make out a long, narrow room. The back wall opens into a courtyard, dusty with old papers and littered, it seems to Sandrofo, with crab shells. Or maybe this is just what he dreams he sees—a dream of exoticism. The light from behind the room is bright enough that what he first observes he sees strictly in silhouette. But days later, when the place has been cleaned out, the plywood knocked down, his original impression will not change. It looks like any lunch place back in Bensonhurst, New York, home to Sandrofo during his honeymoon year and the one year that followed, before he had three children and a wife, now dead with the effort of bearing triplets.

Madeleine's looks like the kind of nondescript place men sit in for years before they look up and notice the faded city portrayed on the wallpaper and remark that it isn't their city. With its turrets and baroque arches, it isn't any city that ever existed in any century when lunch places existed. In fact, there is a city on the wallpaper at Madeleine's . . . though Sandrofo won't see this till later. What he does see now is the long counter running down the right-hand side of the bakery, and even in the dark, he sees—or maybe only senses—that there has to be an old ice box here, a rat's bleached skeleton in a drawer, some shelves, a single old flour bag and two rusty tacks, dreaming of poisoning the bottom of some child's foot.

Gathering place—that has been Sandrofo's fantasy, and he understands and forgives, even respects, his own simplicity. People coming in from the fields to make contact, remind themselves that others know they exist, smell something other than dirt and coffee, the sun baking the green leaves of cane. But the long room in front of Sandrofo suggests drunks hunched over coffee and a doughnut, fueling themselves because eating is one of the few things left that they are supposed to do, that they still can do, even if they have lost a taste for all food that isn't full of sugar.

Angelo taps Sandrofo's shoulder, and the bakery owner turns, momentarily blinded by the brightness of the sun. "You'll make the," Angelo starts to say, "what-is-it-called? The Hostess cupcake?"

"No," Sandrofo draws himself back as if away from the insult and then recites a litany of sweets, his personal prayer words, *"Flan, mantecaditos, budín de pan sencillo."*

Angelo chuckles at the list.

"What's so funny? What's so funny?" Melone calls from the end of the street, where she has wandered with her sisters.

"Girls," Sandrofo shouts, for they are now standing amid a flock of pigeons and stomping their feet, giggling at the commotion this causes. "Don't move," he says, then changes his mind. "Come here," and they do. Sandrofo has been told that the girls have always been fairly docile—at least in public—so he's not surprised by their quick return to his side. Sandrofo turns back to Angelo. "It—the bakery—it won't be the kind of place you are imagining."

This is the dream. Windows full of sugary stuff, surrounded by the basics: bread and a cash register—all of this to be served by a barman of a baker. "Have a crescent roll and tell me your troubles . . . if you have a mind to." He imagines himself being called, like a doctor, to the site of a disaster, bringing wisdom and cake to the aggrieved. "It's the baker!" people will cry with that same sigh of relief they ordinarily reserve for priests and doctors, medicine men and *santos*. Real-world magic . . . that's what a guava-filled puff pastry, dusted in confectionery sugar, could be. Pleasure without a hangover or a pregnancy. Sandrofo isn't thinking of diabetes or the sad, bloated faces who will come to frequent his bakery.

"You have beautiful children," Angelo says and looks down at the three girls clustered at their father's legs. Sandrofo looks down too, looks up and imagines he detects a leer on Angelo's face. His girls are just five years old.

Mistake, he thinks. *The whole thing a mistake and her fault to boot for leaving me these three children and this bakery, for speaking of the bakery so dreamily*. But he doesn't believe any of this, is just amazed to find he is in charge of several lives, not just his own, and his choices will have consequences he cannot imagine for his daughters. Once again, it becomes apparent that he has not arrived on this island with three girls but with three bird's eggs, frail and blue, and he shall have to spend the rest of his life vigilantly protecting them.

"Time to get things started," Sandrofo says.

"What started?" Tata says.

"Things. You'll see, our whole life, we have to get it started," Sandrofo says and reaches down to pat Tata's head.

"Bow wow," she says. "I'm a dog. Bow wow."

"A dog? Here?" Angelo looks quickly to the right and left, and the girls look with him. They look at the bakery again and then across the street at a smooth wall, the color of almond meat, papered with colorful posters for Beck's beer, Bacardi rum and Winston cigarettes. Then Angelo crouches down, cuffs Tata's chin to say, "Here there are no dogs. Save for the wild ones that run in a pack. Are you wild?"

"Bow wow," Tata says, but softly, recoiling a bit, though she does not know at what.

"Ruff," Melone says and giggles. "Bow wow. Ruff." Both girls giggle, and Beatriz sticks her arm out behind her and wags it like a tail.

"Three," Angelo says, as if praising them, "and all wild."

In response, Sandrofo leans down, takes three small wrists firmly—maybe too firmly—in his large hand and says, so viciously that all three girls are instantly quiet . . . and scared, "*Stop* that."

Later in the week, the moon will prove Angelo's words, the words that come from the air around Angelo's neck, true. Installed, for the first night, in the apartment above the bakery, in the civilized street, in the depths of the night, Sandrofo will wake to the mad sound of dog fights, echoing off the stuccoed buildings. He will lie in his sweaty sheets for . . . it will seem to him hours, considering the spareness of his new home, the harsh whiteness of the walls, of the kitchen's straight-backed wood chairs. He plans to buy three beds and small play tables for the girls' room. Organized this way, simply and without much color, he feels he will be able to keep things in order, ward off danger. Leave color to the outside of the building, which will be painted a royal blue next week, or to the insides of pastries, oozing with jelly, or to the yellow and pink surfaces of iced cakes.

Finally, the hysteria of the dogs' barking will pull Sandrofo to his feet. He will draw back the shutters and stick his head out the bedroom window to a night bright with the light of the moon. It will be as if he thinks he can see the sound as it bounces from facade to facade, forever trapped between the buildings of the street.

He will stand at the window and think he is searching for dogs but realize that what he is really doing is letting his imagination wander over his new city, over the colonial homes, the plazas, the churches and finally over the old wall that rings the city. Outside that wall, his imagination will reach water, boats full of passengers. It will make no difference to Sandrofo that his imagination is ignoring the facts: immigrants, these days, go by bus, from the plaza in old San Juan to the airport. From there, they board the famed and horrible Twilight Flight to soar north in unpressurized cabins till they arrive, sick, green worms, in the Big Apple. Nonetheless, Sandrofo lets his imagination go where it wants. He lets it follow the boat's passengers: all men and all leaving, heading north to New York, promised land and obvious destination for those looking for work, though no one has ever proved to anyone on the island—to those who go or to those who stay—that things are better in New York. And everyone knows that poverty, though it is still poverty, feels better in the tropics.

Sandrofo has emigrated backward, an unnatural move that he can equate only with his own sense that he is evolving backward. Once, he was a married man with children; now, he is something less—a man with no wife but with children. *Wards of the state,* he sometimes thinks. He can see so little of himself, of himself physically, in them. And now, beleaguered with loss as he is, he has gone and moved himself from land to sea. Next step? he wonders. The boat full of passengers is rocking in the ocean. He lets some of the passengers be ill, all dirty, most still hopeful. Next step? After land to sea? It will have to be person to lizard. His mind simplifying, his body taking prominence, forcing him to scuttle about thinking about survival, daydreaming about a nice bug to eat. This is what he has wanted all along—the diminution of his brain. For how else to deal with a mind as flooded with grief as his own?

And on that night—it's a night still in the future—Sandrofo will turn from the window, back to his bed and to sleep, where everything will reverse itself to the old order. His body in sleep will be a useless appendage to his brain, an organ that dreams a chemical disaster that leaves his children so disfigured that their chests look like surreal pieces of Swiss cheese. When he wakes the next day, Sandrofo will make his first and firmest resolve on the island: *Avoid sleep, whenever possible.*

Bride-Cake

(Maria Elena—July 1977)

This is the story of how I met and won the recalcitrant heart of one Sandrofo Cordero Lucero, astute student of the mechanics of work habits and—well, to tell the truth—of not much else. It's a fairy tale of sorts, so I always tell the girls to pay attention. They might learn something for the future. Lesson number one, I tell them, is some clichés are true. There is such a thing as love at first sight. How do you think a cliché got to be a cliché in the first place? The truth was repeated till it got boring. But no one wants to think the truth is boring. Listen up, girls, I say, and believe. It's not interesting, but that doesn't matter; opposites *do* attract. Who would have put me, Maria Elena, one-time anarchist, crazy person attached to a fire-engine mouth, with the silent, conservative baker? No one, of course. No one but fate.

I was thirty-five then, a believer in signs and omens, past lives and future ones. The tarot. The patterns of seashells. Advice in the horoscopes of supermarket magazines. I was democratic when it came to other worlds. I still believe today, but at that point, the right words hadn't come my way. I'll confess to being despairing. I was a hen among many hens and only a handful of roosters. You see what I mean. In that age, in this place, it wasn't easy. I'd had the questionable benefits of the sexual revolution. I am talking about years of live-in lovers and only the oldest of old folks disapproving. But where had that got me? On the day I met Sandrofo, I was thirty-five and alone. My parents were dead. My sister, Sisa—whom I had loved desperately—was dead. A heart attack related to her diabetes. I suffered from the disease myself, but I had things more under control. Still, years earlier, I had been in the loony bin, almost dead of grief myself, staring at the rabbit-shaped water stains in the ceiling and crying about my sister. All through my twenties when I dreamed of good times, I dreamed of return visits to the bin. What is this but tragic?

Of course, I had been out of the loony bin too, had been working in a museum and then at a gallery on Calle del Cristo in old San Juan. I was a convert to beauty that year, the middle of my fourth decade of life. The job helped. I took real care with my appearance and with keeping the floor of the gallery clean. I liked the cocktail parties before an exhibit opened. I liked how I held my elbow just so when I poured out wine. I took beauty home with me, started thinking of "wearable art" instead of jewelry. I imagined hanging Japanese silk tapestries in the living room. Needless to say, *dinero*, cash, scratch . . . it was all a problem. And I was still sad all the time. Yes, yes, yes, I'd argue with myself, it was better than the hospital. My neighbors weren't in four-point restraints. But, but, but . . . there was this sadness, this weariness. People know the feeling, or they don't. It's no use trying to explain.

That day, the one when I met my betrothed, started out ordinary enough. Unremarkable weather. The bus didn't break down on my way to work. No terrorists threatened to blow up the governor's bedroom. We were five weeks into an exhibit at the gallery. We were showing that famous series of illustrations to the child's tale "The Emperor's New Clothes." Predictably enough, gallery traffic had slowed to include only tourists and the occasional passerby.

Even though there wasn't much to do that day, I delayed going to lunch. I'd been doing this for weeks. Lucia, who minds the gallery with me, said later she thought it was a way to deny that I was sick. I would have agreed, but it wasn't true. I knew I had diabetes, and I was playing with things. How close could I get to going too far and still pull back? I don't say this was conscious. It was something I puzzled out later.

Anyway, this one day, the game served me well. It was sugar that got me a husband. Sugar got me a sugar, I say in English. A sudden drop in my sugar level that sent me out of the gallery to look for food. I was dizzy for the better part of the noon hour, but I ignored the feeling and set to retyping a smudged price list. It wasn't until I found myself daydreaming about making tiny construction-paper clothes for the Emperor Who Had None that I said, "Lucia, I'm off to lunch."

I stepped out of the cool, air-conditioned gallery into the hot street and felt a bit crazier with every step I took. I had the real feeling that the watercolor paint of the sky had been mixed with too much water and was now running down over the buildings and puddling on the gray-blue ballasts of the street. I knew enough to head for an ice cream vendor in the plaza just at the end of the street.

When I crossed over the street into the plaza, I saw that the vendor who normally operated out of the northwest corner of the square was gone. Ordinarily, I'd have thought, "Well, it's time for some juice," but ordinarily I'm avoiding sugar, not looking for it, and I couldn't think where, in the whole of the old city, I could find what I needed. Just thinking about it made me feel terribly hot. In my mind, I went down one street after another, but I could only see greasy *empanadas* and plump flies under heat lamps. Of course, anyone else would have also seen the bright orange bottles of *parcha,* which are, invariably, lined up by the heat lamps, but my mind wasn't right. In my head, I saw some fried cheese. It made me reel just to picture it. I wiped my forehead with the back of my hand. I could have washed my hair in the water from the sweat at my temples, so I made my way to the center of the plaza to dip my fingers in the fountain and cool off. As I stood at the fountain and bathed my neck, I felt I was about to faint.

"Excuse me," I said to a woman who was standing next to me. She was short haired, stoutly built and rough complected. Clearly, a cold-climate woman, and I wondered what she was doing here. I couldn't really gather much else about her, because the world was turning into a cheap black-and-white TV set with bad reception. "Excuse me," I heard myself say again, "I'm about to faint."

"Oh," the woman said, and it sounded as if she said it with real pleasure. She took my right hand firmly in hers. Presumptuous, I thought, but did feel steadied by the press of her fingers against my own. "It's so good you *told* me. I'm a healer. Lie right down. Right down here."

Mother of God, I thought, I've got a crackpot. Still, I did as she said and put my back on the stones of the plaza. I had enough sense to worry about pigeon droppings and to put my purse under my head. I could feel the sharp clasp of my wallet just below my crown. A pen stuck up into my ear. Why had no one ever invented a cloth writing utensil? I wondered. My best thoughts always came to me when I was depleted of sugar.

I looked up and then turned my head so I wouldn't be staring at the brightness of the sky. The woman was still holding my hand. "Diabetes," I said and shook my medical-alert bracelet. Wearable art and practical too, I said to myself in the voice of a radio announcer. So buy some before midnight tonight. My inner voice pitched and squealed in such an odd way that I wondered if I'd spoken aloud.

"Just breath in deep," the woman told me. I sucked in air. "And out." I blew hair away from my eyes. "In and out. In. Out. Now," she said in that hypnotic voice people use when they want to make sure you're going to follow their instructions, "what I'm going to do is press very hard in the center of your hand. This is called a pressure point, and I'm going to press hard, so you can release the tension in the rest of your body."

I shook my wrist once again to indicate that I had a genuine medical problem.

She said, "Now just let the tension flow down your legs and out of your toes."

She pushed her thumb into the center of my palm. The pressure was so strong and so painful that I thought, for a moment, it would be possible for her to push her thumb right through my hand. Still, it felt weirdly pleasant, like rolling backward slowly into the warmest, gentlest of oceans. I closed my eyes. I opened them. A crowd had gathered above me.

The woman said to me, "My name is Iriamne. Who are you?"

"Maria Elena," I said, but the way my voice came out it sounded like a needle scraping a record, a fingernail scratching a blackboard.

"Well, Maria Elena," she said, as if I were an idiot, "we think it would be a good idea to take you into the bakery. It's cool in there, and we can get you a little something to eat. How do you feel about going to La Madeleine?"

La Madeleine. Why hadn't I thought of it when my mind was wandering the streets?

"Does that sound OK?" Iriamne asked. She went on without waiting for a reply. "We're going to let these men here carry you." *What* men, I thought, though I knew she was referring to some people behind her. "And some other people are going to get an ambulance. Now, can you hold your hands like this?" She rearranged my arms so that I hugged my sides.

"Yes," I said. "I think I can handle that." I counted on the fact that my voice had, of its own accord, risen two octaves to conceal my sarcasm.

I felt her twist my long hair into a single dark rope and tuck it into the collar of my shirt. Then I was aloft. I'm not a heavy woman. I pride myself on my figure. Slim. Nice breasts, I've been told. (That's a side point, I guess, about the breasts. It doesn't directly relate to my tale.) I closed my eyes. (They're brown.) I didn't want to be embarrassed by the faces that were lifting me. Soon enough, I thought, you'll be hiding your eyes when you meet these people on the street. Hands were pushed under my back, and I was in the air. I felt Iriamne tuck my skirt up between my legs so everything was proper. And then the hands kept lifting. This was strange, I thought. They carried me—I felt six, flat palms in all—as if I were a gigantic tray at a fancy restaurant. Their arms must have been nearly outstretched, for instead of holding me at chest level, they had me up in the air. Seven, maybe eight, feet.

I opened my eyes. What a strange way to see the city. I closed my eyes again and then opened them quickly. It was like being dead, I suddenly thought, being carried at this height, out of the plaza and past cornices that, from my vantage point, needed painting. The TV screen flickered again. It went dark, then light, and the words "funeral bier" inserted themselves in my brain like an unwelcome mantra. I panicked and started to shout, "Let me down, let me down, let me down." Then, we were there, and I was being lowered through the door of the bakery. I smelled confectionery sugar and saw the pressed metal of a ceiling that had been painted an ugly yellow. I saw two ceiling fans and six flies. I heard the scrape of chairs being pulled back and people clearing the way. A girl cried, "No, not the floor. It's filthy. Not the floor. Not the floor." Then I was being laid out on the linoleum counter of the coffee shop.

A different voice, male, deep and commanding, approached. "Stand back. Stand back," it said. "Let the lady have some air." Things faded, and then this same voice said, "OK. Tata, Beatriz, push it over here. Lift the wheels over that thing in the floor. OK. I've got it. Good. Now, give her some room."

Even when I am not thinking straight, I am a curious person. I wanted to know what the man was talking about. Wheel *what* over *what* bump *where?* That's just the way my mind works, so I tried very hard to open my eyes and focus on what was going on around me. I saw a fork with a piece of cake looming above my nose. Behind that, things were blurry.

I did my share of drugs in the sixties, and I can honestly say that, as altered states go, I preferred just about everything to what I was feeling at that moment. Still, I could not bring myself to put that bit of cake in my mouth. Now, what happened next takes some time to describe, though it happened in the space of a few seconds. I squinted and focused my eyes on the prongs of the fork. I looked at that piece of cake for what seemed like hours. It was white, and there was a dab of blue icing, smeared like a wayward bit of toothpaste, on part of it. I stared so hard at that cake that it came apart in my mind. I thought about crumbs and how many crumbs make up a single bite of cake. My depth of field was narrow. I saw one end of that bite of cake in perfect focus, but the far end was out of focus and in no way related to the very interesting crumbs on the near side. Then I looked farther, past that fork to a hand. One of the fingers of the hand was deformed, turned, so the knuckle faced the palm. I looked even further to a face. The cake went blurry. A handsome man was holding the fork. Well, this got my attention, as a handsome man is bound to do.

"Have a bite of this?" the man said. He was dark, clean shaven. I saw a long nose and blue eyes. There was brown hair and a single section in the front that was too long and flopped in his eyes. He pushed it back, and I could see he was Spanish, but I guessed right away that he had other blood in him, for he was too pale to be from the island, even if both of his parents had been "white" Puerto Rican. He had a good, an intelligent look about him, but what I noticed was something else: he looked like a man who was used to serious concern about others.

I said to him, "Señor." Again, my voice screeched out of my mouth and sounded nothing like my own. I propped myself up on my elbows. "Señor," I repeated. Later, when I knew him, he confessed it looked as if I was leering at him. "Señor," I said a third time. And here is where the TV set of my vision clicked off. I only remember bits of the rest. Like a child, I have to appropriate the memory of others and claim it as my own.

I said, "Señor, isn't matter funny? Last night, a cake could have killed me. Today, it saves my life."

"Yes," the man replied, almost as if he were talking to himself, "the way the world twists and turns, twists and turns again." Then, apparently, I had a mouse-size nibble of cake. I looked at the handsome man in a funny way. My head was cocked like a perplexed puppy dog's.

"It's good. Right?" the man asked. "It's a wedding cake, but the wedding was called off. I knew it wouldn't go to waste." His tone was friendly, matter-of-fact. This was business, getting the patient to eat. "Have some more," he offered.

"No," I said. People say I sounded flirtatious when I said this.

"Christ," the man said. He turned his head and said something to someone behind him.

"You're very handsome," I said. Again, this is only hearsay, and I can tell you that I don't just up and say something this forward on an average day.

"Just force-feed her," someone suggested.

The man turned back to me and started to stroke the top of my left arm in the slow, rhythmic way a mother pats the back of a child who is throwing up. "Just one bite," he said.

I started to stutter my replies to him. "I just . . . wait . . . I just . . . what did you say? Before? Before the cake?"

"Come on. One bite," he repeated.

"No, you . . . just, you . . . you're . . . it's . . . before the cake?"

"What do you say we have some of this cake?"

"I've got to tell you this one thing, Señor."

A voice again shouted out a suggestion: "Just push it in her mouth. She's not going to spit it up on that silk dress."

I said, "I've just got to tell you this one thing, Señor. Because I'm thinking, but you're saying."

Someone pushed the handsome man's arm closer to my mouth, but he jerked his hand back.

"What?" he said. "What did you say?"

"You're saying what I'm thinking. I think the words, but you say them." I gave him a smile. This, it seemed, was all I had to say, and having said it, I began to eat forkful after forkful of cake.

And here I stop again to do what no storyteller can honestly do. I tell you what the handsome man—but, of course, he was Sandrofo—thought when I said all of this. He told me—much later, to be sure—but he told me. He said the idea so fascinated him—that I was seeing him speak my thoughts—that he didn't mind hesitating a second to hear me say it again. In retrospect, he felt ashamed of the desire. I was sick, and for a brief moment, his curiosity got the better of him, and he forgot that what was important was that I eat the cake, not that I make myself understood, not that he understand me.

But he paused, almost reflexively. It was a real desire. *What* had I said? Sandrofo wasn't a man, by all accounts, of many desires. Even his three daughters by his dead wife—Beatriz, Melone and Tata—confirmed this. Birthdays were impossible; there was nothing the man wanted. But he was curious about what I had said and then. . . . Well, you know how it is. Recognize one desire, even a small one, and the rest come tumbling out, demanding attention.

Red lights flashed over the ceiling and down the far wall of the bakery. I confess to having a memory of this. I remember it because the yellow wallpaper was patterned with brown pen-and-ink drawings of an Italianate city. I remember I thought of the red lights as they fell down the wall as so many sunsets, burning themselves out hysterically over the cities. As I watched, days and days, and then years, whole lifetimes, seemed to pass. It was like one of those calendars in an old movie, one where the pages tear off with frightening speed in the wind. Meanwhile, cheery music plays in the background, so the audience won't notice how horrifying the image they are looking at really is.

The cake must have had its effect, because I started to feel more normal. I turned and saw Sandrofo smiling at me. "It's just the blood," he said. "Soon you'll be fine."

"Yes," I said. Softly, I think, in something more like my own voice. "Thank you."

I imagined that I was in bed and making love to this man. As I moved, there was a moment when my breasts were brushing his chest, and then I didn't experience my body as separate at all from his. Together, I thought, we were one creature. Four-armed, four-legged, I could cartwheel through life with this man to whom I was meant to be attached.

The ambulance was still at the door. I said, "Wedding cake," and Sandrofo used his fingers to put another piece in my mouth. I tasted the dirty salt of his skin underneath the frosting. The sirens started up again, and I said, "Wedding bells."

Some hands lifted me again, and I was carried out. Someone else carried out the wedding cake and put it in the middle of the road, in case I would still accept a forkful of the sweet stuff. Sandrofo remained by my side. "Maybe we'll get married," I said in that joking voice you use when you're frightened about how someone will respond if they take you seriously.

"Maybe," Sandrofo allowed. Then, he said, as if he were musing on the possibility, "The baker's wife."

An IV went into my left arm. The technician said, "We're going to stabilize you here. I'm going to tape this down." White tape went over the crook of my left arm. The technician strapped me to the linen of the ambulance stretcher. For no reason, I felt like crying. Such bad things had happened to me up till that day. Sandrofo's face was still just above me. I thought, I am a loaf of bread. I am ready to rise. And that thought was mine and mine alone. I never, to be honest, heard Sandrofo speak it.

Ancestors

(Rayovac Rodriguez—August 1977)

That's my nose," Rayovac Rodriguez said. "That's my nose." He was not talking to anybody, unless you could call the bronze statue, striding majestically across its pedestal, the pigeon-mottled creature in the center of Mercone Plaza, somebody. Rayovac wasn't pointing either, but had anyone heard him, it would have been clear the nose he was claiming was the bronze one that soared above him. It was a pug nose, remarkable in its stubbiness, remarkable in its resemblance to the squat nose plastered—unceremoniously, Rayovac thought, as if one could come by noses ceremoniously, and he, unlucky as he was, had not—on his own face. The man on the statue was none other than General José Rodriguez.

The General, as he liked to be called, was all those things a man could be: hero, statesman, warrior. Much admired in his day by all manner of people. Much admired today by all manner of birds. Occasionally, a human would even feel called upon to pee on his feet. This was not, of course, what Rayovac was thinking of. He was thinking of how at the base of the statue, he, the grandson of the General, Rayovac Rodriguez, was none of those things a man could be. He had done nothing in his life, a fact he had cherished till very recently. What was life if he couldn't use it to debunk the foolish values of his time? Or at least this is how he defended himself to himself. He came from a good, a noble family, in so far as such a thing was possible on the island, and he cherished his own downward mobility like a prize, hard won, fought for by ignoring his obvious talents and the scorn of others, by letting slackness take over his face and body so that, in spite of his youth, he looked worn out and droopy. Already he was thickening in the waist, though he still occupied a bedroom in his parents' home.

But today, he had brought himself to the base of the statue to summon something like the strength of his ancestors. Rayovac was ready for change. It was a day-old obsession, this obsession for change, but it was a firm one, based on a desire for improvement that Rayovac, self-appointed gadfly of the tropics, a man who lived to disgust his sisters and bother his parents, had never had before. For the first time, the first time ever, he was eager to impress. Love had caught him, off guard, the way it does, and demanded an alteration in his personality.

The object of his affections was the baker's daughter. It sounded Chaucerian to him. The baker's daughter. Was that right? Was he getting confused? He had been sent to the best schools that the island could offer, which meant he went to St. John's and studied in English and spent the better part of the day trying not to get thrown off the porch at the back of the school. He must have read Chaucer there. But it was foolish to try to make literary connections.

The baker's daughter. Her name was Melone, which made no sense to Rayovac, as it was a name that came from nowhere. He, after all, was named after a battery. And most of the people he knew were named after something or, more often, someone—a previous José, another Ramone. He thought, fraternally, of a guy he had once met named Toyota.

For good luck, Rayovac leaned over to touch the first letter of his ancestor's name, engraved on the bronze plaque that was mounted on the pedestal. He pulled his hand back in pain, away from the hot metal. He looked around cautiously to make sure no one had seen him make such a stupid mistake and then slunk out of the plaza.

Melone was a shy girl with messy brown hair. Her nose was pronounced but soft and rounded. Her chin was a bit recessed. The rest of the face was more classically lovely—large eyes, high cheekbones, a sort of olive-complected skin (in the manner of Mediterranean Jews). In later life, she would probably be a true beauty, unless the weakness of the chin and the prominence of the nose went unchecked. Then she might end up with the look of a sniveler. But Rayovac didn't care. He liked the way that, when she concentrated, her brow wrinkled into three distinct parallel snakes. He liked, too, the perpetually worried look on her face. Rayovac dreamed of placing the pads of his fingers on her forehead, smoothing her skin. It would be like a blessing, a laying on of hands, when he whispered, "Don't worry."

She first showed up on a Thursday afternoon. It was an average, too hot day with too many bugs flying about the ears, a day that found Rayovac pushing and pulling a hand mower across his parents' lawn. Inside the house, there were all the most up-to-date electronic gadgets. A microwave for the morning's coffee and the evening's rice and beans. A large television set, a blender, an electric vacuum, a washer and dryer. Rayovac's extensive collection of ham radios. Still, the idea of a motorized lawn mower seemed to repulse his parents. Which only meant, as far as Rayovac was concerned, a lot of blisters and sneezing and bug bites and sweat for Rayovac Rodriguez. On the day in question, Rayovac was feeling about as grumpy as he could feel about his endeavor, without feeling so cranky that he stopped altogether. Still, the sight of his mother's massive old Buick, looming up over the blacktop at the end of the street, seemed heaven sent. It was his chance to take a break.

Rayovac rested on the sly, only looking up in pretend interest when the car came to a full stop in the street, and he saw his mother step out of the driver's side and say, "Pedro will only eat vanilla." Ice cream, she meant, and he knew it and couldn't figure out for the life of him why his mother needed to voice this fact till he saw a young woman, hugging a tub of ice cream, step out of the passenger side of the car. Beads of sweat, from the ice cream, not the girl, dampened her shirt in inconvenient spots, and Rayovac felt so embarrassed for her that he looked away. "We'll get it inside before it melts," Teresa said. "That's my son," Teresa added, all business, in a way one might say, "And this is that lawn chair I was telling you about, the one I got on special at Plaza de las Americas."

"My son, Rayovac Rodriguez," Teresa added. Rayovac grunted in reply. That was his way in those days. But then he said, "*Buenos días,*" and added, in English, "all right," because kids from the States always said, "all right." To use the expression on the island was to declare one's cosmopolitan nature.

Melone smiled and said nothing.

"Rayovac, after the battery," Rayovac said, and the explanation seemed to puff him up.

"Oh," Melone shook her head, "of course. I'm happy to meet you."

"You are, huh?" Rayovac said. This was just one of the ways he cut to the heart of things, made words mean what they meant, or else showed words for what they were: polite, little lies.

"Yeah," Melone said. "I am," she laughed. "I am an honest soul. Really, I swear." She laughed again. "Your mother's a very interesting woman. We've had a wonderful day."

"Oh, sure, she's great," Rayovac nodded in quick agreement, though this seemed to him to be getting off the subject at hand, the subject being Melone's happiness to meet him.

"I think I must have spent the entire day doing everything you did when you were a child. Your mom took me on the ferry over to Cataño, and we met the old woman at the *santería* down there. Then we drove inland and saw your family's old farm." She smiled. "Well, you look busy," she reached over and tapped his forearm as it rested on the lawn mower handle. "And this might melt," she added, hefting the container of ice cream in her right palm, as if it were a melon she were testing for weightiness. She smiled and turned to follow his mother into the house, where she tripped, *tripped sweetly*, Rayovac thought for no reason, over the stone step at the entrance.

You are not falling in love, Rayovac told himself. *You don't know enough to fall in love.* But his step across the lawn lightened. He pushed the mower with real energy and told himself he was not happy for something he was *hoping* would happen—a chance to know Melone better, but something that had already happened—their short conversation, her light touch and, most of all, her words, "I'm an honest soul." She had known, known exactly what he was accusing her of, and she had answered in the best of possible ways.

"What's she coming here for?" Rayovac asked, disgusted, when she was gone.

"What's so horrible?" his mother said. "A pretty girl comes for a visit."

Rayovac, Pedro and Teresa were sitting around the dinner table. They sat far apart and had to shout to make themselves understood. The family had once included others, and the table had been bought for that time when there was an older brother, two sisters, even a maid. They had all gone on to other homes, other jobs. Pedro was nearly deaf, so the arrangement was the most difficult for him. Occasionally, he cupped a hand around his ear and tried to understand what was being said. For the most part, he sat in a silence that seemed like anger, anger at a world that had decided, so late in his life, to start presenting itself in a form he could not understand.

"I want to know what she's here for," Rayovac said. "I'm not complaining about her *being* here."

"Maybe she came to see you."

"I don't think so," Rayovac said, and he scooped some beans and rice into his mouth.

"Sit up straight," Teresa said.

Rayovac, thirty years on this planet, leaned his head closer to his plate, so the forkfuls of food needed to travel only a handful of inches to reach his lips.

"She's here about the bakery, Pedro," Teresa turned to her husband and prounounced her words slowly. "She wants to talk to you about ordering a sign."

"So why is she buying ice cream with you?" Rayovac said. "Why didn't she go to the Company?" The Company was where Pedro had worked all these years, manufacturing colorful signs for rental car agencies, ladies' dress shops, bodegas—naming, in effect, the island.

"Well, we got to talking about how things used to be, about places like the Mallorca and how La Madeleine gets the wrong kind of customers and what could be done to change that."

"What's the wrong kind of customer? One without money?"

"*Turistas*, child. They want it to be an island bakery. Not a place you go to take something back to nibble at the blackjack table. They want it to be *real* Puerto Rican, and they want my advice. On appropriate sweets, things I haven't eaten since I was a girl."

Melone was back the next night, a notebook on her knee, an earnest expression on her face and a box of day-olds from the Mallorca open in front of her. Rayovac sat on the far side of the porch, away from the women, but within listening distance.

"And what's this," she pointed to a pastry full with jelly.

"Oh, *delicias de guayaba*," Teresa said.

"And this?" She pointed to another pastry, a round cookie sandwich, scalloped at the edges, leaking more of the same blood-red jelly.

Melone printed the answers in her notebook with real dedication. Everything about her was neat, save for her dark brown hair, a mess of curls that traveled down her back. "Did you eat these when you were a girl on Calle de la Playa?" she asked, looking up like a reporter waiting for an answer.

Ah, Rayovac sighed from behind his newspaper, so Melone had indeed been taken to the places he was taken as a child. Earlier, they must have been driving around the city while Teresa pointed out everything—all her previous homes, her childhood by the sea and then at the farm, her teenage years in a mansion that went to ruin, then became a hotel, then a boarding house and now, as far as anyone could tell, was a house of ill repute. "Oh, Je-sus," she would have yelped as she told the story of how she had left a doll out on the wooden windowsill of that house turned whorehouse, how the doll's image, its pale silhouette, had burned into the wood and must still be there for the prostitutes to see.

She would have told her all that. It was her standard pitch, Rayovac thought, with no shortage of scorn. Charming at first, he knew that, but later, later it was what she used against people: history, her own sense of belonging. Only Pedro's ancestors, only the Rodriguezes, could match her, decade for decade, for belonging. It drove Rayovac crazy. Still, he eavesdropped in earnest. He figured things out.

Like her age. Fourteen. Even Teresa was surprised and blushed when the number was announced, as if her earlier remarks to Rayovac, those hints about a possible romantic liaison, now made her something perverse, Mother of Humbert Humbert, a matchmaker for lechers.

Melone was careful with Teresa. She spoke slowly, Rayovac guessed, because she thought her sentences out in advance, considered them completely and judged them to be wise or unwise before she spoke. It would have seemed pompous if it weren't accompanied by such pale, trembly hands and a neck that bent downward, looked at the floor for answers.

She was a miracle, Rayovac thought, because she had been born three times over, once in the form of her sister Tata and once in the form of her silent sister, Beatriz. Everyone on the island knew about Beatriz who didn't speak. But, with or without a voice, it was easy to distinguish Melone, because she wore her hair long to her sisters' chin-length style and because of her eyes. One was completely brown. The other was half brown, half hazel, and the hazel seemed to glow, a green moon of color off which Rayovac could not keep his own dark eyes.

At length, the two women were through talking, and Rayovac, having abandoned the lawn for his bedroom, slipped out the front door so he could bump into Melone, carelessly, as she made her way toward the bus stop and home. "Hello," he called, when she had shut the front door behind her.

"Oh, hello," Melone said.

"Rayovac," Rayovac said.

"Yes, of course. I remember," Melone said. "I'm reliving your childhood, after all. And I'm Melone. Well . . ." She looked at her feet. "Bye," she said cheerfully, "bye."

Rayovac sighed deeply. It was clear that he would never be able to make his move here. The front lawn was too close, what with his parents just steps away, what with his bedroom, decorated with maps and ham radios and other relics of his boyhood. Down the street, it would be just as bad. The park where he rode his bike as a kid, the public pool and the lake where he caught eels. The whole neighborhood was too close. All of Santurce was too close. Maybe the whole island was too close.

"Have a good . . ." Rayovac started and couldn't think of how to finish his sentence. "Bus ride. Hope you have a real good bus ride."

"Why, thank you," Melone said and pulled her hair over her right shoulder, shrugged once, and made for the street.

Rayovac bought a van. This was a first-ditch effort at respectability. The money, relatively easily come by, secured on the basis of his good name . . . or more accurately, his father's good name. The whole thing was embarrassing, dragging his father with him to cosign the loan. Only love could undo his pride like this, bring him to the cool, overly air-conditioned offices of the Banco Popular.

It was an old blue van, had once been in commission as a *público*, a sort of bus-taxi that ran, when it pleased, from town to town, making its leisurely paced way across the island. But this particular van seemed cursed. The mechanics would swear on their mothers' graves that the wiring was splendid, that the electrical system was perfect, that the battery was new, and yet, on alternate Wednesdays, the battery wouldn't take a charge. Rayovac, feeling charmed by the coincidence of his name and the clear absurdity of such orderly dysfunction, bought the van for five hundred dollars. He paid cash, placing the bills grandly on the hood of the junker that served as office for Raphael Jiminez. Jiminez, owner of OK Used Cars, was a man long plagued by the assertion that the giant O-K blinking on and off above his lot was unfair, in fact, a drastic overstatement of the actual quality of the goods he had for sale. This embarrassment did not prevent Jiminez from grabbing quickly for the five bills before they fluttered, like green butterflies, away in the wind.

As far as decorating went, Rayovac was not without thoughts. He considered a desert scene for the windows, some cacti and maybe an orange sun? Or maybe two? But this was silly, he knew. He was not that kind of person. His van was no fuck truck, no harbinger of ill will for some poor soul who had defaulted on a loan, no moving drug store. This was a van that would have all the positive attributes a van could have: tools, storage space, special shelves for transporting goods safely. Later on, beds for the kids. But here, Rayovac was getting ahead of himself—as he was still quite single. For the time being, the vehicle would have to be a vehicle of employment. Of that, Rayovac was certain, and with that, he went to visit the baker.

"I have a business proposition for you," Rayovac told Sandrofo as the two men sat at the large round table in the corner of La Madeleine.

"Yes," said Sandrofo, warily.

Donned in his father's pin-striped suit and wearing a white hat and dark sunglasses, Rayovac looked, though this was hardly his intention, like a hit man for the mob. His manner was forthright and assertive, or that's how it had seemed to him earlier when he'd practiced a few choice lines out in front of the mirror. He had had a copy of *How to Be a Fat Cat (Even if You're Just Small Potatoes)* lying on the toilet seat next to him. He had found the book at the public library, crammed in between several copies of *How to Win Friends and Influence People.* The latter looked well worn by many fingers, and Rayovac thought, if he was going to make an impression, he might as well try something a bit different.

Sandrofo gave Rayovac a little smile. Rayovac chose not to smile back. Instead, he scratched his chin. "It is my firm belief," Rayovac began, then stopped and coughed. He had forgotten the importance of keeping his sneakered feet out of the baker's line of sight. *Never sacrifice your standards of professionalism,* the book had declared, but Rayovac figured he could fudge on this one point. Now he tried to hide his feet by wrapping his ankles around the legs of his chair. He began again. "It seems to me that your bakery's profits . . ." He was starting with money. *The benefit to the client,* as the book put it. "Could be improved by transportation. And what I mean by transportation is a van." Sandrofo smiled. "And what I mean by a van is a vehicular mode of transportation to . . . to . . . to *enable* transportation. What I mean is moving goods around, services rendered, supply and demand. What I mean is stocking the supermarkets, hiring out at birthdays. Cake in the tropics."

"Rayovac," Sandrofo said and leaned toward him. "Can I get you something to eat with that?"

Rayovac shook his head. "You understand what I am talking about. You see the enabling power of this van?"

"No, I can't say I do see what you're talking about. I'll get you some cake, and you'll tell me again."

"No, no," Rayovac said and leaned over to grab Sandrofo's wrist.

Sandrofo brushed him off. "What are you so . . ." Sandrofo gestured his hands in the air, as if in imitation of a madwoman, "so nervous about?"

"I . . ." Rayovac stumbled and then said, though it was not what he meant to say, had nothing to do with the business enterprise he was proposing, "I can't eat cake."

"Oh," Sandrofo said, almost sadly. "Well, diabetes, is it? Or something? I'll get you some bread. Can you eat bread?"

Rayovac nodded his head. Sandrofo stood and made his way to the counter to ask his daughter to prepare something. Shyly, Rayovac looked up at her. He let his chest heave, almost comically. It wasn't Melone. He was disappointed but glad. He was safe.

"So what are you saying? And tell me plainly. Plain as you can."

"OK. OK," Rayovac said, and the words sounded like the starting notes of some mediocre song he was about to sing. "I bought a van so I can be your delivery boy." He grimaced on the word "boy."

"We don't really have a need for a delivery boy," Sandrofo said. "But I thank you for your interest."

"But you do. You do. Understand that if you could have branches in the island markets, if you could make home deliveries . . . ."

"It's not a bad idea, I'm sure. It's just we don't produce all that much here. We don't have the business to sustain, and what's more important, we don't have the equipment to sustain an increase in production. We're a small operation. A family business really, and that's the way I like it. I just hire a few women to wait on tables and run the cash register. Otherwise, it's just the girls and me."

Persistence, the Fat Cat book would have advised, but for the moment, the form that his persistence should take eluded Rayovac. "Thank you," he said. "Thank you kindly," and he left.

That night, Rayovac kicked the tires of his van, kicked the tires in revenge. Stupid man, he thought. Stupid, stupid, stupid man. Man with a tax break. Man putting his little girls to work in hideous, sweat-shop-type conditions. And wasn't he a suspicious fellow? Come all the way from Brooklyn without a wife. Come all the way with three girls to open a business that he wanted to fail. There would have to be law on his back somewhere. Rayovac didn't really believe any of this, but he allowed himself to rail on. Sandrofo was a crook. Why else would he defend failure with rhetoric about the virtues of a family-run business?

Wasn't that a trick Rayovac was familiar with? Perhaps he didn't truly understand the profits one could get from a delivery service. Perhaps . . . the sneakers, Rayovac thought. The fatal flaw. He got into his van and headed for the mall, where he walked in air-conditioned peace till he found a pair of dark dress shoes.

The Baker's Wife

(Maria Elena—November 1977)

What I wanted, more than anything else, was for Sandrofo Cordero Lucero to protect me against the past. He was—with his diplomatic manners, his witty children—the dream I'd always used to shield myself against my past romantic liaisons and all the troubles they'd brought me. He was the *worthy* man who treated me well, an unrelenting argument, in his neatly pressed chinos and white cotton shirt, against the cruelties, the stupidities of others.

Sometimes I thought I willed Sandrofo's goodness out of sheer desperation. He appeared on the island, a relative newcomer even after a nine-year stay, because he wasn't what everyone else on the island seemed to be: an old grade-school classmate playing grown-up.

At first, I was frightened of losing him, of his affection drifting, like a sea buoy, away to another woman. I wanted to be an appropriate partner for him, for I sensed that for a man like him, a man so precise and correct in his manner, appropriateness was emotional duct tape, the tie that would bind. I exhausted myself thinking of required changes. He was quiet; perhaps I should shut up? He worked incessantly, never slept. What could I do? I drank coffee. My guts churned angrily till I agreed, after midnight, to embrace the nearest pillow.

Six months into my romance with Sandrofo, Lucia, my boss at the gallery, said, "Who was it who came here, armed with flowers, the day after you decided to sprawl yourself out on the plaza?" Lucia had taken my fainting spell to be a dramatic ploy, an unseemly request for attention.

I gave her a look. "Sandrofo," I said. "Sandrofo came here."

"He came looking for you," Lucia said.

"That's right," I said, unsure why we were narrating history for one another.

"For you," Lucia said, "not some other girl, not some quiet insomniac." Lucia was only fifteen years my senior, but her marriage and three children seemed to age her—morally, not physically, for she'd retained the high glamour, the slim body and unlined face of her youth.

"Well, they're not always so easy to find, those quiet insomniacs."

Lucia rolled her kohl-rimmed eyes and started to apply burgundy lipstick to her mouth, a sign she found my words sufficiently foolish that she needed an additional activity, something beyond this conversation, to occupy her attention. She had been my advisor throughout my romance with Sandrofo—for the many months when he'd stop by, once every few weeks, to say hello, but not to ask me out, and for the past six months, during which we had finally become lovers. "I'm only saying," she started and paused—for effect and to blot her lips in the palm of her hand (a move of planetary concern, she was trying to conserve tissues). "I am only saying you are who you are, and apparently he likes who you are, so leave things be."

"Okay," I said, "you're right," but what I thought was, Who will create who? Out of whose desires? My past relationships had taught me this: you are a paper doll being jammed into the wrong spot, or you are the hand trying to force a paper doll into the wrong spot.

"Love," Lucia said out loud, as if she could read my thoughts. "Don't forget love." I supposed she meant that the emotion made hands and paper dolls immaterial.

I tried not to forget love; perhaps I even felt it. That very night I went to see Sandrofo in the small apartment he occupied, with his three daughters, over the bakery. "We're making you dinner," Tata called, before I even got up the stairs. "But look what she's done to the rice," a steaming pan attached to a slim arm appeared at the top of the staircase.

"I'm not a cook. I'm not," I heard Tata call. "That's Melone's job," Tata said to me, when I reached the apartment.

"Just scrub," Melone said, handing her the pot to clean out. "Don't tell me what to do," Tata said.

"OK," Melone said. Shrugging, she took the pot to the sink and ran cold water over the rice, which made the pot hiss and steam till she was enveloped in a cloud. "It'll be good," she said of dinner. "Fish and rice. It'll just be late. Dad's still downstairs. He's talking to Rayovac."

Beatriz, who was sitting at the table and observing the proceedings, rolled her eyes at this last sentence. Tata said, "Rayovac's hot on Melone."

"He is not," Melone said.

"Oh, please," Tata said.

Just then, Sandrofo came up the back stairs. "Someone wants a job," he said, and the girls hooted with laughter.

"What's going on?" I asked Sandrofo. I hadn't yet found my way into the rhythm of this family, so I had been standing stiffly at the doorway to the kitchen, observing the girls as they chattered around me.

"Rayovac Rodriguez is going on," Tata said. "Right?" She looked at her father who nodded his head. "He's here every day asking for a job."

Beatriz banged her hand on the table for emphasis. "Yeah," Tata said sarcastically, as if echoing Beatriz's point, "like he *needs* a job."

"Explain," I said, raising my eyebrows at Sandrofo.

He put his hand lightly on my back, and I relaxed at his touch, as if his hand meant now I was really in the room, had finally arrived for supper. Sandrofo gestured toward a chair, and I sat as he said, "This has been going on since the end of the summer. Rodriguez, you must know them. Big family in Puerto Rico. Great-great grandfather founded Mercone. Family made a fortune investing in pharmaceuticals. The son, Rayovac . . ."

". . . wants a job in the bakery so he can stare at Melone," Tata said.

"He does not," Melone said.

"The son lives with his family out in Santurce, never got a job, spends his day by the checkerboard by . . ."

"Iglesia de Maria de Croix?" I asked. "The one who wears a T-shirt that says 'Sea World, Land of Dolphins'?"

Sandrofo nodded tiredly.

"Oh, Melone," I said, "you can do better than that."

"I don't even *like* him," Melone said. "Could we please talk about something else?"

"Here, let me help," I said, going to the sink where she was using her fingernails to scrape the last bit of burnt rice from the pot.

"No," Melone said, guarding the pot with her shoulder. "We're doing this for you. You can't help. Why don't you two go out for your walk or something? Then when you come back, we'll have dinner ready. OK?"

Sandrofo looked at me. Winked. "OK," I said.

We didn't go far, just over to Plaza de San José. It was small, quiet and bathed with light. On one side was Iglesia de San José, which is the oldest church on the continent, or at least the oldest one that is still used. On the other side of the plaza was Casa de los Contrafuertes, where Lucia used to work. Lucia said Contrafuertes was the oldest house in the city. She'd worked on a restoration project there, before she left to start her own gallery. Since June, the private residence next to Contrafuertes had been Museo de Casals. I'd only visited in the evening with Sandrofo. Then the plaza was transformed from its daytime quiet to a temporary carnival of drunks and reveling tourists, lured by flyers slipped under hotel room doors, that promised "*almuerzo y* 'happy hour,'" as if the two should be considered one and the same. Not the kind of thing Sandrofo liked, so I never quite understood his attraction to the plaza. Still, el Museo seemed to be our spot, perhaps because I had a key from Lucia, and it allowed us to wander through the place alone, several times a week.

Each visit, Sandrofo would stop in front of the case that had a yellow plaster of Paris cast of Pablo Casals' hands. I had always thought the hands were a little ridiculous . . . and definitely creepy. I used to tell Lucia they should have a plaster of Paris cast of Casals' ears. And that we should try to cast all our artists' eyes, so if they got famous, we would be rich when they died.

Tonight, I thought I'd finally ask Sandrofo why Casals' hands so fascinated him.

"I don't know," he said. "I guess what they could do. Everything they could create."

"How did you hurt *your* hand?" I asked. "I've always wondered." I picked up his right hand. The fourth finger was twisted around so the knuckle faced the palm. Where a wedding band might have been, a deep red scar ringed his finger.

"Just born like this," he said and curved his hand into a fist and opened his hand again. The damaged finger stuck out, useless, unwilling to curve in either direction.

"Really?" I said. "It so looks like a later accident." I touched his scar lightly with the pads of my fingers.

He flinched, pulled his hand back to himself. "Sorry," I said. "I'm sorry."

We walked upstairs to a small, cool hallway, with one large window that opened on a now-empty courtyard. Still, the noise from the plaza floated over the house and inside the window, so we didn't feel quite alone. Sandrofo pulled me toward him, and we kissed, like schoolchildren, passionately because our privacy, however partial, was so hard won. This was our ritual—sex under that open window, in the dimming evening light—but I still felt startled each time by the event: Sandrofo's hands lifting up my skirt, pulling down my underwear and seating me on the tile of the floor, cold from a day's worth of air conditioning. He'd lean over, take off my blouse, let me start to remove his shirt, and I'd feel each button like a gift. Sandrofo always washed before he saw me, scrubbing his face, hands and forearms, but sometimes a small piece of dough, trapped under his shirt, would fall down on me, or I'd reach up and find a papery bit of flour, still pasted to his elbow. I liked all this and the vague smell of butter and sugar that lingered, like evidence of another life, under the smell of soap.

"Kiss me," I said tonight, and he did. Then we were silent, talking only when I said, "Turn over," and he did. We made love quietly, and I looked down at him, then out the window at a teakwood tree with its huge leaves and flowers shaped like Christmas trees. It was a strange tree to find in the city, since it was so big, and I wondered if it wouldn't, soon enough, destroy the museum's foundation. I remembered how, when I was a schoolgirl, we used to paint the tree's big round seeds with demonish grins.

When we were through, both lying on our backs, considering the welts the tile would be making on our skin, I thought to say, once, experimentally, "I love you," but I saw Sandrofo check his watch. "OK," I said instead, pulling myself up and gathering my clothes.

"We'd better head back before the girls burn the place down," he said. I nodded.

Back outside, among the small crowd that had started to gather for night activity, Sandrofo pointed to Iglesia de San José and said, "In 1898, when the U.S. was bombing, a cannonball went through that window and disappeared. No one ever found it."

I squinted up into the purple of the night. "Where could it have gone?"

"I don't know. That's not the only thing that's disappeared. Remember back a handful of years ago?"

"Sure," I said. "I am in the business after all." A Flemish painting, "The Virgin of Bethlehem," had been stolen. Everyone in the art world talked about it, especially since the painting had apparently come to the island in the early 1500s.

"Some people say it wasn't stolen."

"I never heard *that,*" I said.

"A woman told me that she was there the night of the robbery, that she was praying and looking at the Virgin one minute, and it was gone the next. It just disappeared before her eyes."

"Oh, I know who you mean. Pilar. She's crazy. Everyone knows she was cleaning rooms at the Hilton that night. She's thinking of her own girlhood. One night she was looking at a virgin; the next morning she wasn't."

Sandrofo laughed. "Well, perhaps . . . ."

"This doesn't sound like you. You don't believe in magic."

"You're right," he said, then laughed. "But I do believe in things disappearing."

"Like what?"

"Like . . ." he turned and took my hands. I looked down at our four hands, twisted together, a strange bouquet of flesh. "Like Maria Elena Pico. I believe in her disappearing and being replaced by Maria Elena Pico de Lucero."

I stepped back, pulled my hands to my breast. "You're asking me to marry you," I said in what must have sounded like amazement.

"Yes," he said, quietly. "I am."

In the morning, when I told Lucia that I had agreed to be Sandrofo's wife, she started cursing.

"Lucia," I said, surprised. "I thought you would be happy for me."

"*Ay,*" she said, "you don't even know the man."

"Of course I know the man."

"His family?" she asked, pushing her chin-length, slightly graying hair behind her ears. The gesture seemed important, and I remembered how she said she'd refused to dye her hair because she thought the gray made her look stately. "His family?" she said again, prompting me.

"Three daughters, wife dead in childbirth."

"I know that," she said, disgusted. "I mean parents? Siblings?"

"I don't know. No siblings. I guess his parents are dead."

"You guess," she sneered. "And what sort of worker was he? Before he came here?"

"Before the bakery? I don't know. He did something up in New York."

"Age?"

"Thirty-six," I said.

"And the girls?"

"Fourteen," I said.

"Married at twenty-one, I suppose, and this in the States during the sexual revolution?"

"It's not *that* damning," I said.

"Was she pregnant when they married? How long were they married anyway?"

"A year? I don't know."

"*Ay,* how can you not know these things? What do the two of you talk about when you are together?"

I said, "Lucia, just yesterday, you seemed to like Sandrofo."

"Yesterday you weren't getting married. I've seen things. Men robbing their wives. Men who marry so no one will know that they prefer men to women. What if he leaves those three girls with you and disappears? I can't be giving you a raise to support them. There's no more money in the budget."

"These things aren't going to happen. Sandrofo's steady. You've seen it yourself."

Lucia looked as if she were about to nod her head in agreement, but then she clapped her palms together and said, "We'll go to Perez for advice."

"Oh no, no, no," I said. "Not her. I can always be persuaded to go somewhere, but not to Perez." Señora Perez was Lucia's mystic of choice. At Lucia's insistence, I had visited her over a year ago when I was embroiled in an unhappy love affair with a married man. I'd have stayed for her advice, but Perez insisted we sacrifice a donkey first. "A what?" I had asked her. "Bring me a donkey," she had said.

"The woman's a lunatic," I had told Lucia later. "A goat, a chicken. I have heard of these things. But a donkey?" Lucia told me that hard truths often required the sacrificial animal to be large and braying. "And I'm the one who had a three-week stay in a loony bin," I had said, amazed, to Lucia.

Now Lucia said, "Only Perez will tell you the truth. This man, Sandrofo, had a wife. How will you ever know about her unless you go to Perez? You think your husband will tell you? Your husband will not tell you. There are things husbands do not tell."

"OK," I said. "I'll go." Won over, I thought, shamefacedly, by my own damn jealousy. "No donkeys," I said.

"Oh," Lucia said, her voice a model of reason, "of course, no donkeys. Who wants a dead donkey?"

Three days later, Lucia came in late to the gallery with two greenish-brown coconuts tucked under her arms like bowling balls. She placed them on her desk and said, "She'll see you tonight—at eight. So . . ." Lucia stopped and pointed at one of the coconuts. "We'll ask her to give coconut to the saint and that way there'll be no sacrifices." I nodded my head. I knew this most common of divination techniques. The *I Ching,* essentially, Caribbean style. You broke the coconut shell into several pieces, then tossed the shell on the ground. Depending on how the pieces landed—white meat up or brown shell up—you had a pattern that signaled the answer to your question.

That evening, we took the ferry to Cataño, that small enclave across the bay from the gallery. The place was famous for its *santería* and, in my mind, the number of TV sets that faced out of windows. At dusk, when we got there, each window was noisy with a different story, and the streets were clustered with people finishing dinner or sitting on folding chairs atop the road's cracked pavement and following the hapless exploits of Lucille Ball. It was as if everyone's home had been turned inside out, with fights and lovemaking happening on the corners. You'd have to go into someone's kitchen for the relative anonymity of public space.

To get to Perez's, we stepped down a narrow alleyway. Laundry hung, an informal curtain, between the buildings' walls. Behind a drying pair of brown polyester pants, we found Perez, sitting just inside a doorway that opened, almost furtively, on the alley. She wore a yellow and brown plaid shirt over a skirt with blue and red flowers. Dressed smartly for the gallery, Lucia and I looked like foreigners. It seemed that before we were even in her line of vision, Perez was talking to us about sacrificing a wild dog. "I can't do this," I said to Lucia—it seemed to be as much a matter of my working-girl clothes as my squeamishness. College in the States had ruined me for life on the island.

"Perez," I said, leaning toward her dark doorway, "I'm sorry. I can't do this."

Puzzled, Perez said, "I catch the dog myself. You don't catch the dog."

"No, that's not it," I said, shaking my head. Lucia was not stupid. In the gallery, her eye was discriminating, but Perez clearly had a hold over her faculties that defied reason.

"I give you advice, free of charge," Perez said magnanimously. "It's advice from me. Not them," she gestured behind her. I could vaguely see what she was referring to—two shelves were nailed to the wall behind her: one was lined with several of the flat stones that represent the *orishas,* the saints; one was almost collapsing under the weight of a TV set. "You want to know about this man. You just ask him."

It was simple advice. It was advice I meant to take, but I realized the impossibility of the wisdom that weekend when Sandrofo took me out to a restaurant he favored. It was an unpromising place from the outside, just a suburban restaurant off the main road in Río Pedras, but its interior had none of the North American feel of the road. We entered rooms that seemed European, with dim lighting casting everything into shades of brown. Around us, elegantly suited men rose for handshakes with men and for double-sided kisses with women.

"Nice place," I said as a waiter pulled out a chair for me. "Where'd you get such good taste?"

Sandrofo shrugged.

"Previous wife?" I asked playfully.

Sandrofo smiled.

"Really," I said. "*Was* it her?"

Sandrofo smiled again and said, "It's so sad. Let's not talk about it. I never think about that now."

"OK." I was quiet for a bit then said, "But I do wonder about things. Like your parents. What were they like?"

He shrugged. "What is there to say?"

"Well, what did your father do?"

"Flags. He sewed American flags."

"And your mother?"

"She was a housewife."

I nodded my head. "My dad worked in a pineapple-packing plant, after the tobacco plantation went under. We all lived in Cidra." He nodded. He already knew this. "My mom sewed school uniforms for years before . . . ." I waved my hand so he would know I meant "before the stroke" which had killed her. "So your parents," I began again. "What was their background? I mean, culturally?"

"I don't know much. Jews with ancestors from Spain. But they never talked about their childhoods."

"And you didn't push them? I mean, you must have been able to tell some things from their manner." Sandrofo shook his head no.

"Well, at least you knew they were Jewish. And what about . . . let's see . . . the street you grew up on?"

Sandrofo held his hand up as if to stop the questions. "Bensonhurst, a neighborhood in Brooklyn, down the street from the firehouse. The engines . . . they'd go all night, but none of that matters. I have a new life with you." He smiled seductively, tapped a thin brown cigarette against the table and used his free hand to reach over and squeeze my fingers. A candle flame of desire, mimicking the tiny blaze on the table, flared up in me; it was a blue, too hot pressure starting in the groin, a no-color, oxygen-eating emptiness of the gut that moved hotly through the center of my body but tapered off at my throat

"And . . ." I said leadingly, as Sandrofo reached over, as if to put his index finger to my lip and quiet me, but then he didn't touch the center of my mouth with his finger but gently traced my bottom lip.

"OK," I said with resignation, feeling fear work like a bellows to my desire till there I was: a regular conflagration in the suburbs, flames pushing past my throat to my mouth. A shy dragon, I didn't dare drop my jaw. What I mean is I kept quiet, knowing too many questions might make him change his mind about me.

We set the date of our wedding for early September, a few months after the triplets' fifteenth birthday and far enough away that the girls would have a chance to get used to me and to the idea of their father marrying. In the meantime, I began to spend my evenings in Sandrofo's apartment. Soon enough, I was there every night. As the weeks passed, I found myself thinking less about the marriage than about my impending motherhood. I tried to compensate for my deficiencies—notably, the decade during which I'd had the bad taste not to know my own daughters. I made it my project to fill in the details. This was much easier than assembling the facts about Sandrofo's previous marriage. The girls told me what they could. Or rather Tata and Melone did. Beatriz didn't talk, but I didn't sense that she had any objections to my project.

So during the months of my engagement to Sandrofo, I asked questions. For the briefest of time, I let myself be that unheard of thing: a sympathetic journalist. I asked for first memories, because when my sister was dying and when my family was crowded—weeping, clothes damp with tears—around her expiring body, I had thought to say, "What was your earliest memory?" I asked everyone in the family. I even asked the nurses. In the years since my sister's death, I asked the question often. It seemed important to me, just as it always seems important to know a person's dying words. First memories, dying words: not quite bookends to a life but close enough. And I had another question: When did you decide how you would be in the world? When did you decide what life was like? I felt appallingly earnest. I was a history book, ready to digest decades. While Sandrofo worked, I found the girls in the apartment and asked my questions. Hands clasped at the base of my throat, I said, "Tell me everything, everything you remember." As they started to talk, I realized they would tell me too—whether they meant to or not—some of what I still needed to know about their father. Who was he? How did he come to be his own sad self?

First Memory

(Melone—January 1978)

OK," I told her, "I'll tell you everything I remember," but as soon as I said it, I heard the voice of the old rabbi at the Miramar synagogue. "Don't say it," he'd say when we went for our Hebrew lessons. "Don't say it," he'd say again, as if he knew we were on the verge of saying it anyway. I was scared, but I couldn't help sounding out the word, silently, in my brain. *Yawheh.* God. *Adonai.*

To me, he resembled our father.

"Our father," I used to say, as if starting a prayer, but I would finish it up as a statement: "Our father loves us with wrath and mercy—like an Old Testament God." I understood myself correspondingly, as a person with an unhealthy fondness for gold calves and easy miracles.

But I didn't say this to Maria Elena. She didn't want to know all that. What she wanted was my first memory, and that's what I tried to give her. I liked her and didn't mind talking, but it's funny moving when you're little. You lose your old life before you've got anything like a real handle on it, and then when it comes back to you, it comes as a crazy mixture, so what you know to be true is really what you were told was true combined with all the details your imagination provided on an earlier telling.

For Maria Elena, I wanted to pick a full memory. Earlier images flickered in my brain—they came to me as dreamlike stills—but they were all hazy and confused and had to do with when I lived with my grandmother in New York. I remember a cellophane-wrapped block of cheese being thrown against a wall, a small box of flavorless lollipops, a clown puppet. But these memories, perhaps because they are so insubstantial, seem to belong to another person; I'm just storing them as a favor to someone who no longer exists. My first complete memory took place on one of our first days on the island, during the year that we were five and our father was twenty-six.

We had spent the night in the apartment over the bakery. Of course, it wasn't quite a bakery then, and the apartment wasn't quite an apartment, but it was an entire building, and it was ours. I remember thinking that was amazing—a whole building with two floors and a basement just for us. I couldn't believe we were actually going to live in it, though I don't know now what it was that impressed me—the size of the building or the combination of commercial and residential space or the fact that it was on such a well-traveled street. I know it was something different, better, than whatever we had lived in before. Better, I suppose I mean, than our former apartment in New York, a place I barely remember.

The first night in our new home, I slept, with my sisters, in blankets on the floor. Our building was on the corner, and on all sides but one we had windows. The windows were big, and out back there was a courtyard formed by the backsides of four buildings. It wasn't completely enclosed, because a small drive—it would become the place where we left the bakery truck—led away from the back of the first-floor kitchen, down a short hill to the street.

When we were indoors, it felt as if there wasn't really enough building to separate us from the street. The walls seemed more like skin—something to distinguish what was outside from what was inside but not something that kept you out of the outside. I felt, when I curled into my blankets that first night, as if the real floor were the street and not the floor of the building.

The next day Daddy woke us by shouting into our bedroom, "*Arriba!*" That meant "up," as in "get up." He was giving us Spanish lessons. He came in with three towels, three washcloths, three little bars of soap wrapped in paper and three tiny bottles of shampoo. The lights didn't work in the apartment yet, but the water did. Off the kitchen, there was a stall shower, and it was already hot out. Daddy said he'd go out and get us breakfast, and we should clean ourselves up. Tata told him we normally took baths at night, but he said that didn't matter.

Beatriz, Tata and I got in the shower together, and I used my washcloth to block the drain, so it would be like a bathtub. We played bull-in-the-china-shop, a game we liked to play in the tub. We sudsed our hair, and then Beatriz made her hair into two white horns and tried to stab Tata and me in the stomach. In my memory of this, we are all giggling, and I knew I was supposed to be happy, but secretly I felt a sort of nameless despair connected to the newness of my surroundings and the fact that I considered myself, at five, too smart, too wise in the ways of the world, to be a child. I loved the softness of the soap horns, as they stabbed me in the gut, and yet I thought, darkly, of stories I'd overheard about sad children back home who went to the playground unsupervised and never returned.

When the water in the shower came just above our ankles, Tata picked up the washcloth and let the water drain out. We were still playing—only I was the bull—when father came back with breakfast.

"Enough, enough," he said. "You'll wash yourselves away. Dry off and we'll go on a picnic."

Instead of a front door on the second floor, there was a black iron gate at the top of the stairs. We went through the gate and then walked down the stairs to the front door, which was blue and wooden, like a real door. We went out into the street. There were some men milling about in front of the door, and there were some pigeons, but otherwise the street was quiet, and it seemed the city had yet to wake up. It was even a little cold against my sunburned skin, and I wished I had my sweater with the ladybugs embroidered on it.

"Want to look at the bakery again?" our father said, and we said we did, and he moved a board so that there was a hole in the plywood and we could see what was going to be the bakery. I stuck my head in first, but it was just dark and smelled like fish. Then Tata and Beatriz looked, and Daddy said, "OK, breakfast." He gave each of us a bag. I carried the rolls, and Beatriz carried the juice, and Tata carried the chocolate bars. We were going to have chocolate sandwiches for breakfast—a special treat.

"They do it all the time down here," Daddy said, meaning either that the islanders were partial to bread and chocolate or that they were always spoiling themselves with early-morning treats. There were funny blue rocks in the streets, and they were hard to walk on. Daddy said that they were ballasts, a kind of weight that you put in the bottom of a ship to make the ship heavy, and that after the ships came over from Spain, they took out the ballasts and used them to pave the streets.

The houses were all painted like candy. We went past a white church that was so flat and smooth it looked like icing, and it made sense to me that we were going to open a bakery. Then Daddy pointed to a big, brown building.

"That used to be a convent. For nuns. But now it is a fancy hotel." He laughed, though we didn't know what was funny about that.

We walked up a hill, toward another big building. "That used to be a convent," Dad said again, "but now it is the U.S. Antilles Command."

"We're Jewish," Tata said.

Daddy looked down at her. "So I hear," he said.

"Of a special tribe of Jewish people called the . . . called the . . ." Tata let her sentence trail off as she tried to imagine a name. She was always making up stories like this.

"I can say the *Shma*," I said, "but you're not supposed to say it by memory because that means you think you're smart."

Tata said, "Beatriz knows how to say it too, don't you?"

Beatriz nodded her head.

"OK," Tata said, "say it." Beatriz looked at her. "I'm just kidding," Tata said and gave her a hug. "I know you know it."

Our father seemed not to take any of this in, and I vaguely remember we were disappointed by this, that we were used to our grandmother praising us for being clever. "Watch out; there they are now," he said and looked up the street. Two nuns were coming down the hill on the far side of the street. When they passed us, they said, "*Buenos días.*"

"There are a lot of Catholics here," our father said. "Sisters of the Brothers of the Daughters of the *Mishegos*," he said and laughed. "You know *mishegos?*" he said. We nodded, but he told us what the word meant before we had a chance to offer our own definitions. "It means crazy, craziness."

Past the final convent, the street stopped and opened, it seemed, onto the sea, but as we came to the end of the street, we saw that we were high above the beach and the water was still quite far away. There was a short stretch of sparse grass, littered with paper cups, and then a thick stone wall that ran as far as we could see to the right. On the left, the wall ran until it reached what looked like a giant castle that stuck out into the sea. Above the wall, there was nothing but the sky.

"That," Father pointed up the slight incline, past a large stretch of field to the castle, "is El Morro. It is a very famous old fortress. When the enemies of the Spanish came, they sent cannonballs into the sea to defend the people in the town." He gestured to the sea as if it were the water, not some nameless marauders, that had threatened the city. "Later, we can go there."

"Come on," he said, and the three of us followed behind him in a line, like baby ducks. When we got to the wall, Papi brushed the top of it off and lifted us up, one by one, to sit.

"This is a walled city," he said. "There is a wall around the whole city." He explained how the castle up the hill was only a part of that wall and how the wall dropped all the way down to the sea. I turned around to look, but he said, "Don't look," so I didn't see what was below and behind us.

Then Papi took the bags we had been carrying and gave each of us a juice. He unpeeled the chocolate bars and broke open the rolls to make sandwiches.

"I don't know what I am doing," he said. "Of course, you can look around. Look around."

So, my bottle between my thigh and my sandwich held together by the knobs of my knees, I put my palms to the grainy top of the wall and looked. Several hundred feet below the wall was a slum, and from where we sat I could see the backs of apartment buildings. They were in such disrepair that nothing was straight or square. Foundations sagged. Fences tottered. Upstairs porches swung loosely from the bodies of buildings, as if the porches were dress sleeves waiting for arms.

We must have seen slums before, because Tata said, all matter-of-fact, "Oh, Papi. You know, this is a bad neighborhood."

"That's right, girls," he said. "I don't want you ever to go down there. No matter what happens." Just then, a dark-haired, large-pored, greasy-looking man emerged from a break in the wall. He was breathing heavily, having just climbed the stairs from the beach.

"Uh," he said, then looked at my father, gestured to the three of us and said something I didn't understand beyond a few words I'd been taught like "*muchachas*" and "*aquí*." I guessed he didn't think girls should be sitting here. My father said something back, quickly, in Spanish, and the man shrugged and walked away.

"It's called La Perla," our father said, his chin gesturing to the buildings at our backs. "You can look again, if you're curious." So we turned once more to look at the broken-down settlement on the beach. You couldn't see the exact point where sand met water, but people were clearly there, throwing their week's trash into the water; wrappers and debris floated out into the sea, a foamy tongue of garbage in the blue of the ocean.

Another man stumbled up the steps and out from the opening between the wall. He looked over at my sisters and me. Then he looked at my father and made a funny hissing sound, some form of disapproval, before he walked on.

"That's enough," my father said. "Hold onto your breakfasts, and let's go. We'll walk and eat." Tata jumped down from the wall. Feeling a slight scraping at the back of my thighs, I slid off too. Then Beatriz followed. The roll in my hand seemed too big, and I wished I didn't have it and that those men would come back and see me without a roll. I felt sad, the way I had felt earlier when I was in the shower.

We went back across the field to the street. We walked past the convent that wasn't really a convent.

"Let's go see Christopher Columbus," my father said. "You know who he is, don't you?"

"Of course," Tata said.

"Discovered America," I said.

"That's right," our father said. "And there's a statue of him right here in this very city." We walked down the hill and into another section of the city we hadn't been in before. It wasn't like an iced cake here, but it wasn't like La Perla either. It was busy and full of people and trash, but the buildings were all firm, and none of the floors was on a diagonal, and no one looked at us. There were other children here, and they were wearing dresses, as we were, and sandals. All the girls, even babies in carriages, had tiny gold studs in their ears. I saw one girl with black nail polish.

"He sailed the ocean blue," Tata started to sing a song we knew about Columbus. She didn't stop till we were standing in front of him in the center of a big stone plaza.

"Look at this," Tata said, and she climbed up onto the pedestal so she could hug Columbus's knees. She turned to look at what Columbus was looking at: the whole bay of San Juan full of ocean liners and ships and, in the distance, large cranes that took new cars off ships and into automobile showrooms. "Look at this," Tata said again. Beatriz obediently turned to the water. "This is bee-u-ti-ful," Tata exclaimed. "I could just look at this *allll* day!" and she closed her eyes, as if it were too much for her eyes to handle and she would have to give them a break. I saw some adults look up at Tata and smile.

"Oh, Tata," my father said, disapprovingly, "look at that." She had smeared some chocolate from her sandwich on her dress. "Come on," he said and held her hand while she jumped off the pedestal. "Time to go."

We headed out of the park and down a new street. There were lots of people standing around with paper cups of coffee, and there were some newspapers here—either in people's hands or blowing across the street with a swoosh, like some informal broom for pigeon soot. We saw a long line of men apparently waiting for something. The line went halfway down the street and then rounded the corner so it didn't look like a line at all but like a human curb for the sidewalk.

Beatriz tugged my sleeve, and I said, "Beatriz wants to know what everybody's waiting for."

"Don't know," our father said. "Maybe a movie."

Beatriz tugged my sleeve again. Daddy saw this and said, "Well, let's follow them and find out." Beatriz nodded her head and smiled guiltily. This was what she wanted. We walked down the street and turned left and saw that the line of men continued down that street and turned right. We followed it right. It quickly turned right again, although this time the line went down an alley and not a street.

My father stopped for a second. Then he said, as if answering some plea from us, "Well, all right, but hold hands." So we held hands, with Daddy in front and then Tata and then Beatriz and then me in the back. All of us put the right hand out in front and the left in back, so as we went through, we were facing the line of men. A few of them nodded hello as we went by.

"*Pee-yoo*," Tata said, because, halfway down the alley, there was a huge mound of trash that smelled like rotting meat. We pushed by it, arching our backs so that our dresses wouldn't get dirty. When we were past, I looked back and saw that beside the trash there was a man stretched out, as if for a nap. He was dressed in stained, old gray slacks and worn black shoes, but he wasn't wearing a shirt. He had dark hair and a dark moustache. His chest was covered with long, parallel red marks, as if he had been beaten, in a very orderly fashion, with a stick. He wasn't bleeding, but he was badly bruised. Perhaps he was sleeping or, maybe, I thought, dead, because a fly landed on his stomach, just above his belly button, and it wandered over to his bottom rib and back. The man did not try, lazily, to wave the bug away. This worried me, but then I thought, Do people always wipe bugs away when they are asleep? Maybe he was drunk. Perhaps his stomach was invisibly calloused from the years he had spent pushing a cart full of fritters and meat-filled tan ears with his belly. Then I saw a fly crawl out of the small gap between the man's upper and bottom lips. The fly rose off the man's face—*his soul*, I thought, though I didn't believe in souls, *his soul alighting*—to fly around the dank air of the alley.

No one in the line that was just a few feet away, pressed away from the garbage and against the wall of the building opposite, paid the man any mind. In fact, they were so oblivious, I thought perhaps he wasn't there, perhaps my sadness put him there.

I felt the tug of my sister's hand. I turned my head back to my family just as we were emerging onto what happened to be our street, although our bakery was still a few blocks away. We started down along the line of men—it was in the direction of home anyway—when our father stopped short. Some men nodded hellos, but then Father made a sort of harumphing sound of confusion or anger. It was hard to read. "Keep holding hands," he said sharply. It was a reprimand, as if we were already freeing ourselves and fleeing in all directions. We moved down the street, to the end of the line and our home. The line led to our door, and at the front was a man named Angelo whom we already knew, my father reminded us, from a few days earlier.

This man Angelo had a funny voice, like it wasn't a voice at all, and he said to my father, "Señor Lucero, a fine day. I've taken the liberty of telling a few people about the employment opportunities here at La Madeleine."

For a moment, my father looked confused. Then, he started yelling, "Get out of here. I don't think this is funny. Now get out of here." Then, he said something in Spanish. People in the line started to move, but they did not really fall out of line. My father said it again, whatever it was, and he said it in a stern voice so the group responded like torn-out stitching. The line loosened, moved into the street and then, front to back, widened and dissolved.

I looked at Beatriz, and Beatriz looked back at me. It occurred to me—something about the panic in her eyes—that she had seen the man by the trash, too. This worried me, because I still hoped I had made that man up, that I'd never seen him.

My father yelled at the men again, and I felt embarrassed at the way he was talking to grown-ups.

"I dropped my roll," I said and started down the street, in a pretend search for my bread.

My father shouted, "Come back here," but already I had quickened my pace and was running down the street, weaving through the men still scattering up and down the street. I stopped where the alley was. I looked down, and it was an empty alley. I mean, it was full of trash on the left-hand side, but there was no evidence of the line that had been there only moments before. Still, even though it was dark between the buildings, I could see the man's two legs, looking like two fingers, forming a peace sign over the fist of his torso.

"Get back here," I heard my father yell, his voice ferocious. I walked back.

"I guess the pigeons had a snack," I said. "I guess they just went and ate my roll."

"You ate your roll," Tata said. "You're crazy. *You* ate it."

"Don't run away like that," my father said. "Ever." He grabbed my arm and pulled me to him.

"Sorry," I mumbled, since my throat felt tight. "Sorry," I said again, and he let go of my arm. And I was sorry, but it was more about the position I occupied in the world, as a little girl in a clean cotton dress with a meal in her hand, than about the fact that I had run down the street to check my vision against itself. White ovals, prints from the pads of my father's fingertips, were on my forearm. I rubbed them for a long time afterward. All the way up the stairs and, later, when we were in our room, folding up our blankets, I would drop a corner of the blanket to rub my arm. Tata said, "Stop doing that," and we had to start folding all over again. Later, I would forget to rub my skin, but then our father would say something or be looking in my direction, and I would pat my arm lightly. I was just being strong, I wanted him to think. I was aware of what I was doing—this play for attention—but I couldn't stop myself.

And that is it: my first memory. Tata's first memory takes place at school. She remembers walking around a room and shaking maracas, part of an impromptu band that the teacher had formed. And she remembers throwing the maracas on the floor, because she was mad about something and being surprised that the maracas broke and beans spilled out of the center. She says it never occurred to her that they would break if she threw them.

Beatriz's first memory—she wrote it down for me—is of our first day at school. She remembers hearing one of the girls in the classroom saying to her friend, "Did you see those triplets? They all look alike, and they are all so ugly!"

I know, of course, about their first memories because I asked about them, though now what I really want to ask about is second and third memories, but that's like asking about the place you consider "almost home." Still, that is where my curiosity lies, because though I have a first memory, I don't remember much else for a long time after. I *do* remember general facts. I remember going to a private school where we learned Spanish but spoke English, and I remember how my sisters and I used to come into the bakery after school and tell my father what we learned. As for specific memories, however, there is little, especially before that particular day on the island. Which is a funny thing, because, though I know it sounds unreasonable, discrepant with the events of the day, I am sure that morning was the first time I ever had the feeling that—because it had to be the most sincere expression of grief, the most honest response to being in the world in some sort of inappropriate way—I wished I could die.

Days Like This

(Tata—February 1978)

Melone found me in our bedroom and told me that Maria Elena wanted us to tell her stories about our first memories or important moments in our lives, and I said, "You mean she let you talk?" Melone laughed and slapped my arm. "You mean, you were alone with Maria Elena, and she didn't spend the whole time counseling you on your love life?"

"She's not that bad," Melone said.

"She is so," I said, "but I guess I need the advice. First kiss," I added, calling out the bedroom window, "where are you? Where are you?"

Then I went over to the gallery, told Maria Elena she could have my deepest and darkest secrets if she'd buy me an ice cream cone. I'm a sugar slut, I told her. I'll do anything for sweets. She said she probably would too if she didn't have diabetes, so we got an ice cream for me, a diet soda for her, and we went to sit in her boss's office above the gallery. "What can I tell you?" I offered grandly.

"Well," she said, almost shyly, rearranging her pretty smooth hair in a bun as she spoke, "why don't you start with telling me about your dad, and then tell me about an important moment, something that made you who you are."

I tried to tell her about my father, but there was nothing I had to say. Melone hadn't prepared me for this part of the question, and I felt cheated: did she want to know about me or get information about Papi?

I only pretended to answer the question about my father, and then I went ahead and told Maria Elena what it was I really had to say:

I used to think Papi was magic, because he never slept and never cried and only ate meat with corn fritters. I got over that pretty quick though, once the idea of fresh bread had been pushed into my head. He *had* to be up early so the bread would be ready by dawn. Not something I'd ever do. I lived to sleep in. I would get up for a good reason, of course: if something was happening, or Beatriz and Melone felt like flying a kite on a Saturday, or there was wine we could swipe from the church service on Sunday. I'll swear red wine tastes best when it's burning a throat that is out in the early-morning sun. And of course, I got up early two years ago when a girl from school, Rebekah, the one who used to say strange things like, "I *like* to eat flowers," told me that if we went to the plaza in Mercone at noon, we might be considered for a part in a new movie about life on the island.

"What *kind* of movie?" I said, because I'm not naive like Rebekah. She'd think working as a stripper was dancing in the ballet if you didn't set her straight. Still, she could be fun, and I didn't mind her, even though I'd be rich as anyone needs to be if I had a dollar for every time I said, "Oh, Rebekah, just *think,* will you?"

"You sure you don't want to go?" Rebekah said. She was sitting on the edge of my bed, trying to coax me up and into the day. I had to say yes, because it was the first time in a long time I had seen her excited about anything, seeing as her mother, who had only one hand, was dying of something . . . I don't know what.

Rebekah was really Beatriz's friend. Well, that's not quite right. She wasn't all that close to any of us, but I could tell she wanted to be around me because she wanted to be around Beatriz. I think she thought Beatriz was charmed for all that time not talking. I guess it just ran in the family. That's what I'd say. Some ability to make other people stare at your troubles, retreat in amazement . . . and start murmuring compliments.

"So what is this movie all about?" I asked Rebekah.

"What's it about?" Rebekah looked disgusted.

"I'm up. I'm up," I said. "I'm going. You convinced me." I put my feet to the floor. "Just tell me what it's about."

"*Romeo and Juliet.* It's a . . . love story. There are these two families . . ."

"I know what *Romeo and Juliet* is about, Rebekah." It was my turn to be disgusted. "We're going to try out to be Juliet?"

Rebekah nodded, and I just hit my head against the closet door. Oh, Rebekah. Hard not to love her in spite of herself. We were no Juliets. Actually, my looks were OK . . . more or less; I'm being generous here. What I mean is nothing startling in the facial deformity category, but Rebekah was a little scary. She always wore black, and she shaved the top of her forearms. Her skin was pretty pale, but her hair was blacker than black. It made me feel a little sick to see her arms and the underside of her chin dotted with tiny black spots. And there was something else . . . she always seemed as if she wasn't in her body, as if she was standing to the side of herself. Ask her a question, and she'd look foggy for a bit. Then, as if she'd found her brain floating like a tiny, low-lying cloud at the side of her temples, she'd perk up, snatch that brain from the air and pull it into her skull. She'd answer the question and then go dreamy, her brain drifting right back out of her head.

"It's a talent search," Rebekah explained and flipped her hair out of her eyes.

"More like a cattle call. Sounds like."

Rebekah looked hurt, and I had to bite my tongue, so I wouldn't say, "The plaza at Mercone's no Midwest soda fountain." Instead, I said, like sudden inspiration, "We'll take the bus."

"Whose line? Whose line?" Rebekah's fingers drummed the table anxiously. It was true that, particularly on a Saturday morning, you couldn't count on most of the buses to Mercone. Drivers took detours at will, stopping in their hometowns for lunch—and maybe something extra—from their wives. Or they pulled to the side of the road, had a beer with a friend who owned an *empanada* stand. Rules of order—timetables, tires that stayed inflated with air—these things just didn't apply when you were on the road to Mercone. But of course that was part of the thrill, that and all the revolutionary signs hung by the *inde-*

pendistas and the bazaar that you passed through that made you feel you'd left the island behind for Africa.

I had an idea, which perked me right up, as ideas often do.

"Rayovac. We'll get Rayovac."

"Teresa's son?" Rebekah said incredulously. "Teresa Quiñones de Rodriguez?"

"Yes, yes," I said, "he's all taken with Melone. A man in love is easy to manipulate." I didn't really believe that—or at least I didn't think I did—but I thought Rayovac was the kind of man who could be persuaded . . . not to do favors, he seemed too selfish for that—but to do himself a good turn. He'd be playing chess, at any rate, at the park down the street.

We found him slumped over checkers. Games are such a stupid waste of time. I could barely understand why kids played them. If you were running around, that was one thing, but here was this grown man . . . it made one scared about the possibilities of the world. I'd look at him and think, "So *this* is why it's good to be rich? Well, then, forget it."

"Rayovac," I called out, as Rebekah and I approached him. Our feet sent a bunch of pigeon feathers into the air, a dirty, fluffy carpet for our approach.

"Rayovac," I said again. He looked up, blankly. He was one of those people who let the whole world lie heavily on their shoulders. At the same time, he wouldn't do anything about the weight. He just played checkers and acted disgusted with whatever came within his line of sight. Tourists made him particularly sick to his stomach, and though he wasn't a revolutionary, far as I could tell, he was a cultural purist. He'd have hated me if it weren't for Melone. "Rayovac, my good and dear friend, Rebekah, and I . . . right here," I pointed her out, "need to go to Mercone. Will you take us in your van?"

The audacity of the request took him by surprise. I barely knew the man, despite his almost daily visits to the back of the bakery to ask my father for a job.

Rayovac turned back to his checkers and said absolutely nothing.

"I'll take that as a yes?" I said eagerly.

He turned and looked at me. "No, you won't," he said.

"Really?" I said, disappointed.

"Yes, really," Rayovac said. "Now, leave me alone. Get out of here."

"What? This is a public place," I said. "Isn't it?" I asked Rebekah.

"Ah, let's get going," she said.

"No way. I'm staying put. He thinks he owns the goddamn *parque*. Je-sus," I added.

I was overreacting, but I had my reasons. It was the principle of the thing and a sudden heaviness in my legs. I didn't really feel like going to Mercone today. And then the laziness was a sudden and extreme desire: I would *not* go to Mercone today! I would not! I had a Girls' Choir concert tonight, a book report due on Monday, butters to soften at the bakery. I even had a dress, half-sewn for the concert. And Rebekah, Rebekah and her sadness, I was weary of it. If she wanted to go, she could go, but why did I have to humiliate myself, claim beauty when I felt there was none? It wasn't a day to read dusty words, to croak in a tomb, lover at your side. It was a day to make good on my New Year's resolution not to lie.

"Come on," Rebekah tugged at my arm.

"No," I said. I would not lie and say I wanted to do something I did not want to do. "I'm not going. I just don't feel like it."

"But," Rebekah said, in a panic, "your career."

"Oh, career, sch-meer," I said. It was a previous lie about a glamourous nonexistent past that got me in this mess. The very lie that made me give up lying and take up my own life, ordinary as it might be, with a vengeance. I had told everybody about my trips up north, about how I sang jingles for all sorts of soap products on the radio, how I ate spaghetti, for hire, for a noodle company.

Now what could I do? I had lied, and my sisters had obliged me by corroborating each and every one of my stories. I couldn't betray them, so I said, "I don't think I *want* to do commercials anymore. I'm devoting myself to singing."

"Tata . . ." Rebekah said, so my name sounded like a reproach. *Tata . . .* or *I'm not interested in listening to this garbage.*

"I need to rest my voice for tonight," I said, but I said it weakly, knowing Rebekah would never let me get away with putting on airs.

"I'll go alone," she said, stoically. We were always melodramatic in those days. How else to get worth unless you grabbed it where you saw it, bestowed it on yourself?

"You don't mind?" I asked, suddenly guilty.

"Of course she minds," Rayovac offered from behind me.

"Shut up," I said to him.

"Kids don't tell me to shut up." It was true he was thirty-one to my fourteen, but you couldn't gainsay the effect of the tiny teddy bear stitched above the left breast of his polo shirt, couldn't pretend you didn't see the "Go, Yankees!" visor that shielded his face from the sun.

"What *is* it?" I turned back to him, genuinely curious. I couldn't guess what we were fighting about. What had him so ticked off? Could this all be about Melone? Anger at the way his affection had been ignored, ignored politely, but nevertheless dismissed?

"Let's do something tomorrow," I said to Rebekah. "When you get back from church."

"I'm not going to church anymore," she said glumly.

"Well, before church then. Oh, I'm sorry, Rebekah," I said, earnest as possible but miffed as well.

"Good-bye then," she said and embraced me.

"Oh, Rebekah," I said. "A flair for the dramatic." And, then, she was gone.

"Girls," Rayovac said, thoroughly disgusted, and turned back to his game. I didn't care. I sat down on the ground determined to live in the *parque* for the rest of my days rather than leave before Rayovac.

It took only ten minutes before I itched for activity. At my back, making up one wall of the *parque* was Iglesia de Maria de Croix. It was a strange, dark place, and people entered it from the side of the nave which bordered Punto Maya Street. I say "people" but I mean "men," because you never saw anyone in there unless it was someone with gray pants and shirt sleeves. It didn't have the feel of the cathedral or the church just up the hill; they were so obviously holy. Melone said that Beatriz, always given to weird religious fits, used to shudder when she was near the cathedral or the church, but Maria de Croix didn't affect her at all, probably because it seemed so much like a social hall. People prayed here, but they came in with cups of coffee and the morning paper, and they didn't leave till they had chatted with half a dozen others.

A graveyard ran from behind the church and along the length of the *parque.* Only the dead there. Nothing to keep me amused for too long. Across the street, there were always lots of people, moving in and out of restaurants. Tourists came up from the cruise ships docked at the old port. Instinctively, they stopped at Punto Maya Street, didn't cross over to read whatever was printed at the base of the statue in the center of the *parque.* Who could blame them? Why hazard the darkness of the place when there was the sun-bathed plaza with cotton candy vendors by the Old City Hall? When there was the bustling, if dirty, Plaza de Colon over near the bus stop?

I want to say I waited the rest of that day, waited into the night for Rayovac to leave, that I married and bore children and never went more than ten feet from that chess table. But the plain fact is that after thirty minutes or so had passed, the Metatruck pulled to the side of the road. Everyone knew the Metatruck. It served as mode of transportation and occasional bed for Angelo Marti, would-be pervert and general oddball-about-town. The truck was a dusty, red pick-up that had the words "Red Pick-up" painted on the side.

The Metatruck pulled up, and Angelo leaned his head out from the passenger seat. "Rayovac," he called.

Rayovac nodded once in response. Then he stood from his game and went and banged on the wall of the church. Four men came streaming out from the back.

"Have I mentioned," Angelo called to me, "that you are the love of my life. That I have loved you since the day I first laid eyes on you."

"Yeah," I said back. "I think you did say that once or twice."

"Did I tell you that I wake sweating from dreams in which I am kissing the backs of your knees? Did I ever tell you that?"

"Who's driving your truck?" I said, trying to make out who was sitting beside him. I understood men to be peculiarly territorial about motor vehicles, and I didn't understand why Angelo would have surrendered his rights.

"Nobody. It's nobody. It's not anybody who loves you like I do."

I stood and dusted my skirt off. Rayovac was following the men from the church into the back of the truck. I tried to catch his eyes, but he was absorbed in conversation.

"Why you looking at them? I'm your man," Angelo said.

I smiled. "I would be yours if you could tell me my name," I said.

Angelo looked confused. "Melone," he guessed.

I shook my head no. "That's my sister."

"Names? Who needs names?" he shouted out as the driver put the truck in gear. The pick-up pulled away. "I don't need a name," I could hear him say. "I know *you.*"

I smiled again. Then I went home to sew the rest of my dress, so it would be ready in time for Girls' Choir.

My school, like every school, had its unwritten rules. If you wanted to sing, you were in the Glee Club. If you could sing, you were in Girls' Choir. There were twenty of us, and on weekdays, we practiced from seven in the morning till eight, when classes began. Latecomers were dismissed, dismissed forever, from the group. No exceptions were made. A successful year invariably meant a chance to go touring. Not around the island, but somewhere genuinely exciting. Last year, when I was too young to be a member, the group had gone to Spain.

Before concerts, we waited in the front rows of the school auditorium for our leader, Señora Isabel de Visabel, to arrive, pitch pipe in hand, and give us a pep talk. On the day of the auditions for *Romeo and Juliet,* I arrived early for the preconcert lecture. I had finished my dress. All save for the hem, which I had safety-pinned up. I sat in a chair, next to no one, and fingered the pins. I was wondering if anyone would notice the slight pucker at the edge of my dress, and I was wondering if anyone would fill the empty chair next to me.

In the row in front of me, two girls were tormenting a third. "So what does it feel like," one asked, "to have a father who is a camel?"

"He's not a camel," the girl said, confused. "He's a person." Her face looked, for all the world, as mournful as a camel's.

"Don't be ashamed," the second girl said.

"What are you talking about?" the confused girl said. "You're not making any sense."

"You can tell us," the second girl leaned over and said in a confidential tone.

The confused girl was close to tears. "No one's . . . no one's . . . father is a camel."

It was almost time for the preconcert rehearsal, and Señora Isabel, Rebekah and one other girl, Digna, were still not here. I heard the door bang and turned quickly, hoping it was Rebekah. She would be heartbroken if she were kicked out of Girls' Choir. But it wasn't her. It was Digna, hobbling up the center aisle with her single crutch. Digna was a beautiful girl who had been born with one leg shorter than the other. To compensate, she wore a single thick-soled shoe and used the crutch. After fourteen years, you would think she'd have gotten used to the situation, but her gait was still awkward. She seemed older than the rest of us for this reason and because she wore old-fashioned dresses, as if she were an American girl from the prairie. I had seen her once, when she thought she was alone, walk surprisingly briskly and efficiently to get a book she had left in her desk. But no one else had ever seen that, and the entire class coddled her. When she was halfway down the aisle, girls started to shout, "Sit here, Digna. Sit here."

She stopped and looked up. She gave us a smile, as if she were surprised by our kindness, though it could be no surprise. When didn't we beg her to sit next to us? And, even though I'd seen what I'd seen, when didn't I add my voice to the others? Digna slipped into the seat next to me.

"Rebekah's still not here," I whispered in her ear.

"Oh, no," Digna said. "Oh, this is horrible."

I gave Digna a look of concern.

She whispered back to me, "Señora Isabel is in the hall."

And true enough, just as she said it, the door in the back of the auditorium banged shut, and Señora Isabel started saying, as she always did, "So good of you to all come today."

When she got to the front of the auditorium, however, she didn't tap her pitch pipe against the podium and find a note for us. Instead, she said, "I am afraid I have some terrible news. There has been a horrible accident. Apparently, a bomb . . . well, excuse me girls." She cleared her throat to disguise the shaking of her voice. "Girls, you know the road that goes from here to Mercone. A bomb blew up the road, and it seems some people who were traveling—two cars and a bus—have been killed."

"But Rebekah was on that bus!" I shouted.

"Yes," Señora Isabel nodded her head. "There are reports that your classmate, Rebekah, was on that bus."

"Oh, my God!" a girl in front of me whispered and that was all it took. Some people, I am told, have delayed responses to grief. I have never, myself, seen it. We all cried, immediately and loudly. Señora Isabel had no problem joining in. What can I say of our tears save that, at length, Señora Isabel who had been repeating, "What to do, what to do," under her breath, called us to attention.

"Girls," she announced. "We have a concert to do. Up in the old Dominican convent, as I am sure you all know. I . . ." she faltered, then said, "and we are going to do that concert. If you can't go . . . . If you can't, you can't. But I will be there, and I would like to see as many of you there as possible. Here are the instructions." As always, she passed out pieces of paper that explained what bus line we were to take to our destination. Today, since we were going only five stops into the city, she needn't have done it, but I think the formality of the pieces of paper set her at ease. Stationery supplies always seemed to have that effect on her.

I went to the concert, but I waited, didn't get on the first bus with the rest of the girls. When a second bus, relatively empty, arrived, I was ready to travel. I could imagine the voices in the first bus. They would be saying things I was thinking, and I felt that would cheapen my feelings, as if sadness could be true only if it were original. I was never sorry I got on that second bus, even when the bus got a flat tire and I had to get off and wait for another. On the third bus, I sat crying, but quietly, looking down at a crumpled cup on the floor. I was still tracing the safety pins in the hem of my dress. One came undone and stabbed my thumb, and the brief prick made me cry even harder. People, I could tell, were purposely choosing not to sit next to me on the bus. The old man in front of me and the two woman behind me even changed their seats for protection. Then a woman tapped me on the shoulder. She leaned close to me so I could feel her warm, fruity breath on my cheek.

"Excuse me. Do you live in Miramar?" she asked. We were not coming from or going to Miramar, so I couldn't understand why she asked. She was pleasant looking. In a dark blue cotton dress and white sandals. She smiled.

"I do," I said, because even though I didn't, my family was always talking about moving there. "Why do you ask?"

"Well," she said. "I would just like to invite you to a Bible study group."

"I'm Jewish," I said and said it harshly. "I'm Jewish."

"That doesn't matter," she said.

"It does. It does to me," I said and stood. It was almost my stop anyway. It seemed to me her words were a final blow; I had been taught that people, especially on a Catholic island, were likely to think I nailed the hands of God's relatives to crosses for sport.

At the concert, we sang on risers that were placed under the balcony in the central courtyard. We sang badly . . . that was no surprise . . . and the audience kept politely shifting to the back of the courtyard, where coffee and cookies were being dispensed. There will be days like this, I told myself, but I wasn't sure what I meant. But I kept repeating it, over and over, till I discovered something. I didn't get taught a lesson. I figured things out. There will be days and days and days like this. It wasn't something about the world I realized—I'd read history books—but about how I was going to act in the world. "If this is what it's going to be like, I've got to grow up." The concert ended, and the people who took care of the old convent, not aware, I think, about what was happening, asked us to put away the risers and, while we were at it, to mop down the courtyard floor. We were too sleepy with sadness to argue.

And then Rebekah came in.

"Arrgh!" the girl who had been accused of being a camel's daughter screamed. We all looked up.

"Rebekah," Señora Isabel cried and ran up to her and hugged her. Rebekah's face was splattered with mud, and she looked, as always, confused.

"I'm late," she said. "I'm so sorry. Can I still be in the choir?"

"Of course, of course," Señora Isabel cried. "How . . . how did you get back?"

"Back?" Rebekah asked.

"From Mercone?"

"Oh," Rebekah looked glumly at a half-eaten cookie near her feet. "I took the wrong bus. I went to Fajardo. I got out and sat in the center of the plaza, but I couldn't figure out where all the movie people were. So I got . . ."

Isabel didn't care. She hugged Rebekah so that Rebekah's face was crushed against her stomach and the rest of her words were buried in the cloth of Isabel's dress. Other people came and patted Rebekah on the back. It would be days before she understood their reaction and why they weren't sneaking, as they normally did, the leftover cookies from the reception into their pockets.

People would get mad at Rebekah, later, for scaring them so. Me, I didn't feel that way. I felt funny like Romeo or Juliet. I couldn't remember who was responsible for what in that play. But I felt like one of them, as if I'd already taken my poison and found it strangely sweet; the fact that Rebekah was back from the dead couldn't help me now. I'd already made my decision, and in the years to come, I would find it was a good one.

Patron of the Seas

(Maria Elena—March 1978)

It was almost nine o'clock, and Sandrofo was still downstairs in the bakery. I saw Rayovac's van out front, so I knew what was keeping him—a particularly lengthy appeal for employment. Because I was starting to feel cheated of my evening with Sandrofo, I decided to go downstairs. I needed a reason for my descent and settled on a question about the wedding. Earlier that day, I had gone to select a simple dress—there was no point in doing things extravagantly, given our ages—and I thought I might use the fact of the errand as my excuse for interrupting Sandrofo. Not that I really needed his approval. I knew he would like what I picked, a pale, calf-length cotton dress with small pink and yellow flowers. It buttoned up the front and had thin straps. I thought it was sexy, in an understated way. I'd mistaken it for an elaborate slip at first and then realized it was meant to be a dress.

"Hello," I called, as I walked down the narrow staircase into the back room. I meant to announce myself in advance in case they were talking privately. I stepped into the room to hear Sandrofo saying, "My fiancée, well, I had better be going." I saw Rayovac sitting sullenly on a stool. Then my heel hit a wet spot on the floor; my legs slid out from underneath me, and I fell, sprawling into three giant white barrels that stored flour. Because the barrels were empty (and light, they were made of plastic), I knocked them over when I fell. And that's when—bruised and humiliated as I was—I came face-to-face with Sandrofo's butter-stained first wife.

She was lying on her side, in a frame, and she came toppling toward me. I pushed her away and started to say, "Who's . . ." but I already knew, so I just said, "I thought you said you didn't have any pictures of her."

"Good-bye," Sandrofo said gruffly to Rayovac, but Rayovac, unaware that he had been dismissed, bent to pick me up.

"No photographs," Sandrofo said. "I didn't have any photographs, because we didn't have a camera."

"Oh," I said. I brushed flour from my dress and then bent to pick the portrait up. Two wives, I thought. Two wives righted.

"Anya," Sandrofo said, for Rayovac's benefit. "My first wife. The girls' mother."

She was beautiful. What could I say; it took me aback. Her beauty. I pulled myself up straight as I held the portrait. I willed my neck longer, my eyes wider. I tried to hang a heavy baroque frame in the air around me, and as I did, I was conscious of the whirling in my stomach, a discomfort that always made me feel ugly, as if I looked as bloated and sweaty as I suddenly felt. I put the weighty picture back down on the floor, gave my stomach a surreptitious pat to make sure it was still flat and said, "What century are you from anyway?"

"It's archaic, I know," Sandrofo said. "Anya's parents wanted it done."

"Oh," I said. "Who painted it? I mean . . ." I stopped myself for a moment, told myself not to tug my fingers through my hair. "She's very beautiful, but it's not much of a painting."

"No, it's not, but it's not finished."

I was quiet, then said, "When I asked for a picture of her, why didn't you show me this one?"

Sandrofo shrugged his shoulders, reached down to wipe away a small bit of butter stuck to her right shoulder and said, "The girls are there. She's pregnant with the girls in this picture."

"Oh," I said and looked back at the portrait. Anya's maroon dress cloaked an indefinable frame. The face was High Renaissance, rendered in exact detail; the body was more like that of a Giotto monk—there was clear evidence of a leg, but nothing more, under the clothing.

"Why are you storing the picture behind the flour bins?"

"Beatriz. Beatriz thinks the picture is bad luck. The dead woman is depicted; the three living children are hidden in the belly." Sandrofo shrugged his shoulders. "You know how she is." For a moment, I thought he meant Anya, that I knew how Anya was, and I wanted to say, "No, I don't. That's precisely the problem." But that wasn't really the problem. The problem was I didn't know how many more lies would follow this first one.

"You'll have to tell me about her," I said. A statement: since Rayovac was in the room, I gave my words no real inflection.

"You know all there is to know," he said.

"Sandrofo," I started, ready to say I-don't-know-what, to cough up some sound of frustration. I stopped and wondered where polite muteness became repulsive self-deceit. *Here*, I thought, *right here* and I readied my first real cruelty. "Rayovac," I began and swallowed air. I could still stop myself. *Be good* or, at least, *Good for Sandrofo*. I coughed. "Is that your van outside?"

"Yes, my van. It would be excellent for deliveries."

"Of course," I said, clearing my throat. "Sandrofo is always complaining about having to take the cakes over to the hotels at the end of the day. Could you do that? Deliver cakes?"

"Yes," said Rayovac. "It's a van. It has horizontal surfaces. Cakes and horizontal surfaces. A neat equation, wouldn't you say?"

"I would," I said. "I would." Sandrofo glared at me. "Why not give him a chance? I'll pay for it myself. Out of my own salary. It'll be my way of buying more time with you." I kissed him lightly on the cheek. "I'll be upstairs," I added, as if it were all settled, and I made my way quickly out of the room.

I knew to expect his anger when he came upstairs. I waited for it at the kitchen table, where I sat thinking vaguely of the *santero*'s love potion, the one that involved opening a coconut and putting the name of the person you wished to woo in the milk. I had played out all the possible arguments we might have, so that by the time Sandrofo did come into the apartment, I said none of the things I felt. Instead I said, "I'm sorry. It's your business, and I shouldn't have interfered." And rather than yelling, Sandrofo said evenly, "I *could* use help delivering those cakes."

"Can I stay?" I asked, girlishly, hating myself for the way emotion made me drop decades from my life.

"You have somewhere else to go?" Sandrofo asked.

I shook my head no and felt comforted, though I knew the price of the comfort: no more questions about Anya. I was willing to agree. The too beautiful face, the enormous eyes, even the hands (which were left incomplete, bare outlines) suggested a grace I would never have. I already knew too much. And anyway, I had been looking forward all week to my plans for the next day—an outing with the girls. I was taking them to buy dresses for the wedding. I didn't want to postpone the trip because I'd had a fight with Sandrofo.

And the next day I *did* buy them dresses, but not before I paraded them before the portrait. My resolution not to ask questions had lasted all of a day.

"What do you know about her?" I asked, trying to make my manner as offhand as possible. I looked up at the three girls. It seemed, for a moment, that Beatriz was about to say something. I blinked my eyes. Then Tata said, "She was a bitch."

"Really?" I said, trying not to sound hopeful.

"That's the story," Melone said. "Anya Rosado de Codero, graceful and delicate as a banana leaf, though . . ."

"Peculiar ways and a brutal tongue," Tata interrupted.

"Or so Dad says," Melone added. "He says it was a fair-enough trade. God took one foul-mouthed woman from the earth and gave back three gurgling infants. He used to tell us that he'd hear us go 'goo goo' and think he was hearing prayer words."

Tata said, "We'd spit into the dirt on the floor, and he got to thinking of this as holy water."

I stared at the girls.

"This is what he told us," Melone said, defensively. "But maybe he was only touched in the head from grief . . ."

"Or relief . . ." Tata said. "I guess she used to say things like, 'You're ugly, Sandrofi, but I don't mind. It's your inner ugliness that's so unbearable.'"

"Well," I said, "no wonder he doesn't want to talk about her." But I didn't understand how the story could be true. Sandrofo was sharp featured and angular—perhaps a bit too continental for the purists of the island—but he was good-looking, if slightly cross-eyed. As to his spirit, it was puzzling but hardly ugly.

I shook my head at my own thoughts and remembered why I loved Sandrofo: he must have believed those long ago words, for though he was considered something of a catch on the island—what with his well-stocked store and his apparent power in the city's small business association—he seemed to distrust his own fortunes. True, he could affect an angry arrogance, snapping at every fool and foolishness that came his way, but I knew he hadn't convinced himself, and there was something about the way he moved through the world, duck-footed and with face hung low, that made it clear he felt himself entirely incidental, even to his own life.

Just last week, Melone had had a nightmare, and even though she was too big for this sort of thing, I had gone into her room, climbed into her bed, determined to stay till she returned to a better dream. After a long silence, Melone whispered, "If Papa went to war, he'd die." I knew Melone didn't doubt her father's physical strength and wondered if she simply feared his willingness to be sacrificed for a cause he only half-heartedly believed in. Then she mumbled some more words, and I realized she was, and had been all along, fast asleep.

"Beatriz?" I asked tentatively now. "Are you all right?"

She nodded to indicate she was fine.

"Really?" I said. Her mouth was steady, refusing to betray the emotions that, given her father's words, she must have been feeling.

Beatriz nodded and pointed at the picture.

"What?" I said, looking at Melone and Tata for an interpretation.

Melone said, "Beatriz is pointing at her mouth. She's a pretty women, but there's something in her mouth. Isn't there?"

I had to agree. Her hair was rich and full, her eyes the doe eyes I've always longed for, her face a balanced heart, unmarred by plumpness or sharpness, but her mouth was thin and pinched. I imagined her personality had come up from her gut, worked its way up her throat. The frown was the meanness her jaw couldn't hold back. Those lines at her lip were *force of effort*, the struggle, the constant swallowing, to keep her way of being away from the loveliness of her face.

"I don't think," said Melone, "she liked being pregnant."

"Dad said she didn't like us, because when she was carrying us, she was always falling out of bed, because she was confused about where her new body ended," Tata said.

"Oh," I said, puzzled. Why would Sandrofo tell his girls this even if it were true? So they wouldn't feel so bad about the fact that they had, merely by being born, killed her? And if all this were true, why not tell me? I was clearly looking for the comfort these stories provided.

"Well, enough of this," I said, businesslike, as if I had no real interest in the details about Anya, had just asked because I thought they might want to talk about their mother. "Let's go find some dresses for you girls."

"But she liked the bakery," Melone said, almost as an afterthought, as if she needed to say something nice about her mother. "She loved it. It belonged to her grandfather, or something like that, and she used to come in and get madeleines, those shell-like cookies, out of a big jar. Dad said when we first moved here we used to sell them, but the *italeros* —you know, those are the *santeros* who specialize in the reading of shells—they got superstitious, even though the madeleines look nothing like cowrie shells, so we stopped making them."

I nodded and again thought I saw Beatriz making a motion as if she were about to talk. I blinked again, and there was that same softness around the corner of Beatriz's mouth, the distinctive weight that always prevented me from confusing her with her sisters—her mouth muscles hadn't done the same work theirs had.

"Come," I said to the girls, "let's go find dresses. You're going to look lovely." I was imagining them each in a fabric to match the flowers in the dress I had bought. Lemon yellow, hibiscus pink, bamboo tan: we'd make a good composition, and that, of course, was part of why I was marrying Sandrofo: I wanted his children.

I wasn't stupid. A dozen bad love affairs had taught me that the problems of the courtship are the problems of the relationship. Sometimes, I'd stop myself midstep and say, "Why am I in love with this man?" The answer was that the losses involved in this love were acceptable . . . or more acceptable than the losses of other loves. Finally, my sadness about my own life was so profound that I was willing to make a choice that might be wrong.

That night, the girls and I spread out the dresses for Sandrofo to see. He approved each one, complimented the girls on their taste. I sat in Sandrofo's lap, kissed him a thank-you for his kindness to the children, resisted the urge to ask about Anya's sense of style. When he left the room to lock up the bakery, I said to the girls, "Well, your father's pleased." For the third time that day, I had the sense Beatriz was about to talk. I must have given her a peculiar look for Tata said, "What's the matter?"

I said, "It's strange, but Beatriz . . . I thought you were about to talk."

Beatriz smiled and shook her head no.

"Maybe," I said, "no one ever asked you the right question?"

"What's *that* supposed to mean?" Melone said.

"Just that if she were asked the right question, maybe she'd have something she wanted to say."

Melone bristled at this, but I knew I had a point. I was beginning to understand that there was something I knew about Beatriz that others didn't. I just hadn't been able to give words to what that something was yet. "Someone needs to draw her out," I said.

Melone made a harumphing noise. "Oh, yes," she said, sarcastically, "we never thought of that, but then we weren't really alive before you showed up."

"What are you talking about?" I said.

"Nothing," she said. "It's nothing."

"It's not nothing. What?"

"We're Jewish," she said, as if I didn't already know that. "And we don't believe in being damned, so we don't think we're in any need of saving."

"Nobody wants to save anybody," I said, amazed and curiously pleased; I was having my first fight with my daughters. Then, Sandrofo came back into the room. "I hired Rayovac," he announced.

"What?" Tata said.

"How *could* you?" Melone said.

"I gave in and hired Rayovac. He's going to drive a delivery van to the hotels, and I'm thinking of shipping some bread and cake around the island. We're going to need to expand some for when we move."

"Move?" Tata said.

"Well, we can't all live here after the wedding. There's not enough room."

Melone looked at Beatriz and said, "Beatriz thinks we can." Tata started to laugh.

"What's funny?" I said, eager to join the conversation if the mood was going to lighten.

"It's Beatriz," Tata said. "She hates change. She cried for a week when we replaced the old cash register in the bakery with a new electric cash register."

I smiled.

"Who knows," Melone said, with a surprising lack of malice, given the earlier conversation, "why she isn't objecting to you?" I shrugged, agreeably, as if it were the question with which I always struggled: Why is it that they don't object to me?

"I don't know," I said—my tone playful, my meaning somewhat indecipherable, even to me—"why I don't object to you." My hand flew out in front of me, so it was clear I meant the whole family. "Except," I continued, "I love you so." I kissed Sandrofo on the cheek and said, "I've got to go to bed. Too long a day." I hugged the girls good night and felt words tug at my lips. I almost spoke, but then I just let myself think the words: *I succumb to my future.* And my future, for the first time ever, seemed clear to me—a physical thing. It was the ocean, and I was walking backward into it. "*Yemaya,*" Lucia at the gallery would say to me the next day, when I told her what I had thought, "patron of the seas. Your vision means you were calling on her to protect you."

"OK," I said, willing to accept her interpretation. I had thought it meant I was going to drown.

Accidental Contact

(Rayovac Rodriguez—March 1978)

For Rayovac, the struggle to get a job had been a long one. For his friends, it had been a baffling one. It was, after all, an era that respected straightforwardness, and there had been nothing to prevent Rayovac from banging on Melone's front door and extending an innocuous invitation for a walk, a drink, an ice-cream cone down by the park. Still, for Rayovac, the wrongness of such an approach had been obvious. Weeks earlier, he had catalogued the reasons over a chess game in the park with his friend, Luis.

"First," Rayovac had said, leaning over the chess board conspiratorially. "If it's that easy, if it's only a matter of a sentence . . ." But Rayovac couldn't say what he needed to say next. If it were only a matter of a sentence, how explain his failure to speak that sentence, how explain his lengthy bachelorhood? How explain all the things that had accompanied his bachelorhood like the creeping, horrible sensation that his body was beginning to stink with disuse, his flesh turning weirdly odorous because he had failed to touch and be touched for almost a decade? This was definitely not the sort of thought Rayovac was likely to share with Luis. He could barely admit it to himself. Instead he tapped a pawn from the chess game nervously against the table and said, "If it's only a sentence, it doesn't mean anything."

"Mean? You're crazy, man," Luis said.

"I don't see you knocking on any doors with a bunch of flowers."

"Why waste the money, man? I satisfy myself." Luis clenched and unclenched his right hand.

"You make me sick," Rayovac said.

"You crazy, man," Luis said again. It was his habitual refrain for all conversations with Rayovac.

"Second thing is," Rayovac said, ignoring Luis completely, "I've got to give her a chance to see me. You know, out in the world. Doing my thing."

"You ain't got no *thing,*" Luis reminded him.

"What I don't got," Rayovac said angrily, "is some bourgeois career-itis. I don't *haave* the di-sease. Just not in an ab-so-lute panic if I don't have my day filled up with activity."

Luis shook his head. "It's your move," he said and gestured toward the board.

"I just can't make my move when she only knows me as the Rodriguez kid. See?"

"Yeah. I see. I see," Luis said. "It's the classic problem. No one ever makes it in their own hometown. No one ever makes it in their home. Hell . . ." Luis raised his eyes toward the park. It was inhabited strictly by men and pigeons and the smells of plantains and bacon frying in fat. ". . . No one ever makes it." Luis continued to nod slowly, as if amazed by the wisdom of his own words. At the base of the chess table, two sooty pigeons squabbled over a piece of salt pork discarded from a nearby kitchen. "Ah," Luis repeated, giving the park one last, curt bob of the head, "no one makes it anywhere."

"You're a drag," Rayovac said and knocked Luis's king off the table.

Not long after and to prove to Sandrofo that he was responsible, Rayovac had started delivering goods for other merchants in old San Juan. It was a roundabout tactic and ultimately an unsuccessful one. His ultimate goal had been to secure a job that would give him the opportunity for plenty of casual, accidental contact with Melone. He certainly wasn't getting that when he delivered shellacked shells from Star of the Sea Gifts to La Concha Hotel. Distraught, Rayovac had increased his visits to the baker, made particularly emotional appeals for employment.

"The people, they want your cake . . ." Rayovac had said one night, as he sat with Sandrofo at a small table in the rear of the bakery. Rayovac was speaking of the great need for home delivery of La Madeleine's products. To his own ears, it sounded as if he was pleading. His body was leaning forward, foolishly, over the table, and he was using a tone appropriate to a preacher begging the heathen to turn back to God. "They want your cake," Rayovac repeated, "but they can't get it." He collapsed back into his chair as if grieved by the inaccessibility of sweets.

It occurred to him that he should have decided to be a fat man, not a businessman. That would get him where he wanted to be . . . in the bakery gazing at Melone, though he supposed it was not such a good plan if he wanted Melone to gaze back. "Over here," he pictured himself saying, from behind a plate of some forty-odd *rosquillas*. "I'm here," he'd say and then rest his fleshy chin on the mountain of sweets.

Rayovac had other, more specific fantasies about what he hoped would happen between Melone and him. But even he didn't quite realize this at first, for his fantasies (not the fulfillment of them, but the actual creation of them) depended on his ability to rid himself of the unpleasant sense that someone was listening to him. And then he had to get rid of the anger he felt for believing such an absurd thing. *I can daydream if I want*, he thought, angrily defending himself against himself.

Still, there was a residual feeling of shame when he placed himself, in his imagination, in the storeroom. Rayovac had assumed there would have to be a storeroom in the bakery and the room would have to be filled with bags of flour. It would be purely happenstance. Things always had to be like this—unplanned, as if the circumstances of human contact (a room, a closed door, a certain silence) had more to do with the accident of proximity than willful desire. And then . . . but Rayovac's imagination had to skip the next part, because the actual first gesture seemed impossible. He had already convinced himself that when the time was right, he would have to kiss Melone, but when he tried to picture that moment, when he tried to see himself leaning toward her, he saw instead a gigantic canyon that hollowed out the space between them, and he saw himself closing his eyes and madly leaping the few feet while he prepared his ears for that diminishing scream cartoon characters make when they fall into a big pit. In time, Rayovac forced his daydreams to omit the canyon. One second he was chatting shyly with Melone; the next he was kneeling in a bag of flour and scooping his hands up under her apron, her flower print dress. She had unbelievably soft breasts. Rayovac thought of kneading biscuit dough. Her nipples hardened against the palms of his hands. He was unbuttoning and undoing. When he entered her, she made a funny little gasping sound . . . force of Rayovac's skills as a lover, of course. . . . But already the daydream had turned sarcastic.

What people said, during those months before Sandrofo offered him a job, was, "That Rayovac." People in earshot would nod, say: "Crazy in the streets." And he was: driving his new van like a madman because punctuality had achieved a new importance in his life. One day, several months into his project, he found himself racing to the park to meet Luis for their weekly chess game. Luis was always late, but this fact did not lessen Rayovac's need to be there on time. As he drove, he silently but frantically kept repeating his own version of an American poem he had found at the library. "Business, friends, is boring. We must not say so. Ever to confess you're bored means you have no financial resources."

Rayovac swooped down Ponce de Leon and into the old city, where he drove his van down Calle Fortaleza and over into the *parque.* He stopped only when he reached the chess table. Creative parking. It was just one of the little ways he saved money on business expenses. He gazed out the windshield. The usual crowd of regulars lingered by the wall that hugged one side of the *parque.* Others were spread out on the low benches that ran underneath the cemetery, on the north side. Though the day, sunny and cloudless as it was, brightened most corners of the city, the placement of the trees, the shadow of the church . . . everything, really, conspired to make the *parque* an unusually dark spot. Unlike the city's plazas, located two or three blocks away in almost every direction, the *parque* went ungroomed. Its gray slate floor was carpeted with dirt and feathers, cluttered with old newspapers and grease-stained napkins. Rayovac stepped out of the van. With his sunglasses still on, he felt as if he were walking into a dark room. He passed a kid with a gigantic radio, big as the youth's torso and playing an uneven percussion. Not the usual thing one heard coming out of those boxes with their regular, insistent beat. In fact . . . Rayovac stopped and listened carefully . . . it seemed the music had the same tempo as the refrain in his mind, "Business, friends . . . ."

Where was the chapter in the *Fat Cat* book on boredom? How to address that problem? Lack of interest. Sleepy eyelids. Just today, as he made an impassioned pitch for the doorstep delivery of banners that read "Puerto Rico: Star of the Caribbean," Rayovac was so overwhelmed with the dreariness of his endeavor that he thought he might be the first man in the world actually to fall asleep *while* he was speaking.

"One thing about chess I like," Rayovac said later that day. He paused to pick up a knight and move it with a flourish over his own pawn. "Is that it's a game I win at, but I don't always win."

Luis nodded his head. There was no interesting response to Rayovac's words, so he just chimed, as if he were some far-off bell, "Don't you know."

"You see. I don't really like to play if I can't win. I'm *that* competitive. It's why I hated gym class. You know, if I worked my butt off I'd only be average. But I'm not interested in a game I can always win either."

"Like?" Luis said.

Rayovac looked at him. "What are you talking about?"

"Like what are you so good at?" Luis asked. Rayovac gave him a hard stare. "I mean, you are as unemployed as these old farts," Luis gestured to the men in square, "but you don't take the trouble to wait in line for your present from welfare."

"I've got a job. I've got a job," Rayovac said, omitting his usual speech about the career-itis that was rampant on the continent and threatening to ruin the island.

"And," Luis continued, evenhandedly, like a lawyer, presenting his case, "you're no good with women. And you're ugly as a mud fence." Rayovac sneered at his friend. "Now a looker like me could give you a hand."

Rayovac was silent. He remembered how once, in a rare moment of self-reflection, Luis had said, slowly, to him. "You know, I'm not a good-looking guy. I got this car. It's a piece of shit. And I don't have any money. But I can fish like a motherfucker." This was all true. And it was true in other people's minds as well as his own—the skill was a saving grace. Fish, people liked to say, would leap out of the sea and into Luis's boat. Children were told he could fill buckets without ever throwing a net or casting a line.

"Hey. What you being so quiet about? You know it's only a joke."

"The thing I am trying to explain to you is that the game has to be the right game. The one where you bring all your true talents to bear but still run up against the real possibility of your own failure . . . and your own success. See what I mean?"

"Listen," Luis said and leaned over the chess table to place his hands on Rayovac's shoulders. Rayovac started back from his touch.

"Hey," he said, laughing nervously, as if he needed to explain his own, overly strong reaction to Luis's hands. "Everyone'll be saying *maricón.*"

Luis put his hands on the edge of the chess table. "I have to tell you—it's for your own good—she's not interested in you."

"Now, what are *you* talking about?"

Luis shook his head and said, "Ah, man, *you* know," but he wouldn't elaborate beyond that. It was as if he felt the mere uttering of the word "woman" in a park full of leftover men would set the earth to trembling. "Give it up," Luis said. "Just give it up."

"You know. I've got work to do. I don't know what I'm doing hanging out here with you. This place," he gestured to the *parque*, "always gives me the creeps."

That was the night Rayovac had gone to visit Sandrofo, and the baker had finally offered him a job.

"Ah, my friend," Sandrofo had said at first, as Rayovac pushed through the bakery door, "it's no good."

Rayovac had ignored him and said, "Let's talk privately. I have some new suggestions for you."

Sandrofo rolled his eyes and said, "The back room." The two men descended to the basement room and pulled high stools up to a long wooden table that was used, mostly, as a gigantic cutting board. Flowery shapes—from the scalloped cookie cutters used for a jelly sandwich in which the bakery now specialized—were etched into the wood of the table. Rayovac repeated his pitch.

"I don't need a delivery person," Sandrofo said. He spoke slowly and evenly, as is if to an idiot child. "I thought you understood that when we last spoke."

Rayovac nodded but would not leave. "That would be yesterday," he said, to allow for the fact that he had heard Sandrofo's words. He leaned over, picked up a blue vinyl briefcase leaning against his stool, slapped the briefcase on the table and produced a pad of paper from its plastic interior. Pointing to a graph he had already drawn, Rayovac said, "Let me just help you understand how your profit margin would be improved by this sort of investment."

Just then, a door slammed. Maria Elena, Sandrofo's girlfriend, came down the stairs. She started to say something but bit her words off with a yelp as she slipped on the bottom step and plowed, feet first, into some white barrels lined up against the wall behind Sandrofo. There was something impressive and purposeful about her fall. She looked, Rayovac remarked, much like Roberto Clemente, sliding into home base. The barrels toppled around her, revealing a large painting, stored against the wall. It was a picture of a woman, and it, too, started to fall on Maria Elena. The odd perspective of the painting made it seem as if the woman on the canvas was reaching out to embrace Maria Elena, and though the frame was obviously heavy, Rayovac could not bring himself to stand and intercept the loving gesture.

"*Ay*," Maria Elena cried as the frame hit her. She pushed the painting away from her but remained sprawled on the ground. Sandrofo made no move to pick her up. Rayovac glimpsed the lacy edge of her underwear, then Maria Elena tugged her skirt down, and Rayovac, despairing of Sandrofo's rising to help her, climbed off his stool and lifted Maria Elena to her feet. "Are you hurt?" he said.

"No, no," she said, patting her skirt down, as if she were far too dignified to have actually fallen. Rayovac felt reproached as if it was insulting to suggest she could be so affected by the earth that she'd be injured after she slammed into it. A cellophane wrapper, with the letter "L" printed on it, stuck to her hair, but Maria Elena made no move to wipe it away. She was too busy considering the painting that had fallen on her.

And then, as if the woman in the painting had given her instructions, she turned abruptly to Rayovac and asked him if he would like to work for the bakery as a delivery boy. If he wouldn't mind delivering cake to the hotels.

"Yes," Rayovac said. "It would be a wonderful idea. Don't you think?"

"I do, and I'll even pay you out of my own salary," she said, turning to Sandrofo. Rayovac reached over, shook her hand and quickly said, "It's a deal," before Sandrofo could undo her words. Then she kissed Sandrofo and went back upstairs.

Rayovac wondered if his plan had backfired on him, if the baker's wife, instead of his daughter, had fallen in love with him. Why else would she offer to pay him out of her own pocket? He considered the possibility as Sandrofo told him the schedule for delivering tarts to the hotels. She was an attractive woman, closer in age to Rayovac than Melone, and there was certainly something in her experienced air that made it hard not to consider her sexually. Before she was with Sandrofo, Rayovac used to see her about town with a handsome attorney who specialized in prosecuting drug dealers, and after that, she was with a doctor of ambiguous marital status. While Sandrofo spoke of hourly wages, dress codes, cleanliness of hair and hands, Rayovac let himself make love to Sandrofo's fiancée. The sex was fierce, athletic; Rayovac entering Maria Elena from behind, pushing her shoulders to the ground and leaning himself over the expanse of her brown back to twist her dark hair in his left hand and to put his mouth to her right ear so he could instruct her in her own desires: "Like this. This is how you like it." But then Rayovac thought back to Melone and blushed at his daydream, at the notion that a woman who had already had lovers would consider him a man, as opposed to what he always suspected he was—not a man, surely not a woman, but something else, the third gender that included everyone who believed his own ugliness to be oil to the watery possibility of passion.

A Tender Heart

(Maria Elena—April 1978)

Carla Mendota, informal proprietor of the street, stood behind the cash register at La Madeleine, rang up orders, and supervised the goings-on outside. If she saw anything of interest, she called over to one of the triplets, who helped wait tables after school, or one of the other women who was employed in the morning. When Sandrofo was around, however, she was all business, though she was a bit chattier than normal about the fact of the transaction. "OK. What can I do for you? You feel like paying? Well, we like that. We like that in a customer. Let me just ring that right up."

But once Rayovac was hired, things changed. Carla, like everyone else, developed a new interest in the activities in the interior of the bakery. She didn't notice when a young man, eager to make room for himself on the crowded thoroughfare, walked down the street with a boa constrictor wrapped around his torso. She didn't see the vacationing movie star—a particular favorite of Carla's—peel a strip of skin from the top of her sunburnt arm and give it to a fan as a keepsake. She didn't see a handful of fistfights. Not surprisingly, locals began to claim the street was becoming perceptibly more dangerous now that Carla's eyes were turned away from its activities to the drama in the bakery.

In truth, the drama in the bakery wasn't so dramatic. It was just that oldest of stories: unrequited love trying its damnedest to become requited.

At first I wondered what was going on. The girls had told me that

Rayovac had a crush on Melone, but that didn't explain the sudden increase in the number of patrons to the bakery. Nor did it explain why people were coming in during what had previously been the least populated part of the day—that is, after school, when the girls traded off the chores of waiting on customers, cleaning the bakery and preparing the mixes for the next day. But then I never watched soap operas when I was young, so it made sense that I was confused. Lucia, who sometimes stopped by during her afternoon break from the gallery, explained the phenomenon to me; people, she said, were coming in for love.

"What do you mean?" I'd said when she first told me this. "It's not like love is a pastry you can carry away with you."

"I mean they're coming in to see love, to see how love plays out," she said, then added, almost as an afterthought, "with Rayovac."

At first, I didn't believe her. Why would anyone care about Rayovac's desires? But I had to admit people clearly did care. In the back corner of the bakery, there was a round table at which three old men—Cardona, González and Garrido y Mena —sat every day and played cards. Once Rayovac was hired, their wagers shifted from their poker hand to Rayovac. They made bets about the hour of the day when Rayovac would finally get up the courage to talk to Melone.

Thankfully, Melone was at school and never heard the betting. I myself heard it only a handful of times when I came into La Madeleine on my coffee break.

"Three-fifteen, I tell you, three-fifteen," Cardona would say and shake his fist at his friends.

Garrido y Mena would respond, much calmer, "My friend, do not be ridiculous, there is no chance it will happen before sundown."

Cardona, González and Garrido y Mena weren't the only ones. Giggling girls, tireless romantics and even stodgy-faced bureaucrats—gentlemen who seemed not to have a passionate bone in their bodies—stopped in to monitor Rayovac's progress.

No one expected a match between Melone and Rayovac to succeed, so it wasn't entirely clear what it was people wanted to happen. One knew only what they *said* they were watching for: when he would speak to her, when he would make his shy approach. There seemed to be a general belief that Rayovac's persistence should be rewarded, and people cheered at his successes—which consisted primarily of Melone's polite, sororal responses to his questions. Yes, she would be happy to pass the sugar—and the like. At the same time and without any irony, people advised Melone not to succumb to the pressure of Rayovac's affections. He was, they said, a nobody, a loafer, a hanger-on, loitering in the bakery all day to do his one hour of work in the evening. What's more, he was too old for her and didn't always bathe. A cape of white dandruff hung at his shoulders. Last night's meal still lingered in the crevices of his teeth.

Despite the air of expectancy, the amount of actual action in the bakery was limited. Sometimes the most Rayovac could manage was to step Melone's way, then walk purposefully toward the napkins at her elbow, grab one and noisily blow his nose. Other days, he merely managed a hello, and Melone offered a single hello back. Tata and Melone kept up a steady stream of chatter while they worked, and occasionally, one of them would direct a kind "And what do you think?" to Rayovac. Otherwise, the real talk in the bakery was the talk of the spectators; while they waited for worthwhile action, they ate sweets and told each other tales. One woman recalled a bookstore manager she had once loved, how she'd read a library's worth of classics while she lingered in the store, waiting to catch the man's eye. A businessman told of his years teaching in the university, before he was denied tenure, of the students who bumped into him, years later, and said, "Señor Perez, you know, of course, your class changed my life." A biologist spoke of the beauty of the *coquí's* song, of how the sound of that little frog at sundown haunted her memories of childhood, and how when she traveled, she always missed that sound, so she'd decided to import the frog to zoos around the world. But every time she sent the frogs off, they died because, she was to discover, they could only live on the island.

One day, after work, when both Lucia and I were drinking coffee at La Madeleine, I said to her, "Is it my imagination, or is there a pattern to all this talk?"

Lucia looked up at me and smiled vaguely. Her look confessed that she too had been eavesdropping on the conversation at the neighboring table, where a carpenter was telling a young woman that he would like to quit his job, move to a shack in the countryside and raise goats and marijuana.

It didn't seem to me that I was sitting with Lucia in a room full of people looking for love. It seemed I was in a room full of people entranced by the thing they most desired and knew they couldn't have. This was the change Rayovac had wrought. But he didn't have this effect on the family, only on visitors. Sandrofo, the girls and I never had an urge to confess these sorts of fantasies. While customers prattled on, we were sensible as ever.

In truth, Sandrofo was not only sensible as ever; he was remarkably oblivious to what was going on at the bakery, though he did notice the increase in business. He confessed he found himself ordering less sugar for his cakes and altering recipes now that things seemed naturally sweet. I asked him one night what he thought about the situation with Rayovac and Melone, and he said, "What situation?"

"Rayovac's crush," I said.

"Well, Melone isn't going to have anything to do with that boy," he said.

"I wasn't suggesting she should. I meant the way everyone is watching the progress of his efforts."

Sandrofo asked me to explain what I meant, and when I did, he told me I was imagining things.

"I don't think so," I said. "Lucia's noticed it. We talk about it all the time."

"Well, you women," he said, dismissively.

"Sandrofo . . ." I said in a firm voice, readying an argument.

"It's just," he said, trying to wave my anger away with an explanation, "if you only realized how little people think about other people, you'd be quite comforted."

"I would?" I said, not believing such an idea could possibly bring anyone comfort.

In some ways, I supposed he was simply describing himself. I guessed a certain amount of willed blindness was necessary if you were a grown man with three adolescent daughters, and I didn't pursue the conversation.

The girls, however, talked endlessly about the situation. At night—after I was home from work but before their father had come up from the bakery—we'd discuss the day's events.

"Today it was just staring," Melone told me on the same day I'd had the discussion with Sandrofo. We were sitting in the girls' bedroom with Beatriz and I on one bed, Melone and Tata hugging pillows on the other.

"Unbelievable staring," Tata added.

Beatriz nodded in agreement.

"Moony-eyed," Melone said.

"A basset hound face," Tata said.

"And what can I do?" Melone said. "I want to be nice, but I have to back away from him. I literally feel repulsed and have to force myself not to step back."

"Just because he's in love with you, you don't need to be in love with him," Tata said. "You see," she turned to me and said, "Melone thinks she should be in love back, but she doesn't have to be."

Melone pushed her pillow under her knees and said, "What if this is my only chance?"

"Don't be crazy," I said. "You'll have plenty of chances in your life."

"I don't know," Melone said.

"You're fourteen," I said. "Whatever put such an idea in your head? That's no way for a fourteen-year-old to talk."

"Almost fifteen," Melone said, mournfully, as if old maidenhood were slamming down on her like a freight train. Melone was aiming for emotional advancement to match her intellectual skills; she was always being praised as the smartest one in her class. Precociously, I thought, she planned to go through a middle-aged crisis in high school.

Tata looked at Melone and said to me, "See. That's just what I've been telling her. I mean, no one's mooning over me, and I'm not worried."

Melone said, "I'll moon after you." She dropped to her knees on the floor, clasped her hands to her chest and gazed pleadingly up at Tata.

Tata looked lovingly back at her and said, "*Querida*, my love, I can see right up your nose to your beautiful gray brain."

They burst into giggles, then both jumped up and crossed to the bed Beatriz and I were sitting on. They fell to their knees. "The gorgeous wax in your ears," Tata said to Beatriz.

"The bacteria in your stomach," Melone said to me.

Beatriz and I turned our hands to fans and waved at ourselves as if we were British royalty, used to being admired.

"Still, really," Melone said, sitting back on the floor and turning quickly serious, "it's no use for him to go on. And I can't be mean like that girl, remember that girl . . ."

Beatriz nodded, and Tata said, "Let me tell."

"Go ahead," Melone said.

Tata turned to me and explained, "There was this girl at school, a few years ahead of us, named . . ."

"Migene," Melone said.

"Yeah," Tata nodded. "Migene—and there was this guy, Pablo, who was like Rayovac. Everyone knew he was in love with Migene. He'd bring her flowers and chocolates . . . everything."

"So there's this dance," Melone went on, "at the beginning of the school year, and everyone goes. So Pablo goes over to Migene and asks her to dance, and she says, 'I wouldn't dance with you if you were the last man on earth.'"

"Incredible," Tata said.

"I can't be like that," Melone said. "I heard that when he went to university, he tried to slit his wrists in the library."

Beatriz winced and held her left wrist with her right hand, as if in sympathy.

"Well, you're not like that," Tata said sharply. "I mean think about it; how much can he love you if he wants you to do something you don't want to do, which is to love him?"

"That doesn't make sense. He doesn't want me to do something I can't do, he wants me to feel something I don't feel, so that's a *wish*."

"But, if he really cared, he wouldn't wish it. He'd leave you be," Tata said. "*That* would be real love."

"Lord," I said to Tata, "how did you get to be so smart? It took me until my thirties to realize that."

Tata gave me an impatient look, then shrugged and smiled and said, "I don't know. I had a happy love life . . . in another life."

"I thought you didn't believe in other lives," I said. Tata was always making fun of my mystical streak, pointing to mosquitos and saying, "Wasn't that your third cousin a few lifetimes ago?"

"Well, I don't," said Tata with some irritation, "but if I did, it would have been happy."

"Sometimes," I said to Melone, "it's nice to have the attention, even when it's not from a particularly worthy object."

Tata said, "Yeah, and men are always getting crushes on Melone."

"No, they're not," Melone said.

"What about that guy who had you go walk with him down by the old fort, and the one who . . ."

Melone put her hand up. "They were lunatics. The tourist from London who thought everything was 'amusing.' The insurance man with boils. He asked me if I'd ever seen a boil before, and when I said no, he pulled at the neck of his shirt so I could see two red pustules by his collarbone. I think, what does he see in me that makes me seem like an appropriate candidate, and I only feel worse for the attention."

Tata said, "Oh, you're thinking too much. And anyway, it's better than nothing." Tata posed theatrically at the edge of the bed. "As I well know . . . having experienced . . . NOTHING." She threw her hands in the air on the final word, as if she were holding the high, final note of an impossibly difficult song.

Beatriz kicked the bed to indicate her agreement.

"No, it's not," said Melone. "It's worse than nothing. You'll see."

Tata rolled her eyes, as if to dismiss the idea that she would ever have the kind of experience that would give her more knowledge than she currently possessed.

"Girls," I said, "you're so young to be having this conversation. Everything's ahead of you; there's still so much more to happen." Time, I wanted to add, is still a luxury. You can still add future events to your life and have a definition of yourself you like.

I thought later how odd it must be to have obsessive attention from a man just at the age when, as I remember it, one was already so obsessed with one's sexual self and what it could and could not do in the world. And I thought, too, how odd to have the attention just when you are acquiring a stepmother. My own relationship with my mother and sister had been terribly close but also competitive in the realm of sex. As girls, we competed for our father's attention, pitted him against our mother in foolish ways, and then, later, I stole an admirer from my sister—although just long enough to get him to acknowledge his affections for me, because I didn't truly care for him. When my sister died, the long-ago event weighed on me so heavily I could barely offer comfort to her husband, the widower. I stood stiffly by him at the funeral, patted him once on the back, as if he were a soccer buddy who'd missed an easy goal. I rarely called to see how he was doing, and only when he remarried did I allow myself to greet him with a chaste kiss on the cheek.

The day after the bedroom conversation with the girls, I took my coffee break before school let out. Sandrofo saw me come in, waved a hello and said, "If you can wait five minutes, I'll take my break with you."

I nodded my head and pointed to a table by the side wall, where I intended to sit. While I waited, I heard an elderly man, his limbs so arthritically snarled he looked like a tree, say dreamily, "In my youth, in Cuba, we'd sneak out to go dancing. There's no place here like that. Only Havana feels like Havana."

I heard González say, "He's bluffing. He's only saying he thinks six o'clock, but really he thinks seven. He's trying to get you to bet earlier in the day." At a table next to me, a woman leaned confidentially over to a friend. Both were dressed in the blue and white uniforms that bathroom attendants sometimes wore in the fancier hotels. The woman said, "Rumor is, this very afternoon, he's going to ask her to a movie." She sat back in her chair and nodded knowingly.

Sandrofo came over and said, "What do you think about the Hotel Santiago for a wedding reception?"

"I heard that was a hotel for high-level drug dealers."

"No, no," Sandrofo said, "I never heard that. It's for businessmen, but it's respectable. It's quite elegant." I rolled my eyes. Elegance was no argument against drugs. These days, Puerto Rican money was inevitably drug money. Ignoring me, Sandrofo said, "It's continental but not like. . . ." He stopped and waved his hand toward the Condado, the strip of San Juan that was weighted with luxury hotels and shops. His dismissiveness was the standard dismissiveness of everyone on the island. It was the New Yorker's scorn for the World Trade Center, the Bostonian's boredom with Faneuil Hall, but it was amplified by the fact that he wasn't really from here, by the fact that his first wife had been a continental, the term for Puerto Ricans who go to live in North America. "And it's next to the synagogue," he went on, "so we can go straight from the service."

I nodded my head. I was technically a Catholic, though I had no formal religious education, so I'd agreed to convert for the marriage. I was even taking Hebrew classes, once every other week from the rabbi in Miramar.

Sandrofo went on, "We'll get rooms for the night. Put the girls on one floor and ourselves on another. My friend Victor knows the owner and says he can arrange things even if it's all booked up."

"OK," I said. I had met Sandrofo's friend Victor and his wife, Coco, and knew if the Santiago was a place where they did business, it couldn't possibly have drug connections. Victor had made his money through wise investments; he was Sandrofo's only partner and had a controlling interest in a rum distillery. The very cleanness of Victor's cash had always made him seem beautifully anachronistic to me, an impression compounded by his old-world manner. Though he'd benefited from the tax breaks of Operation Bootstrap, he was disdainful of United States businessmen and only reluctantly engaged in ventures that didn't have at least the look of being "purely" Puerto Rican. On the island, this sort of nationalism dissolved class lines. The sleeves of Victor's suits were fastened with gold cuff links, but a man pushing a donkey through the street would talk to him for hours, would inevitably say, "Now, there's an unusual man," when they parted. I felt the same way. Around Victor and Coco, I didn't have my teenage urge to spout Marxist platitudes. Instead, I found myself amazed and frightened by how I so enjoyed their money, the elegance of their easy generosity.

"I'll call Victor and ask him to make the reservations today," Sandrofo said.

"That's a good idea to include the girls in on the hotel stay," I said.

"Yes," Sandrofo said. "We'll have our privacy," he leaned over and kissed me on the nose, "but they'll feel . . ." He couldn't find the word he wanted.

"Safe?" I offered.

"Well, I don't know that they feel unsafe, and, of course, they love you, but to ease them in, to . . ."

I nodded my head. "I know what you mean." I was so busy noticing the times when Sandrofo didn't engage in analytic conversations about the girls' hearts that I was always impressed when I found myself in the middle of a conversation when he revealed himself to be thinking about their needs. Of course, I knew he thought about them all the time. There was that vague look of worry that was always on his face and the way he collapsed into a panic when the girls were not home when they said they'd be. He just didn't talk about his thoughts, and the silence let me imagine he was less concerned than he was. But, I thought, particularly after a conversation like the one I had had the night before, someone did something right somewhere with these girls, for they had such clear affection for one another, and they didn't hesitate to show it. I loved watching them together. The way they would finish each other's stories or prompt the other to tell a particular detail or be sure to articulate Beatriz's thoughts for her.

"I wonder what their feelings are about having a new mother," I said now to Sandrofo. "Not about me, but about the whole situation."

"I think they're excited," Sandrofo said. From across the room, Carla called him to the phone. "Just a second," he called back and stood, kissed me and said, "I'll see you tonight. Don't worry about the girls. You're good for them. There are so many things I haven't been able to do for them, talk to them about." He kissed me again and walked away.

I sat for a bit longer drinking my coffee. Next to me, I saw a man I recognized as a manager at one of the Condado hotels. "My people," I heard him say to a young woman, presumably from elsewhere, "are so stu-pid." There was loving frustration in his voice. "They think," he went on, "that they can get something for nothing."

The woman said, as if continuing his thought, "They want welfare benefits, but they don't want to pay taxes. They want independence without losing the tax benefits that come with commonwealth status."

"Yes," said the manager, as if she had brilliantly deciphered his meaning. "Something for nothing. Stu-pid."

The young woman looked at him expectantly, and I could see why. It looked as if he wanted to say, "And I'm the same way. I want what they want too."

I scooped up my belongings to leave. At the door, I turned back, hoping to catch Sandrofo's eye before I left. He was behind the counter. He looked up from a clipboard where he was writing something and mouthed, "Don't worry." I waved him a good-bye and went back to work.

All afternoon, I hoped Sandrofo was right about the girls' feelings, but I wasn't so confident. Melone was occasionally defensive around me; Tata could be short tempered. Beatriz alone offered complete, if silent, support. Ever since we had announced our engagement, I found myself pausing at doorways before I entered—perhaps I could hear something I wasn't meant to hear? Something that would clarify their true feelings for me?

But the overheard phrase wasn't forthcoming, especially since if I didn't join in their conversations, if after work I went into Sandrofo's and my bedroom to read, they'd pursue me in there. I don't think it occurred to them I might want to be alone; why ever would anyone want such a thing? They, after all, had never been truly alone, even in the womb. Melone joked that she got lonely when she went to the bathroom; she was so used to company. When they'd find me in the apartment, on the rare occasions when I wanted to be by myself, they didn't hesitate to remove reading material from my hands and start talking. They liked to compare their education with my youthful education; they liked to hear about my years trying to be a political activist, about my old boyfriends, about my eventual decision to go into the art world. They liked to hear about my mother and my sister, the tobacco plantation in Cidra, where I grew up. In turn, they told me about their favorite books, classmates and childhood games. They analyzed the customers in the bakery and spoke of going to university and living, perhaps, up

North, where they wouldn't feel so funny about being only partly Puerto Rican.

And Sandrofo was right that there were things I could talk to the girls about that he couldn't. "I'm open about sex," I'd told them weeks earlier. "I was in college in Wisconsin in the sixties, so I've done just about everything, and I don't mind talking about it."

"Wisconsin," they had breathed, fairly amazed. "Why'd you go there?"

I laughed. Said: "You're supposed to ask about men."

Later, once it was clear I was a permanent fixture in their lives, Tata didn't hesitate to ask me the occasional question about sex and then inform the other two of what I had said. (It reminded me of my own sister, how late at night she'd lie in the bed next to me and reveal what she'd learned from our mother: the mysteries—menstruation, armpit sweat, leg hair, the whole jungle of the self—and the necessity of constant care, of pruning and scraping away those endless secretions and growths.)

Indeed, the night of the day we settled on the Santiago as the place we'd have our wedding reception, I stood outside the girls' bedroom door as they talked about whether they had or had not ever had an orgasm. At first, I'd been eavesdropping for information about their feelings for me; then, when I realized what they were talking about, I couldn't bring myself to interrupt. At length, I heard Tata say, knowingly, to Melone, "Oh, well, you must not have ever had one, because you'd know if you had." It was something I'd said to Tata days earlier. I coughed in the hall to stifle a laugh and heard Melone wrap up the conversation by saying in a campy voice, "Well, girls, I don't think we'll ever be closer than this."

I called my greetings from the doorway and then entered into the room, to the flood of words that was a typical conversation with the girls. They were voluble talkers. You could start a sentence and have to wait an entire hour before you had a chance to finish it. When they were talking, I noticed how one would prompt the other, how Tata's eyes would flicker toward Melone, as if she was checking to make sure she was still being appreciated. Then, she'd continue on, a storyteller secure in her audience's admiration. It might have seemed like self-absorption, but then they'd turn their attention intently on me and listen compassionately and intelligently. That night, for instance, we talked for hours, and I was conscious of feeling my throat hoarsen with overuse. Finally, Melone said, "It's ten o'clock. Where's Dad? Let's go get him."

Everyone stood to make for the back staircase, and I thought of how I bored Lucia after I first met Sandrofo, how I wouldn't stop talking or thinking about him. I could devote an afternoon to my fondness for his shoulders and upper arms; three work days to the charming quirks of his Spanish, derived, I supposed, from his junior high school Spanish teacher. It was always like this for me whenever I fell in love. The girls, I thought, were nonstop talkers even when they weren't in love. Either that or they were in love—but with everything. Such possible democracy when it came to one's affections impressed me, for in my own adolescence, I struggled with depression, and after my sister's death, sadness overtook me completely. I don't think I saw what the world had to offer a person with a tender heart.

"Paaa-pi," Tata called playfully as she went down the stairs. The bakery closed at seven, so she felt free to use this voice. "Papi."

Sandrofo wasn't in the bakery. "Where is he?" said Melone, worried. Normally, he came upstairs by eight-thirty at the latest, but he could get lost in his work, and often we'd had to entice him up with a reminder about dinner. All four of us pushed into the back room, where Sandrofo normally did his end-of-the-day paperwork before he brought the day's earnings to the bank. "He's not here," Melone said, although we all could see that. "Maybe he's still at the bank," Tata said, but Beatriz picked up the empty canvas bag Sandrofo used to bring money to the bank's deposit box. Then, Tata opened the door to the storage room and screamed. "What, what?" we cried and all went running. "They're here, they're . . ." Tata paused, trying to find a more descriptive word, and said, "here," once again.

"What?" I said and pushed away her shoulder to see Sandrofo and Carla Mendota, bound to wooden chairs and gagged.

"*Ay, Dios,*" I cried. "Undo them."

Melone yelled, "What happened? What happened?" and Tata pulled at the cloth in Carla's mouth. Carla rolled her eyes as if this were a familiar inconvenience; she really needed to find a less demanding job. Her exasperation was calming, and we all stopped yelling and started picking at the knots, trying to untie them. As soon as the gags were out of their mouths, Carla said, "Robbed. We were robbed."

"Are you hurt?" Melone said.

"No," said Sandrofo, "it was just a robbery, and we're lucky because I went to the bank after lunch, so we only lost the afternoon's earnings."

I rolled my eyes. "Are you *hurt?*"

Carla shook her head no.

"Who did it?" Tata said.

"It was Rayovac, wasn't it?" I said, suddenly stricken. Just last week, I'd told Sandrofo to give the man a copy of the key to the bakery. "It's my fault. I said to hire him."

"No, no," Sandrofo said. "Why would Rayovac rob us? It was kids on drugs. You could tell from their eyes. Heroin."

Carla said, "He's right. Those kids. They stole a tree from my front yard, because they thought they could get ten bucks for it. They dug it right up."

"What? The same kids?" Melone said. "You know who did it?"

"No, no," said Carla. "Some other drug addicts. These people did the thing with the panty hose. We don't know who these people were."

"Wait. I thought you could see their eyes," I said.

"Well, no, I guess I couldn't," Sandrofo said. "But I just know it was heroin. When they came in, they were almost apologetic. They didn't hurt us at all. They said they were doing it because of the wallpaper. You know how the wallpaper has buildings that look like they were from Italy? They said there were little men in the building, and those men had told them to take our money."

"Sounds more like schizophrenia than heroin," I said. I was surprised Sandrofo even hazarded a guess about drugs, because drugs were out of his sphere of reference. It made him seem pure to me. I honestly felt there were some things in the world he just didn't see. In the same way I never noticed cars because cars bored me, he didn't notice things that compromised his vision of life on the island. Around the corner from the bakery, there was a man with a microphone who stood outside a jewelry store. Behind him, the store's windows were filled with rotating mirrored balls. Why someone would do this on a sunny island was beyond me. I kept waiting for lawsuits in which tourists sued the owner for neglectful blinding of a passerby through use of the sun for promotional purposes. The man outside the jewelry store tugged at the cord of the microphone, which snaked through the open door to the shop, and he advertised bargains in English. "Diamonds, diamonds for your loved one. Show her you care. Get a rock on her finger." The man never stopped, but I honestly felt Sandrofo had never heard him. The very sight was beneath him. I was equally convinced Sandrofo had never seen a T-shirt with fluorescent lettering or read the local rag filled with letters to and from the lovelorn. On another man, this might have been snobbery or stupidity. On Sandrofo, it was a fervent and admirable wish taken to extremes. He wanted so badly for the world to be better than it was that he saw it that way—as if that, in and of itself, could change things.

Later, two police officers came and said Sandrofo was probably right about the drugs. The bakery was the fourth business to be robbed in as many days on the street, and the robberies were consistently sloppy and desperate, although the shoddiness of the crime hadn't resulted in anything like a capture, just a hypothesis about hypodermic needle use. The police asked Sandrofo to go to the station the next day and look at photographs of suspects.

"*Ay,* no," he said. "I can't leave the bakery. Carla, you go."

"What?" she said, refusal in her voice.

"You go, you go."

"I'm not going. Police stations," she said and shuddered. "No offense," she added quickly, giving the officers a flirty half-smile.

"Go tomorrow morning, and you can have the rest of the day off."

"The whole day?"

Sandrofo nodded.

Carla turned toward the officers, thrust her arms out and pressed her wrists together, as if readying them for handcuffs or bloodletting. "A day off!" she cried, and then, like a woman begging to be ravished: "Take me. Take me away."

Normally, Sandrofo's days were spent in a handful of places. Before dawn, he was in the back room baking. In the morning, he opened the store, saw to it that things were running smoothly. Then he'd go out to visit his suppliers and the hotels and restaurants that placed special orders. Afternoons, he was back baking and doing setups for the subsequent day. Late afternoons and evenings, he attended to his books. It was rare for him to spend the entire day in the front room, where people nursed cups of coffee for hours on end. But with Carla gone for the day, Sandrofo had no choice but to install himself behind the cash register, atop a high stool that allowed one to survey the events of both the bakery and the street. Although I didn't stop in that day, I was curious to see how this would change his perspective on the Rayovac drama. After all, his myopia in the matter could have been purely circumstantial; he didn't spend enough time in the front of the bakery to judge events accurately. So that night, when I came home and asked the girls how their days were, I hoped for substantial revelations.

Tata said, "Big afternoon. Rayovac asked Melone to go to the movies."

"At three o'clock," Melone said. "I remember because Cardona stood up and started shouting, 'Three, three, three. Pay up, pay up' to his pokermates."

I shrugged, unwilling to explain what that was all about.

"So," Tata continued, "Melone said she was sorry, but she didn't think she could go. Then people in the bakery started to boo at her. Like this is the cock fights or something."

"Maybe I should have just said yes," Melone said.

"Oh, don't be ridiculous," Tata said.

Beatriz started pushing Melone in the upper arm, and Melone said, "OK, OK. I'll tell. So, Maria Elena, listen to what Tata did. She stood up on a chair and ordered everyone who was booing out of the bakery."

"*Dios mío*," I said, laughing. "What did people do? What did Rayovac do? What did your father do?"

"Well," said Tata, "here's the great part. First, Rayovac wasn't there. As soon as Melone said no and people started to boo, he sneaked out back and got in his truck and drove away. But the people, they quieted right down. Then they started clapping for me. It was amazing."

I laughed and thought, Well, they got to see it. If it's true that the customers were in La Madeleine looking for love, they got to see it. I said, "And your father? What was he doing during all this?"

All three of the girls looked at each other. They were stuck for an answer. "I don't know," Tata said. "What *was* he doing?"

"He was there," Melone said, "but, God, I don't know. Beatriz?"

Beatriz shrugged.

It occurred to me that Sandrofo really should have been the one angrily defending his daughter against the crowd.

"How come you did it?" I said to Tata.

Tata, clearly impressed by her own performance, said, "I don't know. It was just automatic. I was angry, and there was this chair, and all of a sudden I'm shouting to the crowd."

Melone and Beatriz laughed. And I wondered to myself how these girls learned to care for each other the way they did.

"We taught each other," Melone said.

"What?" I said.

"You asked how we learned to care for each other, and I said we taught each other."

"I didn't say that. I thought it. But I didn't say that out loud," I said, taken aback and frankly scared.

"Yes, you did," Tata said. "Didn't she?" Beatriz nodded her head.

"That's odd," I said. "I thought that I just thought it. That's very strange."

"I guess we taught each other," Melone repeated, and I sensed that in speaking the sentence she was discovering the lovely, mournful truth of it for the first time. We were all quiet. The girls thinking, I suspect, about each other, while I hoped it didn't take away from Sandrofo's virtues to admit Melone was right; he didn't teach them. They taught each other.

"Sandrofo," I said that night, when we were in bed, "what are you thinking?" He smiled at me. His eyes looked kind, knowledgeable, and he took me in his arms. Wrapped up as I was with him, I thought, "The lines of the family are drawn." At first, I didn't know what I meant, then I realized I thought of the family as a four-piece puzzle. Beatriz and I fit together; Melone and Tata fit together. We made a whole picture. Sandrofo didn't figure in. A question, I supposed, of being male. But the next day, I realized how very wrong I was. My mood was light as I walked through the bakery on my way to work. I was imagining Tata's performance the previous day. But as I stood making small talk with Carla about her visit to the police station, a cloud must have passed overhead; the front room of the bakery temporarily darkened, and I ached suddenly and terribly for my own long-dead sister. I wasn't a member of this family, not really, for I'd passed through the bakery, like any customer, looking for the thing I most desired and would never have.

The Second World

(Beatriz—May 1978)

I talked to myself, first. Then I talked to her. I had to; she wanted my story so badly. I told her everything, even about how you could say I was a murderer. I wanted to explain everything, so she'd understand about how I had to be good. "Slow down," Maria Elena said, because I spoke so fast, but I was making up for lost time. If I talked enough, I knew that in the end, I mean the very end—my deathbed—I'd have spoken the same number of words as anyone else:

Biologically, we were an impossibility, but there it was. A set of triplets with identical chromosomes despite the fact that each of us arrived in the world sheathed in her own placenta. *Solitude in companionship*, my sisters said. I accepted this, as well as the common wisdom that pictured, for who knew what reason, the setup in the womb. Tata, all agreed, would be curled into Melone; they would fit together like two snug spoons, save for the fact that Melone would be leaning back to whisper something in Tata's half-formed ear. Maybe they were more like forks, their prongs tangled together. But my back would be turned to the both of them. Even then, my only real interest, escape, freedom.

An impossible desire, I would learn soon enough, for I could do nothing to escape *myself*. Wherever I looked, there I was. There were my locks of dark brown hair, now short curls, now long tresses. There were my almond eyes, my sallow skin, my weak mouth, that arch of freckles that curved, like two quarter-moons from my cheeks to my brow. I don't need to tell you I resented the glassy stillness of the sea, left behind to pool in old rock. What was water if, when flat, it would only behave like a mirror, like my sisters; it would only give me back to myself?

In the world of the family—and nowhere else—Tata was considered the Star of the Three . . . she shone in public, and we all knew she would be an actress, a performer, that she'd take to lying as a vocation. Melone was the Smart One, and I was the Silent One. From the start, my attributes were all of absence; it was the only way I could figure to get some attention for myself, a ploy really, my weapon against invisibility. What I *wanted* was to be known as the Good One, but everything frustrated me in this.

It's true that, to all appearances, I was a well-behaved girl. At least, that's what everybody said. But I knew evil wafted about me, day and night. I heard it whisper in my ear, *Possibility.*

My story starts the day before my fifteenth birthday. I had been scared, in advance of what the day would bring. Though I was raised a Jew by an atheist father, our island was partially Catholic and completely superstitious. I didn't know what to make of the possibilities for the day. I'd heard fifteen was a bad number because it was really sixteen—if you counted your virtual year in the womb. And that meant you were combining three—the Trinity—and the evil number thirteen. It seemed worse that there were three of us having a birthday on that day. I'd think, *3 and Trinity and 13 and damned.* Up to that day, my life had been governed by the one fact of my silence, though I didn't pretend I couldn't hear and for that reason had an understanding with Tata and Melone. Frequently, they would express their thoughts as my own, and I'd nod in agreement . . . they were never all that wrong. But if I were truly going to recognize the importance of the day, something would have to change. I didn't know what that something was, but I thought it might be my voice. I might have to start talking. But first, I needed to find out if I could talk.

To do this, I went to the pond at the center of the forest, the one that everyone says has no bottom. I took off all my clothes and hid them behind the water tower. I was looking for a thick tree to climb, because I wanted to jump from on high into the water. From the ground, I eyeballed a fat branch that appealed to me. I liked the dip and sway of its center, thought it would make a nice seat if I lost nerve and needed to sit down to consider what I intended to do next. I touched the bark at the base of the tree, selected my jumping off point, and heaved myself on to the lower limbs and, as I did, thought of the funny monkey that climbed the body of the potter whose shop fronted Highway 3 near Luquillo, thought of how he loped his wide-eyed, furry self up the potter's body to sit on the man's bald head. But once I reached the top, I was higher than I thought I'd be. The world was too leafy to think of baldness, and I too scared to sit. Instead, I looked down, tried to make out the soles of my feet against the sky and the clouds and the undersides of the leaves . . . the whole second world below me. Perhaps I wouldn't do it, I thought, as I inched my feet along crusty bark and clutched at the thick leaves from the branch above, but then a handful of leaves tore off in my fist and it seemed I'd do anything to break the glassy stillness of that picture below me. I jumped and thought, *I am in pure air,* and put my hands to my face to push my hair away from my mouth. It was then that I hit—the sudden slap of the water against the soft back of my arms was a reproach, and I thought, *Why didn't my feet feel water and warn my hands?* But already I was slowing my plunge downward. I tried to force my body down a little farther against the water, and then, as I came up, I started to scream, "Ladies and gentlemen, if you please . . ." I had a whole speech, not geared to the contingencies of rise and fall, lung capacity or body buoyancy. But I had done it, and I had heard it, and no one else had, though it sounded like children blowing bubbles in the bathtub.

I swam to the center of the lake and floated on my back and felt the velvety surface of the water along my back, between my legs. I was staring at the sky, watching the movement of one heavy cloud after another. I was trying to right my faulty perception, to understand that I was moving and the clouds were being left behind, but I couldn't do it. Then I closed my eyes and tried to guess, when I opened them again, what pattern I could expect to be formed between the trees. The temperature was a clue. I thought I could feel big clouds as cool wind, absence of cloud as pure hot sky, saying, *Here, Beatriz, take our heat.*

That's when it happened. I felt a chill like no other I'd ever felt; my nipples shriveled and tightened like old fruit, and I thought, though I knew I was alone, to be ashamed. Then the world stopped. I mean it. Everything stopped, and if a bird was singing, I could not hear it, and if I was breathing, my chest didn't heave, and in that moment something happened that has never happened before—I thought without words. I had one thought, and it was pure but I didn't translate it into sounds for my head. I would say what it was I thought, but the thought resists words, even now, so the best I can say is that while my eyes were closed, I felt a huge black cloud, heavy with raindrops, pass over me; except I knew it wasn't a rain cloud. I knew, without doubt and without true understanding, that the shadow of God had passed over me and that if only I knew the time of day, I would know whether that shadow fell in front of Him or behind Him and thus know whether I came before Him or He had passed me by. I didn't dare open my eyes and didn't dare hope for clues about my position.

The rain started falling in plump, cold drops to the pond. But still I couldn't move. I was too frightened, so I pressed my lids shut as the water struck and thought of the times when I woke in the morning and couldn't open my eyes because they had been glued together by sleep, by "fairies' glue," as Melone said when she wiped them clean with a warm cloth. With the first crack of thunder, however, I realized my clothes were not protected under some tree but lying in the open behind the water tower, and I would have a long wet walk back down the hill . . . I swam for the shore and ran for the bus that would take me home.

On the morning of the next day, I woke as I always did, tugged a starched pinafore over my white blouse. I kept the delicate floral print on the pinafore bright by reserving it for special occasions. Papa would already be downstairs at work—he left in the middle of the night—but I knew, from habit, there would be words from him, a note with the jam and the bread he sliced in the dark for our morning meal.

"Hurry up," Melone called from the kitchen.

Tata was still undressed when Melone called for a third time, "Hurry." But I was the last one to the breakfast table. It seemed there was nothing I could do about it. I was considered the slowest, and everything I did bore this out. Even if I woke, on purpose, hours too early, with a plan—I would cook bacon for my sisters!—somehow I'd lose track of my intentions and find myself, once again, the last at the table.

Melone, for her part, couldn't be late if she tried, and I sometimes wondered if we were true to ourselves or true to the family's understanding of ourselves. If Melone was quick because she'd always been the Punctual One. If I was slow only because my sisters called me Put-Put.

"It says," Melone shouted one last time. "For my girls. On their birthday." She would be referring to Papa's note, and then I was finally in the kitchen to see what he meant. A bright red balloon was tied, with string, to each of our chairs and next to the bread and purple jam, we found blood pudding.

"We're adults now," Tata said as she pulled her chair out from the table.

Melone shrugged her shoulders. Said: "Isn't it sixteen when you're considered an adult?" Our sense of time had always been faulty; by silent agreement, we considered our ages to differ by virtue of our birth order. Melone was the oldest, Tata the baby, and I between the two.

"And as an adult," Tata said, paying no attention to Melone, "I refuse to eat this." She looked glumly at the black sausage, sliced in rounds and piled in a cup before her.

"You have to," Melone said.

"No," Tata stopped to consider her answer. Though she was bossy, she was not truly in the habit of disobeying Melone on any important matter. "I don't."

"But you *dooo*. It's been bought special. Try it with milk," she said and poured some milk into Tata's cup.

Tata looked at the result, grimaced and said, "I'm not listening to you." She tilted her head back over her chair, stared at the tarantula-shaped water stain on the ceiling and began to hum.

"I don't think there's ever been a more spoiled girl on this island than you."

"I'm not listening," Tata told the ceiling. "But if I were, I'd tell you to grab a fly and then curl your long tongue back into your mouth."

"Can you believe this?" Melone asked me. I nodded, and she said,

"Oh, you *can.* Well, *of course,* you can. Tata was born a brat. Why do I think she'll be good and eat her blood pudding?"

"Say another word, Melone. And I'll throw it in your face."

"Just one lousy word?" Melone asked.

"Yes," said Tata, her eyes on the ceiling but her fingers curled menacingly about her cup.

Melone folded her hands in her lap, looked coyly at me and then at Tata, cleared her throat and said, as if starting a lyrical poem, so true and lovely only a fool could fail to be moved by her words, "Oh, purple root heart of the banana . . ."

Tata sat straight up in her chair, met Melone's eyes, then threw the contents of her cup in Melone's face. She aimed perfectly—not a spot of the sausage and milk mixture hit her hair or her neck but her face was covered. Tata looked more amazed than Melone; could she possibly have done what she had just done? And then they both started to laugh, but already I was running. For the first time, really, one of my sisters' faces seemed to me to be my own. I thought that this shouldn't be a possible sight on this most dangerous of days, that I shouldn't have seen my own face bathed in milk and blood pudding.

I was thinking of revelation, of terrible insights, of my own damnation as I ran down the stairs and then pushed open the front door and headed out into the street. And I was thinking I hadn't done anything shocking enough to deserve my fate. I hadn't even done anything to deserve my thoughts. It occurred to me that the time had come to show my life who was boss . . . which is only to say that, when I reached the plaza, with its statue of Christopher Colombus, instead of running toward the bus stop for my school, I did something I'd never done. I disobeyed the common order of my days and took the bus inland. I should have gone left, should have been drawn toward water. Girls who weren't headed toward my private school or the public school went right, inland and uphill, away from our classrooms by the sea, to a parochial school with cool white walls and a tin roof that made such thunderous sounds on rainy days that the knees under the blue and green pleated skirts would have to tremble, and only the most devilish girl could doubt the awesome power of the Lord.

I'd need such a blue and green kilt for entrance into the school, and though I'll say, *My thoughts were confused, I hardly knew my own mind,* it seemed my body knew before my mind did that I would go to that school with the pale cross at the edge of the forest. I had been spying—without knowing my purpose in doing so—on that school for years. I don't know how I understood my badness in advance of any crime. I simply did. Sometimes I thought it was because I was the only one who knew about it all . . . about how I woke long nights with evil thoughts, how I dreamed of accidentally slipping into various beds and, while I slumbered, letting my nightgown twist up over my chest. And of how I was not ashamed.

I knew I'd need help to stop thinking of a man's hand as something created only to cup my breast. I knew that our island was polluted with the kind who would take advantage of my night dreams and bring me to ruin so that even the one thing I knew to be true about myself—that I was an honest sort of girl who meant to do good, to steal chickens for the poor and to sacrifice my shoes for orphans—would no longer be true, and I would prove to be something more than a bad and quiet girl. I could, if I allowed myself to fall, lose all my characteristics, become absolutely nothing.

What I mean is: I needed one of those kilts, so I could get into the school and learn what it was the day had to teach me. I had my own white shirt with a round collar underneath my pinafore. The shoes . . . I'd go barefoot and hope those nuns spent so much time dreaming of Heaven they wouldn't dare consider Hell and cast a glance down at the floor.

If only I was ready to start talking, I'd have grabbed that skirt in some playful way—suggested a swap of clothes, and lives, for a day. But since I wasn't ready to start talking, I decided I'd have to try to take the skirt of Elizabeth Peretta —I knew her as Betta—who might give it over without words.

Already, Betta was known to prefer the touch of girls to boys so when I jumped, like a frog, across the path I knew she took to school, she didn't take a single step back. Not even when I stood and pulled her shoulders to me, leaned right through the thickness of the morning air to kiss her red lips.

But she did disappoint me when I found her mouth dry and when I heard her say, "Beaaa-treez" so it sounded like "Bear's trees." And then, "I'm late for school."

I grimaced and tried again, stepping toward her and placing my hands on her hips, pulling her toward me, as I had seen men do in the alley behind the Allegro bar on Punto Maya street.

"Fly . . ." she said affectionately but pushed me away nonetheless. "I don't like your buzzing about when I have things to do."

It was impossible to understand what I was doing wrong or why I *was* beginning to feel like a bug. I grabbed at the hem of my pinafore and pulled it right over my head. It stuck on my ears, so I danced around in a circle till I'd tugged it off. I gave her a smile. She shook her head, as if at the ridiculous goings-on. She was almost twice my size, firmly built and already fully developed as a woman. Still, her features seemed broad, almost masculine, save for her dark brown hair, which was long and beautiful. When she let it down, she was the envy of the whole island, though now she had it tied back in a loose bun. I held my pinafore against her. It was clear it wouldn't fit, but I raised my eyebrows and wondered if she could read my face. *Appreciation and genuine admiration*, I meant to tell her. She scowled. Of course, she wouldn't care for anything so frilly as a dress. Still I held two red berries up to her ears for earrings.

"You city girls," Betta said, looking at my legs, which were not muscled like her own, "should eat more and do more work. Look at you."

I did, as best I could, and was not impressed by the sight. I motioned for her to give me her skirt as my legs were bare.

"I'm always late," she sighed and took my dress in her left hand and my palm in her right and continued down the path toward her school. This would have seemed a good sign if not for the clipped pace of our walk. She still meant to get to school on time, and I still meant to get that skirt! I reached over and touched the giant gold pin that lay, flat as a snake, in the fabric of her garment.

"Do you want that?" she said.

I nodded.

"Why don't you talk, silly?"

I shrugged as if it had never occurred to me, in my fifteen long years of life to consider the matter. She stopped for a moment and shrugged herself. I knew the gesture for I'd used it often. *Well*, she meant, *why don't you?* I looked down, and she looked down too, and for a few moments, I felt she really wanted to hear my answer. I thought the trees would grow in on us, from both sides of the path before I could explain it—that I had nothing to say, but no, that wouldn't be right, that words couldn't say what I had to say, that there was no way to be honest and good with words because with words you're always lying and sinning, even when the whole of your heart and mind is set on truth, on accuracy. It's the impermissible wish for perfection that kept me quiet; it's failure; it's . . . I couldn't say what it was, so I pointed at her kilt pin. She bent down to unfasten it.

"Just a decoration," she said, slipping the needle-like arm of the pin out of the fabric. I confess I *was* surprised the whole skirt didn't fall down when she handed it to me. "This way," she said and walked down a small trail that led off the main path.

"Really, do you ever talk?"

She would know—the entire city knew—I didn't speak, and I decided to pay no attention to this line of questioning. Instead I reached in front of her, as she moved, and I stumbled, falling into the branches by the path, but not before I had undone her top snap and top button.

"Oh, really," Betta said and stopped to refasten her skirt.

I stood up, sheepishly, wiping dirt and pieces of brown leaves from my bare legs and elbows. I really had been defeated, and now I was to be one of those sad characters who, once missing her chance for revelation, never gets another opportunity but goes as baffled to the grave as to grade school. I didn't easily reconcile myself to this defeat, and as Betta proceeded on her way, I walked softly and sulkily behind her, understanding my steps to be the kind of steps the damned took, dangerous and hellish because they were so purposeless. I didn't know why I was walking with Betta anymore and not sitting in the arm of a tree and weeping. I didn't know why I wasn't turning around to go to my own school, the one that glittered by the sea. I didn't know why I even thought I should think of turning. If Tata, all practicality, were along, she'd explain my thoughts in some deflating, but unfortunately accurate, manner. "Oh, she's confused," she'd say with a pay-*her*-no-mind wave of the hand so that I'd want to pull the saddest of sad thoughts from my brain, hold it before me, a belligerent child to my schoolmarm rage. "Aren't you ashamed of yourself?" I'd say and shake that thought, let its loose legs go flying so it would know what a flabby thing it was.

"Oh, I'm too late to even try not to be late," Betta said. She stopped and turned to me. "If I do, will you talk?"

I nodded my head ferociously.

"Promise?"

I bobbed my head up and down.

"You're not really so bad looking," she said and pulled my hair away from my face and held it behind my head.

Her hand dropped my hair and slid down my face, and when she kissed my neck, I started to unfasten her skirt.

"Slow, slow," she said, tapping away my hands, with a gesture I used for bothersome mosquitos. The skirt fell to the leaves, and she stepped one foot, then the other, out of the O of fabric that lay at her feet. And then what came over me? I can't honestly say I didn't like the way her fingers had slipped between the buttons of my blouse and were circling what there were of my breasts. Maybe I liked it too much because I put my hands to her shoulders and pushed as hard as I could, sending her through twigs and low bushes, a button from my blouse jumping after her. She'd be scraped and itchy at the least, maybe a lot worse, but I didn't stop. I grabbed her skirt and ran.

Whatever I expected to find when I went up that hill that led to St. Catilla's, I knew that it required neatened hair and a well-pressed blouse. I did my best to wipe the dirt off my shirt and to arrange Betta's skirt so it did not look too big by folding the waistband, letting the skirt provide a belt of fabric for itself. I took a strong piece of hay and tied my hair back and thought of Betta saying, "You're not really so bad looking," when she pulled my hair out of my face.

Whatever I expected to find, I didn't expect to find an empty house, some insect's carapace, a hollow space, where I thought I'd find life.

The school was low and long, white beneath its tin roof and dark at the windows and the single door that fronted the building. Unreadable orifices, really, no government poster reminding one about the four food groups or infectious diseases. I stepped through the front door expecting sound to guide me, but there was nothing in the unremarkable, dark hall that led from one end of the long building to the other. I turned left to make my way down the hall. . . . I was surprised to find the linoleum here gritty with dirt. I stopped twice to wipe the soles of my feet with my palm and then to wipe my palm on my skirt. The windows cut into the classroom doors let dim parallelograms of light out on to the hall floor. I stepped gingerly to the first one . . . poked just the edge of one eye in and saw . . . nothing. Nothing but a room filled with twenty wooden desks with metal legs bolted to the floor. Each desk had a hole in the top right-hand corner, presumably for a pot of ink, but there was not a single pot of ink in the place. I made my way down the hall and found more of the same. My concept of religion was rapidly revising itself.

From my days of spying on this school, I knew that the girls who went to the school *actually entered* the building. Hadn't I seen them giggling on their way up the hill? And hadn't I remarked at how, though they all wore the same clothes, one could easily distinguish a popular girl from those no one would have anything to do with? I'd concluded it had to do with gait and posture more than anything else, and I was determined not to let my feet wander, flat-footed, side to side, as I walked but to make them proceed like arrows, straight in front of me. This effort caused my legs a good deal of sorrow, and on days when I was particularly diligent, I'd barely have enough energy to eat my dinner; I was so eager to get into bed and give my legs a rest. It was worth it, though, because I couldn't have people hating me when I was trying to do good. It would leave them confused, I thought, and if people needed grace to understand charity, I would have to do my best to combine the two. I know this sounds like vanity, but I swear it wasn't. Walking straight was just one of the little things I tried to do to set myself right with the world.

So girls went into this school every morning, but then they . . . they disappeared. And after, they came back. This would have to have something to do with the soul, something that those of us outside the Church and thus outside Faith couldn't hope to understand. I sat down at a desk in one of the far corners of the room, folded my hands and thought to join them.

"Leave your body," I told myself. But this proved harder than I thought it would. I closed my eyes and suddenly had a vision of a chocolate hazelnut tart—it wasn't something we'd ever made at the bakery, but it just came to me: a small boat-shaped layer of shortbread, filled with hazelnut cream and coated with a thin layer of chocolate. I would suggest it to Papa and even prepare the first batch . . . I added this last offer to mitigate the fact of the thought of the pastry . . . this could not be the soul I was thinking of. I felt the sun warm on the back of my neck and heard a bird sing outside. I thought I could hear wind ruffle the palm tree leaves like waves. Then I realized, in this most holy of places, at the very moment I was trying to think of the soul, I'd come to have the unfamiliar sensation of a man's coarsely shaven cheek on my thigh. It was clear I was in trouble, and at the very moment I started to tell myself to forget the soul, to leave the whole matter behind and realize how chained I was to my body, even though it displaced so little air in this universe and interrupted a fragment of the giant picture of the whole, impressive world, it ruled and diminished me completely. At that very moment, I heard a voice say, "Oh, my, what are you doing here?"

"I'm too late," I thought dreamily, and I meant *to save myself.*

I opened my eyes and found a massive construction before me. The nun wore a heavy black habit with a heavy short coat and thick-soled black shoes. I thought to faint out of sympathy: she would be so hot her head would have to be swimming, but when she put her fingers to my shoulders, I could feel their coolness through my thin blouse. I wondered at the ring on her hand . . . did this mean she was married to God, and if so, did she have visions of His cheek against her thigh? I also wondered at the way the angles of her face so resembled the folds of her . . . whatever did you call a nun's hat? . . . the folds of her hat. And the folds of her hat reminded me of the origami swan I had made in art class, when I was still quite small. If this facial construction was a prerequisite for leaving one's family behind for the family of God, I'd never make it with my round stub of a nose.

"Oh," the Sister said. "You've been left behind."

It was amazing, I thought. She's practically like Melone; she so understands my own thoughts. I nodded.

"Well, let's see if we can catch you up."

I gave her a reverential stare. I didn't know such a thing was possible. I think she thought I was strange, and I guess I didn't blame her.

"Yes, yes," she said, more to herself than me, "let's just go upstairs and see if we can see them."

You can see them! I thought. My amazement was so complete, I felt even the tips of my toes were amazed.

"Up here," she said and beckoned for me to follow her, out of the classroom and up the stairs at the end of the hallway. "You can see practically everything." At the top of the stairs was a small office with a sloping ceiling. The Sister cupped her hands to her eyes and peered out the window. "There they are," she cried, and I joined her at the window, expecting to see wispy, flighty things in the air.

I pulled back, gave her a desperate, lost look. It was just one of those vacuous, blue skies you could see any morning on our island, a know-nothing sky, letting its occasional clouds cast dark shadows on the mountains.

"Why right there!" she said, and a thick, chapped finger tapped the window. Down below, snaking its way through the hill's curlicue road was a clot of artificial blues, greens and whites, speckled with a few points of black. The whole school and a handful of instructors making their way through the brush.

"Can you run?"

I nodded my head solemnly.

"Well, then go ahead," the Sister said. "It's not every day you get to visit the convent."

I did catch up with the others, though by the time I did, my feet were bleeding. It was an easy run, a run downhill after all, but, without shoes, a painful one, even though the path was mostly dirt with only a handful of stones sticking, resolutely, up into the air.

The girls were walking silently down the hill, and though they looked up when I joined their ranks from behind, they remained quiet, though I knew they possessed a knowledge the Sisters supervising their trip didn't have; they knew I didn't belong. A few jabbed their fingers in the air and pointed at me, but I paid them no mind. I was used to being a curiosity.

"These Sisters are excellent women," the apparent leader of the group said. Her name was Felicia, and she was dressed all in white. This seemed much more practical to me . . . particularly for a trip through the heat. Everything about her—the curves of her face, the very folds of her habit's fabric—seemed softer, more human, than the sharp habit I'd seen up on the hill. "How is it that they've reconciled the contradictions of the world?" Felicia was silent. I must have known her name because she'd once picked up an order at the bakery. Or maybe it was Divine inspiration. Either way, I was pleased. "Anybody know?" she tried again. "Ah, girls," she said, "I hope you've all read the material on the Sisters that I gave you."

"We did," someone chirped. She was clearly one of the younger girls, but her brisk, officious manner made me think of a fussy old woman, selecting the two or three most perfect almond horns to bring home to her family. "We did, but we didn't understand it."

"Yeah," said another, "why would anyone want to bash a nun's head in?"

"I believe . . ." Felicia interrupted.

"And *why* . . ." said another, "wouldn't her own family prepare a funeral for her? Were they afraid of the sight of the head?"

" . . . you're confusing," Felicia continued, "the material about the modern-day martyrs with . . ."

"It must have been bloody . . ."

"Girls," Felicia chided, and the assembled group quieted.

"When my papa was in the war," said a small girl with the pinched face of a midget, "he said he saw someone with his brains coming out of his ears."

"I think that's quite enough," Felicia said, and I shrank inside for the midget-faced girl who, being the last to speak, seemed to carry the burden of guilt for the whole of the conversation. "I think," Felicia continued, "*I'll* do some talking now." She stopped the whole group and said, "Sit down right here and close your eyes. We did as she said, sitting in the dirt and gazing up at her figure, which loomed impressively above us. "I want you to pretend you're not at school for a minute."

"Yey!" some of the girls shouted, as they shifted their weight on the floor of the old sugar cane field. The journey downhill was over, and now we had only the flat stretch of two fields and one forest to go through to get to the convent.

"And I want you to pretend you are walking down this road with your mother and father, and in your hand, I want you to feel a smooth cold coin your father has given you so you can buy some milk after church."

"My coin's kinda hot and sticky," said the same girl who had perused but not understood the assigned reading.

"Never mind that; you're not thinking about that coin, because as you walk into the city, you see two legs sticking straight up from a heap of trash. At first, you don't believe your eyes, that there could be a pair of pants and some scuffed up shoes, with a body in them, sticking straight up from the trash. Maybe it's a dead man, you think, but just as you think it, the legs start to kick."

"Oh," a few girls let out an obligatory gasp.

"And an old man climbs out from that hill of trash. He's filthy, of course. And he has a strange look to his face, like maybe he's crazy from hunger. He holds a cape around his shoulder, even though it has an entire egg yolk resting in one of the folds of the cloth. 'Little girl,' he calls to you. 'Will you help me?'"

"I would," offered one girl. I knew her for the way sugar would cake at her lips when she bought breakfast pastry at the store. She was always eating, and the more she ate, the more she looked like her own bones. My sisters named her for her appetite. "Here's Mad-for-Sweets again," . . . but never loud enough so she could hear. She had such an anxious, unhappy look on her face, even as she ate, that we all felt for her secret sorrow.

"Me too, I'd give the coin," said another.

"Sister Felicia . . ." the midget-faced girl called out, but Felicia talked right past her. "I'm glad to hear that. You can all open your eyes now. I have another question. Suppose your father prohibits you from going over to the old beggar. Suppose he says, 'That coin is for the week's supply of milk. You have no business giving it away to a lazy drunkard.' What will you do then? Will you honor your mother and father?"

Not a girl spoke.

"Let me see if I can help. Who was Elizabeth?"

I froze. How ever could she have known?

"Who was she, and what did she do?" Even if I were speaking in those days, I could never have opened my mouth, never have said, "She touched that soft part of my breast with the pads of her fingers."

"St. Elizabeth," a tiny girl from the back, so pale and glassy she looked as if she were made of porcelain, said, "is the mother of John, and *I* am Elizabeth, too. I was named for her."

"Very good, Liz," the Sister said.

"Sister Felicia," the midget-faced girl called again.

"I was thinking," Felicia said, "of Elizabeth of Hungary. Can you tell me about her?"

Elizabeth of the island was silent. She looked at her feet.

"Anybody?" Felicia said, her eyes touring the dark-haired heads spread before her, a bashful carpet of girls. "Oh, girls," she sighed in the kind of mock disappointment that let the gathered know she was *genuinely* dismayed but far too good even to dream of anger as a response. If she had asked us all to put pebbles in our mouths and suck the dirt off as we sat, gazing up at her standing figure, I don't think there was one of us who would have refused. Felicia cleared her throat, and then her voice switched and changed. "Elizabeth of Hungary," she declared, then her voice switched and changed again as if what she had to say next had to do with the ineffable and the ineffable meant your voice would have to lose its warmth, its power to connect with little girls. The voice of the ineffable could only be the personality-less voice of pronouncement.

"Elizabeth of Hungary, married at thirteen, dead at twenty-four, canonized in the year she would have been twenty-eight, was hated by her husband Louis's parents for her love of the poor. Though she needn't have done so, she lived like a pauper. Her in-laws didn't like this sort of behavior, and Louis, bound to his parents' wishes like a mindless barnacle to a shell, prohibited his wife from making her visits to the poor. One day, he caught her sneaking away with a bread basket. He knew where she was going. 'What's in there?' he said without a trace of love in his voice."

"Oh, Felicia," the midget-faced girl called in a panic.

"Don't interrupt," Felicia said gently, but the poor girl's head was swelling with tears, and her face was about to break. Some of the assembled turned their attention to her.

"When she revealed the contents," Felicia went on, "all the bread had turned to roses."

"And so he loved her," a voice from behind me shouted.

"And so," Felicia seemed not to have heard, "he understood his wife to be pious and knew that he would have to do as she did."

"And live in a pigsty," the same voice called.

"It's true," the nun said, broken from her reverie, "that when Louis was dead and buried in the dust, Elizabeth of Hungary was also banished to soil. In her case, the mud of a pigsty. Once her husband was dead and her evil in-laws could do as they pleased with her, they punished her for what they thought was her ugly love of paupers."

There were natural explanations for what happened next, no doubt, but how could anyone, even in this most secular of worlds, not see the necessity of a spiritual reading? Especially since events flew in the face of what we'd learned about weather in science class. The nuns might have anticipated the event—it being the start of hurricane season. They might have known weather would confound reason and nicely illustrate any point Felicia made that sunny morning. The young student who had been calling, "Felicia, Felicia," had seen what the rest of us had only felt in the dimming and greening of the light—something we either read in terms of the portentous nature of the Sister's words . . . or since we all lived on the island, as the daily noontime storm come a little early, even though sound didn't often stop before a storm. If we had been focusing, we would have realized . . . we would have noticed that outside Felicia's voice and the midget-faced girl's shy protests, one could hear nothing. The air was still, and even the animals knew to be quiet in the face of the funnel cloud that, from where I sat, could be perceived as emerging from the center of Felicia's head. *You can't have a tornado on an island,* I thought, but that seemed to make no difference to the tornado itself, as it spun darkly toward us.

"Look," the young girl finally shouted, and Felicia, fully broken from her trance, cried, "Oh, *Dios mío,*" then quickly collected herself. "Girls, I want you to run as fast as you can to the convent. You know where it is. It's the old Díaz plantation. As soon as you get there, go into the basement. Hurry. A holy card for the first ten girls there," she said, surprising me, at least, by this intrusion of capitalistic, competitive sentiment into Catholicism . . . but then America had come to our island in the oddest of ways that year. So the girls ran, and I ran too, trying to imagine what a holy card was.

It had long been a dream of mine . . . a night dream as well as a day wish . . . to see the interior of the colonial mansion on the Díaz plantation. In my dreams, I'd often find myself, by dint of crafty effort, inside the mansion. At last. But once there, I couldn't open my eyes, sealed shut with sleep, to see. Or in other dreams, I saw, but whatever I saw, was so horrible I shrieked . . . soundless screams that brought no help.

Now as we ran, the world seemed to whip itself up like an egg at the mercy of a furious fork, and I tried to keep my thoughts on my destination. Since the Europeans' first colonizing efforts, the old Díaz plantation had been cursed by plague and scandal. But then, at the turn of this youngest of all centuries, a young girl, Catilla, pregnant and just fourteen, had run to the abandoned house to live while she hid her shame. She grew wild, and soon people were calling her the Wolf. One night, Catilla the Wolf clawed through the wood of the door to the single locked room in the house, the one room she hadn't torn up with her fingers, now almost turned to claws. She found crisp, yellowed lace, the whispery sound of paper, thin as fly wings, rattling across the floor, and torn curtains. The Wolf came upon the room in the darkest of night, but she had brought a candle—she was no ordinary wolf—and with it she could see what moonlight wouldn't reveal. She wandered to the window and looked out, expecting to see the wasted sugar cane fields that lay behind the *hacienda.* Instead, the light from the flame gave the room back to her, a full reflection in the old panes of glass, but where she should have been in the picture, she found a face that was not her own. She squinted and leaned close, but her placid reflection did not do the same. That's when the Wolf realized she was looking at Mary Magdalene.

She did what any self-respecting girl, half-wild or not, did in those days. She fainted, and when she woke to morning light, her previously distended belly was flat as a pancake.

The Dominicans would have nothing of this story. They knew she'd thrown her stomach 103 times on the brass railing of the bed in that room, and they trusted the sudden reversal in the Wolf's state had not occurred without loss of blood. But the Wolf didn't care for the Dominicans anymore, for they could do nothing to explain the face she had seen. Others could. A flock of older women clustered around Catilla and proclaimed her a miracle. With their encouragement, Catilla succumbed to visions. She saw how some people's faces were stones cut by diamond and others were molded clay. She saw how you could have sympathy for the back of a woman's arm, how the island had secret lakes, aquifers, that fed the tears of adolescent girls. Bloated as she was with insight, she started her own convent in the old Díaz mansion, and though the Dominicans wouldn't recognize her, she proclaimed herself our island's first saint.

The small group of women who lived there now respected the Wolf completely. They called her Catilla and spoke of her as the small "m" mother of the people.

When we were all huddled in the dampness of the basement with the other Sisters and a giant can of peanuts, Felicia hushed the younger ones who were whimpering about their fathers, whom they imagined being scooped by the wind out of the fields and then tossed into the sea to die.

"Now, now," Felicia said. "We'll pray that everyone will be safe, and remember that if we hadn't been so captivated by the piety of little Elizabeth of Hungary, we might have been more alert to danger."

I thought the midget-faced girl would be insulted by this, but she glowed like a firefly in that dark basement. Perhaps she was an idiot.

"By the way, where is Betta?" said Felicia. She looked over the group and then stood up and yelled once, frantically, "Oh, Betta" and ran out of the cellar, presumably to find her. I jumped up and ran after her, grabbed the hem of her habit. She tugged the edge of the garment right out of my fist, and I was surprised to find such physical strength in a spiritual woman. I leapt for her again, and this time my hold was more tenacious. I threw my body against the steps and would not let go, and when I felt the fabric slipping from my left hand, I bit at a fold in the fabric while she screamed, "Child, you're crazy" and continued to run up the stairs. My chin bumped against each stair, and finally, when she bent to try one last time to push me away, my chin crashed into the hard stone that served as a top step to the basement stairs. I tasted blood then, and two teeth rattled in my head, as they did in my worst dreams.

It seemed I'd have to say my first words. "No, no," I yelled, and my two teeth dropped (like pearls, I thought, for no reason) out of my mouth. Even I was surprised at the animal-like growl of my voice over the gales of the storm. Then I tried again, croaked out a full sentence. "I'm Elizabeth," I said and followed Felicia into the wind. I wiped the back of my hand on my mouth and was shocked at the sight of my own blood. Already, it was clear the world was tornado absurd, as a mattress lay on top of the almond trees at the edge of the woods.

I heard the low mournful bleat of a cow and saw that it had found its home in the small gazebo the nuns apparently used as a shrine. It was in that short turn of my head to the gazebo that I lost sight of Felicia. I stepped further into the turmoil and tried to clarify my sentence. I knew I wasn't Elizabeth. I was just here in her place. It would take more than a sentence to explain, and though I think I spoke, I think I spoke honestly and clearly, the wind took the sound away so fast I couldn't hear my own words, any more than I could hear the cow whose mouth was now open though she was silenced by the rush of air about her and the sudden arrival of a broken-backed flamingo along her own still-intact vertebrae. I held on to a column on the front porch of the mansion and prayed for a wind to swing me toward the door, for though I was just inches from it, I could do nothing to move my body toward it till a gust of wind finally picked up my legs and threw them at the convent door, and I threw myself down the cellar stairs eager to save myself as quickly as possible. I wasn't thinking of the numerous bruises I would incur or the barrage of questions I couldn't answer. "Where's Felicia? Where's Felicia?" and finally, "Who are you?"

Don't we all know no properties genuinely inhere in any object? That anything can, under pressure, completely deny itself? At least that's how we explained the narrow twig that pierced Felicia's heart like a knife when it pinned her to a eucalyptus tree at the edge of the cane field. We found her with her eyes open in surprise, her mouth hanging, loose as her limbs, and I thought I could see that, with her last breath, she'd spoken the word she'd most wanted us to grasp that day. "Elizabeth." I saw how her last syllables were—more or less—my first. I thought about how she couldn't understand me when I said I was Elizabeth, but then I imagined she did understand, and in her last moments she was calling for help from the only one who could give it to her at that time. From me. And I'd killed her. I scratched these words in the dust, "I am the devil." I meant I felt *as if* I were the devil, but my hand shook so badly on those words that my stick couldn't even scratch them out. A few girls shrieked at the sight of my letters, but one of the Sisters came and put her arm around me and said, almost briskly, "Come now, we're all upset." I was instantly ashamed, as if I'd tried to claim for myself a grief greater than anyone else's . . . and wouldn't this, in of itself, be a form of vanity? The nun took me to a white closet, said "Why don't you rest here?" and locked me in.

I took the nun's question as the suggestion it was meant to be, and I sat silently on the floor of the small frescoed room. The world continued its dizzy spin; only now I was more a part of that world's trouble than ever before. I shut my eyes against my thoughts, and when I opened them, I looked around. There was a single step in the room. Two oily dark ovals punctuated its center. Kneecaps, I knew, and placed my own narrow knees, one by one, over the prints. Positioned so, I was face-to-face with a stone relief of the Madonna, pressing the baby Jesus to her cheek. Throughout the closet, there were other images of the Madonna and Child at different stages in life. It was, I thought, not knowing everything I hoped to about Christianity, like a photo album in stone. There was a bust of the Madonna as a young woman. Didn't she look serene? There was Jesus, now a young man, and there were some of his disciples. And there, sad to say, was the cross; there was no way to avoid thinking it: the sculptural equivalent of a snapshot of a funeral.

I banged on the door and called for the nun to let me out. Getting no reply, I turned to pry open a small door, almost rusted shut, underneath what I took to be a prayer table. I was still hoping vaguely for escape, though I knew I was clawing at a door that led to a storage area.

Once I had the door open, my single desire was to hide in that small space filled with nothing but cobwebs and a single water-stained book. But a sudden flapping sound, as if of a bat, made me bang the door shut.

I sat still and wondered about that book. A Bible, I guessed, but couldn't be sure, so I stared at the small door, willing whatever lived behind it to go to sleep. I pressed my ear to the door's wood. I pressed so hard white flakes of paint fell, like petal blossoms, into my ear. Who knows how long I stayed like that? Eventually, the silence from the other side gave me courage. I opened the door and grabbed for the book. Imagining flying rodents following my arm back out of the closet, I pressed the door tightly shut, digging my back up against it to keep it closed.

In my lap, the book was dusty, covered in cracked red leather. The edges of its pages crumbled, like pastry, at my touch. I flipped through and saw that the whole volume was written in longhand, with strokes so elegant and shapely I had an urge to touch them. Maybe Saint Catilla had written it! I turned to the front page and saw the date "1765." "Oh," I said, almost out loud, for it was older than the nuns, older than Catilla. It must have been written when the convent was still a plantation. I read the first sentence: "People died, and yet the graveyards were empty." I slammed the book shut, for it seemed to describe the scene I'd just witnessed. *But how could it?* I thought. It was written over two hundred years ago. Still, people *were* dead and the graveyards *were*, as yet, empty.

Then I knew that I had more evil in me. This murderous day had brought me to this book, and I was willing to steal to get to whatever wisdom it contained. But that was all, I thought: the last bad act I was going to allow myself. I tucked the book in my skirt waistband and rearranged my blouse over the square bulge. *Now*, I told myself, as I knocked on the door and politely asked the nun to let me out, *I would . . . I would . . . have to convert.* There was nothing else for me to do.

So on the day of my fifteenth birthday I decided that if they would have me, I would take steps to join the order. As soon as Felicia had been buried and the island's clean-up had begun. Once sugar cane was wiped off the city's balconies and chests of drawers left the stables, when you couldn't find a wagon wheel in the church, or an almond-paste cake, roses intact, at the foot of the statue that graced one of our city's plazas. When everything was set right, I would begin.

But I didn't begin, though I did start talking. It turned out attending to my spiritual life came in the same category as cooking bacon for my sisters. It was something I wanted to do but could not. In some ways, it was like what I'd always thought about talking: the danger of doing it wrong—praying to false idols, undercooking bacon so worms grew in my sisters' stomachs—was too great.

After the Storm

(Melone—May 1978)

The wreckage from the storm was tremendous. But not on our island. The significant damage—all those household treasures sunk in mud, couches upended in birdbaths, that sort of thing—was limited to neighboring islands to the south and west. Still, we weren't spared completely. A tornado, spun off from the hurricane, cut a narrow, hysterical path through the plains and jumped off into the sea. People who knew about these things said it couldn't have been a tornado, that a tornado needs a large stretch of land to whip itself into such a frenzy. Nonetheless, some wind, funneled or not, tore through the island, sheared the earth like God's mad, lazy lawn mower, clipping a single, twisted row. Everything else was the way it had always been.

Such destruction, random yet focused, put people in a speculative mood. It was worrisome—an entire town of people acting like a farmer who wakes one morning to find his drought-ridden fields under the edge of a cloud. It's storming on his land, while his neighbor's sugar cane is dipped in dust. The farmer feels blessed, which means he's on the path to self-righteousness, busy figuring out his neighbor's faults and his own virtues; he's looking for the obvious reason for Divine intervention. On the island, we were doing the same, tallying up the flaws of those who had fallen victim to the tornado's winds. It wasn't an easy task, since according to the earliest reports, the single victim was a broad-boned nun, and the only building that looked worse for wear was the convent. There was that and some grassland, two cows and one flamingo.

"Well," said Melissa Muñoz, a friend of my father, whom we all called Coco, "it wasn't like the hurricane. I can tell you that. Now, *that* was something." Her husband, Victor, nodded his head solemnly.

"Goddammit," my father said. "Goddammit." He was considering the reports about the death of the nun. But we'd moved past her, on to other victims of other disasters. We wanted to hear what Coco had to say.

"I was just a girl in high school when the hurricane hit."

"So," Tata tapped the table and said, almost impatiently, "so . . . tell us."

"What do you want to know?" Coco said. It would have seemed coquettish on another person, but not on Coco. She had a prideful personality that included frankness and, at the same time, excluded disclosure.

"Well, *what* hurricane?" Tata said.

"What hurricane?" Coco said, disgusted. " '32. What other?"

"The big one," I said and smiled at Tata.

I didn't doubt she was doing what I was doing . . . mentally computing Coco's age. It was a fact we'd never been able to pry loose from her. "Ladies don't," she'd told us. It wasn't as if we had any doubts that she was a lady. Things about our Aunt Coco were never confusing, even though she wasn't really our aunt but the childless wife of Uncle Victor, also no real relation. Victor was my father's business partner, and we accepted the two of them as relations merely because it was their wish.

"The storm, the storm," Tata said, prodding Coco, for we were all sunk into our after-lunch laziness, no one really concentrating on the conversation as much as the final crumbs of birthday cake on the table before us. The bakery had been closed for the afternoon so Rayovac and Carla could go help with the storm clean-up.

Coco picked up some crumbs of cake with the pad of her finger. She placed her finger thoughtfully in her mouth. "We were in the cafeteria, of course. With the water rising." She wiped her hands on her napkin. "We stood on the tables and put the babies in the rafters. The water rose to our necks. If it had risen any farther," she said and then stopped, midsentence. "But then it didn't. It got to our necks, and it got no farther."

Victor looked uncomfortable, the way he always did when our talk turned to the sadder facts of the world. He had a peculiar habit of telling silly riddles and jokes to adults, as if they were small children, still capable of being saved by magic or, at the very least, magic tricks.

"Where's the other pea in your pod?" he asked me.

"Beatriz? I don't know. It's not like her to miss her own cake." I pointed at the table in front of us, and when nobody added anything, I said, "Still dawdling at school, I guess." I said it childishly perhaps because I was lying—Beatriz had skipped school that day—but also because Victor always had this effect on me. His silliness never diminished him, only the person to whom he spoke. It was an odd thing, because I knew it was unintentional on his part. He was enormously generous, embarrassingly so. When we were little, he would always come for visits with bags of toys. "Oh boy!" he would say to my sisters and me. "Have I got presents for you. Presents, presents, presents." It made me sick at heart to say, "How nice to see *you*," cast as I was, already, as a greedy child. I'd try to be thankful while showing I cared nothing for the material things of this world. It was a dizzying effort, and one made on a stomach that had been left, purposefully, empty, for in the evening Victor and Coco took us to opulent hotel restaurants. Everything done "for the girls." More treats. It was hard not to feel ashamed, not to want to smile guiltily at the waiter and make sure he saw your fingernails, sooty from garden work.

"I don't get it," Tata said. "Where's the story? You could always swim. You could have always gone out onto the roof. Right?"

Coco tended to ignore Tata when she spoke. She thought Tata was too much of a child, a status I, apparently, did not share with my sister, though no one could deny we shared an age.

"Right?" Tata said again.

Coco breathed heavily. Her whole chest rising and falling.

"Oh, it's the damnedest thing," Tata said, to no one in particular. "I think I'm talking. I'd swear to God I was, and yet no one can hear me. It must be," she said, in a tone of mock reasonableness, "the beginning of my descent into madness." She gave a sort of monster laugh.

"Tata," my father said sharply.

"Tata, what?"

"Don't you dare. Don't you dare speak to your aunt that way." He was capable of a truly vicious tone of voice, and he was using that tone now.

"Well, the thing is," Tata leaned, conspiratorially, over the table, "she doesn't seem to be able to hear anything I say."

My father stood up so fast I didn't see him stand. "Go to your room."

"I think I'm a bit too old to be sent to my room."

I thought she had a point. Today was our birthday, after all. We were fifteen. In fact, Coco and Victor were here for an after-school celebration.

"Easy," Victor said. "Easy."

"Come on, come on," I added my own voice. "It's nothing. Not worth getting upset about."

Coco was silent. She was a woman who never needed to be defended but who knew, if and when she did, a gentleman would come to her aid. This is all to say she was quietly twisting a fork between her forefinger and thumb when my father stepped around the table and grabbed Tata's forearm and pulled her up, sending her chair scattering backward, like a giant wooden spider with too many legs for coordinated flight.

"Sandrofo," Victor stood up himself.

"Stop it. Stop it," Coco said, and I echoed her words.

"You spoiled brat," my father yelled. "Spoiled, selfish brat."

"What the *hell* are you talking about?" Tata yelled back, while trying, without any luck, to shake herself free.

"Sandrofo," Victor repeated, evenly. His voice always commanded respect, seemed to insist he was the kindly patriarch of the room.

My father threw Tata's arm down in disgust. There were tears in her eyes—how could there not be?—and her voice was breaking, but she was not one to back down. "Sometimes," she said, "you are the biggest jerk." She stepped noisily to the door.

Not a one of us spoke till we could hear her—first through the wall and then through the ceiling—going up the stairs to our apartment. "Well," Coco said, though her voice was flat, her meaning impossible to decipher.

"She is just acting like any kid would," I said to my father, as if her slight rudeness needed to be decoded for him. To me, there seemed nothing peculiar in my doing this.

"My kids," my father faced me to say, "are not like any other kids." I thought of how he always joked that he was a misanthrope, that he didn't like people, especially children, though his own offspring were exceptions to the rule.

Victor turned to me and smiled benevolently. "Where's the other pea in your pod?"

"I can't say," I said, smiling like a half-wit. "I can't say I know."

"Tic-tac-toe," he said, pulling a napkin to him. An elegant pen emerged from his breast pocket.

"Sure," I said. "You first."

"No, no, no," he said. "You first."

After the game, I stepped upstairs to comfort my sister.

I was only fifteen, but already I thought I knew the world, its curious ways, and I felt absolutely secure in the correctness of my responses to things. I wasn't the only one. Each of us—Tata, Beatriz and myself—was privately haughty. The result of too many compliments from my father and our teachers about the quickness of our brains, the charm of our occasional fits of timidity. What I mean is: when I stepped up the stairs to our apartment, when I moved, quickly and importantly into my bedroom, I was already fantasizing about the maturity of my response. I was the first born, after all, though I know, in cases of multiple births, that is not saying much. But an idea is *not* an emotion, though I know some people feel otherwise, and I felt my status to be significant. I was going to take care of the matter.

"Tata," I pushed into our bedroom and sat down on her bed. She was lying face down, her head buried in the white flesh of her pillow. "Tata," I repeated, gently. "Listen, they didn't mean . . ."

"Oh, just you shut up," she leapt to a seated position.

"Hey," I said, calm as could be. "I think you're right."

"They hate me." She meant Coco and Victor.

"Oh, they do not," I said.

"They hate me, because I'm not a little lady," she said and swung her legs over the side of the bed, so she could sit up in mock primness.

"They're just too far away from you is all. They couldn't understand you when you were a kid, and they have a little trouble noticing that *any* of us isn't eight years old."

Tata softened at this. "But they *like* you, and they *like* Beatriz."

"Because we were quiet," I said. "Well, *I* was quiet. And Beatriz . . ." I shrugged and rolled my eyes.

The truth was that, as children, Beatriz and I had acted like miniature adults. At least, this had been our aim. We both had had trouble with childhood, with acting kid-like. Tata was different, though, and sometimes I envied her ability to just *be* what she was supposed to be, not busy racing ahead to some higher rung on the maturation ladder. Beatriz must have felt this way too, because now that she was moving toward adulthood, she was starting to act sillier and sillier. She had a little knit zebra puppet she would put on her hand. Then, she'd run around the house and kiss everyone's ears with her fingertips, the zebra's nose.

"Well, I wasn't quiet, and I'm not quiet, and I'm not going to be quiet."

"Who said you should be?" She sniffed her nose in anger at me. "Listen, your argument's not with me."

"I suppose," she said and was quiet for a bit. "But they do hate me, you know. You've *got* to admit that."

"I do?" I said, but there wasn't much force behind the question. They *didn't* seem to like Tata. Coco always acted as if she were a noisy animal and would sometimes start back from some sudden movement Tata made, as if she couldn't trust Tata not to tip her over, to leave her flat out on her back like a poor beetle unable to flip itself over.

"And the thing that gets me," Tata said "is he sides with them. I mean, I'm his daughter. I'm his real relation."

"He doesn't side with them, Tata."

"Of course, he does."

"No, he doesn't." On this I was firm, for I was certain that my father's sympathies were ultimately with us.

"Yeah," she said. "I guess."

I felt an odd little thrill. I always did when I won a point from Tata.

"You know," I said, "with them it is just a politeness. Manners mean a lot to him, but he loves you."

She shook her head. My father had told us, since we were small, how important we were, how much he loved us. But sometimes I thought my father may have done us real damage by telling us this so often and not simply acting as if he loved us, for the plain fact was he was an impatient man and often seemed bored or irritated with us.

"Yeah, I know, I know," Tata said tiredly, not quite able to summon up the argument she needed.

Part of the problem, I suspect, was it was clear what my sisters and I were to each other, but it was not entirely clear what we were to him. For a long time, I thought I was his favorite, although who knew what that meant? Certainly he knew enough never to suggest such a thing—that he had an order of preference—but I always felt I had an honored spot, function of being the first one out of the womb. Either that or the fact I was, as he apparently had been, the best student at school.

Just then, we heard steps on the stairs. Tata wiped her face off and straightened her clothes, but it was Beatriz, not our father, who came through the bedroom door. She looked, as always, distracted and messy. Her chin was smudged, and she was wearing some oversized shirt that she must have just found at a consignment shop. Her hair, flying about her head, seemed like a handful of wings, desperately trying to lift her off the ground. Instinctively, I smoothed my own hair against my head. Beatriz was clutching an old, dusty book to her chest.

"Hey," Tata said, "what's that?"

"Yeah," I said, "where you been, birthday girl?"

At that, Beatriz burst into tears, and I felt the sort of instant irritation I always felt when Beatriz was sad. I loved Beatriz as much as Tata. In many ways I knew her better. So well, in fact, I could read her mind—not because I am telepathic; I just could tell what she was thinking. Even so, while I relished cheering Tata up and felt proud at my ability to do so, cheering Beatriz was a chore. Once she was sad, her mood never lightened, and it never seemed I had made enough of an effort to help her. The very sight of her slumped shoulders—a sure sign of a low mood—would make me want to rage.

Later that night, Beatriz turned to us at dinner and said, "I am such a bad person," and we, so surpised by sound coming from her mouth, ignored her words, while we celebrated the fact of them.

"She's talking," Tata said.

"Beatriz said something," I said.

"She's got a beautiful voice," Maria Elena allowed.

Someone, I knew, should say, "No, no, you're not a bad person," but I kept quiet. It was as if, early in our preteen years, she had squandered a lifetime supply of comfort, and now I had to scrape away to produce one more spoonful from my heart.

A Private Life

(Maria Elena—June 1978)

It's arrogant, I suppose, to imagine I'm responsible for her starting to talk, but there were so many reasons to think so. Not long after she began speaking, Beatriz found me making *tostones* in the kitchen. She knew I had been asking her sisters to tell me about their lives, so she said, "I have to tell you about me." Her voice was still so new that it came scratchily out of her throat. "But you have to know, before I begin, that I'm a murderer."

I heard Melone yelp from the other room, then say, half-joking, "You'd think you wouldn't want to tell someone who was silent for fifteen years to shut up, wouldn't you?"

"Melone," I called out a reproach, as I folded a bit of brown paper bag over a plantain and ground the heel of my hand into the counter. I wiped my greasy palm on a napkin.

"She starts talking, and what do we learn? We learn she's a kook. Not that anyone ever thought anything else."

"Oh, you shut up," Beatriz called back. "You think you know so much." Her face darkened and twisted. She wore her emotions on her body. Like clothes, I used to think, but once I knew her, I felt otherwise. At first, Beatriz had seemed less sensual than her sisters. She hugged with concave chest, afraid to let her breasts touch another's. When I went to kiss her cheek, she flinched. But then I saw how physical her emotions were. Grief made her hair limp with exhaustion. Joy turned her limbs elastic with happiness. Emotion seeped out of her. It puddled at her feet, and her sisters, when they stepped in it, got angry. Why should the weather of her moods rule their days?

"Beatriz," I said now. "Let's talk privately. Why don't you come to the gallery tomorrow? You can come after school and say what you want to say."

"Good," Melone called—her tone still light, as if she didn't really mean what she was saying, though it was clear she did. "Keep it out of the house."

But Beatriz didn't come to see me. In fact, as soon as she started to talk, she began keeping to herself, ignoring her afternoon hours at the bakery and excusing herself early from dinner. "Homework," she said once, belligerently, to her sisters and father and let that single word explain her retreats to the narrow second-floor balcony, the one that led off the girls' bedroom. On any day, I could walk by the bakery and see her up there, sitting above La Madeleine's sign. Her hips would be wedged between the balcony's black railing and the building's door-length shutters. A book would be balanced on her thighs.

"*What* homework?" Tata finally asked. "What homework does she have that we don't?"

Melone shrugged, and Tata threw open the balcony's shutters and said, "So what's this *home*-work?"

Startled, Beatriz clasped two hands over her book, and even from the hall, where I stood watching all this, the gesture seemed desperate—less like a girl shielding her diary from her sisters than a virgin hiding her nakedness from a stranger.

"What *is* that?" Tata said.

Beatriz closed the volume, bound in cracked red leather, and pressed it to her chest. "Nothing. It's nothing."

"It's something," Tata said. "I know 'cause I'm looking right at it."

"It's none of your business that's what it is."

"Oh, come on," Melone said. "Let's see."

"No, leave me alone."

"Beatriz," Melone said and extended her arm, as if she expected Beatriz to put the book in her hand.

"It's private," Beatriz said.

"Oh, private," Tata said, as if the word itself were ridiculous, and I saw, for them, it always had been. They shared a father, a bedroom, a face. They'd often shared thoughts. Always secrets. What meaning could the word possibly have in the context of this family? "Well, who wants to read your dumb book anyway?" Tata said, turning back to the bedroom.

"Hi." I called, waving, embarrassed to be caught listening, but Tata didn't care.

"*Pri*-vate," she muttered once more in disgust.

Two days later, Beatriz *did* come by the office above the gallery to tell me why she thought she had murdered a nun.

"Beatriz," I said when I'd heard her through, learned about where she'd been and what she'd done on the day of the tornado, "Beatriz, that was an accident, that had nothing to do with you."

"No," she said, in a panic, "didn't you hear what I just told you? About how I stole the skirt and prevented Betta from going to school? If she had been at school, the nun would never have gone out in the storm, and if I had made myself clear, she would never have died and . . ."

"Honey," I said and got up to stroke her head. "You can't think that way. You're stretching the facts to fit your idea of what happened. It was an accident."

"No, no," Beatriz said. "You don't see." She started to cry.

"But I do, I do," I said. "I know what you're thinking—honestly, I do—but you're just not looking at things in the right way." I couldn't figure out how to comfort her, though I didn't doubt I understood her. Beatriz needed systems, cosmologies. That's why she gazed so eagerly at churches and cathedrals. She loved the promise the buildings seemed to offer; they would order the ineffable. I was the same way. Didn't I need something—a job or, in the past, a political party—to tell me what to do? Didn't I need, I thought, a marriage? But I shook this thought away and said, "Beatriz, this book you found at the convent . . . is that the red book you've been reading out on the balcony?"

"No, no, you don't see," she said.

"Beatriz. Please trust that I know what you are feeling . . ." I started, then stopped. I looked at the mask of her face. Why should she trust me?

There was no true way of knowing another's thoughts. I glanced out the window at the passersby, at their heads full of ideas that would never reveal themselves. All that inaccessible wealth hidden behind sweaty pores, within ungainly egg-shaped masses. How exhausting. How much easier to imagine I was the only person who *had* thoughts. "Beatriz, let me change the subject. Tell me about that book. It sounds like it might be interesting."

"It's a . . . I haven't read it yet. I thought I should wait."

"For what?"

"The right day."

"Oh," I said. "OK. I'd love to see it if . . ."

"No," she said sharply. "No, I don't think that would be right."

"OK," I said. "OK."

"What?!" she said. Apparently, my acquiesence shocked her.

"'OK,' I said. I said, 'OK.'" She blinked twice in disbelief. I checked my watch and said, "Listen, honey, I have to go back to work, but we can finish this conversation later, all right?" Beatriz nodded her head and stood for home.

At the door, she turned and said, "You're the only one I've told, you know?" I nodded my head, told her I was flattered that she'd taken me into her confidence. "Well," Beatriz paused and then said, hesitantly, "I'll go." I waved her a good-bye, then went downstairs to the gallery, where I repeated the whole of the conversation to Lucia, stopping only when I'd come to Beatriz's final puzzled look, her gaze that had seemed, for a moment, indistinguishable from terror.

"Sure," Lucia said. "Of course, she'd be frightened. She's never had anything to herself."

"Of course," I said. "You're absolutely right." The point seemed so obvious I wondered at not having considered it.

It was near closing time, and as we spoke, Lucia passed a broom over the gallery's floor, and I filed the last of the afternoon's correspondence.

"You know that girl. I think you should take her to Perez, initiate her in the mysteries."

"Maybe," I said. "Or a linguist."

"A what?" Lucia stopped her broom and gave me a funny look.

"I just think maybe Beatriz's hyperbole, you know, it might be about language. She just might not know how to use subtle phrases, so 'good' is automatically 'heavenly.' 'Bad' is 'evil.'"

"*Ay*," Lucia said, tossing the dust pan with a loud clatter into the back of the utility closet. "What's happening to you? It's this man. You used to believe."

I'd always been a believer, it's true, but now I had something else to believe in: my new family and their concerns. I felt too that these days Beatriz could do the believing for both of us, and there would still be a surfeit of faith.

"You owe it to the girl," Lucia said, "to help her with her talents. You don't ignore a gift like this."

"What I owe her, I think, is her own bedroom. That's what I owe them all, a chance for a private life."

"Yeah, well," Lucia said, shaking her keys from her skirt pocket, getting ready to lock up, "that too."

I knew it was time to get serious about finding a place to live. It was the one clear thing to do for Beatriz since Lucia had rejected the idea of a linguist, I'd rejected the idea of a mystic, and Beatriz, when I'd suggested it, had flatly refused to see a psychiatrist. So that weekend, I told Sandrofo I thought we should start looking in earnest for our future home. He agreed, said, "You're right. Why wait for the wedding?" and the next week, he put the whole thing in motion, setting up appointments at the bank and finding a real estate agent. From the start, we decided to keep the house search from the girls. Our own anxiety about the move—and the money required for it—was tremendous, and it seemed wise not to be so apparently frightened in front of the children.

"A premature honeymoon," I told Sandrofo of the day trips we took to find a place. "Don't you think?"

He had to say yes, for we drove off with meat pies, iced tea and condoms. A kind of a test. Each time we'd ask: Was this a house we wanted to explore more than each other? The answer was no, again and again, and we fled the real estate agent for the nearest hidden spot—a car seat, an unpopulated beach, a particularly leafy stretch of bushes. Sometimes, desperate, we even paid for an hour at a *parador.* I lost track of our purpose and, after several unsuccessful efforts, barely cared that we weren't finding a home; I was stupid with sex, my limbs hollow with desire. The gallery, Lucia, the girls: all just interruptions to my real life, the one that took place after the words, "No, it's not for us" came from Sandrofo's moist throat. Weeks passed this way till Sandrofo rang me up at the gallery and said, "I found it. I found the place. Our love life . . . it's over."

"Really? That's wonderful," I said, twisting the phone cord around my arm.

"Well," Sandrofo said in a low, sexy voice, "not exactly wonderful."

"Oh, no," I said. "I didn't mean that, but where? What?"

Sandrofo cleared his throat and said, "Well, first, it's damaged but . . ."

"But, no, no, that's OK. I mean if it's the place, we'll work on it."

"And it's big. I mean, very big."

"But we want big, right? How big? I mean, you know I'm not much of a housekeeper and—"

"Well, very. But it's affordable, you know, because of the damage. I mean, I don't know, but, financially, I think, with a loan, you know, we'll be able to do it."

"And two incomes," I said, my refrain for the length of the house search, "remember we have two incomes."

"Well, you remember the place that the Catillan sisters had. They had to vacate after the tornado hit because half the building could no longer be used. The remaining half is safe but too small for the nuns, so they're selling it as residential—"

"Um, no, no," I interrupted. "I don't think that's a good place."

"Why? You haven't even—"

I stopped him. What could I do? Beatriz had sworn me to secrecy about the nun, and I wasn't about to break my vow. At the same time, I knew the convent was a painful place for her, and I had no intention of even looking at it. "I just . . . . I don't know, a convent. It gives me the creeps."

"Well, it wasn't always a convent. You'll see. It was built as a *ha-*

cienda. Listen, just come with me. I've already set up the appointment, so just look. It doesn't mean we have to buy it."

"OK," I said. Why object to reason? "OK."

We drove out early the next morning, before work. The road there was a washboard, torn up by rains and left unrepaired. Off it, we crossed one of those zipper-toothed stone bridges the Spaniards built, years ago, over the island's deep ravines. Then, we turned down a drive that was completely red; flame trees were planted on either side and were in full, bloody bloom. Finally, we saw the convent, and I fell into a sort of rapture that was just like love. It was a colonial place—not unlike the buildings in old San Juan but without the gaudy shops. The face of the building was a rosy stone; the eyes of the windows were lashed with dark shutters.

The real estate agent—the overly powdered, red-haired, stupid woman whose name I could never remember—waved to us from the side of the drive. "Here, here," she called, as if there were another house nearby and we might accidentally go to it.

"Inside," she said, shuffling us through the front door. "Señor Lucero, I can guarantee your pleasure with this particular property." She had an irritating habit of addressing her comments only to Sandrofo, and I'd decided to respond by pretending she didn't exist.

We stepped through the front door into a long hallway. "To the right," the agent said, "the parlor. It's where the nuns usually pray. They're off now. A constitutional, whatever that means. They won't be back till noon, though one of them is sick, sleeping, so we'll miss that room. You don't mind?" Sandrofo shook his head, and we stepped into the parlor. I immediately understood why the nuns had selected a *hacienda,* owned at one time by a corrupt government official, for their place of worship. The room had an undeniably liturgical feel. With its creamy, thickly plastered walls, its red tile floors and its windows trimmed in gold, the place looked like a cathedral. Up above, two weighty chandeliers, each consisting of two iron wagon wheels rimmed with electric lights, made me think of dark monks holding candles.

"Why's there a hammock here?" Sandrofo asked.

I followed his gaze to the corner of the room, where an ancient hammock was suspended.

The agent shrugged. "I don't know. Never seen one indoors before." I immediately imagined the nuns in their habits, swinging back and forth on it. I could picture one of them looking about, making sure she was alone and then gleefully crying, "Wheee!" as she flung her body toward the ceiling. "Come," the agent said. "The kitchen is down this way. There's a porch off it that looks out toward the back and a breakfast room that looks out toward the front."

Off the kitchen was a beautiful white sitting room. Stone arches cut into one of its walls and opened onto a courtyard paved with red and yellow tiles. The kitchen led to a slate porch that faced the woods and a tiny gazebo. The gazebo was surrounded by star apple trees, and when we stood in the center of it, we could see a quote from Cervantes printed along the inner cornice: "Every man is as Heaven made him, and sometimes a great deal worse."

Upstairs, even with the damage that had left half the building uninhabitable, there were enough rooms for each of the girls to have her own bedroom. And each room looked south over fields or north over a valley stuffed with mango, avocado and breadfruit trees.

Outside, beyond the sugar, coffee grew, and I thought of the uncultivated fields that ringed my childhood home in Cidra. They'd held tobacco at one time—I remembered how the first planting was always done under mosquito netting—but had gone, in recent years, completely over to beef cattle. Here, the other three sides of the *hacienda* were surrounded by forest. From the second floor, Sandrofo and I could see over the green of the trees to the blue of the sea. If there was a frustration about the place, it was the frustration of not being able to walk out of the house and into that blue. There was some water at the edge of the woods, but it was a sluggish river, not really swimmable since it was chocked with hyacinth.

Ordinarily, such a grand house was well beyond what we could afford, but Sandrofo was right: the nuns were selling the place cheap. The real estate agent told us they had hoped to get more money, but few people were willing to accept such beauty along with such ruin—half the rooms were filled with rubble. The tornado hadn't actually hit the building but touched down on nearby trees, which struck the roof. Then beams fell in on the second-story bedrooms, and this weight had collapsed the top floors into unlikely slides to the first. With an engineer's help, the building had been split in half, with the damaged part left to rot. Animals were already making their homes in the ruined rooms. In fact, as we made our way back to the car, a confused goat with a broken hip hobbled out and greeted us.

Despite what I knew about Beatriz's experiences at the convent, I couldn't quite bring myself to say no to the place or to reject my sense of relief at having possibly found a home. I kept my feelings to myself, however, pretended I didn't like the *hacienda.*

"But, why?" Sandrofo said when we were strapped into the car and heading for old San Juan.

I couldn't think of a reason, so I finally said, "I think it needs another . . . bedroom. For guests."

Sandrofo gave me an odd look. "We never have guests."

"I know but . . ."

"And anyway, there *is* another bedroom," Sandrofo said, grinning. "Remember? The agent didn't show it to us because someone was sleeping in it, but. . . ." Sandrofo did a U-turn on the highway. I clutched my seat. "But I'm sure we can stick our head in."

I looked at him, amazed. "Such enthusiasm," I said.

"I just . . . this house, I just love it," he said. "I want to convince you."

So we drove back, back down the flame-red drive, and this time, with no real estate agent to show us around, we simply slipped off our shoes and walked silently through the house. "I guess she has the flu," Sandrofo whispered, "the one who's here." I nodded my head and followed him up a set of stone stairs, past the bedrooms I'd already seen, to a closed door. Sandrofo cracked the door open and placed his finger against his lips. "Quiet," he whispered, but I gasped anyway. It was the white bedroom of Beatriz's story, the one the so-called Wolf had found when she was still pregnant. "There's a little room off the back of this bedroom," Sandrofo said, still keeping his voice hushed. "You can't see it from this angle, but it's a . . ." Sandrofo stopped to smile at this, "it's a prayer closet. A tiny room with a small round window up by the ceiling and artwork all around."

I nodded but felt frightened, for as Beatriz had told me her story about her day at the convent and what she knew about the convent's history, I had, as one invariably does, a picture in my head—a picture of the girls she told me about, of the school she visited, of the pseudo-saint the convent was named after and of the convent itself. When I saw the white bedroom in the *hacienda,* it looked so much like the room I had imagined that I felt I had, with Beatriz's narrative help, created it myself. The feeling was creepy, made me think for a moment that the world really was, horribly enough, an extension of my thoughts.

Because Beatriz had me in her confidence, I could not, of course, explain to Sandrofo why I was still hesitant about the house he so loved. An extra bedroom, after all. "I'll convince you," he said, taking my hand and walking me back out of the convent. He must have been thinking I had qualms about the ruined half of the building, about not living closer to the sea.

"No," I said, when we were back outside, the morning breeze rippling our clothes. "I'll convince myself," for I knew I had to say yes to the home, yes to Sandrofo's enthusiasm.

"You will?" Sandrofo said and circled his arms around my lower back, held his torso away from me so he could gaze, approvingly, at my face.

"Yes," I said, nodding my head. "Consider it done."

And, by that evening, it was.

I took the rest of the morning off, went and sat in the back of San Juan Cathedral and thought hard about the day of the tornado. I rehearsed the details of Beatriz's experience. The horrible thing in Beatriz's story was the death of the nun; technically, that had not happened in the *hacienda* but in the woods near the *hacienda.* If we mapped out the geography of that day, we'd find a number of places we couldn't live, and I knew that was something we couldn't do. I knew this because, after my own sister died, I had tried to avoid places and things that reminded me of her. Soon enough, the effort proved foolish; the problem was my brain, and there was no avoiding that. Plus, given our many years together, I quickly found myself with nowhere on the island to go.

Later, as I sat at work, wondering how we would ever tell Beatriz about the *hacienda,* I continued to think of all this. I argued fiercely with myself, even shaking my head a few times and with such force that Lucia called over from her desk, told me to stop talking to myself, I was scaring off visitors. For all my conviction that I was doing the right thing, that I couldn't put a life together based on avoiding places associated with bad memories, I couldn't help feeling regret. I thought of my own sister and her youthful nightmares. For years, Sisa had believed the content of her dreams to be related to her slumbering posture. One bad dream and she said she could no longer sleep on her back. Another and she could no longer face the wall. Soon she was sleeping like a contortionist with her right toe toward the floor, her arms hugging her hips, her eyes trained on the left corner of the room.

That memory in my head, I called Sandrofo at the bakery and said, "Let's take it. Let's take the house."

Sandrofo cried out, a sound of boyish pleasure I'd never heard him make before. "Wonderful. I'll start putting the papers together today."

"Great," I said. "Great."

"I love you," he said and hung up.

Good, I thought, *that's settled,* but then I remembered something else, something I had forgotten until just that moment. *How is it,* I wondered, *that these things allow themselves to be buried from consciousness?* I went to the gallery's bathroom, sat down on the toilet seat and wept as I recalled how, in college, I had finally made some comment to Sisa about her sleeping postures. I'd teased her gently but also pointed out that fear was constricting and avoiding danger left one with no way to be in the world. Once I'd said this, Sisa changed her ways. She gave up the whole project of avoiding danger. She walked alone in parks after dark, swam right after eating, bought bloated tin cans of soup. And she forgot—I remembered it all now—she completely forgot, her insulin.

Moving

(Beatriz—October 1978)

Papi explained how Victor and Coco had made it all possible. Tata, Melone and I said, "Thank you," in unison, though we didn't know what "it all" was yet. We were sitting in deck chairs around the pool at the Caribe Hilton, a luxurious place that always made me uncomfortable. I wanted to crawl through my own mouth and leave my skin behind on the chair. I would come back, years later, when economic decline had turned the place into a welfare hotel. Then, I wouldn't mind sitting there. Now, the adults were drinking piña coladas—an embarrassing drink, as far as I was concerned. I smiled at the waiter when they ordered the concoctions. He knew, I believed, that I knew better. All of us were eating stale banana chips out of small brown bowls. The air was sweet with the fragrance of tourists, fresh from an evening shower and ready for dinner.

Victor and Coco stayed here a lot, and when they did, they often had my family over for dinner. In fact, we'd never been to their "real" house. When we were younger, Victor used to invite my sisters and me to come play bingo by the side of the pool. Once I won and bought him a paperweight with my earnings. He still thanked me for it, although I must have given it to him ten years ago.

Victor liked to put his New York business associates up in the hotel. They would meet to do work at the poolside bar. Apparently, he had asked my father to make his announcement here.

Maria Elena was with us. A big red hyacinth was tied up in her hair.

I loved her, though I knew, vaguely, even before my father's news, that Maria Elena would be my downfall. She set things off balance, required too many alterations in the rhythm of my family. We were planetary and couldn't handle a second sun. Our paths became too confused; around what were we supposed to orbit now?

My father was going on, expressing his gratitude to Victor and Coco, when Tata said, in English, "Cut to the chase, Dad. We don't know what you're talking about."

Maria Elena patted Tata's hand, to tell her, I suppose, to be patient.

"We're moving," my father said.

"You're kidding?" said Tata.

"No," Maria Elena said. "All of us. To a house."

"A whole house?" Tata said. "God, that's great."

"Oh," Melone said, as if she couldn't make up her mind if a move was a good or a bad idea.

"Yes," my father said. "Victor and Coco are helping with a down payment."

"But," Melone said, "why a house now? I mean we'll be gone soon."

"What do you mean you'll be gone?" Father said.

"I mean we'll go to college probably in three years, so it seems like a funny time to buy a whole house."

"You'll come live with us in summers," Maria Elena said briskly.

Tata rolled her eyes and said, "I don't *think* so."

Maria Elena ignored her and continued on: "It's a beautiful old *hacienda.* Well, it used to be a *hacienda,* and then it was the convent. You know the place, girls. It was damaged some in the storm on your birthday."

"Oh, no," I said, feeling instantly betrayed as I realized what house she was talking about. "We can't move there."

"What are you talking about?" my father said.

"The Catillan Sisters?" I said.

He nodded his head, and I said, "No, no, we can't move there. Not the Catillan Sisters' place."

My father looked at me. I think he was genuinely puzzled. "What are you talking about, Beatriz?" he said, gently.

"I . . . nothing," I said quietly and listened as he detailed the rooms in the house, talked about the sugar cane field we would gaze on each sunrise.

As I listened, I thought, Maybe I'm just making something out of nothing, maybe I'm crazy, but I didn't genuinely doubt myself. It was bad luck to move to that *hacienda.* If he could hear my thoughts, my father would chide me. More of that magical thinking, he would say, that magical thinking to which I was always falling victim. It's true that I had all sorts of puzzles going on in my head. If I walked under a full moon, my head would ache for a week. If I finished chewing my breakfast cereal at exactly seven o'clock, I would stub my toe on the way to classes . . . that sort of thing. I was trying to break myself of this pattern of thinking. Lately, I'd been encouraging black cats to lope across my path. I'd been prying open ladders, so I could walk under them. Even so, when it came time to leave that evening, when all the information and thanks had been dispensed, I couldn't move. I mean I was frozen to the spot, as if someone had come along and, for a joke, quietly and painlessly severed my spine.

Right away, there was some yelling about this. My father barked at me, told me to snap out of it. Melone groaned. Victor looked worried. Coco said, in a tight, panicked voice, that she was sure it was nothing. Tata told us to all calm down. Finally, Melone went to find a doctor. One of the guests at the hotel came by and pronounced himself a neurologist and my problem one of hysterical paralysis. He asked the group if I had experienced a recent and great shock.

Tata looked at the doctor. "Yeah," she said. "She's turning into a tree. Wouldn't that give you a shock?"

"An emotional upset?" the doctor said, ignoring Tata. "Before she froze, anything like that?"

"Oh, Beatriz, just stop this," my father said. My eyes started to tear. I was not frozen on purpose. "She's just irritated, because we did it before she did," he said to Maria Elena, as if we were all in competition to be the first one to move out of that apartment above the bakery.

"Papi, that's idiotic," Melone said.

"Maybe," Father said to her, "maybe when you're a little more grown up you will be able to understand all this, but for the time being, shut up."

"Oh, for Christ's sake," Melone said. "That's right. Give me another decade or two, because this is much too complicated for a simpleton like me."

"This isn't your argument," Maria Elena instructed Melone.

"Oh . . ." I said, a sort of half-word, half-moan.

My father slapped the table. Everyone else looked worried. Then my father started to look concerned too. "Maybe," he said, grasping at straws and remembering, I suppose, a poster we had in the bakery, "maybe I should do the Heimlich maneuver."

"No, no," Melone said, "that will hurt her."

My father turned to her and said, "You want her to stay frozen, because it will make you look better by comparison."

"What is that supposed to mean?" Melone said and then, when no answer was forthcoming, "Are you serious? My God, what an ugly thing to say."

Father told her that her anger only further proved his point. She was protesting too much, because she did hope for my failure.

"I am protesting too much," Melone said, in the sort of controlled scream one uses for public places, "because that is a horrible, horrible thing to say."

Father raised his hand, as if he couldn't help it; he had only uttered the truth, not created it.

Melone was outraged. "That's right," she said. "And I hope a bird comes along and shits on everyone's head, except mine, so my hair will shine brighter, and I hope . . ."

"The child," Victor interrupted to say. I expected him to be shocked by Melone's anger, not to mention her use of the word "shit," if only because Melone acted so properly girlish around Victor and Coco. "The child," he said again, "is what is important." Everyone turned their attention back to me.

"I think," my father said tensely, "that maybe I should try that Heimlich maneuver. We don't want there to be any permanent damage."

Maria Elena looked at him as if he was crazy. She said, "Listen, let me handle this. I want you to all go home and let me handle this."

My father looked at her, and she said, "No, really. This is the sort of thing I am good at. I'm great in an emergency. You've heard me tell you about when my sister died, when . . ." My father waved her quiet. "What I am saying," she stopped herself short and summarized her approach to life rather than her specific accomplishments, "is that I am good in an emergency. It's everyday life I can't handle." Everyone nodded. It was something she always said: "Blood I can handle. What does me in is making a bed."

"Go, go," Maria Elena insisted. "Home." There were weak objections. After all, it was true that Maria Elena had a gift for crisis. Meanwhile, Maria Elena held firm. She said she'd come back in a taxi and that no one should worry, that she understood me and she wanted to be alone with me.

"I think that's a good idea," I said. No one stood to leave. "Please," I said and then, "I'm sorry."

By the time they were all gone, it was dark, and the hotel guests were all in the dining room, and a sign had been put up by the swimming pool that said there was no lifeguard on duty and people were to swim at their own risk. It seemed like a command rather than a warning.

It took awhile, but I finally tried to explain myself. It was late at night when I began. I told Maria Elena the rest of my story, and that was our bond. Weeks before, I told her the first part of the story, the part about the nun. Now, I started to talk. Just as I did then, I felt as if I were lifting my story up out of myself and putting it into her body, that now there would be two of us who knew. She patted my hand and told me to take my time, but I couldn't. I was always quiet, or I talked in a rush, with huge gulping breaths.

"If we live in the old convent," I said, "something terrible will happen to you."

"Now, why do you think that?"

"Because . . ." I started, but I couldn't finish. Maria Elena was always complimenting me on my intuitive knowledge, but my fear rarely gave way to understanding. It had to do with what I knew about that house. When I was there, I stole something. It was one of the only things I ever stole in my entire life. It was a journal. For a long time, I thought I should do something with it, turn it over to the historical society or something, since some of the material had to do with the early colonial government, important things we'd learned about at school. But I couldn't do it, because I was convinced that, on some level, the family in the journal might be my family. It sounds looped, I know. I don't think I mean something as shallow as reincarnation. What I thought was that my father and Maria Elena were the couple I had read about in the journal. The man in the story—his name was Doroteo Díaz—was my father. The dying woman in the story—she went by Maria—was Maria Elena. They even had the same name—almost. Even the side characters made sense to me. One man reminded me of Rayovac, another of Angelo, that crazy man who went about town impersonating people.

Maria Elena listened silently, then she said, "I'm not sure I can understand all you are saying without hearing the story. I mean, I've been worried about your memories from the day of the tornado and how that would make you feel about the move, and I wondered about the best way to tell you about this, and I can see that the decision to just handle it as if . . ."

"It's not that."

"Then, what?"

"See, I think if we move there, you'll start to have the life of the woman in the story, not your own. And the same with my father. The house just has these powers. It makes people act differently. It's sort of like a haunted house."

Maria Elena was quiet for a moment. I thought, when she opened her mouth again, she was going to talk about the virtues of the beds in the local lunatic asylum, but what she said was, "But why will this happen if we move into the house? I mean, if it's true, it's true, and we can't alter our fate."

"No," I said. "That's just the thing. In the story, there are these unimportant characters. They're barely mentioned, but they're there. There's a man, and his wife is dead, and he has three daughters and they don't live in the *hacienda*, and they like barrettes." Maria Elena nodded her head. "And, you see, I think that we might be those three girls who like to wear barrettes in their hair, and that man is our father. See, it's like we have a choice, but if we move into that house, we won't have a choice." Was it, I wanted to ask Maria Elena, an accident that my sisters and I liked hair accessories? I was feeling a little hysterical. I wanted to shriek, as if the words had undeniable meaning. Pony tail ties! Headbands! Hair barrettes!

Maria Elena looked at the ground. She didn't approve of my father's decision to send my sisters and me to private school, and now I knew she was thinking that too much skill at literary analysis, coupled with a superstitious mind, could get you into all sorts of trouble. I couldn't say I hadn't had the same thought myself.

"Tell me the story," she said, as if coming to a decision. "Tell me." I looked at her and loved her more even than I had before. "Beatriz," Maria Elena whispered. "Tell me." So I started talking, and when I was through, the sun was rising over the pool, a hotel employee had come out to hose down the deck chairs and a stack of newspapers was deposited by the bar.

Maria Elena hugged me when I was done. "Come on," she said, and I stood and walked with her to the front of the hotel where the taxis were. It wasn't until I was in the taxi that it occurred to me I was moving, even though, hours earlier, my legs were like stone. Maybe I wouldn't have moved if I had known what I know now, if I had known that Maria Elena, while she heard my story, understood it in a different way than I did. She went home and read the journal and came up with her own thoughts about what it meant. I couldn't hate her for that, even though one week later, with my hands trembling on the handle of my suitcase, I stepped past the bougainvillea-covered walls of the old *hacienda,* padded up a grand staircase that rose over an interior arch, and walked into my new bedroom. I said, "It's not where I live. Not really," hoping that by merely uttering the sentence, I could unravel the sweater of fate.

At Night, On the Island, In the Dark

28 February 1765.

People died, and yet the graveyards were empty. The island was convulsed with life. There was constant dancing, celebrating, as if bodies were like tree leaves, useful in death, on forest floors, to promote the growth of bananas.

This time, the villagers had converged to celebrate a birth and a death. It was the . . . Doroteo Díaz rolled his eyes heavenward as he counted in his head . . . the nine, ten, eleven, twelfth day of dancing. At first, the dance had been for the benefit of Díaz's chief foreman, Raul Miguel. A celebration! The momentous occasion of the birth of Raul Miguel's first son, Juan Carlos! The foreman's own home, a small shack papered with broad *yagua* leaves, was unsuited for such festivities.

"I won't do it," Díaz had said when Raul Miguel first began to speak to him of his home's small dimensions, its fragile walls. Raul Miguel had yet to make the request, but Díaz knew what he wanted. He had noticed how Raul Miguel had taken to grazing cattle in that portion of the field closest to Díaz's house. He saw the new hardness in his foreman's eyes. At length, fearing a possible shift in his loyalties, Díaz succumbed to the unspoken requests for the use of his home.

Then, after four days of celebrating, the infant died. Díaz felt guilty relief; he dreamed his house empty. But the *isleños,* sparing no opportunity to dance, celebrated at the infant's passing. When the sun bled into the ocean on the evening of the ninth day of dancing, the celebration at the death had lasted longer than the celebration of the birth, and this despite the fact that Díaz and a few of the older *criollos* had insisted that the odor from the corpse was too foul to continue.

But now Doroteo Díaz could smell nothing. He was sitting with a crowd of men on the steps that led to the front door of his house. Inside, the parlor floor shook under the weight of feet. Outside, one could hear the low rumble of steps. It hadn't always been this way. For days, few had thought to enter Díaz's large, Spanish colonial home. The grounds had served well enough. The house had been reserved for the tired. Then rain fell, and the dancers moved indoors for a night. One night became two; two became three . . . . Someone, a minor character in the crowd, recognized the value of exclusion. Those in the parlor became famous. "Who did you see? What are they doing?" people shouted when someone finally left the parlor and a new person was allowed to enter. Some became rich by accepting *pesos* for their spot in the parlor. Within a week, the house had been completely given over to the sleepless. The rest took to napping as they waited for their turn to enter. A line, four people wide, snaked out of the house, down the front stairway and through the grounds till it disappeared into the trees.

The facade of the house faced the edge of the forest; the bank of a river ran parallel to the furrows of a sugar cane field. Together, the borders framed an expanse of purposeless land. The whole of the celebration had been conducted here. Doroteo Díaz owned the house, the purposeless land and the fields beyond. He was, like so many landholders, a Spaniard. And, like so many Spaniards, an official with the government. This year, his title was Acting President of Commerce. Though he waited with the others, Díaz was not impatient for entrance into his own home. This distinguished him, for if not for his right eye—which turned inward, giving the impression he was watching himself—his appearance would have been entirely typical: dark-skinned and dark-haired, trousered and shirted . . . perhaps he was a bit neater than the rest.

A day earlier, on the eleventh day of dancing, Díaz had sent a letter to his wife, Maria, who had been moved to the governor's palace for the duration of the celebration.

Maria, dear. The gardens are mud and the flowers torn up. The bench in the gazebo is now a chair. Children have plucked feathers from our peacocks. I'll have the stairs repaired and the walls cleaned. I've sent a horse; come home when you can. They should be gone soon.

Now Díaz thought the note had been premature. There seemed little chance of an end to the celebration. "Madero," he said, turning to a thick, greasy man to his left, "I'll be back to take my place." Madero smiled, revealing teeth rotted into soft triangles, and Díaz felt permitted to walk toward the forest, in the hope of finding the horse and his wife coming through the trees.

When he was close to the house, no one stepped out of line to talk to him. As he proceeded into the forest, however, people were more and more willing to leave the line and make requests.

"If there is any cloth . . ."

"Another desk like the one I bought during the rains?"

"Chocolates?" another asked.

Cloth, good desks, chocolates . . . And there was more: liquor, a new thing called a steel-nibbed pen. Everyone wanted steel-nibbed pens.

"I've got tobacco," one man said. "Oxen."

No one expected a reply. Díaz couldn't give one. Many men in the government were involved in the flourishing contraband trade with the English and Dutch colonies. Nonetheless, the trade was illegal, and on occasion the government looked for a man to prosecute. A jailed man was to serve as proof to Spain that the local officials were serious about upholding the laws of the continent.

Finally, Díaz caught sight of Maria emerging from the forest. There were her large, deep brown eyes. There was her skin the color of an almond shell and her hair, a bit lighter, almost blonde, long and crimped into tiny waves. And there was her hand, which Lupe Margarita, Raul's wife, grabbed. Lupe pulled Maria quickly past the line and into the parlor. As they went, Díaz heard Lupe proudly announce, "It was the epidemic." Such a death was a distinction; Spaniards were more likely to get it than *isleños,* though plenty of natives had been killed by the disease. People called it the disease of royalty.

Díaz went to join his wife in the parlor, but Madero stopped him on the stairs. "I have something you might like to know." Madero scratched the small scar that nicked his right nostril. Díaz thought he knew what Madero had to tell him. The best information about contraband trade always came from Madero, but Madero said that an inspector would arrive at the end of the season, that he would go to the governor's first, make a tour of the island and then go to the rain forests and the south coast with Díaz.

Díaz smiled at the news—perhaps the inspector would help him with one of his petitions to leave the island—but then he grew suspicious. "No one told me this," Díaz said.

"I am telling you right now."

But Madero was no one to be telling him. Madero had nothing to do with the government, and he hated Spaniards, though he made an exception for Doroteo Díaz and his kind, pale wife. In fact, Madero had nothing to do with any sort of work. The *isleños* loved and respected him all the same. They'd bring him handfuls of sugar cane, yams, bananas, yucca and coconuts if he would only say he had a few minutes for some conversation. He knew the business of everyone on the island, and people who wanted to keep secrets made a point of saying, "Don't give this to Madero."

Rather than push forward, Díaz remained on the steps. He'd have to rely on the meager information that those outside could get of the events inside. By the windows, children sat on the shoulders of the tallest men and gave reports of what they saw.

"Doña Cortez has sugared fruits," a child called from the windows.

"Pepito Armado," began a second child, "has traded his eye for a handful."

"Oh, he has not," an older woman slapped the second child for the lie. "He loves that eye like a brother."

This was true. Díaz himself had arranged for the illegal purchase of the eye from Holland and had lectured Pepito often about the value of the glass and the importance of leaving it in his head instead of popping it out for examination.

"Only a fool would let his wife dance till she drops," Madero said.

Díaz looked at him. He didn't believe she was dancing. Her stay at the governor's house had been arranged to prevent such behavior.

"That so?" Díaz stood and tried to push himself up the remaining two steps and through the doorway, but the people in front of him, mindlessly immobile, held him back. "Excuse me, I have to find my wife, excuse me . . ." he insisted, and two pairs of shoulders parted like a gate. "Excuse me . . ." Díaz said to the next set of shoulders.

The stench in the front hall was unbearable. The parlor even worse. Once there, Díaz saw Raul Miguel twirling Maria around the body of the baby. "That's it," Díaz shouted. "The celebration is over. That's it." People quieted down but did not move. At a loss, Díaz said, "Governor's orders. Everyone out."

Eventually, the house was emptied and the food carried away. Maria's skin turned a slight yellow, and her shaking, what the others had taken for dancing, would not stop.

When everyone was gone, there was a long, long dry spell, and the land, which had been torn into mud, hardened into small, dark waves. Then, months later, there was a Monday, the same Monday the ship with the inspector came, when the air was heavy and wet again. A strong storm wind blew the ship to port days before it was expected. The inspector arrived arguing, and Díaz had to be called to the docks at once. "There's fish rotting aboard," the inspector shouted at Díaz, as if in greeting.

"Fish?" Díaz asked. He looked at the captain who gave him a wink. He imagined the crew had been playing tricks on the inspector since they left Europe. "We haven't much use for fish here. It's a small island, plenty in the ocean. We can get it whenever we want."

The inspector huffed once and turned away. "I suppose," he said softly. Díaz thought he only just realized the absurdity of importing fish from Spain. The inspector brushed the sweat that hung below his nose into his mustache. The man's dress was all wrong for the climate. He wore dark black boots that came up past his knees, stiff black trousers and a heavy black shirt with a jacket. A pair of small glasses with thick lenses rested on his nose in such a way that Díaz couldn't exactly see where his eyes were.

"Well, welcome. Let me take you to the governor's," Díaz pointed with his chin to the hill above them. La Fortaleza, the elegant governor's mansion, was just behind the city wall, on top of a small rise. From the docks, it looked enormous.

They climbed the hill at the height of the day's sun. Díaz looked out to the ocean as they climbed. The sun reflected off the water was white and painful.

The men walked in silence for some time. Díaz wanted to ask the inspector for bits of news from Madrid, anything he'd heard, but didn't feel he could. Still Díaz had the sense he already knew the inspector, not because he supposed he had met him before, but because soon he would know him, and he felt a queer abrogation of time, as if he could dispense with introductory efforts and know the man without knowing him since, by the end of the season, they would be old acquaintances. He wondered whether he knew and liked him or not.

The hill plateaued for a stretch of ten feet, and the inspector stopped to catch his breath. He turned and looked out toward the bay. Then he took off his glasses, rubbed them against his pant leg, replaced them and looked again. "You're Doroteo Díaz," the inspector turned to him to say. "I only just now registered your name. There are letters for you." He pulled four envelopes from his coat. "I almost opened them myself on the way over. I hate a sealed envelope."

Díaz nodded, and the two pushed on to La Fortaleza. Here, the inspector stopped Díaz, wouldn't let him come any further—"You've got to read your letters"—and Díaz left him in the care of an officer at the gate.

The letters were unsurprising and unwanted. One was a letter that should have been delivered with the last ship. It explained that an inspector would arrive with the next ship, that he was sent to undertake a thorough investigation of the island and to propose and initiate reforms. Díaz was to assist him in whatever fashion he could. There was another letter insisting that more taxes be sent home. A third official letter insisted on a halt to contraband trade with other islands. The fourth was personal, a letter addressed specifically to Díaz, rather than to the President of Commerce. In it, the King, Carlos III, refused Díaz's ninth request to return to Spain and chastised him for not fully appreciating an influential government appointment in paradise.

It wasn't good news, but it was news all the same, and Díaz hurried home to share it. The parlor was empty when he arrived, still cleared of furniture from the dance. Raul Miguel had promised to put the room back in order, and Díaz stubbornly refused to do the small task himself. He had been waiting, for months now, for Raul Miguel to rake the dirt out front and to bring his belongings back. There was little to the chore as there had never been much cluttering the parlor—an enormous table with heavy chairs to match the room's heavy chandeliers and the hammock Díaz had hung in the corner for Raul Miguel's use. *This is ridiculous*, he thought, *I can do the job in a matter of minutes.*

"No."

"No." He heard the word trail off softly and, at first, he thought the word was in response to his thought that he do the job himself. No, floating down from nowhere, insisting on the importance of his earlier resolution.

He looked through the doorway and down the hall into the dark breakfast room. It was still light out, so it was the shadow from the gazebo that left the far part of the parlor, the hallway and the whole of the breakfast room in dim light.

"I am not," he heard Maria say, "very happy. But, of course, happiness is not everything."

He had an image of her stroking his face and then accidentally catching her finger's rough nail in his cheek and pulling.

"Of course," the other responded.

By day, the room the two women sat in was white. All white with all white furniture covered by white linens all framed against white walls. Even the other woman, the nurse, was in white. Díaz thought of the uniform as white even when, in the dim light, it was grey. His wife had taught him the trick. "Even in the dark," Maria liked to say, "I can see the brightest of colors."

The interiors of all the foreign homes were white. It was as if the Spaniards thought the tropical disease that afflicted the area always appeared with great color. A faded house inhabited by Spaniards could not prevent illness, yet there was the hope that, when germs did come, they would be more visible in a white home. Spaniards would be able to spot the disease as a dark smudge on the floor, a little bluish blob against the wall or a discoloring in the tablecloth, and take action.

Díaz took two steps into the hallway and stood close to the wall, so he could see without being seen. Maria was twisting one of her hairpins between her fingers. He thought he should not have spent so long at the docks, that he should have returned home earlier and not permitted Maria to be alone with this new nurse. She was the third nurse in four months. Díaz had angrily dismissed the others for their inability to diagnose, let alone cure, Maria's illness.

He looked away from the women now, out through the parlor windows into the forest. The last few months had been hard. As she grew ill, Maria grew inward, as if no one else could hope to understand the exact nature of her troubles. *What are you thinking? What thinking?* Díaz had always asked her these questions, but now Maria acted as if he were inquiring about the weather, offering questions that weren't entirely irrelevant but not at all interesting.

Now he heard Maria trying to explain herself: "I am sorry. I just didn't know. I thought . . ."

He knew she would pause for a moment before she continued. Her eyes would skim over something, distantly; she had the habit of looking at something vaguely and then squinting as though she meant to pull her eyes far back into their sockets and away from what she had seen.

What she thought was that it would have been rude not to dance with Raul Miguel or any man who asked for her hand during the final day of dancing for the death of the infant, Juan Carlos.

"I thought, I thought . . . ." Maria was just repeating the two words.

Well, this is enough. Díaz stepped into the breakfast room. He saw Maria jerk her arm away from the table as if his steps had been unusually forceful, causing a tremor that made its way through the floor to the table leg and up to the tabletop, where it had the power to push her hand away.

"Please finish up," he said to the nurse and turned and walked through the parlor and out of the house. He took a seat on the front steps. He thought of the little jerking movement Maria had made when he walked into the breakfast room and scowled.

Soon after the house had been cleared from the dance, Maria had found him in the library, and she had walked up to him and had spoken to him in her quiet voice. It bothered him, that voice, he always had to say, "What? What are you trying to say?"

"Oh," she had started, "there's something in this." She had taken the book he had been reading. She turned the pages till she reached a barely legible scrawl on one of the blank pages at the back of the book. It read: "Things are apparently quiet but truly noisy and very hard to bear." His first impulse had been to ask who was writing in his books, but he knew that would seem crass, so he said, "Yes, the world is a mystery." But the sentence embarrassed him; it seemed maudlin and simple. She'd been quiet, absorbed in her illness, and now this?

"No," she had said. He hadn't understood, so she took his hand and walked him out on to the porch behind the house, down through the garden to the gazebo.

"What," she said, "do you hear or feel right now?"

He had told her he was happy to be with her. She had turned her head around and looked at him as if he were a fool. This was not what she wanted to hear. She wanted a report from his senses. He thought about it for a bit. What did he feel? What feel? He told her that he thought it was a lovely night and that there was a slight breeze. His voice had trailed off. "Oh," she said, her voice wavering a little. He was surprised to realize she was about to cry. "It's an awful night. Better than others but still terrible. The grass is pulling at my feet and won't let go. The wind is slapping at my face. And the *coquí* . . . they are scratching the leaves' surface with an awful sound. At night," she had said, "I can't sleep next to you because your heart beats so loudly; your blood rushes so noisily through your veins."

When he thought of the incident now, he was almost angry. For his own part, Díaz thought the night she complained of was too quiet. It was at night when he most wanted to leave the island. For though it was true he always hated the island for its lack of order, for the foolishness of trying to govern it, he did love it, during the day, for the richness of its colors, sounds and textures. With nightfall, all that disappeared, and he thought the place worthless.

Díaz pressed his hands to the step and pushed himself to his feet. He abruptly shook his head once to the left, as if he were trying to force the memory, like a drop of water, out of his head, through his ear.

He walked in and interrupted the two women again. "I do believe that will do for the time being." Maria turned her eyes toward her lap. The nurse protested, there were questions still to be asked. In reply, he merely repeated himself, "I do believe that will do for the time being."

"Sir," she said pleasantly, but Díaz detected sarcasm in her voice, "you've called me away from my post, from many sick people, to care for your wife, and yet you refuse to give me sufficient time with her. It's no secret there's an epidemic on, and there are people back at the infirmary . . . ." She stopped and then said, "I would think that a man in your position would have the good sense to . . ."

"A man in my position is accustomed to being listened to when he speaks. You remember where the door is?"

She stared at him, walked to the entrance of the room, turned and said cheerfully—he might as well have offered her an increase in wages —"And when shall I return?"

"Tomorrow will be fine." Maria nodded, and the woman left.

They passed the evening in the room. For a while, he read. Occasionally, he would look at her, but she always felt his eyes on her, and even now, after being married for three years, she would get flustered and start to pull at the hair he had so neatly tied up in a bun at the start of the day. By night, she always looked a little wild with her hair being partially knotted in the back and partially flying about her face. He sometimes wondered if it hurt her to have her hair pulled back. But she insisted. "No one will see you, you know," he had told her. "It would be perfectly proper." But no, she wanted him to keep tying it in the morning.

Sickness gave the days a routine, neat and irritating. Díaz spent the morning in the fields and woke Maria just before he left the *hacienda.* Then he went to town—to the docks or his office at the governor's—to attend to business. Mid-afternoon, he went visiting. Madero, Pepito Armado: these were his favorites, but truthfully, whoever was in town would do. Díaz liked almost everyone. Madero said that this—his lack of discrimination in friends—made him a whore.

In the early evening, the nurse came to question Maria again. The nurse waited upstairs with Maria till Díaz returned from town. Then . . . but it was too dull, always the same . . . he'd read her a book, heat hot water, take her upstairs, pour the water and go to bed himself. The pattern continued for long enough that Díaz's memories of the three years with Maria—the two years on the island and the single year in Spain after the wedding—started to have an unreal quality, an impression sustained by his belief that were he to share his memories with her, Maria would confirm none of them.

After the inspector returned from his tour with the Minister of Agriculture, everything changed. Díaz had to leave Maria for hours on end.

"I want to know everything about these people," the inspector said on the eve of their first long departure; they were to go to Ponce for a few nights. "Everything," the inspector repeated. They were outside La Fortaleza. The night was cool, and the sea was quiet.

Díaz nodded but thought, *The arrogance of this!* "I think," he said quietly, "you would have to be an *isleño* to know everything about them."

"Oh, don't be ridiculous. You don't believe you can know something from the outside? How do you know anyone then?"

Díaz shrugged the question away.

"Ach," the inspector pulled off his glasses and made a gesture as if he intended to throw them into the ocean. But it was just awkwardness that made it seem this way, and while Díaz was trying to see if they had been tossed into the dark, the inspector cleaned them against his pant leg and returned them to his face. "Ach," the inspector made the sound again and then, as if he were having a bit of difficulty speaking, he said, "Jesus, don't agree if you don't agree. We have no need for politeness here."

"No, inspector," Díaz started up slowly, "I don't think it is possible to know everything from the outside. You have to be an *isleño* to truly know the *isleño*."

"And you need to be a coconut to truly know the coconut."

Díaz said, "We'll have to be getting some sleep now; we have to get up early in the morning."

The inspector smiled, "So, that's the way it is."

"I don't get your meaning."

"Díaz," he said, turning to leave, "it will be an interesting trip. You'll learn that I like a good argument more than anything else."

They traveled for days before they arrived in Ponce. It was true the inspector liked to argue. He never left off arguing. He could argue, argue passionately, about anything and nothing at all. In Ponce, a man of six feet said he was tall, and the inspector disagreed with him. "That's not tall."

"For an *isleño,* it's tall," the man said.

"Oh, don't be ridiculous. You're of average height."

They spent only a night in Ponce, then left for the surrounding villages where the inspector asked each *isleño* to express his allegiance to the king. "You do believe in the king, don't you? You are loyal to him, hold him in the highest esteem?"

Everyone knew to agree, and then the inspector would ask for details, for each person to say something they believed to be true about Carlos III.

"What?" they'd say.

"A fact," the inspector would insist. "Any fact. Tell me a fact about Carlos. How can you believe in him if you don't know the first thing about him?"

Then Díaz and the inspector crossed back through the corridor of mountains dividing the island in half. They rode side by side through a narrow path. The flanks of their horses just brushed. Water oozed from the ground under the print of each horse's hoof.

"Why does everyone say 'steel-nibbed' when they are around you?" the inspector asked.

"Oh, that."

"Oh, that," the inspector mimicked him.

"They want me to ask you, ask you about the steel-nibbed pen. We have all heard about it and want to know what it is."

"That can't be it. They could ask me themselves."

"You don't have to believe me," Díaz smiled, "but why would I lie about such a thing?"

"I can't guess . . . and, no, I don't have to believe you."

Before they were out of the hills, the inspector had taken ill. He bathed for an hour in a cold pond and said he would be able to continue, but when he went to mount his horse, he slumped over, and Díaz brought him back to the government's infirmary.

"You know," he said to Díaz on their return. "The governor has taken the king's picture from the wall, and he dances with mulattos in the hallways."

Díaz expressed his astonishment, though this was a famous rumor. "You will find," he told the inspector, "that despite their lack of knowledge, the *isleños* are very loyal to Carlos and to Spain."

"Oh, yes," the inspector coughed in a deep guttural rumble and replied, "you are right, but they are lazy, and this on an island where the rivers are choked with fish, the forests stuffed with fruit. A good many Negroes run free. Excuse me." The inspector coughed violently on his final words.

While he was in the infirmary, Díaz grew to like the inspector. Unlike Maria, the inspector grew expansive and generous during his confinement. He told jokes and complained bitterly, though his illness was small and inconsequential.

The investigation continued from bed. Various people—slave owners, peasants, freemen—were brought to talk to him. During the second week of his confinement, the inspector confessed to having no interest in Spain.

"That's impossible," Díaz said. He was sitting in a chair by the bed. His hands were lying, almost primly, on his knees. "Why all the questions about Spain and the king?"

But the inspector did not answer. "Let me ask you this, Díaz . . . why do you want so badly to leave this island? It's a lovely island. The sun always shines."

Díaz watched the inspector smooth his sheets out with his palms. "It's not that difficult. Everyone who is important to me, save my wife, of course, is back in Spain. My life is on the other side of the ocean."

"What an odd idea!" the inspector exclaimed and sat straight up in bed. He made a move to take his glasses off his face.

"That's an irritating mannerism, my friend."

The inspector looked at him, as if to say, "What?" but he did not utter the word.

"The way you clean your glasses. You clean your glasses on your trousers several times every hour. The only time you don't do it is when you are on a horse."

But the inspector seemed not to have heard him. "I never think about people back home. The way I see it is they hardly exist when I leave them."

Everyone I know is dead, Díaz thought, but he said, "I don't think I could quite bear a thought like that." *To everyone I know, I am dead.*

"I agree it's not the most comforting thing to think, but it frees you up in a way. The best lives . . . . Now here's what I think." The inspector shook his finger like a school teacher. "All true cowards are afraid of it, of leaving. That's because they think life is located somewhere else. Now let's see if I am making myself clear. If you are afraid of leaving anything, but let us just say of leaving Spain, it is because you think it is possible that life could be elsewhere. I mean that life could be somewhere rather than with just you."

"How would anything have value if you could always leave it with no cost to yourself?"

The inspector swung his legs out of his bed and leaned forward to Díaz. "I have always suspected you of having this very thought!" he said with a certain amount of self-congratulation. "You wouldn't be so eager to return if you only knew how wrong you are. You are your place."

I am my place, Díaz thought, but then, because it was his habit to force his thoughts to the mundane when a thought like this came along, Díaz reminded himself of what he needed to do for the rest of the day. *Ask Raul Miguel if he's fixed the ox yoke, find out if the canoes will come this week, speak to the nurse about Maria, bring the cook yucca for dinner.* He would clear these chores away and then think about the inspector's words.

The inspector's foot was gently pushing Díaz's shin.

"Your mind is elsewhere," he said. "Isn't it?"

Díaz smiled.

"Isn't it?"

Díaz's mind had been on contraband trade, and it stayed on contraband trade when he left the inspector's bedside and headed back through town toward his home. When the canoes came, there was much to be done. There was always the excitement, but this was rather vague, of doing something illegal. Mostly, however, what he took pleasure in was the distribution of goods, the taking of things, item by item, out of the canoe and to the customers in town. If not for this occupation, Díaz would never have met most of the people he knew on the island. Still, it amazed him that he could enjoy such a thing; he had not been given, in the past, to disobeying rules. But then he'd never been so high up in the government before, never lived in a large *hacienda.* Really, he thought, it was the house's fault. It had transformed him into a crook. You had, after all, to live up to the requirements of the place you owned, and the place he owned was grand. It asked him to walk with a stiff and formal back, to understand he was above the bureaucracy he administered.

Now, as he walked through town, Díaz considered each house, first according to its occupants, then according to what they wanted from the next group of canoes, and finally according to what he had been able to get for them from past canoes. There was Rabassa who wanted only sweets from abroad. He lived alone and talked too much; he never wanted Díaz to leave. There was Vargas, Cortéz. There was the de Jesus family. Three girls in one family. The mother was dead, and the father was terrified he would never marry them all off, but they were all beautiful, and the family was moderately wealthy, so Díaz thought he had nothing to worry about. Díaz himself would have been happy to have the three as daughters, but the thought bothered him for suggesting his life could have taken a very different turn from the one it did. These girls always wanted those small ivory barrettes to pin up their hair. Díaz was still working on a clock for the father, a machine with a little bird that came out and sang at the hour.

Díaz returned home to find Maria downstairs in the breakfast room with the nurse. They were leaning forward—their foreheads almost touching—over the breakfast table. The scene comforted him, and when the nurse had said good-bye for the evening, he said, "You like that nurse, don't you?"

"Oh, yes, she's very nice."

Maria, he thought, *has the same sense about the nurse that I have about the inspector.*

"I mean," Díaz grinned a bit foolishly, "you really like her, don't you?" He was almost giddy. *I am fine. She is fine. We will both be fine.*

Maria nodded and smiled. "Will you brush my hair?" she asked, sweetly.

"Oh, yes, of course, yes." Her brush was in her lap, and he stood behind her and reached over her with his right hand to get it. He drew the brush down. His left hand followed, lightly smoothing the soft hair. The pads of his palms and fingertips just touched the waves in her hair. *Nothing has been lost; everything is fine.* She pulled his free hand to her mouth and kissed it, then let his hand return to her hair. If only she were well enough for him to really hold her, he thought. But there was no use in thoughts like this. "You can talk to that nurse, can't you? I have a sense you can talk to her."

"I care for her, yes," Maria said.

Oh, Díaz thought with something that was both rapture and envy. *The things you talk about! She tells you about her child, her husband, that doctor. There is a part of the pineapple she favors, and she lets you know about this. You discuss women's problems, monthly pains. Sometimes you tell her about what you write on those bits of paper on your desk.*

But he wouldn't say any of this. Not to her anyway.

"I'll tell you the truth," Díaz said to the inspector one morning. "I am quite frightened for my wife's life. We are eager to get her home so she can have some decent medical attention."

"What? There are no good doctors here?" The inspector picked up his pad and scribbled some notes to himself.

"Ah, materials for your memoirs of disappointment?"

The inspector looked a little shocked, then patted the cool, outer sides of the fresh, white sheets covering him. "I'm not sure I understand your meaning."

"Well, you know the island will be governed as it will, not as you or I will have it. Not, but this is too obvious, as the governor will have it."

"Oh, just leave them be so the British can come in? In my two months on this island, I've seen more disorder than in my thirty years in Spain."

"With all respect," Díaz smiled, "order abounds on this island. It is just not the order you want." Outside, the palm trees looked like green claws against the blue of the sky.

The inspector said in a conciliatory tone, "Doroteo, think of this: in nature, bees pollinate flowers, and it is all very lovely. But also in nature, the black spider eats its mate. We're here to guard against such perversions."

Sometimes this was true, Díaz thought, so he nodded his head. Nature was helplessly stupid, but he couldn't get over the orderliness of bones, the cleverness of having created fruit.

When the month was out, it was time to see what Madero knew of the canoes. Díaz went to his house and found Madero outside, sleeping in his hammock. A full plate of fried plantains was on the ground directly under his head. Díaz woke him with the question, "What can you tell me, Madero?"

"What would you like to know?" he said, before he even had opened his eyes.

Díaz thought for a moment. What he really wanted were facts to clutter up his head, so he could postpone, for the time being, knowing anything. "News of the world," he answered, "whatever you can tell me."

"About the canoes?"

"Yes, that too."

"The Dutch from Curaçao are ready for some tobacco. They suggested Friday night for a delivery."

"That'll be fine."

"No," Madero started slowly, "there is trouble. Luis Camacho's old father seems to have fallen ill with our island's little disease. He says he'll be at home caring for the old man."

"Well, there is still you and me. Raul Miguel always comes."

Madero was silent for a bit. At length, he said, and Díaz expected this, "I am sorry, but I don't think I will be able to attend."

"Jesus, Madero! You don't have to unload anything if you don't want to."

"Perhaps I will be there . . ." Madero nodded as he said this and dragged his fingers through the dirt below him. He stopped suddenly and pointed to the plantains. "Would you like some," he offered. "They're delicious and still hot." Díaz squatted and took a slice. It was cold. He placed another slice in Madero's dirty fingers, while he set his mind to the details of who needed to be told about the arrival of the canoes. Raul Miguel, Maria, the water boy, Pepito Armado . . . and then later, all of the people who had placed orders that were not filled, and there had to be assurances the goods would arrive in later canoes. Things could become complicated if someone got mad at Díaz or the others.

When he returned home, the nurse caught sight of him and called out, "Señor Díaz, how good to see you; perhaps we could talk for a moment?" Díaz agreed to walk the nurse in the direction of the infirmary, as he had to return to visit the inspector. "I am sorry to tell you this," she began, "but I believe your wife may need to be quarantined. For your safety."

Díaz stopped on the path. The news registered on his face like a wave, falling from his forehead to his cheeks to his mouth. "Arch." His first word was unintelligible, but then he said, "It's impossible. She hasn't been near anyone who has it."

"That doesn't necessarily make a difference. If I had to make a guess, I'd say she caught the disease from the corpse of Raul Miguel's son. She won't let me examine her anymore. If I could check her for a bite or the rash, then I could . . ."

Díaz nodded his head furiously, and this stopped the nurse from talking. He knew as well as anyone else on the island what this meant. A small hemorrhage at the point where the bloodsucker had bit and a rash five or six inches in diameter that spread from the point of the bite. Then the hemorrhage spread, and the rash shrank, and the skin wrinkled up . . . but it was impossible to think of Maria like that.

"Doroteo." The inspector always sounded elated when he first saw Díaz. "But what is it? Have you seen a ghost?"

"A ghost during the day? How could I see such a thing?" Díaz took up his position in the chair under the window and beside the bed.

"They have decided to discharge me at the end of the week, and we can resume our travels about the island."

"That's good, that's good," Díaz nodded his head slowly.

"Yes, they just informed me not thirty minutes before you arrived." A woman brought the inspector dinner, and Díaz sat with him through the whole meal before he told him his own news. Then he wept and when he was through, listened to the inspector's words of encouragement. "You can't be sure yet."

"That's true," Díaz said, but what he thought was, *A fatal disease, a woman sick with a fatal disease, a death. There is no point in pretending otherwise.*

"Don't bury her before you need to. No good comes from thinking that way," the inspector said.

Díaz bobbed his head up and down, said, "Well, when shall we continue our travels?" The change in subject matter and tone, for Díaz's voice took on a pleasant, brisk manner, was so forced Díaz himself winced at his words.

"They let me out Friday afternoon," the inspector said. His voice was soothing, as if he were still saying, "I am so sorry to hear that. I am so sorry." *So the words don't matter*, Díaz thought. *It's something else that is important.* The inspector was quiet for a moment, then said, "Why not leave that night?"

"Friday?" Díaz said. "Oh, no, that's when the Dutch come."

Díaz pressed the base of his palms into his legs, as hard as he could. He pushed his short fingernails into his thighs. He needed to hurt himself without the inspector noticing. *What did I just say? Maybe I did not say a thing?*

"What?" the inspector asked.

"It's just a suspicion," Díaz said weakly.

"Of what? Doroteo, you know what I want to know."

Díaz regained courage, but his voice had the shrill sound of a liar. "We, or rather I, suspect there has been some contraband trade with the island. I had a tip and was going to check something out Friday night."

"Well, I'll come along."

"Oh, no, your health." Díaz gestured toward his entire body as if the whole thing could not be trusted.

"I insist," the inspector said. And then, again: "I insist."

Outside in the hall, Díaz made arrangements to borrow a horse from one of the doctors and headed for Madero's.

"I have done a terrible thing," Díaz said as he walked into Madero's hut. Madero was sitting on the dirt floor, stirring the soil with a stick. "The inspector knows about the canoes. I told him about Friday night." Díaz repeated the conversation he had had with the inspector. Madero looked up at him and said, "You Spaniards are so easily upset." Madero did not even think before he devised a plan.

It was simple. Díaz would go down to the shore at eight, load the goods and get the boats quickly to leave the island. He would tell the inspector he would meet him there at ten, and they would find nothing. Díaz would be embarrassed, would say, "You will have to forgive me. I act on my suspicions. I was too hasty." And that would be that. It required only that Madero warn the Dutch to arrive on time and unload quickly. They had to be told that if they were caught, their connections on the island would be seriously punished. And the inspector would have to arrive no sooner than he said he would.

When the night came, Maria said she would not be left alone in the house. Dreams of snaky water monsters and lipless, hairless women had come to her in the past nights, and she did not want to be left with these creatures.

If circumstances were different, Díaz would not have let her come. But there was this: since Wednesday, when the nurse had given him the news, time had seemed odd, a mixture of the time of children and the time of the elderly, so things seemed both endlessly long and precious to him. He wanted to be with Maria as much as he could.

At dusk, Raul Miguel and Madero arrived at the house. Raul Miguel came because his arms were strong and because he could swim the farthest under water without need for air. If the canoes were late, he would swim to the boats and tell them to turn around. Before Díaz and Maria joined the others, they reminded their water boy of his job; he was to make sure the inspector arrived no sooner than he said he would. Pushing, taunting, tripping . . . he was permitted any means to keep the inspector, should he try to arrive early, from the water.

"I imagine there will be steel-nibbed pens in these canoes," Madero said greedily. "I've ordered at least a hundred and plan to go into a little business of my own. I've long suspected I would make a good merchant. Perhaps a little store in my hut."

Moments after they arrived on the beach, the canoes came. They were unloaded with no problem. Others met them on the beach, and together they were able to whisk the boxes away. By nine-thirty, there was no trace of the canoes' arrival. The inspector, despite the diligence of the water boy, arrived fifteen minutes early. He walked backward onto the beach and stopped to throw huge handfuls of mud with every step he took. "Leave me alone, boy. Stupid boy," he called as he threw two last handfuls of mud down the path toward his tormentor. "Je-sus," he turned around and waved at Díaz and the others. "Some idiotic little boy has been persecuting me and . . ." he stopped and looked at Maria. "What's she doing here? She will get us all ill." As soon as the words were out of his mouth, the inspector dropped his head as if he were ashamed.

Madero, Raul Miguel, Díaz and Maria had been standing together away from the water, against a backdrop of sand. Díaz broke from the group and walked up the beach toward the trees and the inspector. "Inspector," he pulled the man by his elbow to his side, "don't say a word. We haven't told her. Please. We will stand off to the side."

"That will be fine," the inspector said, and he nodded his head. "But what are you all doing on the beach? Surely, they will see you. Let's stand over there." He pointed to a clump of tress that jutted out, like a peninsula, into the sand. The group followed his finger. Díaz and Maria moved a few yards away from the others. They waited silently in the shadows of a *yagua* tree for ten o'clock.

The hour came and went without event.

Sometime after the hour, Díaz said, "I'm sorry I must have been mistaken. It was an unreliable sort who suggested the whole idea to me."

"Let's wait a little longer just to be sure," Madero said.

"Yes, let's," said the inspector.

Maria leaned into him and whispered in his ear, so no one else could hear, "The canoes are coming back."

"Don't be ridiculous," he said, under his breath.

"They are. I can hear the paddles hitting the water."

Díaz listened. He heard night insects, but the water was still. The minutes were hours slow.

"I can hear them. They're coming back."

"They are coming back next week," his voice was low and sharp, a manner he almost never used with his wife. "Maybe that's what your remarkable perception perceives."

"I'm not wrong," she said louder, so the others turned to see what was going on.

"What's the matter?" said the inspector.

"It's nothing," Díaz responded, and Maria nodded her head in agreement, then whispered to Díaz. "I'm certain. They are coming closer." She was a bit ferocious now, too, in response to Díaz's harshness.

And then everyone heard the noises.

"Sh!" demanded the inspector. They could all sense shapes on the water, moving in the dark. And then they could make out two long shadows. The canoes were back. Díaz and the others watched them pull the boats ashore. Díaz looked at the others, expecting to see some sign of surprise, but the only man among them who would meet his eyes was the inspector, who smirked and nodded towards the boats as if to say, "Well, there you have it."

Men got out of the boats, wandered to the right a bit, then to the left and then came rushing toward the spot where Díaz and the others were hidden. They called out, "Díaz, Díaz. We have the stuff, Díaz." Díaz saw Madero smile at them.

Jesus, no, Díaz thought, and Maria squeezed his hand as if she had heard his thought.

Díaz denied the charges, of course, but various *isleños* stepped forward with the products he had procured for them. They each claimed that since Díaz was a *blanco* and with the government, they had no idea it was wrong. In many cases, this was true. Pepito Armado displayed his glass eye. Raul Miguel brought a clock, and others showed up with chocolates and cloth and other material. Díaz thought about dragging the rest of the guilty in—naming Madero, Raul Miguel, Luis Camacho—but there was no way to maintain he was innocent and others were guilty. He could only say he was innocent and that it was an evil trick.

The governor who, last year, had bought three whores with the funds intended for a prison, was in a quandary; he'd sent so many favorable reports about Díaz to the King. He said he would allow Díaz to live in his home till they were able to deal with the issue justly. The nurse was permitted to continue her visits to the house, but Díaz's fields and cattle were reallotted. Once, Raul Miguel tried to come to the house to get his hammock back, but Díaz greeted him with a knife. "I'll send you to hell three times," he said and gestured upward with the knife, as though he were pushing it—one, two, three—into Raul's belly. Raul Miguel left without the hammock.

Now, Díaz would go aimlessly through the ground floor of the house, picking through books and cleaning. "Betrayed," he would mutter over and over again. "I have been betrayed," as if the fact would give way to a greater truth. The more Díaz thought, the more the wood floors in the house shone; the more the walls glowed white; the more the kettle in the kitchen was filled with fish. It was, Díaz still believed, however irrationally, the house that was determining the order of his life. If only he had treated it better, had lived up to its requirements. One day, the nurse found Díaz scrubbing the floor in the parlor, and she told him that whatever was making his wife ill had finally affected her mind. "Just today," she explained, "your wife told me that she knows, has known all along, what is making her ill. She believes she hears the noise of something, perhaps a little animal, biting, chewing and swallowing her body."

He ran upstairs. "Where is it?" he demanded. "You hear it. You must know where it is."

He saw she was thinking to pretend she misunderstood him, but then she said, "She promised me she wouldn't tell you."

"What's the matter with you? You know what it is, and you won't stop it?"

There was no point in this. She only insisted on being taken to bed, and Díaz obliged. "Tomorrow," he whispered in her ear, as he placed her on the sheets, "tomorrow you will have to tell me what it is, and we will stop it." During the night, he chastised himself for speaking so harshly. *She is sick. A sick person shouldn't be yelled at.*

In the morning, she did not wake at his shuffling about the room. He called her name and shook her gently. His second emotion was sorrow. His first was anger that even she couldn't be trusted.

The funeral was delayed for two days. Officially, there had to be a European clergyman presiding, and the priest had to be called back from a neighboring village. The nurse, Díaz and the priest were in attendance at the funeral. Several local boys stood by to assist with the coffin. Epidemic victims were buried twice and in two places. They had to wait three years to be moved from their first burial spot to the graveyard. This was a rule everyone followed: the dead must not be infected.

To bury someone in dust, he started to think, seems like a queer perversion of what a burial should be. Something not quite heavy enough about it. One had to dig much further down in this soil to reach the appropriate type of soil. At home, the dark heavy soil was only a few inches under. There, when you put someone in the ground, they stayed. Here, he felt the coffin would just float away.

The priest asked if he would like to say something. "Yes," he said. He would, but when he went to speak, he found there was not really anything. The mourner's platitude—it's not fair—blared in his ear. Nothing else came to him.

When the service was over, he returned home. He remained in the *hacienda* for several weeks without disturbing Maria's room. For a while, he thought he might be tried and sentenced, but that period passed. He almost mourned the loss of an opportunity for a bleak prison existence. There, he imagined, he would share a world with someone.

Once, he sneaked into Maria's room and read from a page she had written. It disgusted him. There were lascivious descriptions of the way the wind caressed her, a description of the grass as a field of worms, of leaves as palms of hands. He didn't look beyond the page. He'd remember her as he would, not as she was.

When he packed his belongings, hers remained. A happy enigma, he hoped, for the person who took his position. A mystery: an empty house with one furnished room. A high bed with white, lace covers. The bowl for the water. White translucent curtains over the windows. The table would be cluttered with books and little things she had written down. He would not read them, but they would.

But then he thought, Why let her version of things stand? He picked up a pen and started to fill a diary, one of the empty ones she kept next to the books in which she wrote. "People," he began, "died . . ." He wrote a paragraph and stopped. He looked back over his words. Why let anyone question his version of the truth? Third person had so much more authority, sounded so much more objective. Why not tell the whole story that way? Where he had written the words, "I rolled my eyes heavenward," he dropped a blob of blue ink. He wrote instead: "Doroteo Díaz rolled his eyes heavenward . . ."

There are so many ways to cheat, he thought, amazed. There were possibilities he hadn't let himself begin to imagine. Still, years later, when he was remarried and working behind a desk in Madrid, imagination failed him; he had to admit that whenever he thought of how others lived in the world, he was at night, on the island, in the dark.

Separate Narratives

(Maria Elena—October 1978)

After I listened to Beatriz's long story about the colonial couple, I felt I had three options: literary analysis, mystical belief or sleep. I chose sleep, since she told me the story through the whole of a long night on the Caribe Hilton terrace. I slept through the day and into the middle of the next night. When I woke, I crept into the girls' room, found the stolen manuscript and set myself down in the kitchen to read.

"I like to go straight to the source," I told Beatriz, when she found me in the morning. "OK?"

"OK," she said, "but it's our secret, right?"

I pressed her hand reassuringly. "Just you and me."

"So," she said, "could you read it in secret?"

"Sure," I said. "I'll take it to the bedroom."

I spent the rest of the day propped up with pillows, finishing the book. The subsequent morning, I succumbed to the urge for literary analysis. It was Sunday, a work day for Sandrofo and the girls but not for me. I woke late, then went downstairs to the bakery for some coffee. All three of the girls were working behind the counter, though given the late hour of the morning, this meant they outnumbered the bakery's customers.

I sat at a table away from the counter, where the girls were flipping through sections of the newspaper. "Beatriz," I called. "Come talk to me for a bit."

Beatriz hurried over, whispered, "So now you see what I'm talking about?"

"Well," I said. "I have to say after reading it myself, I *don't* see what makes you . . ."

Beatriz held up her hand. "See. First, the man in the story, Doroteo Díaz, one of his eyes wanders, just like Dad's. And he has sharp features. And the woman is named Maria."

"Yes?" I said.

"And that's not all. He's an emigré to the island. Just like Papi. He's not really from here."

"Well, Beatriz. If you go back far enough, nobody is really from here. I mean, even I'm not, though I was born here."

"Well, yeah," Beatriz said, "but, you see . . ."

I stopped her, took a sip of coffee and said, "Beatriz, I think because you're, well, the age you are, maybe you don't quite have all the life experience to see . . . ." I stopped, smiled and said, "You're such a smart girl, and I mean no offense by this, but that story about the colonial couple; it's not about what you think. It's just about a couple that doesn't understand one another. When you have boyfriends, you'll see, there's always the narrative that's in your head and the narrative that's in his head. The book is just describing a common phen—"

"Oh, please," Beatriz said. "I *know* that. What sort of idiot do you take me for?"

"Oh, garden variety."

"For Christ's sake," Beatriz pushed back in her chair.

I grabbed her hand. "It's a joke, a joke. Sorry. It wasn't funny."

"Are you talking about the new house?" Tata called over to us.

I said yes, and Beatriz said no at exactly the same time.

"See," I whispered. "Just like the book. Two separate narratives."

"Beatriz," Tata said, "you must be a *little* excited. I mean, you'll get to decorate your own room."

"Course," Melone began, "that'll mean—"

"Come on, Melone," I said. The girls were always arguing over their bedroom decor. It was a fight that invariably pitted Tata and Melone against Beatriz. Their complaint wasn't her taste so much as her lengthy decision making. A lifelong problem, Tata and Melone maintained. "Remember," they'd insist, still bitter, "how when we played dolls, you spent so much time setting up your doll's house that we never got to play? Remember that?"

"Beatriz," I began, as gently as possible, "you know we are going to move to the convent. That's something that is going to happen."

"No!" she said, reaching across the table and grabbing the fingers of my left hand.

"It will be OK, honey, really."

"No, it won't. I know. I see things."

"You mean the future?"

"No, the past."

"What are you saying? About when you were a girl?"

"We can't talk about that."

"Beatriz," I said, shaking my head. "I'm confused. Listen. One thing at a time. We are going to move."

"No," she said violently and jumped up.

"What's going on?" Tata called from behind the counter.

"Nothing." Beatriz slunk back into her chair, said, "His eye wanders."

"Yes, it does," I said. "But your father's no criminal. He's Mister Law and Order."

Beatriz nodded her reluctant agreement, but then she said, "You can't marry him. We can't move there. If we do, someone will betray him. Just like in the story. And you'll die. You'll get a terrible disease."

"Beatriz, I'm nothing like that neurasthenic woman in the story. And who would want to betray your father? It doesn't fit, and even if it did . . ."

"Don't you see? It will be a disastrous pairing. Like her, you're smarter than your husband." I smiled at this. "It's true," Beatriz said. "We pretend otherwise, but you're much smarter than Papi, plus you're in the process of trying to know even more, always asking questions about our real mother's life. And it's not just that. Didn't you read how the man in the story said that the house was making him do things?"

I looked at Beatriz and shook my head. "Beatriz, you're a smart girl. You know that he doesn't mean that literally."

"You can't be too careful," Beatriz said. "Look what happened to the nuns. That house is full of death."

"Beatriz, we're moving. That's not going to change. You're going to have to find a way to reconcile yourself to that."

Beatriz was quiet, her eyes trained on the table, then she said, "Don't marry him. Don't marry my father."

"Oh, Beatriz," I said and stood, kissed her cheek. I had yet to take my morning shower and was ready to leave. "That's not the solution."

But Lucia thought it was. The next day at work, we debated the subject. Finally, as five o'clock drew near and passed, she came to a decision, "Wait on the wedding."

"Oh, come on," I said.

"Don't you believe in prophesy, premonitions?"

I said I did. I also believed in hysteria, and this seemed to be a textbook case.

Lucia said, "I have to tell you again, even if you don't believe anymore, you should take the girl to Sister Perez. At the very least, if there is nothing to fear, it will give her some comfort."

"I guess," I said. We were at the door of the gallery, getting set to depart. Still, we were talking avidly, the stored energy of a dialogue that had been silent all day, because we'd been busy with the bookkeeper. "Actually, that's not a bad idea."

Lucia nodded. "I'll go with you, if you like."

"No, no, I don't think so," I said.

To be polite, I made a physical gesture away from Lucia, to indicate I was respectful of her time, ready to walk down the street and free her if that was what she wanted. But it wasn't what I wanted, so I talked on, thinking it really was true that the body had nothing to do with the soul. "What confuses me most about all this," I said, "is even if we were like the couple in the story—and there are some similarities, though I think she's stretching things—why would this make a difference? Why would their life affect ours?"

"Circular time," Lucia said. "Everything repeats, so your fate is decided, and well, the girl thinks fate is identity." She dropped her keys into her handbag and then pulled them out again and wrapped them around her fist.

I nodded, then slowed my head. "What does that mean: fate is identity?"

"Reverse of existentialism," she said, slumping against the door frame. "You aren't your choices, but you are the product of what is to happen to you."

"Makes a person seem like a beach ball. You get knocked there; then you get knocked over there; that's you."

"Maybe. Perhaps I don't understand it myself," she admitted with a shrug, then pulled herself up and started to turn away from me, down the street toward her car, a magnet stronger than my desire to continue this conversation.

"Identity is fate. Now, that makes sense," I said thinking of how in the past I had unsuccessfully tried to change myself, so I could finally move the rusted rudder of my life and sail off in a different direction. Lucia was quiet. Clearly, she was timing the dinner she would soon prepare. When should she put the *asopao* on the stove if she wanted it heated just when the *tostones* were ready to come out of the frying pan? "Well, bye," I said quickly, eager to be the first one to articulate the fact of the departure. "See you tomorrow."

Despite my words, I didn't seriously consider Lucia's suggestion about going to Sister Perez until a week later. I was sitting with Sandrofo and the girls in the bakery, and we were in the midst of drawing up a guest list for the wedding, when Beatriz started to sob. Sandrofo looked up from the list at me. "What's going on?"

"You know," I said, reaching over to tap the piece of paper he was writing on, "I'm so tired. Let's do this later." Sandrofo shrugged OK. I waved the rest of the family away from the bakery table, pulled Beatriz to my side and said, "What?"

"Really," she sobbed. "How will I stand it when you're gone?"

"Oh, God," I said and held her head to my breasts. "I'm not going to die. I'm not . . . Tata, I mean, Beatriz, what if we don't marry? What if we just all live in the house together?"

"Well, maybe . . ." she said through her tears.

"Marriage," I said with disgust. "It's a stupid institution anyway."

She nodded her head, as if she, too, had never thought much of it. "But, but . . ." she said.

"But what?"

"Keep an eye out for deceit."

"I will," I promised. "I will." What, I wondered, should I look for? Carla Mendota stealing money from the cash register? Rayovac spitting into the dough while no one was looking?

"I'll tell him now," I said and gestured with my head over to the cash register where Sandrofo was standing. "Right now, OK?"

"OK," Beatriz sniffed.

"Hon?" I called to Sandrofo. "Let's go upstairs." He nodded his head, padded behind me to the apartment. As we stepped through the upstairs door, I turned to him, took him in my arms.

"So," he said without malice, "what now in the great drama of my favorite crazy daughter?"

"You know," I said, "let's wait on the wedding. I think we're overwhelming the girls with change." He stepped backward, out of my arms.

"That is ridiculous," he said, instantly angry. "I won't have Beatriz manipulating . . ."

"No, no," I said. "I'll move in with you. It will be just like we were married. We'll just wait on the ceremony." I didn't think he would object; after all, the money saved could be used to pay back part of the house loan from Victor and Coco.

"Don't you *want* to marry me?"

"Yes, yes, of course. It's just the ceremony I want to wait on. For the girls. It has nothing to do with you or with us, with the way I feel about you." As soon as I said it, however, I wondered if it were true. I *did* want to marry Sandrofo, though I had a normal amount of ambivalence. Only idiots, I was convinced, went happily into a union. Those with functioning brains knew that on occasion they'd wake in the middle of the night and realize the thing lying next to them was hot because it was full up with blood. You had to have those flashes of pure disgust at the hair in their nostrils or their weighty stomachs or their tendency to shout instead of simply talk. All those feelings were part and parcel of dealing with the opposite sex, I supposed, since I'd never had these feelings about girlfriends, only boyfriends and, I had to confess, mothers. As far as I was concerned, however, mothers limited their horribleness to food. They left rice on their cheeks when they ate. They made a dreadful licking noise of pleasure when they saw you eating a meat fritter. Asked, asked repeatedly: "How ever do you manage to eat all those fatty foods and keep your hourglass figure?"

"I don't want to wait," Sandrofo said, calling me back to the conversation. "She's got some fantasy about me and can't handle my having a wife, and I think . . ."

I held up my hand. "I don't know that that's it. Let's just do it this way. For me?"

"OK," he said. "OK." I was disappointed by how quickly he agreed—perhaps he had the same set of doubts I did?—but I reminded myself to keep my mouth shut. *No begging for reassurance,* I told myself, and without my alms cup out, he didn't give me any.

Instead, he walked over to the couch, sat and patted the cushion to his side. I curled next to him, resting my head on his shoulders. For a while, we stayed there quietly. We weren't really talkers, and that, I thought, was the problem; my disappointment in Sandrofo was all about words. I missed the frenetic patter of Carlos, the lawyer I used to see, though not, I had to admit, Carlos's unfortunate fondness for other women's beds. Thank God, Sandrofo wasn't like that. He was a good man. That had been my first perception of him, and it hadn't gone away. *He was a man used to concern about others.* Maybe not the most fascinating virtue, but certainly the most important one. I slipped my head into Sandrofo's lap and let myself doze while he stroked my hair. Finally, he shifted my head away, and I woke to hear him softly saying, ". . . left the newspaper. Probably the bedroom." I sat up to watch him. I admired the shift of his leg off his thigh. Something thoughtful in the gesture, I guessed, but I didn't really know. Sleepily, I studied his back as he left the room and wondered what he was really feeling. Then, as if he'd been gone for a decade, I wondered what he looked like. Silence, I realized, had always made him seem physically vague to me. Sometimes, even when I was looking right at him, he could disappear before my eyes.

The next day I joined Beatriz behind the counter at La Madeleine. While helping her refill sugar canisters, I suggested we go to Cataño and find out about the stolen book and what it really meant. I explained Sister Perez's policy: we could each ask one question for free. But, I warned, she was tricky; she counted "How are you?" as question number one. We had to be rude if we wanted to get anything for free beyond a rather revolting description of her indigestion.

"OK," Beatriz said, twisting a dishrag violently in her hands. "I'll do it. I'll ask about the book. But what will you ask?"

"Oh, you know me," I said, "something about your father."

"No, no, you can't do that."

"Beatriz," I said, my voice on the edge of irritation.

"I don't want to go over there," she said, in response. Her voice was so final that I didn't even bother trying to change her mind with a promise that I wouldn't ask about Sandrofo. Eventually, we settled on a compromise. I would go to Cataño alone and ask about the book, then I'd report back on my findings. "No point," I said, "in cutting into your homework time."

"OK," Beatriz said, "but . . ." she hesitated and let her eyes scan the bakery, as if she were looking for an unfilled coffee cup.

"But what?" I said, leaning toward her and raising my eyebrows.

"Deceit," she said.

"I'm on the lookout," I said. "Count on me to be vigilant."

The Book of Names

(Melone—November 1978)

At first, I was like everyone else. I admired Maria Elena and her prophetic ways. I thought she represented a wise addition to our family. She had a liberalizing influence on my father, a calming one on my sisters. Then, sooner than most, I changed my mind. I couldn't hate her, because there was a lot to like, even love. Still, I did wish her out of my family. But by the time I was smart enough to wish her gone, she was already my stepmother, though the relationship had yet to be confirmed by documents, marriage or adoption.

What I didn't like was that she turned her attention to me. It began as a lark, an early evening trip to Cataño to visit Sister Perez, the sometime sorceress. Maria Elena wanted a companion, so she came into the bakery to see whom she could find. Probably she was hoping for Beatriz. They had a special relationship, predicated on Maria Elena's conviction that she understood the quirks of Beatriz's mind and Beatriz's pleasure at Maria Elena's wish—if not her ability—to understand what she was thinking.

"Melone," she called, as she stepped in the door. I sensed disappointment. I was not her favorite of Sandrofo's children. Still, she waved and said, "I've been given the rest of the afternoon off." It was just three o'clock, late of a Tuesday afternoon, the time when the Muzak melodies Rayovac liked to listen to shifted to a more upbeat tempo. I suppose to wake sagging office employees. It always had the opposite effect on me. I'd been daydreaming about stretching out on the bakery counter for a little nap.

"Well, that's nice," I told Maria Elena.

"We're between shows, you know, and we just ran out of work. So, Lucia says, 'Just go, take the day to yourself,' which seemed odd to me, 'Take the day to yourself.' And she was a little smug about it, as if she were giving me chocolates. I was going to say, 'I think my day belongs to me whether you give it to me or not,' but . . ."

"But what?"

"But, you know that old saying: *En la boca cerrada no entran las moscas.*"

I nodded. No flies enter a closed mouth.

"So I decided I should make good use of my time. Which is why I'm here to drag you away from your work."

"Oh," I said and shook my head, "I can't."

"You're not the only one here, are you?" She meant working. There were a few men playing cards at one of the back tables.

"There's Rayovac, out back."

"Oh," Maria Elena said and raised her eyebrows. "Well, then," she started to whisper, "you won't want to come with me."

I gave her a scowl. "You know it's nothing like that."

"And why not?" she said, using a Jewish-grandmother-from-the-Bronx accent. "A young woman like you, pretty." The accent let her say things, while making fun of herself for saying them. I could see it was a liberating trick, and I'd taken to slipping into the voice myself, every now and then. "Sure, sure," she went on, "he's older, but that's no reason to . . ."

"Come on, come on," I said. Maria Elena had converted to Judaism for Father, and though I copied her accent at times, I sometimes felt she had no right to parody the grandmother I barely remembered. It was like the difference between a white and black person saying nigger.

"Now," Maria Elena said, dropping the accent and getting down to business, "maybe you'd like to come on a little adventure? It's a beautiful day."

It was, but then every day on the island was beautiful.

"I'm going to Cataño. I've decided to meet Sister Perez. I hear she's there today, but she won't make any guarantees about tomorrow or tomorrow's tomorrow."

Maria Elena pushed a piece of paper across the counter and tapped it—three times quickly—indicating I should read.

At the top of the paper was a small pen and ink drawing of Christ. He had an impressive, glowing nimbus. His eyes rolled heavenward, so he looked like a basset hound, rather than a man considering his blessed Father. His arms were lifted, his fingers curled into a fist save for the index fingers, which pointed out to either side. He looked as if he might do the Twist.

Underneath were these words:

> You owe it to yourself and your family to see SISTER Perez today for tomorrow maybe too late for she can and will help you as she has helped thousands and thousands.
>
> The religious HOLY woman healer, God's messenger who guarantees to show you your sickness and PAIN, to call all enemies by name.
>
> She will honestly answer one FREE QUESTION for all friends. Enemies must accept and will receive hate-filled lies.

I laughed.

"It will be great," Maria Elena said. "We'll take the ferry over and be back in time for your father. He comes back from the bank at five o'clock, right?" She didn't wait for my answer. This was purely recreational speaking on her part. After all, she knew my father's schedule. "We'll have plenty of time. And—" she started to giggle herself, "tomorrow may be too late."

"And I do owe it to myself," I said. "Not to mention my family. There's that pesky obligation to the family."

"Great. I'll tell Rayovac to mind the place," she said and disappeared into the back room.

I knew Rayovac wouldn't like that. He preferred the bakery's behind-the-scenes activities. He was a fanatic about racking the bread for delivery. Serving customers and working the cash register weren't part of his job description . . . and these tasks made him nervous. Too much human interaction reminded him that he was lonely and unhappy about being lonely.

I could hear him in the back room, objecting to her request. In truth, long before I started to feel hesitant about Maria Elena, Rayovac had developed an apparent, if unspoken, mistrust of her cheerfulness, her openness about her trauma-filled past, her hyperbolic anecdotes. He blamed her entirely for our family's move to the old Díaz plantation, just a field away from the house where his father had been born. He felt the move was evidence of the corrupting influence Maria Elena was having on my family. At first, I thought that was absurd, but I came to see what he meant, though I thought the real problem was that any outsider would have a corrupting influence on our family. There was something about us that didn't admit other people. Other people meant our own version of the world might come under the sort of common scrutiny that it simply couldn't handle.

At length, Maria Elena strolled out of the back room, hooked her arm in mine and said, "It's all settled." Behind her, Rayovac stood sheepishly in the doorway. I knew I'd pay later for deserting him this way. Without saying anything, he could force me into a guilty affection. Enough I-hate-myself looks, I used to say to my sisters, and I'll be saying, "Let's sleep together. How about that? Wouldn't that cheer you up?" Never mind that I had no intention of ever holding hands with Rayovac Rodriguez. At the same time, I disapproved of my inability to love Rayovac, because I knew he was a man who needed love and he'd fastened his hopes on me. Still, I found him repulsive. I'd focused my objections on four bristly hairs that stood on the spine of his nose, but honestly, I wasn't that horribly judgmental. Truth was, he scared me on some level. I knew anything like a real and thorough rejection on my part would put me in the category of all those women—spiritually deplete, caustic bourgeoisie—who had rejected him in the past.

"Sorry, Rayovac," I mumbled. "I'll make it up to you."

Rayovac gave his head a small disapproving nod upward, as if he already saw me decked out in Maria Elena's clothes—the earrings that hung to her shoulders, the purple lipstick to match her purple crepe dress, sleeveless and chic.

"Let's go," Maria Elena pulled my elbow and steered me out the front door. "Sister Perez awaits."

That time of day, the only things down at the docks were two gigantic but empty cruise liners. The tourists were all shopping in the new section of town or deep-sea fishing or sunning on the beaches. The liners seemed odd, too white and big against the blue of the sea, as if they—the boats—thought with their newness and their size they might be able to deny what was unavoidably true about the expanse of the sea. It seemed to me like Moby Dick in reverse. The ocean held a desperate dark whale, a famous character, known by slack-jawed high school students throughout the continent for his failure to tip these two things over.

There was something strangely comforting about ignoring the cruisers and stepping instead onto the rickety ferry that went to Cataño. The ferry had a maybe-you'll-sink feel that seemed pleasantly accurate. Maria Elena and I stood by the rail.

"It's like the Staten Island ferry. Were you ever on the ferry?" Maria Elena was almost my mother now, but there was still so much we didn't know about each other. Even things like this . . . the basic chronology of the geography of our years on the planet.

"Yes, I think I must have been, when I was a little girl in New York."

"Well, so you'll understand this," Maria Elena said. "It's like we're leaving Manhattan and all its sophistication . . . ." Maria Elena turned around to look at the fortress wall that surrounded the whole of the old city. "We're off for more suburban haunts."

"Oh, yes," I said. "Cataño's very suburban. You've heard about the possessed blenders, the talking microwave ovens. The satanic trash compactors."

"Of course. What sort of fool do you take me for? Of course, I've heard about all that." She laughed and patted me, companionably, on the forearm.

Cataño was known to be full of these Sister Perez types. It was the only place in the city with an authentic santería and people who really believed. The area was full of hocus-pocus, and yet it seemed undeniably real. I had always admired the radio clatter, the lack of air conditioning, the difficulty cars had getting through the streets, the way people wired their TV sets to face out of windows—so they could watch them from the road, so they could see what was going on in both worlds, the mystical world of the street and the charmed but unremarkable world of American TV.

When the ferry was under way, the wind hit us full force and swallowed up sound, so it took me awhile to realize Maria Elena was talking to me.

"What?" I finally shouted at her. "What did you say?"

"What are you going to ask?"

"I wasn't going to ask anything," I said.

"No, no," she laughed. "What is the question you want to ask Sister Perez? You get one free one."

"Oh," I shrugged.

"You'll ask about your second lover, of course," Maria Elena said, as if she were a schoolteacher, briskly informing me of the correct answer and disappointed her best student hadn't been able to answer. Maria Elena went on. "It's no good to ask about your first. Your first lover will just be the person you do it with because you are embarrassed about being a virgin. The second one is the one who will count. He's the one you might or might not marry."

"Oh, Maria Elena," I said, as if embarrassed or above concerns about men. "I thought maybe I'd ask—" I was quiet for a moment.

"Not some philosophical question, I hope. That's a lot of rot, you know. I do-not-know-my-way-about sort of stuff. Don't do it. Ask about boys."

I laughed. "What are you going to ask?"

"Don't change the subject," she said. "Boys," she gave me her one-word piece of advice and looked out at the approaching dock.

Maria Elena's thoughts were often on the edge of my own. I *did* want to ask something romantic, but thought I should ask something soulful. Maybe I was just disappointed by my own lack of originality, since in her mouth, my thoughts quickly seemed like nothing.

"Boys," she repeated, as if I might not have heard her. "Don't forget."

I was surprised by her insistence, if only because Maria Elena was possessive about her ability to attract men. It was clear she thought her skill was one other women did not share. She had a sly way of making me understand myself as hopelessly manless, even when she was telling me how young I was, how I had my whole life ahead of me. The words were right, but the tone made me feel miserable. When Maria Elena was around, I started fussing with my clothing, thinking I should stop gobbling leftover dough before I cleaned mixing bowls. I started to hate myself, since she already seemed to have a clear sense of my failures with men, failures that stretched into a long, lonely future where I, bobbing on a rocker and out of pure desperation, regretted my failure to take Rayovac in my arms.

Finally, the boat made its sloppy arrival on shore. We bumped several times against the pier till a thin, somber-faced boy came down the dock, kneeled and picked a seaweed-covered rope out of the water. He tied it to the pier and pulled a rickety wooden gangplank to shore. We followed it onto firm ground.

"Can I tell you a secret?" Maria Elena said. "Let's sit down for a bit right here. Our appointment isn't for another fifteen minutes." We sat on a bench by the ferry station's phones. It was an ugly place to sit, and we didn't make it any better by facing the water. Instead, we faced the swinging door to the men's bathroom. Bits of trash scampered by at our feet as if they—the scraps—couldn't believe they weren't living. "A secret?" Maria Elena asked again.

"Sure," I said.

I'm the kind of person people always tell secrets. Strangers on buses, even. I put on the face I like to wear when people are getting set to tell me a secret. It's a face that says, *It's all the same to me.*

I don't know how many people are genuinely fooled by this.

"I'm going to ask about your father. I'm going to ask . . ." she stopped dramatically and gave me a little look.

Oh, please, I thought, don't say anything about your sex life. It wasn't something I would put past Maria Elena, and I'd have to tell her about how we'd learned a bit about Freud while studying *Oedipus* in

English class, and if she would please just shut up, I would appreciate it very much.

"I'm going to ask who he is."

"What do you mean 'who he is'?"

"Ah, you know. You can't tell me you don't know."

"I can't?" I said and hoped I sounded forlorn.

"The big mystery of your father." I was quiet. "When your father first asked me out, you know what everyone around said? I mean, the women? They said, 'Sandrofo Cordero Lucero, he's never asked a woman out, not once in all these years.' And then he offered to teach me how to sail. That's what we did on our first date. Everyone said, 'He must like you, Maria Elena, because we've never seen him on a sailboat before.' You see, what I am saying?"

"No," I said. "I don't think I do."

"So, I thought I'd cracked the puzzle, the big mystery. He'd finished grieving your mother—I mean no disrespect by that—and he was ready to reveal himself to someone new." I both wanted to ask Maria Elena to be quiet and wanted her to go on, so I was silent. "But I don't know him. Nobody does. I thought I was so unusual and that . . . Well, it was an arrogant thought, really, that I'd figure him out, that I'd know him, you see, but I don't, so I have to ask Sister Perez about it."

"He's just quiet," I said, as if with all her agonizing about his identity, this possible solution had not occurred to her.

"Quiet like the *coquí*'s invisible," Maria Elena said. The *coquí* was a small frog, a transparent creature that graced almost all the island's tourist pamphlets. At dusk, they made a racket when they came out and started to sing a funny song that sounded like their own name: *co-kee, co-kee, co-kee.* The sound drove me crazy. On the porch of our new home, I'd look around desperately. *Goddammit,* I'd think, *now that I live in the country, I intend to see one,* but I hadn't yet.

"Melone," Maria Elena prompted me for a response, "your father."

"I don't know," I said in the way you say those words to end a conversation.

Maria Elena stood up from the bench and motioned for me to do the same. "You're right. You don't know. But Sister Perez does. Come on." She put her arm around my shoulder, and I put my arm around her waist, so we both understood no harm had come from our disagreement. She was a new mother, I reminded myself, even if I, at fifteen, was an outsized baby. She was doing what I imagined new mothers always did: revised their view of the world daily to correspond with the miracle of their new position in the world.

To get to Sister Perez's, we had to walk three blocks inland and then turn left down a short path between two buildings till we emerged on a narrow, empty street. The road seemed, for its lack of activity, more like an alleyway, but apartments, either in the basement or one to two stories up, fronted on the street. We found Sister Perez's place tucked under a short staircase. She had two fire-hydrant-level windows, and in one of them, laced through the iron of the window grill, was a paper sign. With blue magic marker, someone had written, "*Perez y su hija superior. La mujer subterránea.*"

"Hmm," Maria Elena said. "She's come up in the world. Last time I saw her, she was operating out of a door that opened into that alley over there." She pointed across the street. I saw the alley and then looked to the front of the building, where I saw Perez and, I suppose, her superior daughter. They were sitting in lawn chairs, a few feet from the doorway. When Maria Elena and I crossed the street, however, the angle made it impossible to see a thing, and I couldn't tell if Perez and her daughter saw our approach. I hoped not, because as we crossed over I said, "I can't do this. It's . . . too much money."

Maria Elena stopped and looked at me. "You don't even know how much it costs. And anyway, the first question is free. If you have more questions, I'll pay. Come on." She tugged gently at my arm, and we continued walking.

My objection was about the fact that I didn't believe and knew that, if I didn't believe, I was going to receive one of those hate-filled lies Sister Perez liked to dole out to enemies and, faith or no faith, I wasn't in the mood for a hate-filled lie.

"I'll just wait outside while you go in."

Maria Elena looked up at the sky, as if it might give her some child-rearing tips. "Mother of God," she said and shook her head. "You're a loon. Just like your father."

I felt oddly complimented. "I'll sit right on those steps," I said and pointed to the stairs keeping Sister Perez's front door in shadows. "How long will you be?"

Maria Elena looked at me. "Will you go get something to eat?"

I could see if there was some purpose in my being there, if I fed myself, she wouldn't feel guilty. "Yes," I said. "Actually, I'm starved."

"I'll be about one hour, I think."

"One hour," I said.

Maria Elena looked at me warily, but then she said, "Have it your way. Just don't leave with someone else. Just don't find some boy and be wandering about, forgetting all about me, inside, learning about everything."

"I won't. I won't forget you," I said and she kissed my cheek and descended into Sister Perez's parlor.

An hour, I thought, when I turned back to the street. The possibilities seemed wonderful—an hour in an area of town I didn't know, where I was totally anonymous, where I might be anybody I cared to be. Of course, since my hormones were a mess, the first thing that occurred to me was that I could be a slut. I could go pick somebody up in a bar and so forth, but the plain fact was I didn't have the nerve, for that. I mean, my imagination had the nerve, but I didn't. Even when opportunities presented themselves, as they often did, with some boys at the University of Puerto Rico, I wasn't able to act. I was forever jumping up from couches, tearing my hand away from another hand, rebuttoning my blouse, and saying, "Sorry. I forgot. Turns out I *have* a boyfriend. I forgot all about him. He lives in Miami. I don't know how I could have been so absent-minded." I'd hit my head with the palm of my hand. "Isn't that something?" I'd say, apologetically.

Once, after one of these performances, a graduate student whom I was with—a man who, one of my friends used to say, just reeked sex—gently pulled me back to the couch we were sitting on. "That's OK," he said. "In fact, as long as we are being honest, I'm married."

"Oh," I said, as if this were good news. "Well." He pulled my legs up over his and languidly stroked my legs and breasts. He seemed in no rush. I kept my knees pressed tightly together, thinking I could really go ahead and do it, have sex and all. It seemed, given the tenor of the times, shameful to be cautious about sleeping with someone. "Well," I said at length, "wouldn't this upset your wife?"

"Oh," he said. "You know, I don't know. We've never really talked about it."

I gave him a look.

"Well," he said. "We haven't been married that long."

"Listen," I said and sat up quickly, tugging my skirt back down toward my knees. "I'm going to take a guess that this would bother her. Go ahead. *Call* me psychic."

He looked hurt, so I said, as if I had all the experience in the world, "No, no, this is a good thing. It will keep us from doing something we might regret." We continued, nonetheless, to kiss, as we stood by the door to his apartment. "Maybe I'd better go," I said, and eventually I did.

While I waited for Maria Elena, I sat down on the stairs above Sister Perez's. I was disappointed with myself, but I decided to move into a philosophical mode, be contemplative and intense and observant. Be Present to the World, which I knew, from philosophy class was a rare and impossible trait. I tried not to think of anything but what was going on at the moment.

Across the street was an apartment building. Four stories high. It was a relative rarity, since buildings in Cataño tended to be one or two stories. I looked from apartment to apartment and tried to figure out what was going on in each of them. But I couldn't see much. In the first-floor window, a family was getting ready for supper. I saw a young couple and their son. I guessed he was about four. The boy was bouncing a ball. The mother was setting dishes on the table, and the man was reading a newspaper. I saw her call the men to dinner and saw how the men—the father and the son—didn't adjust themselves toward the table in a way that suggested they had heard her. Then the boy said something, something that clearly had to do with his proficiency at bouncing the ball and catching it. But he bounced the ball, and it rolled across the room, and the mother looked panicked and then angry. It was as if she thought the child had been hopelessly arrogant by claiming he could bounce the ball and catch it and since he could not, indeed, do that, she was disgusted and worried. He would be like her, hopelessly incompetent for the rest of his life.

I can't say how I knew this was going on, but I was certain I had read the scene correctly. What a strange woman, I thought. I tried to look into other apartment windows but could see little past some gauzy curtains in one and, in another, a bit of a pink ceiling with exposed wire running to a bare light bulb in the center, I guessed, of a room.

I looked back to the family I could see fully. They all seemed turned inside out, but instead of blood and guts, what I saw was how they were each wronged by the other, misunderstood and disappointed.

This voyeur business was ceasing to be the sort of dark fun I had hoped it would be.

I looked again and saw the woman run around the table to kiss her husband playfully on the neck. So maybe I was wrong. I had a sudden respect for Sister Perez. After all, the impossibility of accurately reading another's life. What a brave thing to set up a sign and call it a profession. I started to wonder not what Sister Perez would know but what she wouldn't know about Maria Elena's life.

A greasy smell wafted over to me. Probably from down the street and then, with another wind, came the smell of fish. Perhaps a boat had just unloaded, although it seemed late in the day for that.

I thought back to that graduate student. I used to see him from time to time after the day we had kissed, and I would always feel embarrassed. At the door to his apartment, he had wrapped his arms around me and pulled me, by my buttocks, into him. He was wearing shorts and no underwear, as I could tell when the front of my thighs butted against his large erection. I wanted him so purely, the only thing I could do was go away. Even thinking about it now, I wanted him.

I was starting to feel angry with my own line of thinking, all this impossible longing. I occupied such a small physical space in the world, but my desires were tremendous. I thought of them, my disproportionate desires, as a giant octopus suspended over the island. Its tentacles floated over the surface of the sea and eventually—this was the size of the horrible creature—they creeped up to rest on the shores of Miami (in one direction) and (in others) Cuba and Haiti. I looked at the door to

Sister Perez's and willed Maria Elena out. It took fifteen minutes for my brand of magic to work. When Maria Elena came out, she looked a little pale, a little stricken.

"What is it?" I called from my spot on the steps. She shook her head vaguely. "Not bad news, I hope," I said.

"Mmm," she hummed, thoughtfully, as if she didn't know.

"Figure out who Dad is?"

She brushed her palms down along her purple dress and cleared her throat. "No, they couldn't find him. Couldn't find his name in the Book of Names. So . . . ." She pulled some sunglasses out of her bag and placed them, importantly, on her nose. "Let's walk," she said, putting her arm in mine as we made our way back to the dock. "I didn't learn a thing. See, the Book of Names in the santería is a little like the Book of the Living and the Book of the Dead for Jews." I suppose I must have looked at her blankly, for she pulled her arm away from mine, turned to look directly at me, and said, "It's true what the rabbi told my Hebrew class. Those of us who are converts will always seem more religious—certainly we'll always know more—than you real Jews. You must have noticed on Yom Kippur when you go to services, how everyone who has died, how their names are read out loud." I nodded my head. "Their names are being crossed out of the Book of the Living and put in the Book of the Dead. Santería has the same thing. All the living are in the Book of Names, but when I asked about your father, they couldn't find his name."

"Oh," I said, unsure how to respond because now she seemed clearly upset by this fact. We had arrived back at the docks, and Maria Elena was fishing in her pocketbook for coins so she could buy a soda.

"So," Maria Elena said, "don't you see? Your father doesn't exist." She clawed agitatedly at the bottom of her bag. "Why won't this . . . oh . . ." she cried out and pulled a bloodied finger from her bag. "I put my razor in my bag this morning. I forgot. Because I didn't have time to shave my legs before . . . look." She waved her finger in the air. "Oh," she said, her eyes starting to tear. She pulled a napkin from her bag and wrapped it tightly around her cut.

"Maria Elena," I said. "Maybe I should get you a . . ."

"No, no, it's fine," she said, though blood was seeping through the napkin. She wrapped a tissue on top of the napkin and said, "*Dios*, I feel lightheaded. Let's sit down." We sat on a bench facing the water. She twisted her hands in front of her in such a way I could tell her interior voice was telling her to keep calm. "Your father," she began.

"Yes," I said. "What did you mean before?"

"Just . . . oh, I don't know," she said, flustered.

"It's OK. I mean, you know I don't believe in this stuff, but even if I did, I wouldn't really get upset, because . . ." I couldn't think of a good reason not to get upset, but I didn't need to because Maria Elena—who hated to be comforted by someone younger than her—snapped her purse briskly shut and said abruptly, "Diet Coke?" She turned and held her uncut hand out to the soda machine on the wall behind us.

"OK," I said. "I'll get them." I took her money. Two cans clunked out of the machine. We both absent mindedly rubbed the cold cans on our foreheads and the back of our necks before opening them to drink.

"I had another question about a book of Beatriz's I meant to ask Perez, but I didn't even get a chance to ask it." I nodded my head. "Couldn't find his name," Maria Elena said out loud but as if musing to herself. Then she laughed and addressed herself clearly to me, saying, "Who would have thought even psychics have problems with filing things in the wrong folder?"

I laughed but lost my sense of humor on the ferry ride back, when Maria Elena spent the crossing telling me about what Sister Perez *did* tell her, in lieu of facts about my father. Perez told her about the divorce I would have, ten years in the future. I was surprised. It wasn't the date of the tale, but the main character of the story—me, feeling as I always knew I would—and the narrator—Maria Elena, knowing things she couldn't know and not because they were in the future but because they were in my head. They were part of the private narrative no one ever tells, the clamorous story that goes on in quiet rooms, that never stops, that dreams into the night, when the world of events and facts and senses are nothing. I would have to live another decade to know if what she was saying was right, whether my skepticism about psychic powers would be borne out or not. But I didn't need anything—not knowledge about future events or wisdom about the world—to hate her for saying all this and to hate her for the way she was saying it.

"You're just like me," she said enthusiastically, when she was through detailing the way in which I would get irritated at my first husband and then turn that irritation into self-hate and then daydream about killing myself.

"I am not," I said ferociously. "I am not just like you."

Surprised, she looked at me, then said, "But of course, you aren't. Everybody is different. What I meant is that the events of our lives are so similar."

Maybe this was a line of thinking Beatriz liked, but I would have none of it. "No, they are not," I said, emphatically. Then, meanly, "My sister isn't going to die."

Maria Elena blanched, and I said, quickly, "I'm sorry, that was a horrible thing to say, I'm sorry."

"It's OK," Maria Elena said. "I upset you. I wasn't thinking you'd be making that connection. Really. I'm the one who is sorry."

Maybe, I thought, Maria Elena really *had* been torn up by her sister's death. It had always seemed to me that in the years since the death, Maria Elena's sister had become just another one of those anecdotes that proved Maria Elena's favorite theory about herself: she was a champ when it came to disasters; everyday life was what she found impossible. It was hard not to be irritated by this, not to want to say, "That's the way we all deal with things." I would never reduce a loved one's death to an anecdote, and I hated the suggestion, implicit in Maria Elena's comparing of our lives, that something bad would happen to my sister and once the horrible event was in the past, I would be breezily using it to pad my emotional resume.

But of course, there was another part of her prediction. I would, like her, have love and then be frustrated in that love. For all my anger about the suggestions about my sister, I needed her to finish the story about my future divorce and subsequent suicidal ideation. "Tell me the rest," I said. On some level, I believed she knew what she was talking about, how, down the line, romantic dissatisfaction would make me mad.

She shook her head no. "I'm done," she said. "I told you all I have to tell."

I thought she was just trying not to bother me. "Please," I said. "Tell me the rest."

"There is no rest. I already told you. A guy who leaves his underwear under the bed. You respond by punching yourself, and one-two-three you are divorced. Actually, not divorced. You never married. You've been living together, but this underwear and punching, it makes you leave."

"No," I whined at her. "Then, what? Tell me the rest." I wasn't even sure what I was asking for, but finally she relented.

"Well," she said. "OK. I didn't really have anything else to say. I mean the story is over. It was just . . ." She concluded her story with the same sort of breathless enthusiasm she had begun it. It was the voice she always used when she was telling a story or complimenting herself. She said, "It was just that I was right. It was your second lover. And you were right. Rayovac never figures into this."

"And?" I asked. The ferry crunched against the dock, and all the sitting passengers bounced to their feet. The trip was over.

"And what? That's it."

"Oh," I sighed, feeling, I thought, the first bit of that disappointment she was talking about, that anger at something not pushed through to a satisfactory conclusion.

The Year of Our Father

(Melone—1979)

Every year, Angelo Marti was someone else. For him, it was a form of organized madness, governed by calendars and his one true talent—his ability to perceive essential yet hidden traits about the people around him. January 1 to December 31 of any single year, he dressed up as a person on the island. One year, it was the governor. Another year, it was the beggar with no voice box. Still another, it was a Catholic drug lord; possessed by money and guilt, he would (in Angelo's incarnation of him) accost lawyers in elegant restaurants and beg for punishment. And then, one year, he was my father.

It was something of an island sport, after the celebrations for the new year, to try to be the first person to discover who Angelo would be for the next three hundred sixty-five days. The morning of the fateful year, the honor went to Tata.

"Melone," she shrieked from the counter of the coffee shop, and I left off sweeping flour to look up and see Angelo, dressed in tan chinos and a plain white shirt, amble into La Madeleine.

It was just ten thirty, January 1, 1979. The first rush of business was over, and the morning stragglers were guiltily brushing crumbs from their laps, leaving their money on the table, and heading into the harsh whiteness of a too sunny day. Angelo smiled broadly and sat down at the counter. He fingered a single, coffee-stained paper that I was about to push into the trash.

"Hello, my girls," he said to Tata and me.

"Oh, no," I said. It didn't take Tata any longer to figure out what Angelo had in mind.

"Papi's going to have a fit. A complete fit," she said to me. And, then, to Angelo, "Hello, Pops," before she broke out into her own fit of giggles.

"You know, girls," Angelo said, "this place is my heart's desire." I guessed he was referring to the bakery. "Which makes me, I know, the luckiest of men. Escape is an old dream. Change: a story that never got written. But I did it."

"Angelo, you need help," Tata said. "That sounds nothing like Dad. But we'll give you pointers, won't we?" She pinched me in the waist—something that always drove me nuts.

"We will not," I said, pinching her back. And then, more to myself, "He is going to be so upset."

My father was an essentially shy man. He could be quite genial, particularly when doing business, but the shyness made him defensive, and he wasn't above lashing out with a sharp-tongued comment if people were upsetting him. When you were in a room with him, you often felt he was the most important person in that room; at the same time, you knew it was necessary not to draw attention to him. He was the kind of person who was always around cameras, but you could never get a picture of him. If that makes sense. In fact, the one time some tourist *did* take a picture of him, my father reached over the counter and snapped open the back of the camera to expose the film. "I am not," he said, by way of explanation, "a slide for a living room wall."

I could already hear my father saying, "No, no, this I won't stand for," when he saw Angelo.

"How do you feel about picking a different person, Angelo?" I asked. Angelo didn't respond. That was part of the game. "Dad," I tried again, "how about being someone else for this year?"

"What an odd thing to say," Angelo allowed.

"Oh, God." I rolled my eyes and said to Tata, "We've got to deprogram him or something. Dad is really going to lose it."

Of course, the chances of changing Angelo's mind were as slim as the chances my father would not be upset. Rumor had it that only once in the history of his transformations had Angelo switched identities midyear. And that was the year he decided the island was too boring. There were no interesting personalities to adopt for a year, so he created a fictitious one. He decided to be a maiden, determined to throw herself into a volcano. So he went to the island's single volcano, only to discover (and this was hardly news on the island) that the volcano was inactive; a golf course, a luscious, green circle, had been built in its crater. After that, Angelo distrusted his imagination. He drove a bus for the remainder of the year. The next January, he went back to being a mimic.

But my father, it would turn out, was no easy person to mimic. It wasn't just the fact that he was a hopeless insomniac that made that year so hard. It was the impossibility of wrestling my father's identity away from him. For the first time, really, I think, Angelo had come up against his own inability to carry his odd project through, and the inability wore on him in the saddest of ways. He looked less and less like my father as the days passed. He kept on wearing chinos and pale shirts, my father's trademark uniform. But he let his hair get unruly and then abandoned the dye that had kept it brown instead of a pigeon gray-white. I suspect he was trying to live without sleeping, because he was exhausted and sometimes would come into the bakery raving.

The truth may have been that he was becoming himself. But who knew what the real Angelo was like? He was a product of institutions—the orphanage, then a mental institution, until the great liberalizing of the sixties. He disappeared into the army for a few years, and then he was Angelo, regular fixture of San Juan, someone who was nobody because he was too many people.

What was strange was my father's response to all of this. From the beginning, he surprised us all. He didn't get angry, though Tata and I were sure he would. He didn't shout, "Stop following me. Get away," as Angelo's victims, in the past, were known to do. Rather, he struck up a peculiar friendship with Angelo.

They had had a loose connection for years. Apparently, Angelo was the first person who really spoke to my father when we arrived on the island, some ten years earlier. I don't remember meeting him, but my father said Angelo had been a beggar then, and he had asked for a job. My father had turned him down right away. From the start, my father knew he wanted Madeleine's to be a family business. He thought he'd done a perfectly good job of communicating this to Angelo. His Spanish was good, after all, and he was not a man who ever had trouble articulating his thoughts. Thus, it was something of a surprise to awake the next morning to find a line of men—a line so long it curled, like a tail, away from the body of the bakery and around the corner—waiting for Sandrofo to arrive at the bakery, so they could fill out job applications. In the ten years since then, Angelo had occasion to come into Madeleine's in one guise or another. Always as a customer, however, after that first year, an earnest eater of cake or drinker of coffee. Now he tried to arrive as owner at four in the morning.

"Sit down," my father would tell him and turn over a milk crate for Angelo. "Sit down right here." My father let Angelo watch him while he worked. They listened, in silence, to the radio. If Angelo tried to talk, my father would wave his hand. No, it was a time to be quiet. Later in the day, he would entertain small suggestions. Angelo wanted to change the wallpaper of the bakery. Angelo wanted to put cake in the bakery window (a suggestion my father took). Angelo wanted to put a pineapple on top of the cash register.

Sometimes, someone might come into the bakery and find Angelo dozing at the small corner table (behind a pillar and partially hidden by the cash register). To tease him, that person would say, "So, Sandrofo, you're clearly not from the island, though you've got Spanish blood and speak with a bit of an accent—maybe from New England—where are you from?"

"My life," Angelo would say at those times, "is none of your concern." He would say it in perfect English.

Maybe I hoped for hidden clues about my father. Maybe that was why I started to watch Angelo so carefully. But the only thing Angelo seemed to have right was that terse phrase "My life is none of your concern." There was no denying my father guarded his privacy. There was also no denying he did it in such a way that you felt his life was more complicated, more enthralling than any other. No matter that I was as much a witness to his life as any child is to her parent's life. He seemed to engage in the same activities as the rest of us. Well, almost. Work. No sleep. Love, I assume, now that Maria Elena was around. A sparse social life and a quirky intellectual life that included politics and science, excluded arts and letters. One thing his life did not include was alcohol. Which was why I was so surprised to realize, as the months progressed in their regular order, that Angelo was drinking too much.

By March, I was ready to say something about it. I slid into an unoccupied chair at Angelo's favorite table and said, "We need to talk."

Angelo looked up at me, almost confused, as if he couldn't guess who I was. Then he said, "It's boy trouble, isn't it?"

"No," I said.

"I'll tell you, he's not good enough for you. I don't know who he is, but he's not good enough for you. If he were, I wouldn't see you mooning about this bakery, crabbing at your sisters."

I fought the urge to deny I was mooning or crabbing. "I want to tell you a story. It's one I think about a lot," I said. I had decided, early in January, to pretend, whenever it was convenient, that I couldn't hear Angelo. "My story is about how my father was always permissive with us girls. But in a funny way, so he took all the fun out of being wild. We were ten years old, and he would insist on giving us cigarettes to try or ask us if we wanted some wine with dinner. When we were eight, he made us get our ears pierced. I mean, that's nothing down here, where everyone gets their ears pierced at birth, but up where we came from, that's something only grown women do."

Angelo gave me a look I recognized from my father. It wasn't unkind, but it demanded that I get to the point.

"Alcohol," I said. "That's what I want to talk about. My father, it turns out, has never had any. Not even one lousy sip of wine. Doesn't even know what the stuff tastes like. And we're Jewish, you know, so sometimes in religious ceremonies, you'll have to have some wine. But from the start, it was always grape juice with my father."

"Why," Angelo said, "are you talking about me as if I am not here?"

"And when I finally asked him about it, he told me he'd seen enough people ruin themselves with alcohol that he knew, very early on, that wasn't something he was going to do. At all."

Angelo stared at me then rubbed the back of his hand against his nose. He squirmed a bit in his chair, as if he were unbearably itchy.

"Do you see what I am saying?" I asked. I didn't think he would say, Yes, because I was saying, "If you want to pretend to be my father, you can't drink."

Instead, he said something I had heard my father say before. "I rather like the idea of bars. They seem so congenial, but no, I'm not a drinker. If I did drink, I think I would drink to excess, so I don't drink at all. Will you excuse me?"

Yes, I said, I would. It wasn't until Tata found the empty vodka bottles in the men's room that I realized he must have been excusing himself for a drink.

"My father was a drinker," my father said, with regret, when I approached him with my realization about Angelo. It was just after closing, and we were drying the last of the dishes. Soon, Maria Elena would come by, and we'd all head out to our new house, a reconverted convent, in the country.

"Oh," I said eagerly, hoping for some more information about him. "At home or at some bar in your neighborhood?" My father ignored me.

"I should have seen the signs. Stupid. Stupid," he said and slammed a metal bowl into place under a giant mixing fork. I thought, for a moment, he was referring to Angelo and Angelo's behavior, but then I realized he was referring to himself and his own failure to notice what I had picked up. "I can't say I haven't offered him a scotch." Though my father did not drink, there was a bar at home, stocked with bourbons and whiskeys. All things my father guessed would be appropriate to offer a business associate. There was nothing sweet and, surprisingly enough, no rum. I think he thought it would be insulting to offer travelers rum. It would mean you thought they were tourists and that wasn't a nice thing to think about a person. "Okay, okay," my father said, clearly in response to some private petitioner, for I was being quiet. "I'll have to see what I can do."

But already it was too late. We knew this because sometimes Angelo would fail to show up for . . . I suppose I want to say work, though of course that's not quite right, but he wouldn't be there, for his early-morning session with Father. We'd ask about him at breakfast. Had anyone seen him? There were always too many answers to trust anyone. He had been out whoring in La Perla. He was swimming around the island. An improbable task, to be sure. But wasn't everything about the man unlikely? And then the more reasonable suggestions: he was passed out in a bathroom in the Chamber of Commerce; he was bathing himself, washing away the stink of liquor in a public fountain; he was snoring, sleeping the deep sleep that is no sleep at all but an alcoholic stupor, under a bench at Ponce de Leon's old house.

Finally one day, Beatriz came into the shop crying.

"What is it?" my father said, in an instant panic. He was terribly protective of his children and had a mind that easily imagined disasters.

"Angelo's fallen down, face first, by the docks. The police came and took him away so you couldn't see him from the cruise ships."

"Oh, God," Father said. "You mind the store," he said to me.

Beatriz said, "I'll take care of things." I knew she was hurt he hadn't asked her to watch things. I had to fight back a sick wave of pleasure at having been favored, favored as more competent, and I took this skill to mean the world, as if it could work like a hex sign, ward off danger with the sheer power of the orderliness it produced.

Father went to the cash register and took out some bills from under the change drawer. "Bail money," Beatriz said, quickly, almost proudly.

"Yes?" my father said to Beatriz in such a way that the "yes" sounded like a question and a reprimand, a slap on the wrist for articulating the obvious.

When my father was gone, Beatriz said, "It's just like the people here. Clean things up so no one on the cruise ships sees anything ugly. Keep it pretty, keep it pretty."

"Oh, come on," Tata said.

"Come on, what?" Beatriz said. "The world's no cannoli."

"What are you talking about?"

It was one of Beatriz's jokes, in those days, to let us know life wasn't a piece of cake by referring to international pastries.

"I am talking about suffering, ever hear of it?" Beatriz said.

"Oh, yeah, once, I think I heard of it once," Tata snapped back. "I hate it when you start this, this Miss-Holier-Than-Thou Thing. No one should have to look at a drunk, face down in the street."

"Why not?" Beatriz said. "It's a part of life. It's there. Whether you look at it or not. I see no problem in asking people to confront reality. I don't think it's the police's job to drag reality away from the cruise ships."

I shook my head at all this. "You know, they didn't take him in because he was passed out in front of the cruise ships."

"That's right," Tata said, happy to have someone on her side. "He was probably choking on his own spit or something."

"Bluck," Beatriz said, and that sound of disgust ended the conversation. It turned out Tata was right; Angelo had been taken to the hospital rather than the police station. He was out that afternoon, and he told my father that he, Angelo, was not a drunk but that my father did have a point, and he was going to restrict his drinking till after five.

"It seems more appropriate," Angelo told my father, knowing, of course, that my father always liked things to be appropriate.

One night, not long after, Father invited Angelo home for dinner. He had been an occasional guest before. At first, it was unavoidable . . . if he was going to hang about our new house, peering in windows and such, we might as well ask him in. But this night was different. Father invited him over like any visitor . . . named a date and fixed a time.

Maria Elena was much more social than Father, but this particular occasion was not one that interested her. She wasn't fond of Angelo or the idea of Angelo as dinner guest. By the end of January, Father had been able to get Angelo to stop making passes at Maria Elena, so it wasn't that—or even the whole project of pretending to be my father—that irked Maria Elena. It was his table manners, which were, it is true, disgusting. At the bakery, Angelo would lean over his plate, almost protectively, and eat with a desperate, panicked concentration. He ate this way no matter what year it was, no matter whom he was imitating. Carla Mendota said she had heard he ate like that because of his years in institutions. He was still frightened he might not get enough to eat. That made us all sufficiently heartsick that we excused him his manners. Maria Elena wasn't hopelessly hardhearted, but she said she didn't know what to do when he was eating. She couldn't bear to look at him. He chewed with an open mouth and bits of his meal were likely to fly across the table. I said, "Just look over his left shoulder. Don't look him in the face." But Maria Elena thought that was a spooky idea—to talk to a person and avoid not only his eyes but also his entire face.

Despite her objections, Maria Elena cooked dinner that night. She made codfish and bataya and plantains. "Just a simple peasant meal," she said cheerfully. We were eating on a small linoleum table—a relic from our cramped apartment kitchen—but we were in a grand room that had once been a parlor. "What peasants?" I thought to grumble, but it was my favorite meal, washed down, at it was, with a red wine Maria Elena favored. Only the girls had anything to drink. One glass each. I think Father thought Maria Elena was stupid to have bought the bottle of wine, but she would have argued it was Angelo's job to live with his problem, not ours to deny that there was a responsible way to drink. At any rate, Angelo didn't touch a drop of the wine, and we were all impressed by his abstention.

Angelo was strangely quiet throughout the meal. Occasionally, he would say, "Excuse me," and depart for the bathroom. Then, he would return to his plate and eat his meal, though he would pay no attention to the conversation around him. At length, he turned and said, quite sweetly, to Maria Elena, "A very delicious meal." His eyes turned puppy dog sad, as if he were humiliated by the privilege of getting to eat.

"Well, I'm glad you liked it," Maria Elena said to Angelo. "You know," she went on, "I was hoping you could tell us a little about yourself tonight. Why don't you tell us about your boyhood?"

"Oh, that won't work," Tata said. "This is what happens when you try to find out what Dad was like when he was young. He admits to having one toy, a clown named Corky, then he denies it, says he never was a kid, just appeared in the world at age thirty. Ask him again, and he stops joking around and gets mad at you."

This was a fairly accurate description, but tonight my father was in a good mood. He laughed and said, "I don't know what you want from me. I really don't remember. I do remember playing stickball. On the curb. There. That's something about my boyhood. We played a game called Catch-a-Fly-Is-Up."

"Well," said Maria Elena, in a joking tone, "there's only one way to find out. That's why I asked." She turned and looked directly at Angelo so there could be no question to whom her words were directed. "Why don't *you* tell us about *your* boyhood?"

Angelo shrugged. "What is there to say? The facts are so sad."

"What facts?" Tata said.

"The dope smuggling, the grand larceny, the mother hoping to save me from myself."

"Is this true?" Tata said, laughing, to my father.

"Every word," my father said.

"It isn't funny," said Beatriz.

"The deceit, the women, the whores, the piles of whores," Angelo continued.

"Hmmm," Maria Elena said, looking in a flirtatious way at my father. "All your secrets."

"The urinating in the synagogue, the fights with the wife, the sex with the wife, the sex with my brother, the sex up the ass of my brother."

Everyone was quiet. It was like the day, not long after we'd moved into the *hacienda*, when Maria Elena had some sort of insulin reaction. We all thought she was just being silly, saying, "Look at this *great* house we're moving into with its *great* black shutters that run the whole *great* length of the *great* door-size windows, which all have *great* little balconies, and the *great* gazebo and the *great* river with the *great* fish who are just sing-ing *great* songs." Her voice screeched out of control then, and though Tata and I had been joking with her, saying, "And the great *this* and the great *that*," we realized something was wrong. "Call your father," she'd said, her eyes bugging out, as she toppled forward. "Lord," Tata whispered to me later that night, "just when you think you're a good time." I nodded in agreement, said, "That's when you're doing the most damage."

Now in the parlor, Maria Elena looked down at her lap and quietly said, "You don't have a brother."

Father nodded his head slowly as if he were saying, "That's right. I don't have a brother."

"Oh, that's right," Angelo said, looking vaguely at the group of us arched around him at the table.

We all looked at my father for guidance. How should we handle this? For a moment, he looked at a loss, then he tapped the tablecloth lightly with his two forefingers.

"Let's clear the table," Beatriz said brightly, as if she were suggesting an unusual after-dinner card game. Tata and Beatriz stood to clear the dishes, and I stood to go into the kitchen and start washing pots, but Maria Elena said, "No, no, sit. We can leave it."

Tata looked at her as if she were sick; hadn't she seen my father tap the table? "Normally," Tata turned to Angelo to say, "normally, she whisks the plate away as soon as you've lifted the last bite off your plate. You sit there, fork in hand, feeling crazy."

"It's true, it's true," Maria Elena laughed. "But I can't help it. I can't think when the house is messy."

"You don't need to think after dinner," Father said. "All your blood is in your stomach anyway. Why bother it by asking it to go up to the brain?"

"It's a good point," Maria Elena said. "And you're a wise man." She leaned over the corner of the table and kissed him on his left temple.

"Excuse me," Angelo said, "if you would." He left the table for what was the fifth or sixth time that evening. This time, however, he did not come back. We cleared the table and heated the water for coffee. We put cups and saucers out, and still he had not returned. For a long time, we all pretended we weren't concerned, and Tata sat quietly grinding sugar cubes into her corner of the tablecloth.

"Maybe," Maria Elena finally said, "you had better . . ."

"I'm going, I'm going," my father said. And he went down the long dark hall that led to a large modern bathroom with three stalls; it had been installed years ago to accommodate the hoards of nuns who came for retreats each June. My father found Angelo blacked out on the bathroom floor. He had a short glass tumbler near his hand. It was half filled with liquid. Behind one of the toilet seats, Angelo had hid our small wicker wastepaper basket. In it was a bottle of vodka, almost completely consumed. My father scooped Angelo up in his arms and carried him, like a new bride, over the threshold of the bathroom. Father brought him out to the parlor and rested him, for a bit, on the back of the couch that we kept in the corner of the room. Then he said, "Open the door. Get my keys and open the door." We asked the usual questions, expressed the standard range of emotions—a little shock, some pity, a bit of disappointment. My father was breathing too hard to answer, for though he was a strong man, Angelo was substantial. Still, he heaved him up off the couch and carried him out the front door and into the car. He drove away without saying another word.

We spent the next three months visiting Angelo. He was in detox, another public institution, which called up, at least for me, horrible, and it turns out, inaccurate pictures. The place he ended up at—a psychiatric hospital with a special unit for "substance abusers"—was almost elegant. It was located in the mountains south of town and consisted of a series of stuccoed, red-capped buildings. I went with Beatriz for my first visit. Maria Elena dropped us off at the front door and promised to be back in an hour, after she'd finished visiting her aunt in Cidra. Beatriz and I stepped through the front door, into a foyer with high ceilings and plenty of plants. To our right was a table with little pieces of paper. We had to write our names down, along with other important facts: whom we were seeing, what we were bringing in with us. To the left of the door was a glass window with a microphone in it—the kind you see at movie theatres, normally with a uniformed ticket taker behind it. Only our ticket taker was a plump Cuban woman with dark hair and a big smile. As a metaphor for what we were about to do—not visiting a person but viewing something—it seemed unfortunate. I was almost happy when she stepped out from behind the window to frisk Beatriz and me lightly.

"No drugs, girls?" she asked.

"No, no, of course not," I said.

"How about any guns? Did you bring any guns?"

Beatriz shook her head no.

"Well," said the woman. "I would like you to show me your firearms."

"Uh," I said. "We don't have any." Was this supposed to be a trick? We said we didn't have guns, but when she asked about firearms, we were to pull out rifles from our stockings and then stop, say, "Hey, wait a minute. You fooled us."

"Go ahead, girls. Take a right out of this building, and it will be the last building on your right."

Beatriz and I walked down the path. We were both looking around, taking things in.

"Good thing I started talking when I did. Or they would have put me here," Beatriz said.

"Oh, come on. You know that would never happen."

"I suppose." Beatriz chewed at her lower lip.

We knocked on the locked door at the end of the building, and Angelo came to answer the door.

"God," he said. "God, it is really nice of you to come." He sounded nothing like my father or anyone else I had ever heard Angelo pretend to be. His eyes trained themselves on the floor as if he were too embarrassed to look up. But it was a funny kind of embarrassment—too much "Aw shucks" in it to seem real, too much unhappiness in it to seem false. Instead it was on the edge of the two—neither honest nor dishonest—nor aware of what it would mean to aim for either quality.

"Hey, it's nice in here," I said. The room looked like a parlor in an English girls' boarding school. There were fancy overstuffed chairs and carpet everywhere. The air conditioning was turned up high.

"Here. We can sit here," Angelo said and shuffled us to a back room that wasn't quite as elegant. It was clearly the smoking room, and cigarette butts and half-empty bottles of soda were scattered about. In the far corner of the room, a woman with dark red lipstick and blue eye shadow was talking to three or four men. Clearly, she was the patient, because, even with all the makeup, it seemed as if her face wasn't being quite held together by her skin. I had a sudden image of the whole thing just sloughing off and lying there, like a carnival mask, at her feet.

"Well, you're looking good," Beatriz said.

Angelo looked down at his body as if only just noticing it was attached to his head.

"A little thinner, I think," I said, the way one says such things, obligatory compliments about the body, as a courtesy to the mind.

"Yeah, well," Angelo said. Then: "I guess I was pretty bloated when I came in. But all I do is eat here. They've got this great flan."

We all nodded our heads.

"Wait. Why I am I nodding my head?" I said. "I hate flan."

"How can anyone hate flan?" Angelo asked.

"I don't like my food to move. No moving, wriggling, shaking. It's an absolute requirement. I mean," I said, "if we're talking desserts and not dance partners."

"You want some Cokes?" Angelo asked. "I can get us some Cokes from the basement."

"Sure," I said. "That would be good. One each?" I looked at Beatriz, and she nodded.

"Right back," Angelo said and left for the basement.

"Maybe," Beatriz said quietly, "we shouldn't be, you know, talking about stuff like flan."

"Why not?"

"It just doesn't seem appropriate . . . to the situation, you know."

"As opposed to what? How nice a glass of whiskey would be right now?"

"No, no. You know. How's he doing? How's the program? Or maybe just more serious stuff."

Angelo came up with three of the old glass bottles of Coke, the kind you didn't see around the island much anymore. I drank mine quickly, just one inch from the bottom, in a few big gulps. "Sorry. A bit thirsty," I said. "It's pretty here. Nice grounds outside and some blossoming whatchamacallits. What do you call those trees?"

Angelo shrugged. "I can't go out for another ten weeks. And they've got bars on all the windows."

"Well," I said.

Angelo lit a cigarette. "Excuse me girls. You'll have to excuse me."

"Maria Elena says to say hi," Beatriz said. "She's gonna stop by later in the week and . . . oh, we almost forgot, we've got a present for you." Beatriz reached into her pocket and pulled out a small yellow box with tiny dabs of pink and green paint decorating the lid. "These are Guatemalan trouble dolls. Have you seen these?" Angelo shook his head no, and Beatriz opened the box and took out some dolls, so tiny they could have bathed together in a thimble. "What you're supposed to do is tell these dolls your troubles. Each night. One trouble a doll. And while you're sleeping, the dolls work on them. But there's only six of them. So you can have only six troubles."

"You just tell 'em your problems and—" Angelo started to ask.

"Yes," Beatriz interrupted. "You say . . ." She held up one of the trouble dolls, so it was right in front of her nose. "Oh, great and mighty trouble doll, I got no job." She put that doll down on the floor we were sitting on and picked up another. "Oh, great and mighty trouble doll, my husband's a lout. I mean, really, Señorita Trouble Doll. He prefers pigs to people. You get the idea."

"Ah . . . that's sweet of you. It is." Angelo said this then tapped the ash from his cigarette into the inch of Coke that remained in my bottle.

"Personally," I said, "I whine way too much ever to be satisfied by this six-trouble-limit thing."

We were all quiet for a bit, and then I said, "So how do you like the people here?"

"They're a bunch of drunks."

"Oh," I said. "Actually I was asking about the staff."

"Them? Well, what can you say?"

"Me? I can say lots of things."

Abruptly, Angelo ground his cigarette out on the floor and said, "Are you mad at me?"

"No, of course not," I said. "Why should I be mad at you?"

"Because if you're mad at me," Angelo said, quite angrily, "I just want to know right now."

"I'm not mad. Honestly. I'm not."

"Oh, this is a joke," Angelo said and rose to walk out the door. "I'm just going to go if you're not going to tell the truth."

I stood up, grabbed his arm and said, "No, no. Everything's fine." I wasn't angry, but I was embarrassed when I leapt to my feet. He was making me feel awful even if his motives weren't all that hard to figure out. He was interested in being a bad boy, interested in my disapproval. At least, then, he'd be something. How frustrating on a certain level not to have even that, ridiculous identity though it might be—given his age and my composure.

"I'm not mad at you," I said, and we sat back down.

"Well . . ." he allowed, then stood again and said, "I've got to get another Coke."

As he left, I mouthed to Beatriz, "I feel terrible."

"Don't let him *do* that to you," Beatriz whispered back.

"Yeah, I know," I said. And I did know she was right, but it didn't stop me from feeling I had done something wrong and should try to make amends.

Later, when we left Angelo, all I could think about was a drink.

"Maria Elena," I said, from the backseat of the car, "do you mind?" I asked and told her about my desire.

"Me, too," Beatriz said. "Isn't that wild?"Beatriz had the least interest in liquor of anyone I knew. "All I thought about while I was in there was how much I'd like one of those drinks that's half whiskey and half soda water."

We were too young, I suppose, to be having these desires, and Maria Elena knew that. But she also knew we were responsible, that she was no model adolescent and still she'd grown up safe, sober, and, in her own mind, reasonably sane. So we went home via the liquor store and bought a bottle of Irish whiskey that Maria Elena favored. We were giddy as we pulled into the driveway. The plan to have several drinks instead of dinner made us feel as looped as if we already had our whiskey meal behind us and were staggering to bed.

"I'll get the ice bucket," Maria Elena said and dragged it out along with several other dusty implements—ice tongs, shot glasses, swizzle sticks—all reserved for the parties my father never had.

Father was out that night. He was having dinner with an exporter of bakery ovens from New York, so it was easy enough to forget about the chicken in the refrigerator while we sat out back, watching what we could of the sky through the trees surrounding the outdoor patio.

"What do you think it is about him?" Tata said. Her feet were propped up on the green metal chair that would have been my father's if he were home.

"Well, it's not schizophrenia. I know that," Maria Elena said. "People confuse multiple personalities with schizophrenia, but they're not the same thing." Maria Elena's own brief hospitalization for depression made her an expert on all troubles of the mind.

"No," Tata said. "I meant Dad. Why couldn't Angelo be Dad for a year?"

"Good point," I said. "That's the root of his trouble."

"Oh, it has nothing to do with your father," Maria Elena said. "The man just finally cracked."

"Probably right," Tata said. And then, in English, "I'm as drunk as a skunk."

We all were, I suppose. So we can't be faulted for our thoughts, not entirely. But it still seemed like a good question, and I puzzled it out as I lay in bed that night. Now that Angelo was safe—in the hospital, after all, under lock and key—it seemed permissible to turn my thoughts away from him. What *was* it about my father that had made him impossible to imitate? Duplication. Triplication was what (some of us) were so good at. Not that I thought I was either of my sisters or they were me. We seemed to be entirely different, emotionally, and though people still confused us, our personalities had worn on us in distinct ways, so most people could tell us apart. Still, it seemed imitation—partial or false though it might be—should have been easier. At least for Angelo, given that he had always been good at deciphering identities. Right before I fell asleep, I had one of those sudden realizations you have late at night. The kind that seem like the key to everything so that you're frightened about what will happen if you don't get up and write it down. Still, you know it's way too important for you to forget in the morning. My father, I thought, was not who he said he was.

The Lit Room

(Rayovac Rodriguez—August 1979)

After the first few nightfalls, that particular drive, around the corner and up the steep little hill leading to the bakery's back door, felt as familiar to Rayovac as his own skin. Actually, more familiar than his own skin, that bug-bitten, rash-prone container, that sack Rayovac dreamed of escaping, freeing himself to feel all those things he normally didn't feel . . . comfortable, satisfied, at home in the world.

As the months went by, the routine of driving the van pleased him more than he ever thought it would. As a delivery person, he had brief encounters with other lives. He didn't have to like any of these lives—those of the men at the docks, the guys in the flour company's garage, the chef and his nervous assistant at the hotel—to love visiting them for a few minutes. And, he thought, by virtue of being at the tail end of so many projects—the shipment of goods, the manufacture of flour, the mixing of sugar and eggs—he was a welcome sight. Rayovac's arrival meant something was completed.

And Rayovac found he liked the routine of work. He smiled every time he made the fish-hook turn that took his van around the corner of the bakery and up into the drive. Then he'd get a little nervous as he unloaded the bags of sugar, the tarts, whatever it was. But, he'd think, he was just a man doing his job, and if Melone was working, he would stay for a cup of coffee, fuel for working men and all. True enough, conversation between Melone and Rayovac remained difficult. Still, Rayovac's discomfort did not alter his fondness for her or his sense that there was something very appropriate in his slow, indirect method of winning her heart.

In his head, Rayovac argued that he was waiting for the age difference between Melone and him to narrow. It was as if he thought that as she turned (as she had since his infatuation had begun) from fourteen to fifteen to sixteen, he stayed thirty. "I got a painting in my attic," Rayovac said when Luis called him on this line of thinking. Luis, who had dropped out of school at age six, looked at him and said, "Huh?"

"Never mind," Rayovac said. "It was something I learned in school."

Luis said, "Yeah, yeah. I keep forgetting you a rich boy."

"Hey, hey," Tata said one late afternoon when Rayovac walked in with a carton of butter. "How you doing?"

"I'm good. Real good," he said, pleased to use four whole words before pausing, even though he was using one of those words twice. "How was school today?"

"School was quite fine, Rayovac," she said, in a sort of stagy voice, though he couldn't tell what it was she was imitating. "I found myself instructed in many manners."

Melone chimed in, "I, too, found myself educated today."

"*Dios mío,*" Tata shrieked in a voice a little more appropriate to a teenager, "did I tell you about what that new teacher said to Ramon?"

"No," Melone said.

"Well, apparently there was a scholarship contest or something like that for the graduating class and Ramon," Tata stopped and said for Rayovac's benefit, "Ramon is this really sweet guy at school, but he's very nervous, and he is always making jokes at the wrong time, and sometimes he is so skinny you think he'll disappear."

Odd, Rayovac thought, as if Ramon's presence in the world, in terms of pounds of flesh and all, was something he could change according to mood. One day, the adolescent would feel unnoticeable, and a handful of limbs would disappear. Feeling important, he'd grow a nose on his forehead.

"Anyway, Ramon screws up all his courage and says he wants to try for the scholarship. This teacher . . . she's," Tata stopped again. "I don't know. Her father's some businessman from California. She doesn't speak a word of Spanish—"

"How—" Rayovac started to interrupt.

"We have classes in English at our school, 'cause it's private, and I guess she never gets out of San Juan, so she can get away with it. Anyway, she's like an old-fashioned schoolmarm, except she's not smart at all. She acts like Miss I Am Going to Educate You Idiots, Thank You. Anyway, Ramon asks her, and she says, 'Ramon, I don't see you in college. I see you dying in the army.'"

"Terrible," Melone said.

"Somebody came by from the nurse's station and gave her a shot, and then she was taken away, I think to the hospital. She's fired, of course."

This might have been the opportunity for Rayovac to say something, what with Melone primed to be polite to people requesting scholarship applications or, in his case, hands in marriage. But the moment passed. He sat quietly, playing with the sugar packets on the counter. Later, he moved to a table and practiced balancing the edge of the salt shaker on a grain of salt. He was still practicing when the store closed. While the girls cleaned up, he breathed hotly onto spoons and hung them off the end of his nose. Evening came on and darkened.

"I'll go now," Rayovac finally said, as if it were a decision with which he had been struggling.

"Bye-bye," the girls called together. "See you tomorrow," Melone said, and her words gave him hope, even though she'd refused, five times in a row, to go to the movies with him. He drove back to his parents' place, thinking his conversations at the bakery—indeed his whole life at the bakery—were a real respite from his family life. The girls saw him, he was sure, as the man he was. It was a freeing thought, and this particular night, as he drove home in the dark, he felt as if his life might go in directions he had not yet dreamed of. Along the highway, electrically lit rooms emerged, one interior after the next, and though he didn't know what was in them, all those interiors seemed like lives—full and complicated and sorrowful (but sorrowful in a good sort of way)—that he might lead. For the first time in years, Rayovac turned off the radio and listened to the sweep of air past his window. All those lit rooms were settled in under the blackness of night, like luminous fish in the dark ink of the sea. Momentarily, Rayovac let his imagination descend into one of those rooms. He saw an ear (not his) and a hand (this time his) in the hair near that ear. He saw his hand stroking the hair next to the ear and his lips whispering the name so often on his mind. Then his imagination was off again, off in the great big world, with the black sky and black sea, filled with endless interiors and possibilities too numerous to mention. He could descend into any one of them at will.

A week later, his truck ran over Tata.

He was in the bakery, behind the counter and talking with Melone when it happened. Beatriz was staying late at school, so she wasn't around. Their father was at a table in the corner puzzling over some bills and a bank statement. For his part, Rayovac had just dragged two bags of flour to the back room when he stopped, as if winded, next to Melone, and said, "Hello." Tata was there at the time, and there was some brief teasing about the way Rayovac transported fruit tarts. He wasn't as gentle as he might be, and the tarts often ended up kissing the cover of the bakery box, so there was no telling, when you opened the box, which side you should look at for saleable products. Then Tata disappeared, presumably to go to the bathroom or to help a customer. Rayovac wasn't paying attention, but it turns out that, as some sort of joke, she was going to carry the tarts in for him. She went out the back door and, failing to have the large set of keys Rayovac carried around, she climbed through the open driver's seat window to get four brown boxes. Rayovac always pictured her, half-in, half-out of the window, like some storybook child being slid, by a witch, into an oven. He imagined her legs hanging out, the front door cutting into her stomach, and her hands reaching to the passenger seat to get the cake. He wanted to see her hand accidentally knocking the emergency brake down, although he knew he didn't set the brake, that it really was his fault the truck started to roll backward down the hill, slowly, at first, then quickly because it was a steep hill.

Inside, Rayovac, Sandrofo, Melone and the other customers heard a crash. They ran out the back door to see Tata, lying bloodied on the pavement in the alley. Below and behind her at the end of the darkened alley, there was the light space of the street, and across the street, a blaze of flame in front of what had been, luckily enough, a recently abandoned jewelry store. Out of the flame, one could see what remained of Rayovac's van.

There wasn't screaming, as Rayovac thought there should be—he had watched a lot of TV disasters in his life—but there was a lot of running and voices saying, "Oh, my God," and "No, no," and "Is she going to be all right?" Panama-hatted men wanted explanations: "How had this happened?" And hairy wrists with thick watches landed on Rayovac's shoulder, and the voices above the wrists said it wasn't his fault.

Back home, waiting for the call from the hospital to hear how she was doing, Rayovac huddled on his bed. On the sheet next to him was what remained of an entire round of guava paste and Gouda cheese. With a furious intensity, he was demolishing the whole thing, along with a bag of crackers. As he ate, he thought, "Why am I eating?" Then he crammed another cracker he had assembled—first the cracker, then the guava, then the cheese—into his mouth, not bothering to bite the thing in half. He chewed while he prepared himself another cracker. White bits of cracker flew out of his shirt and landed on his red polo shirt. "Oh, my God," he thought, and sometimes he would even half-mumble the words aloud. "What am I doing?" he said and looked at the sticky knife cutting into the guava, the separate waxy blade making its way through the Gouda. There was a mirror attached to the dresser in his room. When he happened to catch sight of his face in it, he finally began to do something he hadn't, as best as he could remember, ever done. He cried.

He thought of what it was he wanted from Melone, and then he couldn't imagine what it was. What did he want? It had to be important to end this badly. A girlfriend? That was so embarrassing and seemed wrong, as if desire were necessarily exotic and, tainted with the ordinary, even in the form of a word, had to disappear. But, he thought, trying to argue his own case, it was *his* desire. *His.* And then that stupid possessive word seemed so horrible—a word as embarrassing as "girlfriend" or words like "party" or "cotton candy"—that the very idea of Melone seemed to fade away. Oh, he thought in a panic, he had loved his own desire, not the girl. He'd loved the experience of it, of charting all the times she noticed him. For a brief moment, he hated Melone, as if she were responsible for his feelings, had created them to hurt him. It was, secretly, what he had thought about sex during high school . . . that it was something other people invented and pretended to enjoy simply to upset him. But he didn't really believe this. These feelings about loving his desire and not the girl weren't right either. He put another cracker in his mouth, and it actually tasted salty because one of his own tears had added a final layer to the snack. He was moved to further sobbing by this detail.

Rayovac continued this way until the phone rang, and Sandrofo said Tata was not dead, but her torso had been badly bruised and cut, and two ribs had been broken. They were going to check for damage to the voice box, but otherwise, she was going to be fine. The front right tire was what had got her. It had cut up her torso and then sort of zigzagged up across her throat. Sandrofo's voice sounded constricted, as if someone were strangling him on the other end of the phone line. There was some unrecognizable sound; then Melone got on the phone and said the doctors said Tata was lucky to be alive, and they kept on saying it, and every time they said it, her father would make a funny gurgling sound in the back of his throat and then say, low, almost under his breath, "Lucky? You are a pig."

"Oh," Rayovac said, too sad to utter the abject apologies he'd been rehearsing. "But," he said, "but she'll be all right?"

"Oh, yes," Melone said. "I think so. Well, no one is really saying anything one way or another, but . . . listen, I have to go. Just, you know, it was an accident, and you should remember that."

"If you need anything," Rayovac started to say.

"Oh, well . . ." and Melone, who had seemed composed to him, started to cry and talk quickly. "Well, my father just left the room. I didn't want to get upset in front of him. It's so horrible. Her front is all strange. There really is the imprint of a tire track up over her stomach and breasts. She woke up, and she's grimacing, and you know she's not really a complainer. They gave her morphine, and she can't breath very well, so they have this tube in her throat and . . ." Her voice changed again. Someone must have walked back into the room. "Of course," she said, as if in answer to some request. "That is quite fine. But she'll just be sleeping, so visitors later would probably be better. Well, bye-bye."

Rayovac hung up the phone. He went into his bedroom and then, at a loss, decided to go for a walk. It was late, almost eleven, but his parents' street was a safe one. In fact, most of the people in the neighboring houses were relatives of his mother. He hoped when his parents returned . . . for they should be back any moment from a dinner out . . . they would be informed by one of these relatives, someone, perhaps, who knew someone who had been in the bakery at the time. He walked down the street toward the park with the swimming pool. He was thinking of climbing over the fence . . . for the pool was locked at this time of night . . . and going for a swim.

When he got to the fence, he stared at it for a while. What would people think, he wondered, if they saw him doing this? What would people who knew about the accident think? In fact, those who did see Rayovac thought just what he feared they would. They turned to their spouses and said, "Heart of a reptile." They found their children, dragged them to the window and pointed a cautionary finger before they said, "No good." Rayovac climbed the wire fence anyway. It shook and buckled with his weight. Of all the rooms he could have fallen in, he thought, remembering his winged imagination, which only a week earlier was dipping into various houses, thinking of possible lives, this was one room he did not want to fall into. Rayovac jumped down off the fence and walked toward the pool. "I want the house next door," he thought, as if his imagination, wings unfairly clipped, had dropped from the sky and, as it fell, been pushed by a wayward wind into the wrong house, a life not his own.

Rayovac took off his clothes and climbed, carefully, using the ladder, into the shallow end of the pool. He didn't really swim. He just squatted down so the water covered his shoulders and then spread out, like a gigantic rectangular cape from his neck. He stuck his legs out and floated and thought, *I am nowhere at all*, though he knew where he was, and he knew he would be there till the end of his days.

The City Where Memory is Traded

(Maria Elena—September 1979)

A week after the accident, piousness gave way to recriminations. No more bargaining with God, for, first, her life, then for her good health, then for minimal physical damage. The air was litigious. Who had made that faulty emergency brake? Rayovac was forgiven. He'd set the brake. What more could he have done? But the used car salesman, the car manufacturer. We had to find evil somewhere.

Beatriz, no surprise, found it in me.

Plots, I know, give life order, and guilt in and of itself is a kind of plot, allowing one to dream responsibility where there is none. At least, that's what I thought when Beatriz found me inside the gazebo late on a Sunday afternoon. I was reading the paper, and she interrupted me to say, "It's your fault."

"Beatriz," I said, reproachfully.

"Didn't I tell you about this house? Didn't I?" Her face trembled a bit, as she paused for an answer. She was just sixteen, but as I looked at her, it was clear what she would look like if she ever succumbed to Parkinson's disease—all that loose flapping of the cheeks. I was quiet, so she said, "Didn't I?" again.

She seemed so eager to be sure she'd discharged her duty that I said, "Yes, you did, but it was an accident. You know that as well as I."

"My sister's a highway," Beatriz said. She'd be mumbling this ever since the accident, and she had a point, since there was a tire track scar on Tata's torso.

Still, I reviewed the facts for Beatriz, in the hope that history, unadorned, would reveal itself to be meaningless chronology. This happened; then this happened; then this. No causality, no reason why, things just were. I told Beatriz things as if she didn't already know them. All that had happened, I said, was Rayovac left his truck in the alley behind the bakery. The alley ran, steeply, down toward the center of old San Juan. Tata had climbed into the back seat to get the leftover boxes of tarts Rayovac was bringing in from the hotel. Something happened—the emergency brake gave way, or, I suspected but wouldn't say, Rayovac never set it—and the truck started to roll backward. Later, we learned about Tata's thoughts: how she'd thought maybe she should try to reach the brake, but the fastest way to safety seemed to be out the passenger window and—what she couldn't have guessed—under the front left tire. She had a tire track on her. And three broken ribs. Soon enough, her voice box would heal, though she probably would always sound as if she were talking with a ball of cotton stuffed into her throat. "That's all," I said when I was through, "that's bad, but that's all that's going on. She's fine."

Beatriz shook her head and said, "It's already too much. My sister's a highway."

I asked her what she meant, and she said, "It's your fault. You're ruining this family." Her mouth twisted sadly in on itself, as if she were a felt puppet.

"I'm sorry," I said and drew her to me on the bench we were sitting on. "I promise it will be all right. OK?"

"OK," Beatriz said suspiciously, though she compliantly put her arm around my neck and whispered, "She's so much older now. Don't you think?"

I nodded my head. I imagined I knew what she meant. Over the past seven days, Tata had shown herself to be far more mature than any of us had ever suspected. Once she had been assured she would be all right, she did a good job of handling the initial pain from the accident, as well as the news about the large scar and damage to her voice box. Already I could see how her father and sisters were beginning to change their perception of her age and thus her right, in the lopsided logic of the family, to hold opinions. Before, everyone thought of her as the youngest since she was the last born. Now she seemed like the oldest, aged by experiences unfamiliar to the rest of us.

"Even older than Papi," Beatriz whispered sleepily, as if she was following my line of thinking. She had worn herself out crying this past week, and she was nodding off on my shoulder. I looked down at her face. Her lower lip slid out from under her upper, so she looked like an infant, puffy in sleep. I realized now what her panic was. She thought Tata was going to go through life first, and that must have meant she was thinking about Tata's death. I knew that feeling. I had had it for twenty-four hours before my own sister died. It felt like the surface of the earth cracking open, then waiting patiently for you to notice, as if gravity only obtained when you realized it was time for you to fall.

Beatriz was fully asleep now, and I reached up and stroked the curls of her long, thick hair—something she'd never let me do if she were awake. I understood her renewed fears about the house. My own superstitious streak had started in those twenty-four hours before my sister's death. I remember sitting in the hospital waiting room with a novel. My mother called to me, panicked, from down the hall where she was sitting with my sister, but I would not jump up at her cry, for I was on page thirteen of my book.

"Honey," I said and shook Beatriz awake. "Honey, go inside and get under the covers. Go to sleep."

"No," Beatriz said, in a sleep daze, "I've got to go back to the hospital." We'd been taking turns, rotating hours on and off so Tata, even if she woke in the dead of the night, would not be alone. "Get outta here. You're all making me crazy," Tata had been saying all week, but it was her single wish no one would grant.

"Beatriz," I reminded her, "it's Sunday. She's coming home today. Go rest up, so you'll be ready when she gets here."

"OK," Beatriz said, clearly pleased to be ordered to do the thing she most wanted to do.

I sat in the darkening light, absentmindedly reading the paper and daydreaming. In front of me, trees by the riverbank heaved up and down in the wind, as if they were taking giant breaths of air then exhaling in low, showy whistles. An occasional leaf blew on me, and my urge was to inhale it, to offer it up later out of my own lungs. Behind me, unlit, my new home seemed mountainous, a silhouette in the night sky. Growing up in Cidra, I never thought I'd get to live in such a nice home. Now it made me sad to think I had what I'd always wanted. After all, empires toppled, blood ran like sewer water in the gutters, human skin dropped like vegetable peels for this satisfaction. But, perhaps, my unhappiness had nothing to do with all this; perhaps it was just the way my own desires ran against Beatriz's. Still, I reminded myself, Tata and Melone liked the *hacienda*, though they complained about how house poor we were. Our rooms were empty or furnished with items that looked so diminutive under the high ceilings that we all felt a bit like toy people, living with our toy things in a real house. The wind was picking up slightly, blowing the newspaper at my feet into a giant carnation of print. I stepped on the sheets, messily folded the paper and sat on it.

I liked the feel of the wind on my bare shoulders. If I had never had a lover, I thought this touch might make up for a man's fingers . . . if I could always feel the wind just as it felt now. Out at the edge of the water, something stirred. It was a peacock, probably from the neighboring *hacienda*. I had heard they raised the mean-spirited creatures. I wondered now if it would show its feathers, what beauty I could expect, but it walked stubbornly along, uninterested in display.

This is the world, I thought, the one we're so desperate not to leave. Our attachment seemed beautiful, but an endless puzzle. Why? Why do we want to stay here? Why do we care so much? I thought suddenly of how my own sister reminded me of Tata. I couldn't think why I hadn't made the connection before. Tata had the same impatience with me Sisa once had. There was something in Sisa's brisk competence and comfort with overstatement that always made me seem foolishly analytical. Sisa cut through pretensions, and I had pretensions, and I knew I had them, and I cherished them, the way they protected me.

As I thought of this, I remembered something I had long forgotten. About a year after my sister's death, I was lying in bed. I slept on my side with my hands pressed together, prayer-style, at my cheek, and with my knees curled up. It was a restful position, one I'd recently and consciously adopted when I realized I'd been sleeping coffin-style: on my back with my arms folded over my chest and my opposite hand to my opposite shoulder. It was late afternoon in Wisconsin. I'd skipped my afternoon classes so I could go home to sleep. I was always sleeping in those days. "Recreational sleeping," I'd said cheerfully to my college roommate, "just something I do." As opposed, I meant, to taking up sailing or joining the drama club. As I was lying there, I realized I was feeling my face grow into my sister's face. It was as if I was inside her, waiting to fill up the space she once occupied. I was most aware of my head and how it didn't quite fill her head, how much farther I needed to go to reach the soft contours of her nose, the small blackheads in the crease of her chin, the pillows of her cheeks. After, I knew I could think myself back to this feeling at any time, but was always aware, as I was the first time, that I was holding myself back from something, that I was allowing myself to feel this much but not allowing myself to collapse into grief.

How odd to have forgotten all this till this very moment, for I certainly remember how, when people used to ask my age, I once, accidentally, gave my sister's age at the time of her death instead of my own. And how, not long after, I was placed in the University hospital for depression. And whenever they'd ask me about myself—what my major was, what my interests were—I'd say, Sisa was going to be a singer; Sisa once found a scorpion on our porch chair; Sisa didn't like to eat ices in the square unless the ice was blue and the day was rainy.

Tata and Melone were almost in front of me before I heard them. "Hello, welcome home," I said jumping up. "Can I give you a hug?"

"Yes," Tata said. "It only hurts when I laugh. Ha-ha. Ouch."

Melone rolled her eyes. "She's been doing that 'Ha-ha. Ouch' joke for the whole car ride, but it actually doesn't really hurt her that much."

"I can talk for myself," Tata snapped at Melone. Then she turned to me and said proudly, "They said they'd never seen anyone go off morphine and then off Tylenol as fast as me."

"Isn't she clever?" Melone said.

"Very, I'd say. Come. Into the house. We're going to have a special dinner." We turned and walked toward the house. Sandrofo was standing on the back porch, and he gave us a wave, then pointed at Tata proudly, as if to say, "Look at her. She's doing quite well."

"You don't even look as if you're having any problem walking," I said.

"God," Tata said, suddenly angry, "can everyone please stop commenting on every little thing I do?"

"I'm sorry," I said softly and noticed the silence following my apology. Sandrofo wasn't going to reprimand her for her temper.

That night after dinner, Melone found me in the reading room. We'd taken one of the empty rooms on the first floor of the house and put a lamp, two chairs and a bookcase in one corner. The length of the room stretched from this arrangement to three large windows overlooking the sugar fields. For some reason, we'd set the chairs far away from them, and whenever we were in the room, we'd find ourselves doing laps of the floor between chapters of our books. "Maria Elena," Melone said in a confidential tone I associated more with Beatriz. "I've got to talk to you about something." She closed the door behind her, sat down, and said, "When we were checking out of the hospital, there was this brief tussle because of birth certificates, because Dad didn't have any birth certificates for us. He said he lost them, and when he said that, I started to think . . . well, I started to think this a little while ago, that there's something going on with Dad that he's not telling. I mean *really* not telling. Then I thought about the Book of Names and how the woman at the santería couldn't find Dad's name in the Book of Names."

"Yes," I said, willing my eyes to stay unrounded, unsurprised, but I felt myself flush hotly, all that blood rushing to the skin to protect me from my fears. Wasn't this more evidence something wasn't quite right about Sandrofo's silence about his past? "But," I said, "I thought you didn't believe in santería and all that."

"I don't, but . . ." Melone looked down, then up. "But you know, I feel as if I should believe, just in case. I mean, in the hospital last week, right after the accident, I thought, 'I'm not superstitious, but I'm willing to be superstitious for my sister's good health.'"

I laughed, and Melone looked surprised. "I'm laughing because I used to think—" I stopped myself. "I'm laughing because I was just thinking the same thing today."

"So what I'm wondering is," Melone paused, as if stumped by herself. What was it she was thinking? "I'm just wondering if all this seems a little strange to you."

"Not at all," I said confidently, though I was conscious my hands were trembling. "You know how your father is."

"See, I do, and he's so organized, how could he have lost—"

"Well, that may have had nothing to do with him. Your mother . . . perhaps she wasn't as meticulous."

"And maybe it's silly, but that whole thing with Angelo."

"Angelo!" I said, forgetting he'd called earlier. He was getting out of rehab in a month, and I was to tell everyone. "He just cracked. I don't think that means anything. I hear he's better now, though one of the nurses at rehab thinks he's been imitating her. The rest of the nurses say she's just imagining things; normally, she thinks the patients are in love with her, but since it's clear Angelo doesn't like her, she imagines he's trying to be her. But . . . ." I lost my train of thought; then I remembered. "Your father. He's OK. Really, he is." I reached out and pressed her hand. "Really," I said firmly. "Lord, I don't think I could find my birth certificate if I tried." Melone smiled. I sensed, for the second time today, I'd made someone happy by telling her what she wanted to hear, not what she believed to be true. "It's been a long week," I said. "Why don't we both get some sleep?"

In the morning, I called in sick to work, said to myself, "Enough is enough." I had been looking at things the wrong way: psychology was of no use to me when it came to Sandrofo. Why hadn't I seen this from the beginning? This was a library project.

I don't like the weasely face of a sneak, but I don't take aesthetics or principles to the point of insanity. What I'm saying is: I took myself off to the University of Puerto Rico's periodical room and sat myself down amid obituaries. Dates were no problem for me. Sandrofo's first wife died on the girls' birthday. How many days would Sandrofo have waited to tell her parents, for the paper to print the notice? A week or two at the most.

A vacuous-faced boy with meaty hands showed me how to use the microfilm machine and brought me a stack of small boxes—several weeks of newspapers—to consider. Behind the scratchy gray screen, the paper seemed appropriately immaterial, ghostly, as if the events of which I was reading were preserved from the touch of human emotion, just as the image was sealed off from fingerprints.

After some searching, I found this:

> Anya Rosado de Pardes, 21. May 17, 1963. In childbirth. Leaves behind her mother, Esperanza Arruza de Rosado of Mayagüez; three infants; and her husband, Stephen Pardes of New York. Memorial service: May 25th at Nuestra Iglesia. In lieu of flowers, please send donations to the church.

Stephen Pardes? *Not related, must be another set of triplets born to* . . . . I closed my eyes, aware there was no way to think this away. But perhaps the information didn't mean something bad? I quieted myself, thought for a moment of absolutely nothing. Then I had that powerful moment of perfect clarity I always have in a crisis. It's the clarity of an idiot, I know that. But so what? It helps me all the same. I ask myself one simple question and answer it. I ask myself another question and answer it. I do this till I'm able to piece things together, to decide how to act. My mental equivalent of grabbing a railing and walking up the stairs like a toddler: putting the right foot on the step, dragging the left foot up to join it, then moving the right foot onto the next step, bringing the left . . . . *So,* I thought, *first thing I need to know is what to make of the unfamiliar name. Pardes. Who is Pardes?* Had Anya had a different husband? There was no question the girls were Sandrofo's. They looked like him. Perhaps Sandrofo had never married Anya; perhaps he had been her lover, and Pardes was the legal husband. But why would this Pardes part with his wife's children? Perhaps Sandrofo had kidnapped them? I shook my head at this thought. That was crazy, although not much crazier than discovering my husband hadn't married the woman he'd said he'd married.

I looked back at the obituary. Esperanza was dead. I knew that. Or thought I did. After all, that's how the bakery came to be in Sandrofo's possession, but clearly the bakery belonged to this Pardes. Perhaps Pardes had sold it to Sandrofo? And the memorial service in the church? That made a certain sense. Sandrofo had told me that Anya was Catholic and that the match with Sandrofo, a Jew, had infuriated her parents. They had refused to come north for the wedding, and they had disinherited Anya. At least, they had threatened disinheritance. But, Sandrofo had said, when Esperanza died, the will left the family bakery to Anya. Either her parents had forgotten to change the will or never really meant to follow through on the threat, although from the day she married Sandrofo till the day she died, Anya never spoke to her father and only once spoke to her mother. Sandrofo said she knew her father was gone only because, months after his death, an old childhood friend sent her a postcard telling her about the fatal heart attack. When Anya placed a call to her mother, Esperanza refused to listen to her, shouted into the phone, "What kind of daughter doesn't even attend her father's funeral?" There was no convincing her one couldn't attend a funeral one didn't know about. Esperanza cried, "A daughter knows death. She feels it in her blood. You remember that night when you felt there was air in your veins? That was his spirit, come to remind you." Sandrofo said Anya had hung up the phone, turned to him and admitted she had, months earlier, felt a strange lightness in her limbs, just as she was drifting off to sleep. He'd wondered what sort of lightness Esperanza felt when he sent a telegram with news of Anya's death. Enough, he'd hoped, to lift her like a helium balloon off the island and carry her to the middle of the sea.

OK, I thought, staring at the obituary, *no more information here.* I stood, leaving the stack of microfilm for the boy with the meaty hands. My thoughts were too riotous for alphabetization. My heels clicked against the library floor, and I thought of all the surfaces we cover the world with, the whole man-made shell that protects us from mud and animals and water, and I thought as my heels clicked along, "Break, break, break."

Maybe Sandrofo was . . . maybe. *Oh, Lord,* I thought, for I couldn't even think of a possibility that would explain things. My heart raced; blood pushed too quickly through my veins. Light-headed, I had the vague feeling I was a motor car, idle set too high. Maybe he had had a ménage à trois with Anya and Pardes, and after Anya died, Pardes tossed himself off the Rockefeller building because he couldn't admit to himself that he, like Sandrofo, really preferred men to women and was secretly happy that Anya was gone . . . . I stopped my story, said, "Not funny," to myself. Still, even this outlandish possibility made its own sense. When he first started courting me, hadn't everyone remarked on how long it had been since he'd dated anyone? Hadn't unmarried women said, jealously, when I passed them on the street, "So it's you, is it? You're what he was after," as if they'd finally solved the puzzle of his failure to woo a decade's worth of would-be mates. Lucia had even warned me he might be gay. How else explain his apparent lack of interest in women for so many years? But our sex life was happy, his appetites prodigious, and I'd found him patient and imaginative when it came to my desires. Just last night, hadn't he, at my request, traced a whole tray of ice over my body, around each breast, then down over my belly. "Make love to me now," I'd said, when he slipped the ice between my legs and up inside me. He'd laughed, said, "Always something new." And when I'd asked him how it was, he said, once thoughtfully, "Cold," then kissed my mouth quiet.

"Miss," a curly-haired, slim-hipped college boy was looking at me. "Are you all right?" My thoughts had stopped me on the steps outside the library. I wasn't really aware of having left the building till the boy spoke to me. I don't know how long I'd been standing there, statue-like, unable to pick a direction—down the steps and to the right or the left? How, I thought, do people ever make such momentous decisions? How is it that I've been making these decisions all my life without thinking about what they mean? "Miss," the boy said again, "it's just that I noticed you were standing here looking kind of . . . ." He shrugged his shoulders flirtatiously.

"No, no, I'm fine, just thinking is all."

"Well," he said, "then, I mean, I know you don't know me and all, but, like I said, I was watching you, and you looked so . . . and I'm going out for a beer . . ." He nodded toward a nearby parking lot. "And I thought I'd ask you to come with me. I mean, it might . . ."

"No, thank you," I said crisply and smoothed my palms over my skirt and walked away, thinking all the while, Go with him. Why not? A beer, then up to his college room. Sex with an eighteen-year-old. How erotic. And what did I have to lose? I mean, *who* was I being faithful to? This was the only life I'd ever have, and for the stupidest of reasons, I'd let it be much smaller than it might have been. I turned around and saw the student's back as he loped away. *Silly, a boy,* I thought. *A boy you don't even know.* Then, *So what?* I'd had a lifetime of encounters I never succumbed to (save in my imagination). I'd had endless chances to change my life in small or dramatic ways, but I remained the same, an emotional agoraphobe; there was only so far I was willing to go.

That night, I was back at the *hacienda* before anyone else, and I started a small supper. Once things were heating, I took a glass of wine and went out to sit in the gazebo. I couldn't tell what I was thinking, though I felt on the edge of panic. Years ago, I thought I had become incapable of surprise. For me, the sixties had drained the world of shock value, but now if the things I was thinking were true, I had to admit I was surprised. Thank God, you didn't marry him, I told myself, though the thought was no comfort. I was as good as married. My old apartment, my old life, had drifted away as soon as I got involved with Sandrofo, and could I honestly say I wanted to go back to that? My single-girl life, with my endless affairs, my sad, frozen-dinner evenings? And I loved Sandrofo, or thought I did. It's true he wasn't completely what I wanted, but a dream isn't a person, and I couldn't hold him to my fantasies. After all, I was attracted to him, and I'd learned, as my thirties wore on, how rare that was. He was a good person, and I wanted him. I loved his children. What more did one get in a life?

Oh, God, I thought, pushing my right knuckle into my eye to hold back tears. Who was he? Wasn't it true I could look at him, look right at him, and have a feeling he wasn't there? There was something vague about him. Why hadn't I paid attention to my own perceptions? Why hadn't I let myself ask more questions? It was nothing other than a horrible lack of faith in self—a repulsive false politeness, an eagerness not to offend—that had brought me here. Here, being alone in a gazebo, at the edge of a green river, waiting for my pseudo-husband and his daughters to arrive so I could serve them rice and beans, say, "How was school? How was work?" And to Tata, "What happened at the physical therapist?" And this, I thought, was what I wanted, what I wanted to do and ask.

I sat late in the gazebo. I heard the girls come home and settle into the house. I heard Sandrofo come home. I heard their voices, through the window, wondering where I was. Finally, Sandrofo came out to the porch and saw me. I waved once, pointed at my wineglass to show him just what it was I was doing out here. He waved back, then went into the kitchen. I felt abandoned but then realized he was coming out to be with me. He came back with a bottle of seltzer in his left hand, a bottle of wine in his right.

"Nice night," he said, stepping into the gazebo. He reached over and kissed my neck, then sat to my right, put the bottle between his feet and started to undo it with a corkscrew he had in his pocket. He was handsome, even now, to me. The wave of his muscles on his shoulders, the slight tilt of his face, his dark hair, which fell sloppily in his eyes. He lifted the bottle and cocked his head, Did I want some? I nodded my head yes. If I could get drunk, I could ask what I needed to ask tonight.

"Are you all right?" he said. Then as if he'd noticed something was wrong, "What is it? It's not Tata. Tata's OK, isn't she? She looks fine." I nodded my head, Yes, she was fine. "Oh, good," he said.

"I . . ." I said and started to cry.

"What, what is it?" reaching, with concern, for my hand.

"Nothing," I said and sniffed. "I'm in a mood. No good reason."

He put his arms around me. "M.E.," he said, the letters his latest nickname for me. "What is it?"

I wanted him to comfort me, though he was the problem. It reminded me of when I was leaving the doctor I had dated for many years. I didn't want to leave him but knew he would never marry me. One night, I told him I had kissed another man, an attorney, whom I'd met at the gallery. This attorney had pursued me enthusiastically, and I wasn't interested in anything beyond his interest; still, he was single, an eager-to-marry professional. When I told the doctor about my infidelity, I wept. Whom else would I go to for comfort? "It's all right," he'd said as he held me. "It's all right." And I'd sobbed, thinking, There are so many ways for a life to go wrong.

Now, I thought, No. This is not the man who can comfort you. He can't cure you of himself.

Quietly, I whispered, "Stephen."

Sandrofo looked at me, searchingly. No sense he knew what I was talking about.

"Stephen," I said again, more firmly.

"Who's Stephen?" Sandrofo said, suspiciously, as if I'd taken a lover.

"You, I think, had better tell me."

He was quiet. His face trained on the floor of the gazebo.

"Stephen Pardes," I said. "Go ahead. We have all night."

"I . . ." he hesitated, looked up once at the ceiling of the gazebo, the words printed on the cornice. Then he pushed his right hand through his hair. Normally, I found the gesture charming, but now it seemed evasive, merely a way to get his elbow between my eyes and his face.

"Don't think to lie," I said. "That's the one thing you can't do now."

He picked up the wineglass at his feet and had a large sip. "Who have you been talking to?" he said, seriously, in a tone I didn't recognize.

"Nobody."

"So what is this all about?" he said—casual this time, continuing to sip.

I pressed my lips together and glared at him.

"Maria Elena, I asked you a question." Was his tone threatening? I couldn't tell. Lord, maybe I was engaged to a mobster. Maybe my body would be floating in that green river in the morning. I felt like crying again, like running to my bedroom, into Sandrofo's arms and saying, breathlessly, "And it was so scary. And then he said in this weird voice, 'I asked you a question.' And I didn't know who he was."

For a moment, I thought to back down, not to press him, for something horrible—horror movie horrible—might happen to me, but then, I thought, Your sister died. You can die too. Couldn't you always do what she could do? Weren't you that competitive? What is a life, anyway? You hold on to it too tight, and you find you've allowed yourself nothing, nothing in the name of a safety that isn't guaranteed anyway. I had a sudden, intense stab of regret at not having slept with that college boy. *Oh, his smooth body*, I thought, *avidly entering yours.*

"Tell me," I said, darkly, film noir style.

"What . . ." he said, "what are you going to do to me?" I realized he was scared. And his fear frightened me too. It was that familiar disorienting sensation from my dating days: you wanted to win a person over so badly; you were charming; you were flirtatious, and then, sickeningly, you realized you had done it; you were a horrible spider; they were stuck in your web, and now they wanted you back. They pursued your friendship; they stroked your arm, gazed at your ass. All of a sudden the terms of the world had changed, and you were backing away from affection, looking at these repulsive bugs dying in your web. You had to look down at yourself and think, What were you anyway? How could you have gotten so confused about the terms of the relationship?

"I'm not going to do anything to you," I said harshly. Then, kindly, "God, Sandrofo, I need to know who you are. I need to know who it is I'm going to marry," and I started to cry again, and I felt something dissolve in him too, and I realized we were fine, if fine meant we weren't determined to be cruel to one another. We were each operating from a point of ignorance.

"All it is," he said and coughed, "is I changed my name before I moved down here."

I nodded and said, "From Stephen . . ."

"Yes," he said, "from Stephen Pardes to Sandrofo Codero Lucero." He smiled at me, hopefully, as if I'd say, "Well, OK, then, everything's clear now, let's go in and have some dinner." But when I was silent, he said, "So, you're going to ask me why? Why did I change my name?"

"I think that's exactly what I'm going to do," I said.

"This is hard for me," he said.

"I don't think," I said, my voice icy, "I don't think I care right now if it's hard for you or not."

He nodded, as if just beginning to understand how angry I was. "You hate me?" he said, almost hopefully.

"Just tell me the truth. And keep talking till I know what I need to know."

"Well, you know Esperanza, Anya's mother, died and after that I changed my name and came down here to get the inheritance, and I wanted to start a new life."

"But the name? Why?"

"I'd done some things I was ashamed of. I just wanted to be somebody else."

I wanted to be sympathetic, so I leaned over and patted his leg. "We all feel this way."

"Mmm," he said absentmindedly. Then his voice cracked, and he said, in a voice so pained and without pretense I knew it was true, "Really terrible things, Maria Elena. Terrible." His words were almost physical, cold water in the face, and I jerked back. It wasn't what he was saying but his tone of voice. I knew this was the first honest sentence he had ever spoken to me.

"What?" I whispered, my stomach clenching itself and everything, even my hair follicles, saying, *we don't want to know.* Still, I heard myself say, "What did you do?"

"Do?" he said, as if confused.

"Yeah," I said breezily, thinking my tone might change what he had to say next, "what did you do so awful that you had to change your identity?" I cocked my head, smiled as if to say, "What I expect next is a grotesque story about burning ants with a magnifying glass."

"Well," he said, not seeming to understand this was not an answer to my question, "the girls used to live with my mother. After Anya died, they didn't live with me. I was off. I was . . . I came back and took them away. I told her, I told my mother, that I had to go away, that the mob was on my back."

"Oh," I said, as if this were ordinary information. Lord knows, I'd dated a drug prosecutor; I knew how to fake sophistication in this world. "Well, that was cruel of you, wasn't it?" When he didn't respond, I said, "Well, *was* the mob after you?"

"No," he said and shook his head once sorrowfully.

"What was it then?" I felt kind as I asked. I did love him, I thought. I should try to help him out here. He didn't respond, so I said, "It's true that Anya is dead, right?"

"Yes," he said.

"And her family?"

"Dead. All dead."

"And your mother?"

He was quiet.

"Your mother is still alive?"

"No," he said. "I thought, you know, she'd be OK. I mean she'd been in the camps and all, and I thought, Well, this isn't the greatest thing to do, but she can survive."

This stopped me. During my lessons with the rabbi, I had been in the uncomfortable position of attending Hebrew school classes with pimply children studying for their *bar* and *bat mitzvahs*. They were badly behaved, selfish kids, but I'd been impressed by them on the day the rabbi invited Holocaust survivors to class. The children's uncommon gentleness made me think they knew, even though they were just twelve years old, that their responsibility was to ensure these survivors experienced no more harm.

"Your mother was in the camps and . . ."

"And, yes, I know, I know, I left her alone there."

"With no way of supporting herself?"

"No, no," Sandrofo said quickly. "She had her pension and my father's life insurance policy. I told you that. She'd been a dress buyer for Saks."

"Well, how do I know what to make of what you've told me?"

Sandrofo shrugged in agitation, pulled a cigarette from his pocket and started to tap it against the gazebo bench as if in preparation for smoking, though he made no move to light it.

"And your father?"

"Dead. Died when I was a kid. See, my mother had been in the camps when she was younger, had had glass pushed into her knees because the Germans thought she was a spy. She had these scars on her knees. Both of my parents escaped, but my father didn't last long in this country. His mind was overloaded, I guess, with horror, and he'd just bought a life insurance policy, so he had a heart attack, supposedly, though there was some talk that he'd figured out how to induce the heart attack. But . . . my mother was different. She raised me alone. She played," Sandrofo stopped and smiled at this, "mah johng in Bensonhurst, had ferocious discussions about borscht recipes. She was a survivor. I'd known that my whole life, so she wouldn't be ruined by my leaving with the girls. She wouldn't, I mean I hoped she wouldn't spend, I don't know, the rest of her life examining the features of street prostitutes, wondering which ones were her grandchildren. I mean, she had to know me, at least, that well."

I shook my head. If she believed the threats, if she imagined mobsters ready to put bullets in the backs of her beautiful grandchildren's necks, how could she believe Sandrofo was capable of creating a good life for them? "So she was alone?"

"Well, yes," Sandrofo said impatiently, "after I came and got the girls, she was alone."

"So, wait a second, you were . . . where were you? I mean how long was she taking care of your children for you?"

"The whole time."

"The whole *what* time?"

"The whole time between when Anya died and I moved here."

I shook my head. "So what were you doing all that time?"

As if he'd misheard me, Sandrofo angrily responded to some unarticulated criticism. "Listen, you want to hear the story; I'm telling you the story. It happened. I can't undo it now. I stole some cars. I robbed some stores. I had a gun, but no one was ever hurt."

I was quiet, absorbing this information, thinking of medicine burning my hand as it entered through an IV, the way the quick branching of pain through my arm always made me realize how much human beings owed to trees. "But what did you do that was so horrible you had to change your identity and begin all over? I mean were you going to jail? Were you going to get killed?"

"No, no, nothing like that," Sandrofo said. His voice barely a whisper.

"Then, what," I said, "was it?"

"I tried to kill someone."

"Tri-ied?" I said, hysteria finally pushing my voice up an octave.

"It didn't work," he said, almost offhandedly.

"Then, what? What?" I said in a whisper of a scream. "You were afraid he would come after you? You were so ashamed you had done it you couldn't stand to be yourself anymore?"

Sandrofo shook his head slowly, back and forth. They were long sweeps of his face, like a clock's pendulum, ticking no, no, no, no, no.

"It was just . . . nothing. Do you see? It was nothing. There wasn't any reason. I just did it. It wasn't so horrible, but it felt so horrible, so I had to leave. I couldn't see how to do it without a clean slate."

"But . . ." I started to say.

He held out his hand, "Don't ask me any more questions. I told you the reason. There was no reason. That's it. There is nothing to tell, except that you can't tell anybody. Nobody. Promise?"

"I promise," I said and felt scared. Sandrofo tossed his unlit cigarette to the floor of the gazebo.

"Let it be for tonight," he said.

"Let it be? Are you kidding me? Lord, we're not talking about . . . a . . . a . . . an I-don't-know-what . . . a bad report card from one of the kids."

"I know, I know, you have a right to be mad. I just . . . forgive me for the night, and I'll find a way to . . . I don't know, just let it be for tonight. Please? And I'll make it all right. I promise."

"Oh—" I started to say, and Sandrofo said quickly, "K?" He gave me a hammy grin. "Oh-Kay?" I had to laugh.

He reached over and touched the dried tears on my cheek. "I'm so sorry," he said. "The kids. We should go in for dinner. They'll be wondering . . . ."

I really was too tired to do anything but agree. We went toward the house. "Wait," I said, as I stepped onto the porch. "Do they know?" I pointed at the house.

"No."

"But they must remember. They were old enough to remember their grandmother."

"Yes, yes," Sandrofo said chummily, and he put his arm around my back. "But you know how it is with children; they believe what you tell them."

I pulled his arm away from my waist, pushed it down toward his side. "Tell the girls I don't feel well, that I won't be able to join you for dinner."

"No, listen, Maria Elena," he said and grabbed my hand, pressed it warmly between his own palms. "I thought it through. Back in New York, I settled on a plan. I asked everyone at the hospital what their first memory was. See. I'm just like you, I know . . . I mean the way you've been asking the girls about their memories . . . it was like that, and what I found was the memories all began around three or four, so it seemed to me I could recreate the girls' past. I mean, I know that has the ring of bad science fiction to it, but there it is. When we first came here, I told the girls a past I wanted them to remember. I would correct them, tell them they misremembered when they did indeed remember. I made my long absence from their lives go away. Don't you see? I became a good person. It was me, not my mother, who cared for them in their infancy and toddler years. It was me . . ."

I held up my hand to quiet him. "Wait, remember when you told me about the way they learned to walk . . ."

Sandrofo nodded his head and began to recite. "Yes, yes, I told you about how they first learned to walk by standing on each other's heads. I told you about the way Tata used to punch Beatriz, and Beatriz would refuse to hit back no matter how hard Tata punched. Told you about the floppy clown Melone liked to sleep with. The day when, looking into the mirror in the small bathroom in Bensonhurst, the three of them collapsed in giggles because they realized they all looked alike."

"And that's?" I tilted my head, as if to say, "Fill in the blank. True or false."

"Well, it's true now, but no, no, it never happened."

"Unbelievable," I said and shook my head and found myself starting to cry again, but softly, so the girls wouldn't hear. "But, but . . ."

We were standing just outside the door to the kitchen. "Are you coming in or not?" Tata called out impatiently.

"Just a second," I said.

"But what?" Sandrofo said.

"But . . . I don't know," I sniffed and said, "Pretty good stories." I looked at Sandrofo, thought of all the accommodations I had made to enter his life. "Are you Jewish?"

He laughed, said he was. "See, when I got here, there were a lot of things to decide, but religion . . . I thought: You can't fake Catholicism on a Catholic island. But we were Sephardic Jews, and it's true my ancestors were from Spain."

"But you said your parents were in Germany."

"Well, they moved to Germany so my father could take a management position in a women's dress factory."

I nodded. Poor man, I thought. Given the little bit Sandrofo had told me about his father's melancholy, I wondered if he'd felt compelled, however unconsciously, to emigrate to the geographic center of pain for his people. Born too late for the Inquisition, he had to accept the managerial position, move inland so as to be in the right place for the Holocaust.

"And when I got here," Sandrofo whispered, "it wasn't only religion. What language to speak? Spanish or English?" Sandrofo went on in hushed tones. He said he knew only a clean slate could provide him and his daughters with a good life. This was the hypothesis of his new identity. It was a hypothesis based less on facts than a sort of blind faith. Still, it was Sandrofo's organizing principle; though from the start, he saw how impossible it was, how the chalk dust of memory settled on the slate and insisted he choose certain things—Judaism, the bakery, education as a primary value—over others. It was, he said, the reason for his insomnia. He'd walk the circumference of his bedroom to stay awake, to think about everything he needed to do to reestablish himself as a legal lie. What neighborhood would he say he grew up in? Say Spanish Harlem, and people would know soon enough that he didn't know the names of any of the *bodegas* or streets over there. Say Staten Island, and they'd look at him. What was he doing there? He settled on the truth, Bensonhurst, because there was a small, but distinct Puerto Rican population in Bensonhurst, and he knew, through his wife, a few inside details: which places, for instance, had bugs in their rice. And soon Sandrofo realized he'd have to add quietness and forgetfulness to sleeplessness; these would be his virtues. Without them, he'd be caught in endless lies.

Thinking about these and a thousand other matters, he'd wander the edge of his bedroom, letting his hand trail along the length of the walls, so that even though he washed his hands diligently every night, a smudgy line of sweat appeared, four feet above the floor. For Sandrofo, this giant ring of sweat seemed accurate, since inside the confines of his bedroom, he felt married to his fears. And there were, he assured me, an endless list of horrors: nympholeptic men, scorpions—all that and the countless tasks to guarantee his children a good life.

Tata called again from the window. "Listen, everyone has to do what I want since I'm sick . . . or hurt . . . or whatever." She laughed. "So get in here and talk to us." We heard her turn back to her sisters and say, "Probably kissing. Can't keep their hands off one another, can they?"

"OK, OK," Sandrofo said, and he steered me gently toward the door.

In the middle of the night, when I heard Sandrofo dressing to go to the bakery, I woke, stunned by what I'd heard just hours earlier. I gulped air, bit my lip, wondered if I should find an apartment to rent. But I didn't want to move. I closed my eyes, reminding myself of everything I now knew. My body twitched once in bed, the way it does when you wake, with a jerk, from a dream about falling. Earlier in the night, had he said something about a hospital? Or had I just dreamed that?

I called from my pillow, "You didn't tell me everything, did you?"

"No," he said, in a loving voice. He crossed to the bed, and I could not manage the cruelty—spitting, yelling, threats to tell the girls—I was planning. "Tell me," I said without malice. "The bread can wait."

He shook his head. "Leave it be. Please," he said.

"Sandrofo," I shouted, already half-crying. "Sandrofo, no. No, I'm not going to leave anything alone. Lord, tell me, or I'll . . . I'll . . . I don't know what I'll do. I mean I'll certainly leave you. At least, I'll do that, I . . ."

"It's OK. It's OK," he said soothingly and crawled back into bed to hold me. "Lie down." I lay on my side, and he scooped up behind me, put his arms around my waist. "I'll tell you," he breathed into my ear. "But it's not me anymore. Please know that. It's the story of somebody else. It's the story of Stephen Pardes. Not someone we like."

"Not someone," I somberly agreed, "we like one bit."

Pardes

(1968)

On his first and final day as a hit man, Stephen Pardes traded the fourth finger of his right hand for a spotty daydream, one that he didn't even know he had when the gun pointed at Jeff Pallace backfired and blew part of his own hand onto the sidewalk. Stephen was so drunk it didn't even hurt at first, and he was less amazed by the sound of the soles of Pallace's boots, thundering down the path, and the severed finger on the tar than by the fact that he, Stephen Pardes, was holding a gun and thinking he had failed at this, his latest job, killing for hire.

But that thought was fleeting too. Pardes picked up his finger with his left hand and started running, not down the path after Pallace but through a narrow strip of grass, up a few stairs, and across the park—crowded with trees and abandoned by people—which hugged the trolley tracks. He stopped at the street to catch his breath. Then he crossed the traffic, ran through a small campus for a college—a girls' school, he had heard, though he didn't know; this wasn't his town—and across another street and through the front door of the Beth Israel Hospital. He couldn't talk for exhaustion, so he showed the finger in his left hand to a blue-smocked woman standing in the lobby. She gasped, a sort of muted half-scream, and then there was a kid with a bloody hand who was crying and, after that, Pardes heard himself screaming, "I killed your mother. I killed your mother."

Some time later, he woke up to a voice that was saying, "All right, all right." There was a young Asian man—Korean, Pardes guessed; he didn't know why—and the young man said, "We're going to be able to take care of that for you." And, Pardes started again, "I killed your mother. I killed your mother. Pearl Harbor, I killed your mother. She's dead. I killed her." He was confused. The Koreans and Pearl Harbor? Surely, he had made a mistake. He was very, very drunk. He tried to remember if drugs were involved too, but he didn't do drugs. He'd always thought that was an important distinction between him and . . . everyone else, whoever they were. But there must have been an entire bottle of whiskey involved; sometime around breakfast, there must have been something like that. Then a huge and long whiteness till Stephen Pardes came to himself in a different hospital, in a narrow bed, with a fully restored hand. Only, something was different. The fourth finger of his right hand was turned around backward, with the knuckle sharing the same plane as the palm of his hand. His thought when he woke—and he was shaking, the DTs—was that he should go to a palm reader and give her a good scare.

He looked about the room he had been placed in. It was a small, standard-issue hospital room, and he was alone, save for a folding chair and a TV mounted on the wall. Still, the walls were thin and cheaply constructed, so he could hear voices coming from all sides of him, and he didn't feel alone, though he couldn't make out a specific conversation from all the sounds. He wondered which one of the voices could help him find a drink.

Then, he thought, dimly—this was the spotty daydream—about changing his life.

This was his life:

He was Stephen Pardes, twenty-five years old, father of three, husband of nobody, out of work, and without prospects. He'd married young—very young, at nineteen—to a Puerto Rican girl who lived, like Pardes, in Brooklyn, New York. She was dead two years later, died in childbirth. *People still did that*, Pardes would sometimes think, shaking his head, as if the death were something outdated and hysterical his anachronistic wife had done on purpose, just to upset him.

He had managed three children in one year thanks to a fertility drug Anya had been taking. They had had triplets. The doctor said it had nothing to do with the drug. If it had been the drug, the girls wouldn't have looked alike, but they were identical, not sororal, triplets. Then the doctor said, "What's a twenty-one-year-old girl doing with fertility drugs?" That was a question that never got answered and accounted, in a weird way, for Pardes's own abstinence from drugs, if not alcohol. It didn't make any more sense than if Anya had, say, slit her wrists and he had taken to avoiding open windows, but it was a rule he had made for himself. It was one he stuck to because, though he was broke and without prospects, he did think he was better than the people he hung around with. He certainly thought he had a lot over the guy who had paid him the equivalent of six months' rent to kill Jeff Pallace. That guy—Lorenzo, if you could believe it, was his name—had no morals whatsoever. He was having him kill Jeff Pallace over a grudge. This Pallace guy had not only fucked Lorenzo's wife but had also given her the clap.

Pardes thought of the fee he was going to get for offing Pallace in terms of rent money even though, it is true, he was paying no rent. His three girls were living with his mother, in the same apartment in Bensonhurst where he had spent his childhood. It was an arrangement that was meant to be temporary, but there was no obvious end in sight. The girls—they were four years old now—were sleeping on the green, vinyl couch in the small room off the living room. Pardes had spent his boyhood pulling that same couch out into a double bed at night and pushing it back into a couch for the day. He'd heard the word "daybed" once when he was little, and he assumed that was what his couch was. Pardes's mother's apartment was down the street from the firehouse, and all night the red lights of the fire engines would swoop across the ceiling and disappear with the sounds of gradually fading sirens. That was something he would always share with his girls, even though, things being what they were, he didn't actually spend all that much time with them, didn't really get to see them on a regular basis. He was trying to get some money together so he could rent a place for them, and he was trying to figure out how to get things together for himself—a regular job that wouldn't drive him nuts. Maybe there was no such thing.

And now, he thought, as he lay in his hospital bed, he was probably going to jail. Some life for his kids. He even thought, shortly after he woke up in the hospital, that he might *be* in jail, but after a nurse showed up and drew some blood, that seemed not to be the case. And, then, as time passed, it became clear that no one knew what he had done, that his principal crime had been to be a drunk, a racist drunk who had come to the hospital so disorganized he hadn't even managed to keep his limbs attached before he arrived. Soon enough, Pardes bought that interpretation of himself as well. So he had come to the hospital without a finger. So what? It wasn't a goddamn interview, was it? Had he ever tried to kill a man? No, he had not.

Still, on occasions, when he looked in the mirror in the bathroom off his hospital room, he saw a slightly fugitive look in his own eyes. Once, he'd even called to a young doctor standing in the hall. "Look," Pardes had said, "do you see something there?" The doctor had come into the room, peered into Pardes's bathroom, and said, "Yeah, this place was so badly done. All the black is coming through." Pardes had no idea what he meant until, a few days later, he was in another bathroom in the unit and noticed the mirror's silver paint had flaked off in big chunks, so when he looked at himself, he seemed to have a horrible skin disease.

At the hospital, Pardes's mind was like a camera lens jiggling into focus. As time went on, he understood events with increasing clarity. Still, the process was slow. Things revealed to him on his first day at the hospital—things like what town he was in, what was going to happen to him—only became apparent to him several weeks into his stay. For him, the chronology of events became the chronology of his understanding of events, so plans for the future were revealed only when the future was already history.

On his third week at the hospital, Pardes absorbed the fact that the doctors had put him on a six-week plan, that he had a regular schedule of meals to eat, meetings to go to and urine samples to give to nurses. He was to dry out for four weeks and then take halting steps into the world on the fifth and sixth weeks. The fact that this particular world—

suburban Boston, where the hospital was located—was not his world seemed to complicate his treatment. There were no beleaguered relatives to come take Pardes to an afternoon movie and observe him as he did *not* swerve into every package store between the hospital and the cinema. There was no job for Pardes to try to get back. He hadn't told a soul he was here, which meant he hadn't told his mother, who was, by now, used to his month-long absences. She would be no angrier than usual. He knew she considered her grandchildren her children and knew not to expect steady financial help from Pardes. It made him furious, but things being what they were, anger was not an emotion he could indulge. He had no way of providing for his children, and here the state, not even *his* state proper, was providing for him.

He had come, he thought (part of the increasing lucidity as the days wore on), to a very bad spot in his life.

He started recognizing things: the names of nurses, the variations in his daily schedule that occurred on Tuesday and Thursday afternoons, the patter of talk during the various "meetings" he was sent to, the names of other people in the unit, the fact that he was in a "detoxification unit" and that most of his companions were older than he, had lived in refrigerator boxes. He felt, all the time, much older than he really was and as if he had lived many lifetimes and through many experiences that were, in truth, quite foreign to him.

There was a particular doctor who seemed to take a special interest in Pardes. It was in his third week that Pardes learned that his name was Jack, Jack Kelly. He remembered a specific conversation with the doctor on the same day he realized he had been talking to him, every day, two times a day, for three weeks. *When,* Jack had asked him, *had he started drinking?*

Pardes didn't remember how he'd answered, but later that day, he remembered thinking, *When I was eight, when else?* When else, because third grade, in his neighborhood, was the grade that separated boy from adolescent, and since so many of the adults he knew were perpetual adolescents, that meant, of course, boy from man.

"Finding it hard to talk to people?" Jack asked him on the subsequent day. They were in a triangle-shaped room, one they had been in every day, but Pardes was just now taking it in. It was a room at the end of the hall. All the patients had small single rooms off this hall, and each room had its own small bathroom with a sink and toilet. There were fifteen people in the unit, and they gathered in the purple and orange vinyl chairs that were here, in the triangular room, and had conversations. One of the bedrooms off the hall was converted into a small lab, and that was where urine samples were left and blood tests were done.

Pardes knew it was time for him to respond to Kelly, so he said, "No, I can talk." He was putting other things together. Every day, the patients went to a room off the main cafeteria and ate their meals off brown trays. They went through a line and picked up Saran-wrapped items from metal shelves. Often, lunch was an ice cream scoop of egg salad with a single black olive pressed in the center. Pardes couldn't leave off thinking of this meal as Psychedelic-Breast-in-a-Dish—to match the Chicken-in-the-Basket dinners.

"You seem kind of quiet, though," Jack Kelly said. "You know, alcohol makes some people more social, gets things going."

Pardes nodded his head. He knew what Jack was suggesting, but that wasn't it. He had always been relatively shy. He wasn't more social when he was drinking; he was smarter. He'd always been proud of that. He wasn't the cliché—the man who drank for ease—he drank for smarts, and to a point, it worked. As he got drunk, he got smarter and smarter, and then, things fell apart and he was incapacitated. That's why he did so well in high school. He was always at that point right before things fell apart.

"Stephen?" Jack Kelly said, as if calling him to attention, but Pardes couldn't keep his mind in the room with Jack Kelly and the purple and orange vinyl chairs. He was thinking about how he'd done so well in high school they'd sent him off to Brooklyn College for classes when he was still a senior. Then when high school was over, he didn't go to college. He loved that. He was supposed to go. He was prime fodder, but he showed them. Again, *them.* He was smart enough to know that *them* was a construction he'd fabricated to account for his own failure, and he was angry enough not to care. So what if he knew better? He'd show them. He took a job as a salesman at the English Muffin Corporation of America. But the problem was, though his intelligence was a product of alcohol, his diligence, his work habits, were entirely a product of a clear head.

He was not, he had to admit, after being demoted to mail clerk at the English Muffin Corporation of America and then fired from that position, eminently hireable.

And women. The plain fact was, it was hard to romance anyone when you had three kids to your name and were still living in friends' apartments or sleeping at mama's house.

It was the classic dilemma—one he recognized in novels and movies but not as it played out in his own life. Early disdain had turned into an arrogance that made him reject everything. That arrogance became self-doubt, because as time passed, Pardes could no longer be admitted into the system, couldn't have all those jobs he'd snubbed before. His credentials were no longer in order, and once out of order, his adult life seemed like a mass of unaccounted-for years. He thought of the phone book as a list of people who wouldn't recommend him or hire him for jobs.

Jack Kelly, either realizing he wasn't getting anywhere with his discussion of sociability or being possessed of unusual telepathic abilities, tried something else. He laid Pardes's life out in front of him: the lack of employment, health insurance and mailing address.

"All good reasons to lay off the sauce, no?" he said, affably.

"Sure," Pardes said and nodded his head. He was confused. He wasn't drinking now, but he guessed they were talking about the future, when his habits wouldn't be monitored. "Sure," Pardes said again. He admitted it. He wasn't denying his life was a mess. He'd always been a realist, but how to explain his bigger fear, now that he was left with his thick tongue and the vocabulary of a sober man? He'd been drunk his whole life. Alcohol was just not something that you could take away and still have . . . well, still have him.

"Are you with me?" Jack Kelly said. He was never angered by Pardes's failure to respond, only, it seemed, a little confused.

"I'm . . ." he began and then looked at Kelly. He took in the man's curly dark brown hair, his wire-rimmed glasses, as if he were seeing them for the first time.

"I'm," he started again, "softer stone than all that."

"Huh? That's interesting," Kelly said. "Softer stone, what do you mean by that?"

Pardes shook his head, disgusted by how inarticulate he had become. "Like those statues in the arches. You know, in the cathedrals in France?"

Kelly looked confused and then delighted. "The jamb statues? Like at Chartres?"

"Sure," Pardes said to make Kelly feel good, though he didn't know what he was talking about. "Say you want to clean the dirt off by sandblasting, but you don't want to overdo it."

Kelly shook his head eagerly. "God," he said. "That's great. I get it. You blow their features away."

That was it, Pardes thought. His features were going to blow away without alcohol. At first, he thought he was afraid that without alcohol he would return to the only sober period of his life, that he'd turn into a seven year old, but then he realized his true fear was that the real world would work away at him like an eraser. He'd get vaguer and vaguer, and soon he wouldn't be there at all.

"That's great," Kelly said again. "What a great way to describe it."

Pardes felt complimented. He was being an interesting patient. So there had to be something still there, even though he had been in the hospital, without liquor, for three weeks. This seemed like a discovery. He wouldn't disappear because his fear would distinguish him.

How they found him, a week later, in the hospital with news of his mother-in-law's death is anyone's guess. After all, he was a New Yorker and had gone to Boston only for that Jeff Pallace job. As far as he knew, no one else even knew he had left town, though he hoped people were beginning to say, "Anyone seen Pardes in a while? I miss that guy." The hospital he had ended up in was a small one in an ugly, Irish Catholic town. So even if they traced him, through his train ticket (although he'd paid cash) to Boston, how would they have found him in that town, in that hospital, in that unit located off the main part of the hospital, in some buildings that were really "mobile classrooms" originally intended for the high school and now hastily subdivided into patients' quarters?

"Stephen Pardes," a man came in and announced one day, "I'm

Harvey Masters, attorney of the law." He was a short man who seemed more round than fat. His dark brown hair was combed forward over a bald patch. "Just a few things, Mr. Pardes," he said. "May I?" he said and gestured to the folding chair.

Pardes nodded his head. He was propped up in his bed and waiting for the sound of the shower at the end of the hall to stop, so he could take his shower. It was just seven in the morning.

Harvey Masters opened his briefcase on the folding chair and pushed Pardes's legs gently to the side, so he could sit at the edge of the bed. He smiled at Pardes's knees, under the covers, as if to apologize for displacing them. "Let's see," he said, when he had settled his buttocks a little further back from the edge of the mattress. "Just a few things, Mr. Pardes. Related to the death of your mother-in-law."

"What?" Pardes said and then, feeling garrulous, "What?" again.

"It seems," Masters began, speaking with the speed of a farm auctioneer, "what with your wife dead and your wife being the main beneficiary and then, after your wife, your children, but with your children being minors (as we say in the law, that's what we call them, minors, children, you know)." Perhaps, Pardes thought, the lawyer thought he was mentally disturbed.

Masters went on, not noticing the expression of amazement on Pardes's face. "There's the matter of an inheritance. But," Masters slowed a bit and looked at Pardes. "But you must be shaken up by this, grieving, distressed. I'm so sorry. Allow me to offer my condolences." With that, Masters extended his hand. Pardes shook it and felt surprised by how warm it was. *All that blood under the skin*, Pardes thought, for no particular reason.

"It must be a shock," Masters said.

Pardes squinted at him. "I'm holding myself together," he allowed, flatly, "but thank you for being so very kind."

The plain fact was Pardes had never met his in-laws. His father-in-law died soon after the marriage. Anya had been a late, accidental birth. Her father was crowding eighty when she left Puerto Rico for college. As for Anya's mother, when she realized Pardes was Jewish, she had refused to come to the wedding in New York. In fact, she had made a huge fuss over the phone, had screamed at Anya and threatened to sue the Brooklyn family with whom she had been living. (In those early days, before they married, Anya had been able to afford Brooklyn College by living with some old friends of her parents. For her room and board, Anya helped out with the cleaning and did a little babysitting. This was the sort of nut Anya's mother had been; she would sue her own friends, friends who were willing to house Anya for four years.)

"It's not that you're Jewish," Anya had told Pardes when her fights with her mother finally subsided. "It's that you're not Spanish."

"Well," Pardes had said then and let himself be satisfied, though it later occurred to him he was every bit as much Spanish as she was, since he was a Sephardic Jew. They had, in Spain, the same ancestral country and, in America, the same, more or less, birthplace, although Anya always said, "Nobody considers Puerto Rico part of America but you."

The lawyer interrupted these thoughts to say, "My experience with grief, my friend, is this: it must be allowed to blossom and flower and then, like any old tulip, die when the season is right. Excuse me," he stopped himself and then whispered, "I didn't mean to say, 'Die,'"

"Fine. It's fine," Pardes said. The woman was hardly dying before her time.

"Umm," Pardes said, and Masters leaned toward him eagerly to say, "Yes?"

Pardes had nothing to say. "Um," he tried again. "How did you find me?"

"Social Security number. Never believe them when they say they won't give it out. They always do. Easiest way to track someone down. Now," he said and leaned over to pluck a sheaf of papers out of his open briefcase, "nurses said make it quick, don't disturb the patient and etcetera, etcetera, as I am sure you can imagine, so I'll get right to the point." He cleared his throat and continued, quickly, "The point is that there is some money, not much, but—" He stopped and gave Pardes an appraising look. Pardes guessed he wanted to say, "But it looks to me that some money would be a definite advantage in a case like yours." But he did not. Instead, he said, "Also, there is a small piece of property, been abandoned for some years, but it is apparently in the heart of a semifashionable urban district . . . this is what I am told . . . I don't travel myself except like this from Boston out to the suburbs and back again.

You won't even find me driving to the Cape, no, you won't. But to the point, to the point. Yes, hum. You'll want to think about selling the property, I suspect. It's a relatively small commercial space with some residential space on the upper floors, though there is the possibility of converting that to offices. There's a courtyard, but I am told that that is not at all unusual in the southern climes, so I can't say that will be a selling point, although I, myself, would find it quite lovely. Again, all this is what I am told; I don't guarantee my own eyes have verified any of this. We can arrange for the sale. The space is in old San Juan. You'll want someone bilingual, of course. Best to get someone down there."

Pardes smiled, "It's not La Madeleine, is it?"

"What?" said Masters. "Oh, yes," he said, fumbling through his papers, "that's absolutely right, that's the name of the property. Queer, isn't it? Well, there you go. Le or la Madeleine and your mother-in-law's savings account. That is it. That is the point. I have gotten to it. Now, I don't want the nurses to say that I am upsetting you. Here is my card. I'll leave you the papers that need signing. Here's an envelope with postage. You call me if you have any questions, and as soon as this is processed, there will be inheritance taxes and all. She had her money in a bank on the mainland for some reason. As soon as it's all done, I'll send you the title and the check."

He stood up off the bed and closed his briefcase. "Well, I'll be off. Glad to know you."

"Glad to know you," Pardes mumbled, stopping in his mind on the phrase *know you.* He was thinking about the fact that he was being bailed out. It was shameless but true. He was getting bailed out, a chance when he hadn't earned a chance. That couldn't happen more than once, the gods grinning so broadly at you and all. He would have to make it work—the money, the property. People got second chances but never third chances. It wasn't, he thought, fear that would distinguish him, though that thought was so strong when he had talked a week earlier with Kelly. It was will. His will would distinguish him.

Masters reached down to shake Pardes's hand. Pardes pulled his hand out from underneath his sheet. At the door, the lawyer turned and said, "I am sure when this terrible sadness passes, you will be happy for the inheritance." Then he lifted his arm and flapped his hand up and down in a childlike wave. "Bye-bye," he said, in a voice that was almost sweet. Pardes took it as the only true prognosis he would get at the hospital. He, Pardes, was going away. No, he stopped and thought, not liking the sound of that; if he went away, he might come back. He, Pardes, was gone.

Missing

(Tata—October 1979)

So," Maria Elena said, giving the table a final slap, "there it is, the story of your father." We were all sitting in the back room of the bakery, and for once, I have to say it, my family was quiet. I'd have listened, mouthed the word "lunatic" to my sisters and left it at that, but there was my father, sitting next to Maria Elena, looking sheepish and adding an occasional, "Yes, it's true." Finally, I said, "Whoa. And I thought I was the family liar."

But nobody laughed.

"This is something you must not tell anyone," my father said. "It can't go beyond this family." I made a face and pointed toward the storage room. Rayovac was rearranging flour bags back there, and I didn't know why we were all assuming the door to that room was soundproof.

"Rayovac," I whispered. My father waved his hand, as if to say that Rayovac couldn't hear us or that he didn't really count.

"Well, that explains a lot, I guess," Melone said quietly.

Beatriz turned to Maria Elena and said, "Well, it's decided then. We have to move out of the *hacienda*."

"What are you talking about?" I said to her. I was sick of how she was always trying to get us to move out of the *hacienda*. "Let me talk to you again, Beatriz, about the virtues of a private bedroom. But," I added in a stage whisper, "not in front of Dad."

Beatriz paid me no mind. Instead, her eyes widened and she got that slightly hysterical look that made me feel instant disdain for her.

"He's a crook, I told you, a small-time crook," she said, addressing her words to Maria Elena.

"Enough of that," Father said sharply and slapped the table himself. Bits of granulated sugar jumped up off the cutting board in front of him.

"Don't . . . don't tell me what to do," Beatriz said.

"Calm down," my father said.

Beatriz was furious. "If I'm not allowed to get upset about this, what *am* I allowed to get upset about?"

"Beatriz," Melone said tightly, "it's not *what* you are upset about but *how* you get upset."

"Well," Beatriz said, shaking her hair about her face so she looked like an upright mop, "how can I help *how* I get upset?" Then she turned to my father and Maria Elena and said, "Can't you see what you're doing? I've warned you again and again."

"None of that witchcraft," Father said and reached across the table and grabbed her wrist tightly, as if that was where the words were coming from.

Beatriz pulled her hand away and started to scream, "Don't touch. You can't touch me, ever. You're just the most evil person."

"Quiet," he said, for surely her words were traveling up the bakery stairs and into the ears of late-afternoon patrons.

"I'll . . . no, no . . ."

"Stop it," Melone said. "Just stop it, Beatriz."

"Oh, don't you gang up on me," Beatriz spit at her.

"*Sha*," my father said, Yiddish for "quiet." I don't think I'd ever heard him use the word before, then he leaned over the table and slapped Beatriz across the face. She looked confused, as if her skull were still recording the fact of the blow, while his handprint stayed on her face, a red glove of hurt. Then blood started pouring from her nose, and Maria Elena said, "Mother of God, look what you've done." She went over and wrapped Beatriz's head in her arms. Melone jumped up for a napkin, and I said, icily, "So what's next?"

But I felt bad for saying it, because it was clear my father was ashamed. He opened his mouth as if to say something, but he said only, "I'm . . ." and shook his head once in apology and stood and turned quickly to go up the stairs. "Rayovac," we heard him saying before he got to the top of the stairs, and then he walked back down the stairs, opened the door to the storeroom and said, "Rayovac, will you lock up for me tonight?"

"Yes, sir," Rayovac said. Was there a sneer in his voice? "Yes, sir." He followed my father back up the stairs.

"Do you think he heard?" Maria Elena asked, but Melone said, "No, that door's thick as they come."

"Hey," I said, turning to my sisters, "talk about drama!"

Beatriz sniffed a laugh.

"Hey," I said, "it's like that thing I saw on TV, about the program Bobby Kennedy founded in the sixties. You know, the Witness Security Program or something, to get people to testify. We're a test case. We could go up to the Justice Department and say, 'Sorry, boys and girls, it was a cute idea, but these things never work. These manufactured identities . . .'" I shrugged and held out my hands as if I were holding a new brand of cleaning fluid, "'we find they just break down.'"

"Poor Gerry," Melone said.

"Who?" Maria Elena asked.

"Gerald Ford," Melone said. "Remember him? First a crazy Puerto Rican threatens to kill him." She was referring to Carlos Irizarry, a political painter. Maria Elena nodded her head. Just the other week, she'd told us Irizarry would probably have had a show at her gallery if he hadn't been led away in chains for his threat against Ford and for a brief stint as a hijacker—all for the nationalist cause. "Then after that," Melone went on, "no one votes for him, and we show up with our bad news about the war against crime."

"You know," Maria Elena said, paying no attention to the thrust of what Melone was saying, "I don't like Irizarry's work. It's too simple—in message and composition, but Lucia said just the other day we should capitalize on this terrorist thing; that now that he's going to jail, we definitely should try to show some of his work."

"What," I said, "are you trying to say? Crime sells? That we should turn Dad's story to our advantage? Have a Two-for-One Rolls and Robbers Special?" Maria Elena lifted the right side of her upper lip to acknowledge my attempt at humor, and then we were all quiet, trying, I suppose, to guess at our own thoughts. What did we think of Papi now? What did we think of ourselves? Finally, I said, "Murderers' Meringues?" and let out a little snort of a giggle.

"Not funny," Beatriz said, a napkin still cupped at her nose.

"Pinch here," Melone said, pointing to her own nose, "right here under the bone. It stops the bleeding." Beatriz did as she was told, and Melone said, "and tilt your head back and . . ." Melone smirked slightly and added, very quietly, "*Y besitos de bandido.*" Bandits' kisses, instead of the sticky *besitos de coco,* coconut kisses, we made on Thursdays.

"*Azucardo de* Anabuse," said Maria Elena, a bit louder. "Anabuse icing," I echoed in English. "Good idea, the baker's special. Well, *this* baker's special and the perfect topping to . . ."

Melone giggled, "*Bizcocho de bandido.* No . . . rum cake!"

"It really isn't funny," Beatriz said, smiling a little herself.

"She's right, girls. We're being terrible," Maria Elena said. "How's that nose?" Beatriz held out the napkin with the blood on it and touched the red stain.

"It's stopped, I think."

"OK, then. Let's go home and see how your father is." Maria Elena was quiet for a moment. "OK?" she addressed us all. We nodded, then she turned to Beatriz. "You'll forgive him," she said and clearly it was a statement not a question. But Beatriz said, "I will not."

Maria Elena started to argue with her, but I said, "I don't want to listen to this anymore. Let's go home. It's time for me to change the bandages on my chest anyway. I'm all itchy inside." It wasn't really true, but in the last few weeks, I'd learned I could use my body to shut my family up.

Despite my joking, I *did* spend the whole ride home wondering about Maria Elena's words about our father. There was something so right about the portrait she had just drawn I had the feeling I'd seen it all along. It was as if she'd found the final piece in a jigsaw puzzle, a piece missing for years, but when she presented it to us, we were unsurprised. We'd done the puzzle so many times. We knew the shape by its absence; after all, it was the only piece missing. Still, it seemed things would have to be different in the family now. I wondered what we would say when we came home or if Papi would even be home when we arrived.

What happened was we found him washing rice in the kitchen, and we assumed a strained politeness, that seemed, for the stretch of the evening, like acceptable behavior. I thought it was only that night—we were all too shocked and all, so we weren't going to do anything. Tomorrow, whatever would happen would happen. But in the morning, we were all the same, no one willing to tip the status-quo boat over and leave us flailing in unfamiliar waters. Another day went by, and still nothing happened, and then another. Within a week things seemed, strange to say, normal. We were like grinning depressives, noticing how falsehood becomes reality; you do cheer up a bit when you have to pretend you're happy.

Things continued on this way for several weeks, through October and into November. I looked everywhere for changes. There were some things. Affection had clearly altered our sense of morality. My sisters and I developed familial feelings for loan sharks and remembered, with real fondness, childhood games of Cops and Robbers, games, to tell the truth, we never played. We found ourselves newly interested in phrases like "extenuating circumstances."

We were, I knew, in a dark place, but darkness couldn't find us. Who knows why? Lord knows, we glittered, showy night stars begging the dark: "Come get us; we don't make any sense without you."

It took Rayovac, of all people, to put things in order. It started with a phone call. Rayovac rang the house and asked to speak to Melone. This wasn't a surprise in and of itself, but once she was on the line, he whispered a single word, "Sorry," and hung up. Melone figured he was talking about my accident. He'd been so hangdog sad about it that he'd transferred his hovering affections to me, although I knew, of course, his solicitousness was guilt, not love. "Want," he used to say, generously, when we were at the bakery, "to play my game?" And he'd slip a tiny pinball game out of his pocket and hand it to me. "I don't *think* so, Rayovac," I'd say and roll my eyes. One day, I even allowed myself a "Oh-grow-up, will-you?" and he didn't shout at me, just mumbled, "Plenty of adults like these sorts of things. Plenty." I got so sick of him I threatened to cartwheel across the floor or polka on the bakery counter, just to prove I was in good physical condition. Finally, I said, "Listen, the only thing about this accident that bugs me is this stupid tire track on my chest. So basically we're talking about my problems shopping for bathing suits. You want to help me; get into fashion design."

A week after the phone call from Rayovac, we figured out what he was apologizing for. We were cleaning the dinner dishes when there was a knock on the door. The police. Three blue-capped men with a warrant.

"What can I do for you?" Maria Elena said, as she stood politely at the door, and the rest of us gathered around her, wondering what was going on. "We're looking for a Stephen Pardes, alias Sandrofo Codero Lucero."

Melone looked at me. How could they know?

"I'm Sandrofo," my father said, stepping around Maria Elena onto the front steps.

"Señor Lucero, you are under arrest for . . ." said one policeman, but no one heard the charges because Maria Elena got instantly hysterical, "What's this about? What's this about?" she cried. Finally, one of the policemen said, "Trafficking in drugs."

"You've made a terrible mistake," Maria Elena said, and the policeman asked her if she could please be quiet for a brief moment so he could discharge his duty. "No," Maria Elena said and squared her shoulders like any old Girl Scout, "not if your duty gets in the way of justice."

Over her protests, the policeman read my father his rights. As he spoke, my father said calmly, "It's OK, girls. It's OK."

"I'll come with you," Maria Elena said, grabbing a sweater and her purse.

"No," my father said, "no." He seemed relaxed, convinced this was a mistake and ready to help the police uncover their errors.

"Yes, I'm coming. What if they keep you the night? You'll need a toothbrush and . . . they've clearly made a mistake." She ran from the door and into the kitchen. "Wait," she called from the other room, "just wait." Papi shook his head at the police and smiled, as if in apology for Maria Elena's behavior. "I'm ready," Maria Elena said, running back to the front door, her purse now hanging at her side.

"Stay here," my father snapped at her, and Maria Elena said, ferociously back, "No. I told you I'm coming." And then they were gone.

Melone, Beatriz and I didn't know what to do, so we sat in an anxious silence punctuated by an occasional, "I'm sure it'll prove to be nothing," until Maria Elena's headlights swept up the drive. We raced to the door, but she was alone when she stepped out of the car. "We'll get you some tea," Melone offered, and we hustled her through the house. No one said a word till we were in the kitchen, and then we all said, "What? What's going on?"

"Jesus," she said, slumping into a kitchen chair, throwing her forehead into her left hand and slinging the pocketbook over the table.

"What?" someone said again, and there was a brief silence during which our world was still the old world we knew and understood, and then we knew things would be irrevocably different.

Maria Elena breathed deeply. "The police came here to pick him up, and I went with him to the station."

"We know that," Melone said impatiently. "We were right here when it happened."

"I knew," Maria Elena said, "that this couldn't be about those crimes he committed in Brooklyn. Statute of limitations and all. And how would they know anyway? I knew you girls wouldn't talk but . . . Rayovac. Rayovac talked."

"The little shit," Melone said, her face contorting.

"He heard your father that day. You remember. The day I told you everything, and he was in the storage room? He went down to the station, and he told them your father's real name. Which shouldn't have meant anything, but it turns out, the police did know the name of this Stephen Pardes, because it has been associated with some drug deals on the island. Now, I sat there and thought, *It can't be so.* Remember: Sandrofo changed his name. Stephen Pardes doesn't, in effect, exist anymore. And I thought, Well, maybe someone used your father's name, and . . . well, it turns out the person who used your father's name was your father."

"What?" I said. "What the hell are you talking about?"

"Listen," Maria Elena said. And she told exactly what happened when she went into the police station.

They had sat in the hall outside the room where Maria Elena knew, from TV shows, Sandrofo would be questioned. She assumed the room had one-way mirrors and electronic bugs, so she thought now was the only time she could get the truth out of him. "If," she hissed through her teeth, "you don't tell me everything I need to know, I will tell these police what you told me. I'll defend you to the end if you tell me the truth, but not if you lie to me. What have you done?"

Sandrofo leaned his head down, talked softly into his own chest, and Maria Elena pushed her ear toward his chin so she could hear him. "There were a few loose ends when I first moved here. There wasn't enough liquid cash, and I didn't want to sell the bakery, so I arranged for a few . . . transactions, to get things going. It wasn't anything I was going to pursue . . . once I was on my feet and all. But that's how I met Victor and Coco."

Maria Elena gasped, then bit her own index finger, so she would be quiet. "So Victor agreed to be my partner, if I'd just do a little work for him over the years."

Maria Elena couldn't be quiet any longer. Her voice trembling, she said, "At this rate, tomorrow I expect to wake up and find that, I don't know, that my toast can talk." She must have sounded, she confessed now, a little mad. Certainly, she felt a little mad.

"Maria Elena . . ." Sandrofo said, for her voice was rising.

"And it will turn out my breakfast toast can also sing and, and . . ." Maria Elena burst into tears. "Why?" she said. "There had to be another way. What sort of drugs?"

"Oh, Maria Elena," Sandrofo said.

"What?"

"The standard."

"Heroin?" Maria Elena asked, and Sandrofo nodded his head. "Oh, Mother of God," Maria Elena said. "Don't you see what you've done?"

"It's not so bad," Sandrofo whispered. "It's not what you imagine. I'd just deliver an occasional . . ."

"Oh, shut up," Maria Elena said. "Don't you ever think? Don't you care about the people you're hurting? Don't you care about people at all?"

"Of course, I do. I love my girls. I love you. I love . . . the whole reason I started a bakery was because of other people, because I wanted to give them . . ."

"But at someone's expense. Someone, somewhere has to drop off the planet. Cities have to fold; people have to be machine gunned to death so you can pass out cake to people."

Sandrofo lifted his head abruptly. "Oh," he said in a condescending tone. "Don't be such a child. You sound like Beatriz."

"Why did you do it? There had to be another way."

"Why?" he said, thoughtful, his snideness gone. "I guess I missed . . ."

"Oh, God," Maria Elena said, as if she suddenly understood everything, "and I always thought you were mourning your wife."

"No," Sandrofo said, and Maria Elena said it was like the day she first met Father, like the day she was convinced their thoughts were so united that he spoke her thoughts, and she realized she hadn't had this feeling for the whole of the time she had been with Sandrofo. And Father said, "I guess you're right. It was me. I missed me."

Two days later, they moved my father to a jail in Río Pedras to await trial. We sat in the kitchen, wondering about bail money, regretting the fact we hadn't sued somebody—Rayovac or the car manufacturer—after my accident. If we could sell the house or the bakery, there might be enough. If we could hit up Victor and Coco? But Victor and Coco were gone, off the island, on a vacation to nobody-knew-where. Among the four of us, there was not a person who knew what to do. Even Beatriz was too confused to offer her panacea, "Sell the house," although that was clearly what she thought we should do. Maria Elena thought to ask her old boyfriend, Carlos, the drug attorney, what to do, but she feared a conflict of interest; she just might help convict my father by seeking advice. Our father was no help. Ashamed, he refused to see us. Apparently, the jail gave him a piece of paper on which he was to write the names of all the people who could come to visiting hours, and he wouldn't write our names down, so we couldn't go visit. He didn't even respond to our letters.

Two weeks passed this way, and finally we all agreed we couldn't let Father stay in jail while we debated. We decided to put both the house and bakery up for sale. We would see which offer looked best. No sooner were the properties on the market than we got a call, from Rayovac. It was just as it had been when we'd gotten the first phone call from Rayovac. We were all in the library. Melone and Maria Elena were sitting in the room's two chairs. Beatriz and I were sitting cross-legged on the floor and trying to distract ourselves with magazines. The only difference was that Maria Elena picked up the ringing phone. "*Dios,*" she said as she hung up. "It was Rayovac. He wants to buy the bakery. Jesus Christ, what should we do?" It was entirely unclear what loyalty consisted of here. Everyone shrugged. I said, "Do it." And she said she would. She'd race the transaction through, so we'd have money for bail. It was hard to imagine that we would no longer spend our days at the bakery. It was hard to imagine what we would live on now, but Maria Elena said, "I have a salary, girls. Remember that. I'll always take care of you." I rolled my eyes. She wasn't even our mother. Now it didn't look as if she was ever going to be our father's wife. But then, I reached up and gave her a hug. She looked startled, then said, "It's OK. I guess we are all scared."

Though Maria Elena didn't confide in Carlos, she did let him help us through the court's bureaucracy. Carlos even went down with Maria Elena to pay the bail and get Father out of jail. By the time we got the money from the sale of the bakery, Papi had been there for four weeks, and we were all worried. What would he look like? How would he feel? Maria Elena and Carlos went first thing in the morning. Maria Elena packed a cooler of food—"Lord knows what he's been eating in there"—so he could have breakfast on the ride home. She brought fresh towels and bars of soap and a bottle of water. She wasn't too embarrassed to carry these things with her into jail. And that—when she entered the jail with Carlos—was when all hell broke loose because my father wasn't in the jail. "What do you mean?" Carlos demanded. "What do you mean he's not here?" Soon enough, there were dozens of reporters at Maria

Elena and Carlos's side, asking the warden the same question. This wasn't the first time a suspect with drug connections had vanished from a Puerto Rican jail. All of a sudden, a podium was being set up in front of Maria Elena; more people were gathering. Finally, the jail warden arrived, stepped behind the podium, tapped the mike, breathed dust from its head and said, "He has not escaped. He is just temporarily lost."

Maria Elena fainted at this news. Later, she tried to convince everyone she wasn't upset. She was just having a bit of trouble with her diabetes.

I was upset, however. Beatriz was upset. Melone was upset. After all, our father had disappeared. We slept in the same bed that night, all together for comfort, and we trembled so that we eventually shook each other to sleep. "Reminds me of the good old days in the womb," I said, as I lay sandwiched between Beatriz and Melone. Nobody laughed. I knew we were all staring out the window at the fingernail clipping of a moon, and we were thinking: If he'd escaped—and even grade-school idiots knew he had escaped—why hadn't he come back for us? Why hadn't he tried to contact us? In the morning at breakfast, Melone said she thought his escape must have been recent. But Beatriz thought the reason he never wrote our name on the list or responded to our letters was he'd been "temporarily misplaced" since the beginning of his stay at Río Pedras. Maria Elena didn't allow herself such speculations. She just said, "Well, girls, we have something to live on now."

"Let's buy the bakery back," Beatriz said, but it turned out Maria Elena had already tried that. On the previous day, smelling salts still tickling her nose, sugar still caking at her lips, she went straight from the jail to the bakery. "Nothing doing," Rayovac had said. He had grand designs. He was going to turn La Madeleine into a video arcade.

"The little shit," Melone said.

"How could he?" I said, and Beatriz answered by drawing a long parallel between our family and the family in that strange book she was always reading. She told us that story had ended with a terrible betrayal and our story was ending with a terrible betrayal.

"Shut up," I said. "I really can't stand to hear another word about that book."

Beatriz started to argue with me, but Maria Elena cut in. "I'll tell you how Rayovac can do it. Guilt. It's how he's absolving himself. He's demonizing your father and all of us. We're the bad guys."

I nodded my head, as if to say, "OK, that seems reasonable enough." But then I said out loud, "Who cares *why* everything is happening? What are we going to do now?"

I looked around the room, but no one would open her mouth to give an answer.

Stories About Men

(Melone—January 1980)

I don't know how we survived those first days after my father's disappearance. Nothing seemed real. I kept expecting to step out of bed in the morning and float to the ceiling. Why should gravity be more constant than anything else? I had no idea how to orient myself to the world. There were decisions to be made—endless decisions about how we would live, where we would live and what we would live on. There were emotions to be felt—the betrayal of Rayovac, the—what?—disappearance of my father, which might have been abandonment or death or . . . I had not a clue. The news that my father's morals were so far from the morals by which he had strictly raised us. For months, I walked around slack-jawed, staring stupidly at the truth of our situation and feeling a sudden desire for food. There had to be something I could eat to take care of this feeling, I'd think, and open the refrigerator and close it.

Finally, I went looking for Angelo. I found him, horribly enough, in La Madeleine, which now was a video arcade, full of boys and young men, pushing into electronic games with their hips. There was no question it looked like they were making love to the machines, and when they finished by slapping the games in frustration and bumping their pelvises angrily against the side of the machine, my impression didn't change. I just felt sad about having thought of it as making love instead of as having sex or committing rape.

I tapped Angelo on the shoulder, said, school-girl polite, "Remember the year you were my father? What did you know? What did you know then?" But Angelo was already another person.

"Who is he?" I said to a lanky, young woman with an expression of magnificent boredom on her face. She tugged at the short blue-jean shorts that barely covered her ass and said, "Victoria Manuel." Victoria was an unrepentant gossip. "It's not gossip," she liked to say. "It's concern about others. It makes our community more . . . more digestible." One hardly expected Victoria to be in a video arcade, but I suppose it was a good place to get stories about men.

"Found out anything good?" I said sarcastically to the woman in shorts. She didn't pick up on my tone or chose to ignore it. She said, "Eh, nothing I didn't know already. Victoria, she's a little," the woman touched her head, "simple, you know?" Then, when Angelo's eyes started to tear, as if he were offended, she said, "I'm talking about a different Victoria. Don't worry."

I couldn't resist asking about Rayovac. "How is he?" I said, and though the woman was about to answer, Angelo glanced over from the video game that was illuminating his face in underwater greens and blues and said, "Still in love with that pretty girl, the one whose eyes are two colors. Like yours."

The answer pleased me, for these days I fantasized about my power to destroy Rayovac with a few cruel words, but the plain truth was Victoria was behind on the gossip. Rayovac didn't love me any longer. How could he? Maria Elena was right. He'd clearly turned those years of frustration and then guilt to hate, and I wanted to leave the arcade before I ran into him. Though I'd never liked him, I saw how I had come to rely on the constancy of his affection, and it unnerved me that that, too, was gone.

When my father vanished, I suddenly understood why one speaks, in English, of someone becoming unglued. For a solid week, Maria Elena was not herself but her component parts, scattered about the house. It impressed me: there were more parts than I'd imagined. I'd walk into the parlor, and she'd be sitting there, telling stories to cheer Beatriz and Tata. Her manner would be riotous, her eyes glassy. Handfuls of bracelets would clank at her wrist. She'd tie scarves in her hair and say, "Don't I look like Madame Marie? Here to reassure you about your fortunes?" I'd find her in the kitchen with Carlos, our lawyer, her old boyfriend, and be struck by her willingness to play the part of the flirty coquette. Up in the bedroom, I'd spy on her as she talked on the phone to her friend Lucia. She'd cry so deeply I had to resit the urge to run in and embrace her slim shoulders. Her eyes were big and beautiful and sponge-like; how could so much water be in any one head? When the police would come to ask questions, she was a virtual hysteric. She'd get that mad, bugged-out look of the insane; her throat seemed to bulge, frog-like, from under her chin. I couldn't help but notice the fly-sized pulse, pulse, pulse of an artery in her neck. Always the same artery, ticking away her anxiety. Then, the police would be gone, and she'd be a smooth-necked, cheerful mother. She'd efficiently wipe crumbs off the table and say, even if no one was in the room: "Girls, it's going to be all right." I'd heard her say it once when I was on the porch, and she was alone in the kitchen.

A week after Papi's disappearance, however, Maria Elena collapsed into self-promotion. Reminded us about how she was good in disasters, said this disappearance counted as a disaster, and as soon as she said it, the house filled up with forms: life insurance, adoption papers, bank statements. She wrote away for college pamphlets, scholarship information. "It's never too early to plan for the future," she said. Her mouth was always moving; as she did a household chore, she'd say, "I'm the kind of person who knows how to take care of things," and, "I'm the kind of person who alphabetizes her books." As soon as she gave into arrogance, I could see she was a whole person again. Glued, not unglued.

And our family was "glued" too, even though the weeks passed and my father did not reappear, even though our days were no longer spent at the bakery. Maybe this was what shocked me more than his disappearance: the way we didn't fall apart, the way certain things didn't change, like the way my sisters and I acted, like Maria Elena's presence in our lives. Maria Elena had Lucia hire my sisters and me to do occasional work in the gallery. After school, we each got part-time jobs—Beatriz read books to a blind student at the University of Puerto Rico; Tata waited tables at an open-air restaurant in Miramar; and Maria Elena convinced Carlos to give me some typing to do in his law office.

Without these occupations, our afternoon hours, the hours that always belonged to the bakery, would have been unbearable, a hopeless reproach for our failure to hold onto our father.

"So," Tata asked me one night, "what do you remember about Grandma?" Though we'd stopped sleeping together in one big bed, we were still nervously sleeping in the same bedroom. "I'm talking to you," Tata said crankily and tossed her pillow through the dark and onto my bed. It landed on my stomach. "Jerk," I said.

"Tell me," she said, her voice strained, her mood bad. She was ready for a fight. I started to say something about the clown Grandma had bought for us, but Tata hissed at me. "Liar. He just told you that."

"No," I said. "It had a red nose and a little hat with a blue star on top."

"Like all clowns. What clown doesn't have a red nose? You don't remember a thing," she said, disgusted. I argued with her, but as I did, I realized I didn't know if I truly remembered the clown or not.

"I was locked in a closet once," Beatriz said, and I jumped a bit at her voice. I had thought she was asleep. "I think by a teacher at nursery school or something. For years, I didn't understand how I could have a memory of something that didn't happen. Papi said we never went to nursery school. So I figured I'd seen a kid on TV who was locked in a closet . . . or something like that. But I really do remember it. I remember how the door was outlined in yellow light and how coats fell into my hair."

"Where's Maria Elena?" I said.

"Sleeping, where do you think?" Tata said. "Why is it that you can't stand to have this conversation? We could piece a whole life together if you'd just tell us what you *really* remember."

I turned over and stuffed my head into my pillow.

"Why?" Tata said again, her tone angry. She wasn't truly curious. Still, since her accident, it was impossible to get angry with Tata. You somehow felt harsh words wouldn't enter her ears but leave your mouth, head straight for her chest and start to open up the wounds there. "I said, 'Why?' Don't you wonder about *anything*?"

"I wonder," I said, tightly, "about Social Secuity numbers. I wonder how he pulled that off, getting a new Social Security number for himself."

"Is that all?" Tata said, as if she were sickened by my lack of imagination.

"Come on, Tata," Beatriz said. "Leave her alone."

"Why should I? She's too good to share her precious thoughts with the likes of . . ."

"Shut up," I sat up in my bed and screamed. "Shut up, shut up, shut up, shut up."

"No," Tata said cutely, pretend quiet, but I was in no mood for her dumb joking. I was already raging. "I don't," I said, "I don't want to collect memories with you. I don't want to be you, and I don't want to be her." I gestured with my chin to Beatriz. "Miss I'm Too Funny for Anything to Hurt Me and Miss Doom. What a pair."

"I was only asking . . ." Tata started.

"Oh, yeah, I know, only asking about memories." I stopped and gave a sort of Frankenstein laugh and said, "Then you'll want to dress alike and then . . ." I threw my arm out and cracked the back of my hand against the wall. "Didn't hurt me," I said, between tears, because I'd hit myself harder than I intended to. "Didn't hurt me, but you're supposed to wonder at that sudden pain in your hand." I started to cry.

"Yeah," Tata said with disgust. "Like I'd want to be like you two loons."

"Hey," Beatriz said, softly, a single word of protest—this wasn't her argument, but she'd been attacked by both sides—and then we all stuffed ourselves back under our sheets and tried to cry without letting the other two notice we'd been hurt.

The next day, Maria Elena said, "Now, that was quite a display last night. I heard you right through the walls. Girls, don't take this out on each other." We nodded, sleep having mellowed us. "Come on," she said. "I'm going out to the gazebo and need some help gardening." We followed her out.

"Men just leave. It's what they do well," Maria Elena instructed us, as she pulled at the weeds that were growing between the cracks of wood in the gazebo. Beatriz, Tata and I sat on the floor of the gazebo and picked at the grass, not one of us willing to match her energy. "You'll see, unfortunately, for yourselves, as you grow up and have strings of ruinous affairs."

"Is that a prediction?" I said.

"It's not a prediction," said Maria Elena. "It's just the way things work out for women of intelligence."

"She thinks we're intelligent," Tata said, in a silly voice.

Beatriz said, "I don't think it has to necessarily work out that way."

I thought they'd all missed the point. Our father hadn't left, I felt, but had slipped through our fingers. He was water poured over our palms, and if we'd only thought to cup our hands, we would still be holding onto him. But water being what it was, we'd hold onto only some of him, then eventually something would happen—evaporation or a sudden urge to dry our hands on our pants—and he'd be gone altogether. But then I thought that wasn't right either. And I thought of the way Maria Elena would sometimes say, out loud, but absentmindedly, so it was clear the question was rhetorical, "Who can tell me what I need to know?" I wondered the same thing all the time. Who could tell us what we needed to know to understand our lives?

The Baker's Wife

(Anya—January 1980)

I could have been anything, but what I was was the dead wife of Stephen Pardes. Plugs of dirt in each nostril, a stalk of wild asparagus sprouting from my throat, white, worm-like roots growing from my fingertips, I felt, in death, wicked pleasure at the things going on, a mere continent to the south of where I was buried. There is no denying I had what I'd always wished for: influence beyond the grave.

It took long enough, for if I weren't dead, I'd have divorced Stephen a few years ago. He had been a no-account, a braggart with less brains than he thought he had when I married him. I loved him just the same. What happened was I fell, like any knee-socked schoolgirl, for his looks and for his disdain. He had no use for others; still, he wanted me, and I could not think to say no. My fall was literal and bloody. Once I'd tripped over the stone of him, I never could get the scabs off my knees.

I'd believed Stephen would make something of himself. But in my life, it had not happened. During my pregnancy, he was a degenerate, drinking to excess and stealing groceries. After I died, he was no better than a thug, procuring watches and TV sets through broken glass windows.

From the start, we were an unlikely pair. I'd been the baby of my family, a late birth, and I was used to the tired affection of everyone around me. I got what I wanted, because it was too exhausting to refuse me. That's why I remembered La Madeleine. Though my family lived across the island from San Juan in Mayagüez, we regularly visited that old bakery. Within La Madeleine's walls, black licorice fell from uncles' hands and aunts' pockets. It came dusted in the confectionery sugar sprinkled indiscriminately over all the pastries at the bakery. When I asked for more, I always got it. That's the way things were my whole life. Ribbons, new dresses. I was bedecked. Until Stephen.

I went north for education. I'd been only a fair student in high school, though I did have a real enthusiasm for books and was looking forward to college in the States. But when my parents abandoned me, I had to leave school, take some work in the handbag department of an elegant women's clothing store. At first, it was only part time, because Stephen was still working for the English Muffin Corporation. I didn't really mind. It made me feel pleased and grown-up to be snapping on stockings and going to work. Then Stephen was demoted and demoted again, till he lost his job. To pay the rent, I had to work full time at the store. I stood all the time, and at night, I was too sleepy to read. In the morning, my feet hurt as soon as they touched the floor.

When I married, I married in a synagogue. Though I was born a Catholic, I'd converted for Stephen. The rabbi told us that, in Judaism, when a couple marries, their souls wrap around one another. If we were ever to get divorced, he said (in a tone that suggested he thought that might be a good idea), we would have to remember to get a Jewish divorce as well as a legal divorce. Otherwise, our souls would stay wrapped together. We nodded vaguely at the rabbi and then at Ben, the single school friend we had asked to attend the ceremony. Could he, we meant to say, hold onto this information for us? After all, throughout the day, he'd done such a good job with everything else: rings and flowers, prayer books and official certificates. Ben smirked sadly back at us, as if to indicate that he too thought this an unwise union.

Within a month, we saw what Ben and the rabbi saw: that we were fooled by sexual attraction, that we had no business trying to set up a life for ourselves, that we were magnificent, stunning fighters. We fought in cars, on sidewalks, in bed, over the phone. We pushed each other's heads into the floor and whispered evil things: threatened to leave, to take lovers, to lie in bed and never get up. Food flew, glasses shattered. When we were together, everything was aloft: vases, picture frames, sandwiches. Gravity departed; our anger ruled. And our reconciliations were equally magnificent. We sobbed for forgiveness. We drenched our apartment with tears. We swam laps in the salty water spilled on the floor. We made love for centuries in the apartment building's foyer because we couldn't wait to get upstairs. We swore never to leave each other, and then we swore it again, and again.

And then, in the morning, we'd talk peaceably, without rancor, about our faults. We tried to be adult, to act educated; we earnestly applied what I remembered from Civ 101 to our lives. "You don't like anything," Stephen said, before we rose from bed one morning. "You are always complaining. What do you *like?*"

"That's not true," I said, too in love to be concerned about the accusation. "What I hate," and I thought dreamily of the object of my disgust, "is civilization."

"No, no," Stephen said. "The question is what do you like?"

"Well, you, of course," I said and reached over to stroke his chest. "Cigarettes," I said and tapped one from the pack that lay on the floor by the bed. "I liked school, and if you had a job, I could go back." Stephen didn't argue this point. "I like to swim and . . ." And I never told him the rest: I liked the pills a woman at the department store sold me to help me get through the day. They were good for aching calves and a mind that couldn't let go of the fact that Stephen kept our money in a shoe box and not a bank.

"When you say you don't like civilization," Stephen said, "what are you opposing it to?"

"I don't know. The world as it is. Nature."

"Hmph," Stephen made an angry laughing sound, told me that while I may have hated New York City, I didn't do much better with nature. Walks in the woods made me jumpy. I saw the shadows of leaves as bats, twisted sticks as snakes. I was disproportionately annoyed by bugs.

I remember I told him not to be stupid, that I did like nature, though I knew I was lying. I'd grown up in a relatively small village, but that didn't mean I had some peasant love of the fields. I'd always kept to buildings: to the plaza, the church, my school and home. The prospect of a day in the country terrified me. What was really true was I would have *liked* to like nature.

Later, when I was pregnant, Stephen would remind me of this conversation. "It's just nature," he'd say cheerfully, while he held my forehead as I puked into our small apartment's toilet bowl. Though my body responded as any body would to a pregnancy, I felt no love for the life inside me. I wasn't worrying about where the children would sleep in our one-room apartment. I didn't find myself out at the Woolworth's pricing baby booties. Instead, I considered the unhappy alterations of my body: the repulsive swelling of my abdomen, the weight of my breasts, my own undeniable animality. I bought more and more pills from the department store friend. I felt everything acutely: I felt the touch of the breeze like a man's calloused palm slapping my face; fire engine sirens exploded in my head; the sea at Coney Island seemed agitated to me, like a piece of veal that sickeningly managed to be both overcooked and alive at the same time. Inside me, I could feel myself being slowly eaten up. "For the baby," I said, once, when Stephen found me swallowing pills. "Fertility drugs," I said, and perhaps he was even stupider than I thought because he didn't seem to question that explanation. Fertility, he must have thought, wasn't just about conception but about carrying a baby to term. Even with the drugs that made me feel as if my individual cells were separated with lovely, light bubbles of air, I barely lasted through the pregnancy. The delivery itself was too much. My terror at the natural world undid me—all that mess, that pain, the future soreness. I imagined myself nursing triplets—having to do it in rounds, having one at each breast. I almost died at the thought, but it turned out I didn't need to worry about nursing, for I hemorrhaged through the delivery, and I floated, on a river of blood, right out of the world.

He didn't come to visit. I waited for his period of excessive grief to pass, but I didn't see him, even then. It wasn't till I was almost five years dead that he came. He stood over me, said, "Oh, Anya," and rubbed his hand over the stone his mother had placed above me. Then he turned, pulled a pad of paper out of his coat pocket. A note, I thought, a note for me! I saw how he might fold the paper, might put it by my name and put a stone over it. I saw how all this might happen, but then I saw him walk away, across the street from the Jewish graveyard to the lavish Catholic cemetery. I felt for him. So many people to mourn. In the other graveyard, though, he didn't head for a specific stone. Instead, he walked up and down the rows of headstones. He spent hours there, and when he was through, he had what he wanted. On the piece of paper, the one I thought was for me, he had scribbled these words: Sandrofo Cordero Lucero, 1906–1912.

Above me now, there is a crazy amount of ornamentation. Orange-pink snapdragons, petunias, cut irises, even pots of geraniums. None of these petals was brought for me, but I don't mind. When my mother-in-law was alive, she came and scattered bread crumbs, so my grave would be decorated with birds. I know she was hoping I would be visited by small purple finches, though, often enough, only large, ugly starlings swooped down from the sky. I'd feel the weight of their oily blackness, even all the way down here. It's amazing what gets through.

After Stephen left New York, his mother's mind quickly disintegrated. Without the job of taking care of her grandchildren or her own long-dead husband, she grew stupid. I'd hear her above my grave, talking to the friends who accompanied her to the cemetery. She had no interest in discussing anything but meals—what were her friends going to have for dinner, what had they had for breakfast, what degree of gastric disturbance did milk products cause them? When she wasn't talking about food, she showered people with mindless compliments. I could tell her friends had trouble tolerating her. They tried to get her onto other topics, things like Golda Meir that had interested her in the past. "Israeli statehood," they would start, and she would say, "You have such lovely, lovely smooth skin."

When she was gone, her friends buried her right here. I flank her left side; her husband hugs her right. But what good is that to me? No one talks to each other here.

Still, I'm not alone. When we married, the rabbi forgot to tell us what happens to the soul when you lose a spouse through death instead of divorce, but I don't need to be told. The details of his life—the meddling second wife, the children with their gaping mouths, their stumblings—mean nothing. I feel his soul, right here with me. Its fingers at my hips, its lips at my neck. I have always felt it here with me.

Where We Live Now

(Maria Elena—March 1980)

It was late of a Friday afternoon, and the gallery was closed. Tonight, we would hang the work of a political painter, Luis Cardona. The artist was unavailable to hang the show himself because he'd been jailed for trying to blow up the car of a Virginian state representative who'd been vacationing in Condado with his family. Lucia didn't think Cardona's work would attract the attention it might because his crime was only a copycat crime. Apparently, Cardona had always admired Irizarry, would-be assassin of the mild, potato-faced ex-President Gerald Ford. Cardona's work, like his crime, was derivative of Irizarry's. Now his paintings were leaning against a wall in the center room of the gallery. Lucia and I were spackling over the holes from the previous exhibition. Later, Beatriz, Melone and Tata were going to come by and help us paint the gallery's walls. We always had a crowd during the opening months of a new exhibit, and we wanted everything to look perfect.

Cardona painted the portraits of significant Puerto Rican left-wing leaders, then cut his canvases into different-sized triangles. He scattered the triangles on a new canvas and photographed the result. He'd turn the photograph into a slide, project the slide on yet another new canvas and then use the projected image as a sort-of high-tech paint-by-numbers guide. This final painting was the one he displayed. As an image, I didn't think it made much sense, since it was all about randomness and not at all about perception. Cardona's enthusiasm for fracturing images owed more, I decided, to his fondness for explosives than for Picasso.

Before the girls arrived, I told Lucia I was still worried about Beatriz. I had read her journal and found these lines: "No one believes me about this house. Since my father disappeared, we sit around. We wait for someone to die."

Lucia clucked her tongue once at me and said, "When did this happen?"

"A few weeks ago," I said. "I didn't tell you right away, because . . ." I shrugged my shoulders. "Well, you know." I returned to filling in a hole on the wall in front of me.

Lucia was standing on a ladder to my right. She looked down at me to say, "You have about as much wisdom as my big toe. Don't you know not to read an adolescent's journal?"

I shook my head but said, "It's not interfering the way you think. If she found out, she'd be mad, but she'd like it too. Think of how you were at that age."

Lucia grimaced but then nodded. "It's true. There was a period when I loved to be questioned. I had fantasies about being held as a political prisoner," she gestured with her chin to the other room where Cardona's work was being stored. "There was something seductive about the attention, about imagining someone cared that much about your words."

"Hm . . . we should talk to Cardona about this. Interrogation as a form of love."

"That's what you think. You can't deny it," Lucia said. "You think it is a form of love."

"Oh, please," I said, but I couldn't disabuse her of the notion, anymore than I could convince her that the girls accepted me, that they hadn't run from the house, visions of Hansel and Gretel's new mother in their head, when Sandrofo first told them about his plan to marry me, or later when I said, husband or not, I was planning on staying with them. She remained unconvinced, even when I told her about how, just last week, as a joke, they had started a campaign to have all the inanimate objects in the house say hello to me. I'd open a drawer, and there would be a small piece of paper saying, "Hi, Maria Elena. We're good for stirring, and what's more, we can be hung off a nose. Love, The Spoons." Still, Lucia persisted in believing in the impossibility of a functioning stepfamily, especially one that had such unofficial bonds as ours did.

When the girls finally arrived, it was with the news that we'd have to put off our painting for a day or so. A tropical storm, hovering out in the Atlantic, was supposed to come our way. The radio was advising everyone to go home to tape up windows, Tata said.

"Well," I said, "we don't have glass in our windows, so I don't see why we have to go home." The girls nodded. "I mean we could stay, though we might be forced into an overnight on the gallery floor. After all, you closed the shutters."

"Who, me?" Melone said.

"Well, one of you. Didn't one of you close the shutters before you left this morning?" They shook their heads. "Oh," I said. The black shutters ran the length of the door-size windows of the *hacienda.* Closed, they offered real protection. Open, they'd let enough of the island through the windows that tonight we'd be dining on a carpet of soggy leaves.

"I'll go back and do it and then come back here," Tata offered.

"What?" I said, "By bus? And then walk home in the storm? I don't *think* so. We'll all go."

While they were piling into the car, Beatriz said she thought she felt the first drops of rain. "I don't *think* so," Tata said, mimicking my phrase from earlier. Or . . . actually it occurred to me that I'd originally stolen the phrase—with its inflection on *think*—from her. We waved our goodbyes to Lucia, promised to come back over the weekend to get the rest of the work done. By the time I pulled around the corner, it was raining in earnest.

"See?" Beatriz said, pointing at the sky.

Before we were even out of old San Juan, rain was slamming down on us. We could see, as we dipped down onto the highway, its gray spread over the sea. "Wow," Tata allowed. And then the rain was too heavy on the car's windshield to see much of anything beyond the interior of the car and the lights of other commuters, trying to make it home.

"White-knuckle driving," I said, my hands clenched at the wheel.

"Don't go so fast," said Melone.

"I'm not going so fast," I said.

"Oh, you two," Tata sighed. "You should have let me do the driving."

"You don't even have your license," I said.

"Yes, but I know how to drive. Pull over and let me."

"Not in this storm, I will not."

"Come on," Tata said.

Both Beatriz and Melone told her to shut up. By the time we were out of the city, I wouldn't have minded letting Tata drive. I was exhausted, the way one always is when a familiar ten-minute drive takes, as this one promised to, forty-five minutes. The rain lightened for the final stretch, and by the time we were pulling into the drive to the *hacienda,* it had stopped completely.

"See, if we'd stayed and helped . . ." Melone started to say, and I knew she meant to say we would have avoided the rain, but she couldn't finish the sentence, because if we had stayed to help, we wouldn't have seen our house rising in the storm. We all gasped, as I rounded a curve and we saw our home. The *hacienda,* shimmering in yellow storm light, was floating above its foundation.

But it was only an optical illusion. Before the rain, the earth had been hot. Now steam hissed off the ground and hugged the house so nothing between our land and our home seemed solid. No one spoke, and I didn't let reason try to undo the impression. Our house, I thought, the whole weighty thing, was being carried away by the flimsiest mist. But then the house stayed put; the mist disappeared; and I thought I was wrong. Our house was being supported by the flimsiest mist.

"This would have never happened if Papi were here," Melone said, without regret. I saw what she meant: magic and love—maybe they were the same thing—who knew what he ever had to do with it?

Later that night, Beatriz crept into my room to say, "I've been thinking about that book I stole and I wonder, well . . ." She was shy, frightened, it seemed, by what she was about to say. "Do you think it's possible we're that man's second family and not his first?"

"What are you talking about?"

"Well, remember in that story about Doroteo Díaz; remember at the very end, there's a line about how his first life always confused him." I shook my head no, turning my cold nose into my pillow. Beatriz shook the top of my arm. "No, wake up for this. See, Doroteo goes back to Spain and is remarried and has a new life. You remember that?"

"I do," I said.

"Then when he thinks back to his first life, the one on the island, he can't make any sense of it."

"Mmm," I said, drifting back to sleep.

"Well, I'm wondering about this family he has after he leaves the island and goes back home to Spain, the one we don't know anything about because it's not in the book. Don't you think that it's possible I've been wrong all along, that we're not Doroteo's first family but his second one?"

"Yes," I said. "I think it's a definite possibility."

She smiled at me. The grin transformed her face so she was really quite beautiful.

"OK," she said. Clearly, that was all she wanted from me. "Sleep well."

"Night," I said, and she padded out of the room. I tried to keep myself awake for a bit longer. I always listened at the walls till I thought the girls were asleep. I wanted to know when they cried, but I heard nothing that night. I'd have felt instantly hopeful, but I'd heard plenty of soft sobs on other nights. And despite my wishes, for a long time after, things were still sad, and then it was unclear, I think, what we'd all lost. It became vaguer and vaguer till we remembered it distantly, like the events of a poorly recalled dream. And then just when it seemed to me the girls had never had a father and I had never romanced a handsome baker, Melone said, "Remember the year Angelo was my father? Remember he came into the bakery and said, 'This place is my heart's desire'?" I nodded. Beatriz and Tata did the same. "This place is my heart's desire," meaning: our love is a place, and we reside there. And if we had the power to create our lives all over again, this is just how we would will things to be.